ACCLAIM FOR MICHAEL PYE'S

THE PIECES FROM BERLIN

"Only superior fiction can take us here, a river of shadows more complicating than any film." —*Harper's Magazine*

"Intriguing. . . . [Pye] probes the varied ways in which memory can be put at the service of rationalization and self-deception, the myriad ways in which the past can permeate latter-day decisions." —*The New York Times*

"A story about memory and accountability, about the need to understand the past and the oftentimes even greater need to look away. . . . Pye writes with an impressive crispness and clarity. . . . How completely we are in thrall to passionate intensity is one of the lessons of this sad, spare and rigorous novel." —*The Washington Post Book World*

"Stunning but understated. . . . A finely wrought character study about quiet evil and the importance of remembering." —*The Seattle Times*

"Sandblasts the overused topic of World War II terror and guilt into your consciousness and makes you think it is your own story. . . . Mr. Pye is in turn a poet, a historian and a priest. He leaves the reader aware and unsettled." —*The Washington Times*

"Engrossing. . . . Pye conjures the nightmare world of the dying city with rich and decadent detail."

—*The Memphis Commercial Appeal*

"His taut narrative language is direct, strong and original, with a restrained lyricism full of trenchant observations. Particularly outstanding are the descriptions of Berlin crumbling from war and the oppressive ordinariness that accompanies apocalypse." —*The Madison Capital Times*

"A stylistic tour de force . . . a beautifully crafted and finely nuanced tale of guilt and moral complicity, it possesses a psychological depth that sets it apart from other novels dealing with the Holocaust." —*Library Journal*

"To be read and savored."—*Kirkus Reviews* (starred review)

MICHAEL PYE

THE PIECES FROM BERLIN

Novelist, historian, journalist, and broadcaster Michael Pye
is the author of ten other books including *The Drowning
Room* and *Taking Lives*, soon to be a major motion picture
starring Angelina Jolie. He is currently raising from the
dead the criminal king of the nineteenth century for a
novel.

THE PIECES FROM BERLIN

THE
PIECES
FROM
BERLIN

a novel by

MICHAEL PYE

VINTAGE BOOKS

A DIVISION OF RANDOM HOUSE, INC.

NEW YORK

FIRST VINTAGE BOOKS EDITION, FEBRUARY 2004

The Library of Congress has cataloged the Knopf edition as follows:
Pye, Michael.
The pieces from Berlin / by Michael Pye.—1st American edition.
p. cm.
1. World War, 1939–1945—Germany—Berlin—Fiction.
2. British—Switzerland—Fiction. 3. Art treasures in war—Fiction.
4. Zurich (Switzerland)—Fiction. 5. Berlin (Germany)—Fiction.
6. Antique dealers—Fiction. 7. Art thefts—Fiction. I. Title.
PR6066.Y4 P94 2002
823'.914—dc21   2002020524

Vintage ISBN: 0-375-71416-2

Book design by M. Kristen Bearse

www.vintagebooks.com

Printed in the United States of America
10 9 8 7 6 5 4

FOR ANNA, MARIO, AND PASQUALE

WITH MY LOVE

THE PIECES FROM BERLIN

ONE

He went rolling down into the city, his coat like a cone of green felt all around him, like some round wooden toy: so good and kind and clever, so big and so kind, so that everyone knew he must be a truly happy man. Helen watched her father striding past the dark shine of wet shrubbery and the high suburban walls. One minute he was in a puddle of streetlamp light, then the dark, then the next light: a flickerbook man.

She double-locked the apartment door, ran down the stairs instead of waiting for the elevator, and she followed him. She was afraid of what he might do next.

The cold ached on her skin. There was mist lying sodden among the plain buildings and gray squares of Zurich, gilt clocks poking up out of lanes, the last relentless red geraniums, with linden trees bare, and blue trams snaking by the water, the lake steamers and beyond them shops that glowed with their own gold, armored with huge glass.

He mustn't see her.

He was a brisk, effortless walker, used to scampering on mountains; she followed a block or two back, just able to make sure he was still ahead: the round man, in late middle age, under the shell of his green felt loden coat. His hair was white, and carefully wild: a professorial head. He had never once been ashamed of the great globe of his belly because he was not a self-conscious man.

Purposeful people were lined up for trams. The first shop and office lights were burning. At this blank time of the morning, hardly any light yet, the fact that he was moving was enough to make him stand out. Helen shivered as she walked. Her father retired from this kind of purpose years ago, had no obligation now to stride out on a bleak morning with the frost still standing in the trees.

He turned down the hill to the lake. He didn't nod at any of the galleries on the street, not even the one that belonged to her husband, Jeremy: didn't pause at all. She thought maybe he would catch a tram at the great turntable station down at Bellevue, but he didn't. He wanted to keep moving. He didn't even have time to wait to be carried where he was going.

Along the gray Limmat now, quiet and decorous: a triangle rushing along on his broad base, not bothering to look at the city around him. It was, in any case, already perfectly clean, no condom, ticket, newspaper, or candy wrapper left on the streets to anchor it even in the history of last night.

Nicholas Müller-Rossi knew better. He remembered things, which was what made him ominous.

In ordinary circumstances, he was happy to share in the official civic memory of the city: the memory that makes James Joyce an eye patient, Wagner a bit too showy, Lenin a good quiet tenant although he had visitors the night the Winter Palace fell. He liked the anesthesia of all that convention, to feel at home in a city whose great art is the window display, whose local poet is honored for being a good government clerk, although also a drunk.

But the circumstances were not ordinary at all. Nicholas cut across the Limmat and through the lanes up to the open space of Lindenhof. Helen slowed down, even though the cold caught at her legs. Only a few lanes led up to Lindenhof, and the park itself was small, and she did not want him to see her.

He could make his own mind up, she told herself. She thought he might just need her.

———

He stood looking down on the houses racked up each side of the valley, little terraces and squares, an ingrown city full of plain fountains.

Three days ago, Nicholas Müller-Rossi read in the newspaper that his father had died: ancient, at ninety-five, in a small town in a valley with a lake.

Two days ago, he had gone to see if he could pay for a wreath or subsidize the funeral masses; first the local florist and then the local priest said there was no need. Everything had been attended to. Everything had been considered.

So today he would be a spectator at the funeral, not taking part because he had been told he was not welcome.

Helen watched him stamp one foot and then the other: like a windup toy that's frustrated by a rug, she thought. She'd like to give him coffee, courage, anything he needed. She couldn't tell if he had yet decided to go or not to go.

All Nicholas did, for a moment, was stand under the bare trees, on a path of soft leafmeal, and brood.

He once had a friend who was a pharmacist. Every morning at nine, this friend went to the end of a tramline and opened the doors of a bright white confessional, a shop with shining walls and neat drawers, him in a starched white coat with young women, such graceful young women perfumed with oxygen, fetching and whispering. And everyone came, citizens and neighbors, the ones who kept such a perfect facade, the ones with good credit, fine names, a seat in church and a slot in the graveyard: and they told him things.

This one had a bruise that couldn't be explained, a yeast was infiltrating decent households, tiny, armored insects got in the private parts of the nicest people; this one needs vitamin B and codeine on account of the mornings after drinking, and this one needs eyedrops, homeopathic number 2, on account of the pills; and you could chart the cracks in marriages through the times they suddenly needed hair dyes, anti-flatulents, and tonics. He even knew the most terrible secrets of all: the antidepressants and tranquilizers and barbiturates which revealed when they lacked confidence for a moment in the perfect order of their lives.

Then the pharmacist retired. He said the whole business had changed him; he couldn't even buy aspirin without wondering what the pharmacist knew. His conversation was mostly hints: he knew where the whole city itched.

Then there were the secrets kept in dealers' safes, in the vaults of banks, in files and archives. Nicholas Müller-Rossi looked at the lake mist and the low cloud and it seemed to him the outward, visible sign of some great communal silence.

Standing around isn't proper in Zurich; you need a purpose, a destination. Nicholas, when he went traveling, wandered canals in Venice or Amsterdam, prowled boulevards in Paris, spent imaginary money up and down New York. But here, close to home, going somewhere in particular was a moral matter.

Helen thought for a moment he was going to turn back. She wasn't good at tucking into doorways like some private eye; the shops were not yet open; if she ran, she'd be conspicuous, but he'd outwalk her if he chose the same lane.

So she didn't see him leave Lindenhof at all, bustling down to the lovely, empty riches of Bahnhofstrasse, passing easily by the windows that used to fascinate him as a boy—the painted fruit, the spotlit hats, the occasional Chagall next door to fur and lace.

He bought his ticket from the machine at the main station, wonderfully efficient with the coins. He checked the information board, sorted out his train from the grand expresses and the suburban shuttles.

She knew he'd have to take the train. She checked the times and platforms so she could see him waiting.

She wouldn't offer to go with him. She had seen her grandfather once or twice, so her parents had told her. He was a bit of biology somewhere in the past, the necessary condition of her father and of Helen. But he wasn't there to be loved.

Nicholas settled on the upper deck of the Lucerne train.

He'd gone to see the priest, of course, to offer to pay for the seventh-day Mass, the year Mass. The priest said that was already arranged. He went to the graveyard gardener, thinking the man would be glad to set up the usual twenty-year contract to tend some flowers and clean the grave, but the man wouldn't listen to him.

The train streamed through trees that were prickled with ice.

He had his condolence card in the pocket of his loden coat: black-bordered, inlaid with paper that wanted to be parchment, a Rembrandt sketch of a bridge in a black landscape on the cover. He had paid ten francs for it, carefully chosen the middle range of price. "Heartfelt sympathy," it said, which was not at all what he meant, but that was what all the cards said: the proper thing to say.

They hadn't even told him.

His fists balled and unballed, whatever he thought. He could recite a sonnet and his fists kept getting ready for a fight. He wished the train was already in Lucerne, that he could be on the connection up to the little mountain town where his father was to be buried. He'd already had far too much time to think.

He was the first family: the scandal, not to be mentioned. When his father and mother divorced in 1945 there must also have been an annulment; his father was a good Catholic. His father had simply started life all over again, a banking automaton living in Zug, and started a new family who would all today stand around the grave and be allowed to see the body and pray their father into death. They had been told, he gathered, first that his mother died with Nicholas in the bombing of Berlin; and then, when one of the kids came home with one of Nicholas's books, on the early historical plays of Shakespeare, the story had been changed. Nicholas was as good as dead, even if technically alive, and his mother was written out of his father's story altogether.

He found the name of one of his half brothers in the phone book, and called to ask if he could do anything for the funeral. The man had said: "Yes. You can stay away."

But Nicholas was much too good a man to imagine a solidarity that depended on keeping someone out. A family couldn't be that frail.

He was hungry for tears. He had to see his father one last time, make the reconciliation that had been impossible in life; he had to cry.

Stepping down into Lucerne station, he lost his breath for a moment, as though he'd lost his concentration on living.

He didn't have a choice, he told himself.

He walked down the platform to find the Brünig train, and he saw himself from a distance: a man in his late sixties, too respectable and too old to be troublesome, the kind people trust instinctively when they want a suitcase watched or directions to the ticket office. The very idea of agony in such a man would seem ridiculous to all his fellow passengers if he expressed it for a moment, maybe the first sign of senile dementia, maybe he was drunk, maybe he was simply too old to hold himself in the official and orderly present tense.

He wanted to howl. He bought a sandwich to stuff his mouth and stop himself.

All Helen could do was wait. She went to the kitchen, full of dustless and unsparkling light, and she began to tug ingredients out of shelves and wrappers: two black shining aubergines, some leeks that looked too clean to have grown in earth, red chicory, zucchini, hothouse peppers with skins like armor. She sliced and trimmed and cleaned with a big knife: took the immaculate objects and broke them up and brought out the fine brown seeds that stained the aubergine flesh, the seeds and fiber inside the shine of the peppers. The room took on a faint scent. She tasted olive oil on her finger, and mixed it with hot pepper, soy sauce, and a little balsamic vinegar; then painted the vegetables and laid them onto a hot grill pan. And then the room had a subtle, sugary smoke to catch at the bright light: the air caramelized.

Not enough. The corridor shone, but it didn't smell of cedar, beeswax, pine. The windows were immaculate; she couldn't smell the slightest trace of the ammonia that the twice-weekly woman used to clean them.

She tugged the *Federbett* out of the way and threw herself down on the bed. She rolled to one side, then the other.

She buried her face in the sheets. She was glad she hadn't changed them since Jeremy left.

She was too damned young to collect souvenirs.

She was lying here, thinking about bliss. But thoughts of bliss, before you knew it, had a way of emptying out and leaving you with calculated pictures: with thoughts of roses, gardens, Alpine stars, of reef water, brilliant pink mornings, no surprises, of opera at seven and escapes on express trains, nothing that could not be put in a brochure or a timetable. She didn't want that; she wanted something particular to her.

Nicholas should not have gone to the funeral, she thought. Then she tried to smother herself again in the smell of the sheets.

His train arrived at nine twenty-four. He would need a taxi to the church, which was in the next small town. He would arrive there by nine forty-five. The funeral announcement in the newspaper was for ten o'clock, so perhaps he would have time to leave his condolence card, to see his father's face in the coffin one last time, and then shadow the services that followed.

He was quite still inside his coat: tense and impassive. The mists were shifting, so he could see the white shine and the black skin of the mountains, and catch faint color in the lake waters.

He brought no flowers. He had thought about it, but it seemed too much of a provocation, and too easy to have his wreath put aside or lost. But he wanted to bring flowers. There was a shop by the station, and he asked for white asters. They had them, but in wreaths. He said he didn't want a wreath; he wanted a loose bunch of white flowers. The assistant brought them surreptitiously and with a bit of a sneer, as though she was selling him something irregular. She couldn't see why a cross old man would want white asters. If he was going to a funeral, he shouldn't be cross.

He didn't mean to shout at her, but he lost time buying flowers and he was anxious. At ten o'clock the mourners would have formed a wall at the graveyard chapel.

The taxi driver was a huge woman with a silver tooth. She saw him with the white asters and said: "Church?" He said yes, but the next town. "The graveyard," he said.

She drove at a decorous speed, which annoyed him more, and left him by the graveyard.

The mist was still flirting with the ground, pulling up and settling back again. The chapel was an oblong of dark. In front of it was the cart on four wheels they used for moving new trees, old dung, and now his father's coffin. There was a flat bowl set out to take the condolence cards.

He knew the coffin would be open to show his father's face. He didn't know his father's face, not the ways it must have changed in forty years. If he could see the face, he would at least know his father, know him by sight which was all that there was left to him.

He took his glasses and polished them, absently, as though he was standing in front of some seminar.

He heard a car. There must be cars coming and going on the road; you couldn't expect perfect silence for a funeral even here in the bowl of white mountains. He stepped forward. One of the graveyard workers looked up at him. He put his card into the bowl.

He moved in the heavy, meaningful way that people use in church. He turned toward the cart with the coffin.

The first mourners were coming through the white curtain of mist, straggling up the path to the chapel.

He saw them, but he didn't want to see them. He wanted to see his father.

The graveyard worker cleared his throat.

The mourners, all in proper black, came forward. The men, he could see, wore overcoats and suits that were far too tight; they kept the black for funerals, and funerals were not that common in their lives. They were younger, naturally.

Nicholas passed the coffin. Inside he saw his own face, but drawn and ruckled in ways he hadn't yet seen in the morning mirror: himself, worn out. He wanted to kiss the face.

The mourners were close now.

He must protect his father's dignity. He walked briskly away. The graveyard workers, out of instinct, made a guard around the coffin.

One of the women looked in the bowl of condolence cards. There was, of course, only one so far. She opened it, she read the signature, she tore it into pieces.

He sat on a cold wood bench and looked down at the mourners around the grave. He asked himself if his father would have wanted him there.

They were praying in a knot about the black gap in the ground.

Then the coffin was lowered on strong ropes. Then they were blessing the coffin, one by one, with a spray of holy water. The ground was white with chrysanthemums and asters.

He remembered the last time he saw his father, except briskly or by chance or at some occasion where they were not obliged to talk. It was in the 1950s, when Nicholas was twenty and angry on principle with most of the real world.

All his long life had been full. His life had been his. It had only this peculiar quality: that it began when he was twenty or so, that he had to put away everything that happened before then.

His father was in Zug. He'd come out of the wartime army and into the bank, same rank, same manners, better pay. Most people did much the same: the men glided into work, the women went home again, somehow the fact of Armageddon on every border did not break up the usual life of Switzerland. His mother was in business for herself by then, and she was wholly exceptional; during the war, women only worked unofficially, as stopgaps and temps, so they were simply replaced when peace started. Everybody went back to their places.

Every year in the army Nicholas, a professor with a doctorate, wanted to peel potatoes. Every year, everyone was shocked.

Nicholas's father had already started his second family: two girls, pretty but stolid. He loved Nicholas, but did not want to be reminded of everything that went with him, his mother included, so the meeting was peculiarly tense. Nicholas was not so much a son as an anomaly. And Nicholas was self-righteous, and drank too much beer at lunch and his father thought him sloppy.

The mourners had walked away from the grave now, gone to the church for the funeral Mass. The priest, duly briefed, would extol the past of Nicholas's father, gild his story and make it sound like a moral tale. Nicholas would not be mentioned, nor his mother.

In that moment he thought he could move like a ghost, not quite seen. He carried white asters in both his hands, loose bunches of them. The gravediggers had a flask of coffee, maybe with pear *Trasch* in it; they were busy.

He threw all the flowers at once into the grave. They spilled out like stars against the black earth.

He would have liked some comfortable memory, but all he had was his father producing an official booklet from the war years, with brown covers. His father said he'd thought of sending it to Nicholas's mother. It seemed that since the men had brown notebooks to keep a log of their days on active service, women were expected to have one too.

So Nicholas read: "The homeland requires our resolute will for freedom, honor and humanity. Our homeland in these times requires," and then the list. Number one: "Women who don't complain." Number two: "Women who willingly take deprivation upon themselves." Three: "Women who raise strong children prepared for sacrifice." Four: "Women who conscientiously use household appliances."

He had burst out laughing. His father was half offended, as though he'd giggled at the creed, and half agreed. He said: "You can see why I never sent it. Read on." Nicholas was very aware that his father was watching him closely.

Eight, he read, "Women who with open eyes and warm hearts recognize the need of their neighbors and who support those in need of help."

He looked up at his father and his father inspected him. They were a conspiracy of two, agreed not to make too clear a mental picture of Mama Lucia helping neighbors with a warm heart. He had read on, with some relief, out loud: ". . . stand up for the future of our country."

"It's not a terrible thing," his father said. "Standing up for the future of your country."

Nicholas said he had to get back.

"It's not a terrible thing," his father said. "It wouldn't be so terrible a thing to have children. To stand up for your country."

"If you know what your country is," Nicholas said.

"We knew."

Nicholas tried to make a joke of it, asking his father to imagine his mother being "conscientious" with a household appliance. But they were in terrible trouble: father and son trouble, fueled with the beer. They went for a walk, bristling.

Nicholas was very aware of the dead smell of the earth, of the shine where the spades had cut his father's grave.

It was the streets that had started it. They were clean. They were neat. The buildings were all bunker solid and gray and decent and regular and somehow untouched. Nicholas thought the town was like a necropolis: a garden necropolis, architect-designed. Balconies for the dead to water their petunias. Sidewalks to step away from their black, black cars. Buses that took them to places nobody could particularly want to go, and took them regularly.

He was furious, but his father took this decorous world for granted, and kept smiling so that nobody else would notice how angry or how drunk or how—how shamefully, irresponsibly young his son was. He wore that smile like his suit and tie: his uniform disguise.

And Nicholas remembered thinking: They're not in this century. They hadn't been bombed or starved or tortured or burned. They'd been spared the whole terrible process of changing and even growing up. So when the war ended, all they cared about was keeping very, very still, like an animal that's been cornered.

He said all that.

He wondered if there was a spell to call back words from the ears of the dead.

His father had been quiet, reasonable, as though he was talking about the content of his son's last literature course or the last book he'd read. But he insisted on his words. Nicholas tried to talk over him, but he heard him, all the same. He was saying he'd worn a uniform, been prepared to fight, had gone to the Alps with the army to save the nation.

And Nicholas, all righteous, had said: Then what about all the flatlands where everybody lived? What about the women and children who were down on the plains while you were up the mountains playing at cowherds?

His father had talked, matter of fact, about sacrifice. About there not being money. About being billeted on some family near the border by France; it was where he met his second wife. He said people were hungry. They were afraid.

Nicholas asked why he never wrote to tell him all this truth. He said: How could he? He couldn't write anything like the truth in a letter that was going to Berlin. He couldn't tell his son how they were pulling every last old gun out of the cellars, rusty ones, ones with wormhole in the stocks. Or how all the best kind of people left town suddenly when the Germans were supposed to march in, and then for five years everybody else just sat around waiting and waiting and waiting.

Nicholas had said: "You did write to me. You told me about how the central heating was cut, and how maybe people were all the healthier for it. And you mentioned gas masks, and the blackout."

Until that moment, Nicholas now thought, his father might have regretted the distance between them.

But he turned then. They were on the steps of some big civic building in Zug, columns and pediments and maybe lions in stone. The building was like propaganda. And he said: "I know you were in Berlin. I know things weren't good. But don't think you can come here and try to be like the damned Germans—always arrogant, always sure you have the best music, the best poetry. Then the best wickedness. Then the greatest heroism in facing the best damned pain."

Nicholas said his father had no idea what Nicholas and his mother had been through in Berlin. He said his father hadn't lived it, and he couldn't now make up for it.

His father sat down on the steps.

It was an outrageous thing to do. He was a proper banking gentleman, who might well go for a brisk walk with his young son, who'd be entitled to walk away complaining if his son shouted too loud; and there he was, down on the stone ground. He looked up at Nicholas.

"You belong to her," he said. "Don't you?"

Nicholas was so angry he didn't know what to say anymore. He walked away. His father sat there, looking after him. The one time Nicholas looked back, he seemed so sad, so shocked all at once, as though it was a catastrophe to have the perfect surfaces of his world challenged.

He wrote a letter to Nicholas that evening. In it, he listed the charges against his first wife, mother of Nicholas, after the war: blackmail, extortion, receiving stolen goods. That was all. And he sent his love.

The mourners would go to lunch now, schnapps and wine, three solid courses, maybe venison because it was the season, and a half pear filled with red-currant jelly and the small white noodles. Nicholas could taste it all. A bottle of Fendant. A bottle of Dôle. They wouldn't cry and they wouldn't laugh, not until they had the schnapps.

He walked out of the graveyard, a shade much too solid not to draw attention. He thought of going back in the afternoon to see the grave settled and dressed with flowers, but he did not want to meet the others. He kept walking in the cold, and now that the mist had lifted off the lake, his face burned with the bright, metallic light off the high slopes.

He was an old man, officially. He had cards to prove he was an old man. He was a widower, a father, a retiree; there was nothing left to change in his life. He had lacked a father almost all his life, forfeited his father's attention completely at the age of twenty, made a good marriage, made a life that was perfectly sufficient and self-contained, a fort from which to watch the world. But now that his father was gone, he was shivering.

He had to walk Bahnhofstrasse on his way home. He passed his mother's shop. He wondered if she even knew that Herr Müller, half her name, much of her credibility, was dead, and that he had been buried that day.

The shop was painted rooms, lights as gold and rose as anything on a stage, a nice commercial dawn in between chemists and book-shops. The shine of the place was inventoried: its wax and glazes, glass, gilt and biscuit. In the window, a few small Meissen pieces: a dwarf with whiskers like a cat, two porcelain heads of children that would obviously be the originals, a pretty beaker with stooped Chinese and a baby dragon. Beyond that, a defensive wall of marquetry and plush and ormolu: engulfing sofas, tables spiked with orna-ment, bureaus which could fortify entire new social classes. Beyond that front line, the far interior of the shop was a warm, welcoming confusion of pretty things, china and glass, delicate bent legs, enam-els and inlays shining against fine rosewood. Tapestry hung on the walls: a zebra, a hunt.

He could see her through the windows: a porcelain figure, sug-gested with paint, in her plain round chair—Louis Delanois, still underpriced, no provenance to speak of—surveying her empire. It was pretty. It was profitable. It was pleasant. Nothing here would challenge unduly, unless it challenged someone's wallet. She had spent half a century dealing in the refined and elegant trivia of a civilization, trying to imbue it with significance: a date here, the name of an artisan, a place in history for a pot, a chair, a bit of porcelain which would not even hold a meal or support a visitor.

Nicholas stood at the door and thought about going to talk with her. But they were not used to being spontaneous.

An assistant stood by her, the keeper of keys, making the nightly checks: the alarm systems, the storeroom lights and dehumidifiers, whether the coffee machine was shut down. Nicholas sympathized: it must be hard in these last half hours before the shop was locked, because Lucia was no longer the authority, the patron, but a body to be inspected in an almost scientific way.

She was so old now that age had become her very nature; Nicholas could see that. And yet she traded still on the remains of bright eyes, dark eyes. The hair was dyed the color of old flames. The skin was like cloth, ridged and draped, but over bones so strong and fine that the features stole your whole attention. He saw her as something out of a storybook, where being old always has its own dark meaning: wisdom or evil or magic.

She checked the answering machine again. She always did that herself.

Nicholas read her lips. "That will be all," she was saying.

The front lights went down. She was left in the gleam of the back of the shop, in the warmth of rosewood and gold and kind lights, and she stood up. She was making a phone call.

Nicholas decided not to wait.

She would go home now, and have a glass of Madeira, to which she had become accustomed in old age. Someone would bring her eggs.

Nicholas went briskly into the lanes of the old town. He thought he might spend the night with Helen and Jeremy again. He liked the notion of playing drums with their son Henry, of setting out the Lego train and running it.

But he couldn't bear to talk. So he took the train and then the bus to Sonnenberg: to his house, to the house he made with Nora, to the place where Nora was still alive to him.

Helen paced the white rooms, huge steps. She liked order, but she liked it more when Henry was here, crabwise shuffling on one buttock over the floor, beating on his tin drums, assembling his train and taking the tracks apart to make proper crashes. She wanted handprints on the immaculate surfaces, a sense of breath and action.

She thought of Nicholas. Then she tried to think of her grandfather, who was an absence in her mind; she hadn't even bothered to invent some whiskery, selfless, beaming grandfather, so Alpine his breath would be wildflowers, just to fill the gap. She thought of Nicholas's loss, and, not knowing the man he was mourning, she could think of it only in the most general terms, which helped nobody.

And as for her grandmother, the cause of all this, she knew nothing Lucia did not want her to know.

She'd been taken to tea at the Grand Hotel Dolder, in the formidable propriety of the old-fashioned rooms; and sometimes to buy clothes, which did not much interest her own mother; sometimes to the Kunsthaus where Lucia talked very sensibly about Giacometti's sketches, for which she had a clever passion; sometimes on a walk where Helen could confess, happily, anything that crossed her mind, but never somehow confessed any questions, a walk which always ended with chocolate and cream. Lucia knew things, and Lucia gave things. Given the closeness of her father and her mother, which was like claustrophobia to Helen as a child, this old woman had been the vent, the breath, the frivolity in her very young life.

She'd always assumed Lucia was too busy with the shop to see her often. But perhaps her parents rationed out such a heady treat. They must have had their reasons.

TWO

Lucia knew all the places everyone knows from postcards; she'd just been there before everyone else, sometimes when there was still time to discover things.

She knew Paris, for example, but the Paris of 1914 when she was a very small child.

The Rossi family had habits: a few days in some German spa, often Baden-Baden, or a Swiss mountain and lake, or at weekends the house in Piedmont which stood on pudding-basin hills with a view of the Alps, or somebody else's house around Lake Como or Lago Maggiore. They went to Paris, briefly, to be properly dazzled. The city was further, larger, lighter, grander, and truly foreign in its grandness, and her parents had shone with its reflected glory.

But now there was a war coming. Everyone said so. They had to get home to Milan.

They drew up outside the great iron vaults of the railway station, father in an overcoat in a hot July, mother veiled and ringed with a fox, the taxi smelling of roses because of her; on the outside of the cab, hefty cases. The station halls were stale, air unmoving where there was air, with people pressed back into doorways, scrapping at doors, leaking into the roadways and ebbing and backing and suddenly stopping up against walls. Some looked as though they had slept the night on the road, not even the benches of the waiting rooms. And all of them sounded Italian, except for the fussy officials.

Two porters swung the cases to make a way for the Rossis: metal-edged leather cases, not easy to swing. A nun turned with her mouth open. A pair of soldiers stood like fair angels, but wouldn't part to let the family through. Small men sat bundled on the ground.

"We all want to go home," a man said.

Lucia was nestled up in her father's arms, watching the crowd like a show: watching how they were usually short, usually poor, dressed in thick cloth in summer, how there were blondes in among them, how none of the men had shaved that morning except for her shining father, how none of the women was quite as pretty as her mother. She watched happily.

A tiny man, absurdly in pince-nez, in a railway uniform that bagged and sagged around him, was trying to throw the third-class passengers out of the second-class waiting room; and as one group left, another entered, constantly.

Her mother shouted. *"Via! Via!"*

Her father held her tightly. The porters now had stalled and they had still not reached the platform, let alone the train, let alone the proper and appointed first-class carriage for the long haul back to Milan.

Her father shouted about a sick child, although she'd never in her life felt more alert and lively. Several parents nodded in sympathy and produced their own sick children.

Her father was taller than most of the men, she noticed. She looked out onto caps and hats and heads, some of them almost bald like monks.

Her mother lowered her shoulder and she charged.

The porters evicted boys from a cart that had ground to a halt in the crowd. They stashed the cases on the cart, helped Lucia's mother onto the front of it, and then her father surrendered Lucia to her mother and the porters strained on the handle of the cart and started rolling into the crowd. People were startled, resentful, but the ones they had bruised could not fight their way forward to where the cart now bumped along the platform. There was a smell, tired onions, tired sweat, that she had never smelt before in her well-washed world.

She knew worlds that were entirely alien to the bright young assistants in her store, with their manicured sense of history, and the dealers she knew, who knew nothing inessential, and even her well-heeled, well-aged customers, who were all of them younger. But she turned her memories over like stock in the shop: nothing to treasure, everything moving on.

She stood at the window of the train and watched the confusion on the other side of the glass, men who hit and spat and shouted, who broke against each other. She thought it was like an aquarium.

Lucia, older now, and such a girl: tiny in pink, being tugged past the glitter of shop windows and the other decent people on the street, very aware that she ought to be marching with proper grace and acknowledging exactly her own kind. But her arm hurt in its socket.

She saw the street filled up with people, banners, people she didn't know. She heard bawling and whistles and drums. She needed the sidewalk to show off her fine pink dress, and, instead, she found herself being rushed out of the parade of the streets and in through the door that was cut into the front door, into the cool and quiet of the hall.

Her mother said: "There. Dear. Go and change." Her mother would need a drink now.

Lucia went up the wide marble stairs, pulled herself up on the balustrade since there was nobody to see, like a sailor up the side of a huge ocean ship, like a monkey on its bars.

She'd always lived with the filigree gold, the mosaic floors made up to look like Persian carpet, the carving and the gallery of paintings. But she'd always known there was a world boiling just outside the cool, shaded glass of the windows. Inside, between solid tables and decent velvet, family and servants walked judiciously, guardedly; outside, even on cold lightless days, people milled and muscled into each other, fought and paraded and stopped work and changed party and showed their anger and ambition. She saw riots, she saw funerals.

Inside, Papa like a good banker took orders and made it seem he was in control, listened to what the Germans told him to do and listened to their account of precisely what the Italians needed. Outside, whole orders fell. Governments balanced on a single stone. There were rumors of violence in the countryside, men bludgeoned, rinsed out with castor oil until they were broken and lost, sometimes shot for the wrong attitudes. There were parades of girls and mothers in support of D'Annunzio's snatch at Fiume, a mad bit of nationalism held together with a few poems and arias and many very inefficient guns. There were trains that did not move because of strikes, streets that suddenly came to a stop, like the moment she remembered from the afternoon movies: when the film stopped running through the gate, when reality froze and began to catch fire from the bottom left-hand corner.

At the top of the stairs, she paused for a moment.

She was eleven years old. She had nowhere to show off her pink dress.

She could hear the men talking: barks and whispers, seals and snakes. She could tell they were keeping their voices down. They fussed over words. They cut up sentences and then sucked in their breath and looked solemn. They even made notes.

Lucia, in her pink dress, danced into the room. They looked up. She swirled her skirt, to the left, to the right, then tugged it up, all graceful like a ballerina, flourishing neat white knickers.

The skirt went over her head.

The men coughed.

She smiled, and then, as a dancer runs with more deliberation than speed, she ran back out of the room.

"Signori," she heard her father say.

The house was the shape of her life: staircases with marble, the gilt, the verandas at the back looking out onto trees and walks, and the giddy pretension of some of the rooms: maps set in mosaic on the floors, a room named for peacocks. In the best 1900s manner, the house carried a frieze of huge copper bees: a gesture to nature that quickly turned green and sooty. It once had its own stone women by the front door, one either side, but they were too ample and too friendly-looking, so, after some fit of public morality, they had to be taken down.

The house did not impress all her schoolfriends; they seemed to think it was entirely too grand, too new, and they were either amused or intimidated by it. But it was the shape of her life; if they didn't like the house, they couldn't like her. She couldn't be bothered with the children of her father's colleagues, and she couldn't make friends with the grander girls.

She floundered until she broke out of the house, afternoon and evenings.

Seventeen, eighteen, she'd go sometimes to the cinema, the afternoon shows, mostly women there. She'd go out like a tomboy in the best American style. She'd go to the Galleria, the great commercial cathedral that stood opposite the Duomo, its high glass and iron vaults inside, all up against the sugar-white mountain of spiky church marble. It was always open.

On her own, this wasn't easy. A woman couldn't seem available, but she wanted to know people. The cafés hummed. She heard heels clatter, kept walking. She passed women and men, packages in their hands, heads down. She felt eyes on her; she was decor to the crowd.

She walked more quickly, not wanting to seem as though she, Lucia Rossi, was unsure of anything.

It was tough just to overlap with others. She was the great banker's daughter, but it wasn't such a grand thing to be a banker;

banks did not yet have the kind of power that interested people, not like the makers of cloth or cars or steel. She was too grand for some parties, not quite grand enough for the best parties. She saw the girls linger at the shop windows, chatting. She saw the police smile under their black helmets. She wanted to flirt, but correctly.

At least in the Galleria she felt a little insulated: no weather, no stench from the engines in the street, no beggars, no truly poor people. She could find, in the echo and bustle, all those men who'd be happy to talk, but she had no excuse to talk to any one of them in particular.

She thought how much easier it would have been if she had brothers, who could lend her their friends.

A young man stopped in front of her. She failed to dodge him. He said: "Signorina, I am a singer." She said nothing. "I am a singer," he said, "who has heard the applause of the French." Since he blocked her, she looked him over: tall, narrow shoulders, too much chest, pipe legs, and all wrapped in a cloak that could have warmed half a chorus. "Unfortunately," he said, "at this particular season, the impresarios have chosen not to favor talent. Not at all." She thought of kicking him. "I was wondering," he said, "if I could buy you a coffee."

She stared at him. She had already, in her mind, counted the change in her purse.

They sat in the way of the crowds, a table by potted plants. Lucia told the man nothing, which did not seem to matter since he told her everything about a brilliant career now briefly and only temporarily spoiled by unemployment. His name was Giorgio. He was, of course, a tenor.

She bought him pasta in the end. She thought of him as a clue: how to find a different city, how to get out and not just to wait for her life to begin. And for a little while, quite chastely, she did move out into a city she had only glimpsed as she walked past the cafés: a minor Bohemia of resting musicians, all waiting for the next season's contracts, all hungry to go sing in some tiny box of a theater in far Piedmont rather than live without an audience at all.

She went to his house one afternoon when her parents assumed she was with friends at the cinema. Giorgio lived off the main avenues, down cobbled streets with no sidewalk, on the wrong side of an unused church.

She sat on the edge of a chair and drank coffee he made with a metal espresso pot on a gas ring. She could smell stale water somewhere.

She learned that the stars her parents followed at La Scala were all fakes and frauds and failing, that only the conspiracy of managers stopped a whole new generation showing them up. She learned a little, too, about singing Pagliacci, but she got the impression Giorgio had never actually done that in public.

She heard voices, one after another, through the whole afternoon: uncertain sopranos, rustbucket basses, a mezzo whose breath swelled and failed like a graph. There was a double bass being bowed, a sound just under her conscious hearing. There was a harpist, not good.

One of the two shutters on Giorgio's window slammed into place.

"Don't worry," Giorgio said.

Lucia wondered why the half shade was supposed to make her anxious.

"There's still light enough," Giorgio said.

She used to think she learned everything that mattered in that moment: that Giorgio couldn't go on, could hardly think until she gave him an excuse. He wanted her, but he couldn't place her: not a working girl, clearly of good family, and so dangerous. She couldn't possibly want what he wanted. But then, why was she there?

Lucia didn't move.

"Unless," Giorgio said, "you'd like me to close the other shutter."

But she had learned her lesson already. She remembered that she had to meet someone, so she said, and she left, and after that Giorgio hailed her in the Galleria any time she wanted, presented her to his friends, sometimes took her to a party, once took her to a tiny theater where the lights and the seats squeaked with rust and made her sit through an evening of mangled lieder.

They were never again alone in the same room.

She watched the others flash their reviews, the reviews that Giorgio still sent home to his family in the Veneto even when they were bought notices, two lire a line, of some minimal performance. She got to know one older man, who talked about the Paris Opera and the velvets and silks he wore to sing something in *Faust*, about the sound of applause in London and the prospects in Leipzig, but who was now working part-time as a slow, shuffling butt among waiters in a trattoria.

She was studying, not living; she knew that. She went home to salons, dinners, weekends in the country, weekends at Lake Como, to being discreet around a house where politicians now quite often dined with bankers.

Then Giorgio produced his friend Paolo, from somewhere in Umbria, who played the cello. He was skinny, quick, and small. He fixed on the cello like prey, hunched forward to play, as though the bow might fall short of the strings. Then he extended himself by sheer will, made the body of the instrument sound out.

"He shouldn't play cello," Giorgio said. "Really."

"He plays very well," Lucia said.

That was when she started asking her friends about birth control. She thought they were stalling, since the whole subject had just been put outside the law, but in fact they did not want to show how little they knew. They'd skim the movie magazines, see two people in the same frame, and they could usually tell biting from kissing, the lovers from the heroine's last-reel struggle with the villain, but not always.

Paolo danced well, but he danced rather under her chin. He danced with her in the Blu-room, in the Golden Gate, between swirls of cigarette smoke, where a little perfume did battle with cheap soap. He moved busily, immaculately, while she reared up above him, shaking out the red hair that smothered and bound him in his dreams. He orchestrated a grand turn, and his sigh tickled her breasts.

She went home to dinner with her family. There had to be a way out.

She tried to listen to Paolo's story, when he volunteered it. A little farm near Todi, indeed. Olive trees; there had to be olive trees. Hunters out with guns, high moon, nightjars singing. More pudding-basin hills, all green. A father who worked on the roads, a mother who sold mushrooms in the market. It was too picturesque to be real, and she could not imagine what it would be to come from such a place, and never to be able to shut a good door on the world.

"One day," Paolo said, "you'll have to come to Todi."

A long, rough table, with big plates covered in cooked tomatoes. She imagined herself smiling: the exemplary mother, the exemplary wife who might one day be. There would be all those hopeful faces.

This trip to another class was growing tedious.

"We should go for a walk," Paolo said.

She said good-bye to Giorgio. She looked back at him, once: he was holding forth on the late music of Rossini, and nobody was listening.

She walked beside Paolo and, together, they demanded space from the people who walked, heads down, toward them. She put out a hand, took his; it was an experiment, to see what walking this way on a public street would feel like. It felt fine. Paolo and she became a couple: a ceremonial fact on narrow pavements, to be respected and indulged. As a couple, she noticed that his palms were wonderfully dry, and that his hands did not quite enclose hers.

They turned off the street of bright windows. They bundled together along the side of narrow streets. His eyes turned up to her, hungry and almost dependent eyes: like some sort of child.

"We could walk in the gardens," Paolo said. "In the moonlight."

She saw the family house on the Corso. They passed under its windows, by the heavy portico, with the heavy stone cherubim looking down. Far up the facade, she wanted to giggle at the thought, those great copper bees were watching too. She thought of saying "Good night" and turning in through the narrow doorway, but she didn't want her name and address to be known, and the price of anonymity was walking on.

Tall iron gates, but with a gap to the side. They took the gap. Paolo could smell the lindens in flower; she saw sad parched shapes on either side of an avenue of stone and sand. Behind the trees, residual light and shapes of green bushes. The garden felt on the edge of everything.

She watched herself walk into the dark between the patches of faint light. Paolo tugged at her hand.

They sat on a wood bench for a moment. Since Paolo couldn't speak, she kissed him.

He tugged at her hand again. He led her back behind the avenue trees, behind the bushes, to a patch of grass. She sat down. He lay down. She lay down now, and he kissed her left breast through the cotton of her dress. She liked the rasp, and then the wetness. He said: "*Ti voglio bene.*"

Her skirt had ridden up as she lay down, and she helped it ride higher. She smelt dust, felt tiny sand against her bare legs and buttocks. She was waiting now, to be shown.

She felt fingers, working into her. She heard Paolo's breath. And then:

"*Gesu!*" Paolo said. He had red on his fingers.

She stared at him.

"I didn't know," Paolo said. He had pulled a handkerchief from his trousers, and in doing so he had bloodied the opening of his pocket, and he was wiping his fingers and his trousers.

She said: "*Ti voglio bene.*" He looked funny, trying to shake his hand dry, trying to shake it loose.

He couldn't bring himself to listen. He was up now and panicking. He was signing that she should wipe herself, bring down her skirt, prepare to return all proper to the streets. She wanted to ask: But what would they think we were doing in the bushes except this?

At the park gates, Paolo said: "I'll find a taxi for you."

"I don't need a taxi," she said.

She watched him disappear into the light between the trees.

And she walked.

She didn't want to go home at once. She would give everything away; her mother would know. She thought she might wander back into the side streets, away from the Corso, where the musicians lived.

There was overlooked washing still on the balconies, crowded together. There was talk in the windows and the doorways, as though the houses had no depth and no light and everything happened just off the road. And she heard the musicians all around her, heard the untuned jar of wind notes, piano, forced soprano scales, of clarinets wailing, of trumpets blasting over violins and the thumping chords of some other bad cello player. She felt the noise now like a wall, and even when she stood still, as she did when she waited to cross a street or catch her breath, it was as though she was running faster and faster into that wall. Or else the music was massing against her, each half aria, each unaccompanied Bach piece, each mutant arpeggio played on a keyboard in the damp, was forcing her back and away.

She stopped her ears. She started running.

At home, she washed and washed.

———

For as long as she was panicking, she stayed in her nice gilt box. And then it was winter, and a Milan winter, mostly mist and soot and half-light. So everyone talked about leaving, skiing, and she just couldn't face being sportive with all those other good local families, being the one to whom everyone was polite.

Her mother fixed the invitation: foreign associates of her father's, bankers' kids, nothing in common except the fact that their fathers handled money for respect. One shining winter day, she was driven to Central Station. The trees were gold and the shadows so deep they could drown people. And the driver carried her cases, and she could stride out up the station steps and the whole station was one great new tunnel of glass and light, marble and stone, like a church, with pictures in tiles; and the smells, leather and creams and fish, suits and skirts that hadn't been washed recently, coffee, cheap soap, wet paper. Then the tracks spread out beyond the great hall into a huge and brilliant sky.

She was exhilarated by Monza, which is not what people usually make of Monza, and she loved passing through Como. She'd been too often to Como in the summers. If she could just get past Como, she wouldn't be a banker's daughter anymore, wouldn't even be Milanese.

And then she was past the border, the uniforms, the questions from the customs officers; and the train was still moving, she was on her own and it didn't matter if these lakes and Alps were the ones she already knew, which she'd seen years before with her parents. She changed trains, and changed trains again, always in the glamour of steam and smoke, and each time she was further from cities she knew, names she knew. She wasn't responsible to the world outside the windows anymore.

Then she was on a train that had a snowplow up front, shining curtains of frost either side of the line, and the windows were open for the cut of the clean air. She watched out for the station, and it was the perfect model of a station in the perfect model of a village.

The sunset on the mountain blinded her, great flares of red and silver. She got vertigo in the cable car going up to the chalet. "It's a very international party," said the wife of the colleague of her father's. "People from everywhere. Some English boys. Very clever. Some of the Jewish persuasion. No Italians, I'm afraid."

She first saw Hans Peter Müller against the light. He might as well have been naked in his close clothes.

She'd seen so many poses, and so many suits, and so many people wrapped in cloaks and talking about their futures; and here was a man whose skill was written on his body. She watched the power and the elegance of his legs, so sure on the snow even when it sifted like sand on a mirror. And he was magnified by the thin brilliance of the mountain air.

They couldn't not talk. He spoke Italian, but in serious, Germanic gobbets. She tried to speak German, and she sounded absurdly like the bankers to whom she'd been polite all her life.

He helped her on the ski lift, which was a hook on a cable on a wire. Then he helped her on the snow. She didn't need to be touched; she balanced exactly, flung herself down slopes with no fear at all. He followed, overtook, turned in and out of her path without flurrying her, danced an arcing, whispering dance around her.

The snow was still wonderfully empty in those days. You felt you had come out into a wilderness, not a playground. At lunchtime, skis racked against a rope, poles jammed in the snow like a strong metallic bush, you looked out onto unmarked white.

She was entirely dazzled. She laughed hugely.

At night, the silence was perfect. Houses enclosed all the music and talk. And she walked beside Müller under a white moon, and she saw shooting stars for the first time in her life, each one arbitrary and lovely, no use watching out for them.

He skied; she knew that much. He was some kind of banker or accountant; that meant he was like her father. Her father had been a perfectly ordinary clerk, out of a small Piedmont town, with ambition, so the question of status did not necessarily arise. He was tall, hard, graceful; she loved to watch him. She thought she would be able to long for him properly when she went back to Milan. Longing was what she had in mind, even then.

The last day, he hired a sleigh. They put the luggage on the back, and the horses took off and neither one of them had worked out how the story was supposed to end.

The breath from the horses smoked out ahead of them. And the woods opened out and they saw new valleys, new rock, and water frozen as it fell. They weren't high on the mountain anymore.

He helped her onto the train, like a gentleman. Then he jumped aboard too. She didn't know how far he thought he was going, but he wouldn't step down, and the train rolled slowly down the mountain between banks of still white.

He didn't have his passport, so he got off the second train just before the Gotthard.

The night they married was also the first night they made love. Lucia remembered so clearly how she anticipated glory at last, and what she got was comfort, which was nowhere near enough.

Müller surrounded her body with his, was infinitely patient, was considerate and gentle, was absorbed in her beauty, which was, in the circumstances, of very little interest to her. She wanted to be shocked and excited, but he was always waiting for her.

Her parents did not seem to mind that she was leaving Italy. Her mother was making sharp little jokes about the "interests of the state" nowadays, and how Mussolini wouldn't allow pictures of women too thin or too wiry to bear babies; "It's an offense to be smart," she said. "Think of that." Her father's authority had grown a little dusty. He said he wished he'd been a proper captain of industry, which required inheritance, and not a moneylender, which kept you a kind of omnipotent clerk. It was important that someone do what you did; but you did not matter in particular.

Lucia, in the next few years, had all too much time to think. She wondered if her parents would have had the same easy tolerance if she had presented some carpet man from Turkey, an ironworker from Lille, a peasant from the Alsace; she wondered if they would still have been glad for her to go. She at least produced an accountant who might have ambitions, and a Swiss who could get her out of the flag-ridden streets and the thuggish countryside and keep her safe.

So Lucia Rossi went to live with Hans Peter Müller in a small town in Bavaria. He was the accountant in a firm that made buttons.

He knew things. He knew about bone and horn and glass and Bakelite and brass and the knock-on pricing differential between hole and shank. He talked about such things. He once explained to her, when she'd run out of ways to stop him, that it took phenol and formaldehyde to make Bakelite.

She had every reason to resent him. He remained such a ruthlessly kind man. She woke up beside him, and he was kind. She drank coffee with someone sweet and generous. And when he finally walked down the garden path to go to work, checking the five flowering shrubs, then she'd go deep into the house, the inner rooms, and she learned to bellow into the corners without making a sound, her face red, her cheeks out, not even the sound of breathing.

She'd have coffee again, and read the social columns: Bella Fromm, she remembered, in the *Vossische Zeitung*. She started to be able to remember all the dinners and musicales and galas and picnics Bella went to, not just imagine them. There weren't many galas in their small town.

And it was a town so small that nobody looked directly at anyone else; everything was a rumor. The mayor shot himself and everyone said the police made him do it, but they didn't know if he was a crook or a pervert or Hitler's best friend or all three. Everyone resented everything—the price of meat because everything had to be sent to Berlin, the fact that you couldn't get asparagus in tins. Lucia learned something. In small places, it isn't that people know everything about you, because that would be tolerable. Each of them makes you up and sticks to his story, and each of them has a slightly different version.

She had to get out, obviously. But she couldn't simply run. She was a wife, and as such had a proper place, guaranteed by papers. She was a foreigner, too. Her parents did not want her back in the muddle of fascist Italy. She thought perhaps she could find herself a lover, pick someone out of the main street, someone from the button factory or the butcher's shop.

She decided, instead, on art.

The Herr Doktor Professor liked to talk about Siennese painting, about Beccafiumi and the Roman career of Il Sodoma, and about Meissen porcelain. He knew everything about Meissen, and passed it on. He also insisted that the Nazis were excellent persons because they would bring back the Kaiser, and the glorious great estates, and there would again be a shining culture all through Germany.

Lucia thought she knew better. Lucia said nothing.

The Herr Doktor Professor was a bit of a footnote to the human race, insistent on every one of his three degrees, a belly trailed with vines of stuck hair, limbs like badly rolled cigarettes to hold the belly up, the perfect antidote if your husband is Adonis. She found herself an appetite surrounded by lard. She could rely on his selfishness, a grunting, sweating, demanding person, a man so wedded to the importance of what he'd read twenty years ago that he'd shout out abstract, compound nouns as he came.

She learned what he had to teach: how the making of porcelain had once been an occult wonder; how Meissen loved the arcane too much and almost went bankrupt guarding a secret that everyone else had already guessed; and how Heinrich Kühn threw out the alchemists, cut out the jargon, and let in the bracing, progressive, scientific air of the nineteenth century. The Herr Doktor Professor dearly loved a reformer like Kühn, the more violent, the better. Somehow in his mind everything circled back so simply to the glories of National Socialism, so nothing in particular did, so it did not seem to matter.

She did see flags, banners, slogans, prisoners, and houses that were empty. But what she remembered mostly was lectures on how well Meissen did when Germany was strong and united, or at least without customs barriers, and what a lesson that was for the modern state; and she remembered waiting, as she listened, for the good doctor to pounce on her breasts.

He said it was good they were both married, made them free. "You don't have to explain yourself," he said. He was always on his mettle to keep her happy, by books, by talking about glory, by fucking her fast and rough, and most of all by allowing her to expect and anticipate, which kept her in a state of constant excitement much more than the actual touch of his sausage fingers, or his unusually rough skin.

She didn't want to come alive this way. She knew she'd depend on him.

He carried about with him the odd vegetable smell of old, deep dirt. He talked about personality and genius, about style and temperament, about the variation between pulls of a particular design and in their decoration. He talked about paste upon paste, and shaded flowers, as he held her by her hair.

Then she was pregnant.

There was a neat, blond man called Müller, rather tall, and a stubby little professor who was rather dark. There would not be any ambiguity about the father of her child. She simply decided that it could only be Müller's. She wouldn't let herself think anything else.

The professor liked to feel her belly as it grew, pressing and scratching. Müller attended to her, gently and calmly and on the exact timetable of the hours he could spare from his work.

And Nicholas was born: undoubtedly the child of Hans Peter Müller.

At the beginning, Nicholas was her portable lover. She loved the connection of having him suckle at her breast; she only stopped when he was already three. She loved his company, his utter absorption in her face, his willingness to be always at her disposal.

Hans Peter Müller, she decided, saw the boy as nothing more than the appropriate result of a marriage. But she was busy with the professor, and she never saw Müller playing football with his small, unsteady son, or teaching him how to pick berries on a hot afternoon, or easing him into the run of the river to swim. She was not interested in Müller's emotions, which she had long ago decided did not count, so she missed the wild and generous look in his eyes when he saw his boy.

However, she still needed the professor. She was afraid of need, except for Nicholas, who had a whole life ahead to need to be with her.

So she stopped suckling her son. She knew she would need currency: her mind, her body, her knowledge. She couldn't count on powerful men quizzing her about the paintings of Simone Martini, or being impressed by her command of logic. The breasts, then, mattered.

Everything was becoming uncertain. She never imagined living in Switzerland. She couldn't go home to Milan. She thought it best to pretend to a feeling of ease in Germany, since she was there; but Müller never bothered with that. He didn't live in Germany; he was only employed there.

She wasn't Swiss, but because of Müller she lived as a Swiss. There was a shortage of skilled workers, factories working overtime, money was good; so there were immigrants out of Switzerland all around them. Müller wanted their company. She didn't see the point.

She made the food, brought the bottles. They'd listen to the radio, communally. There was a football game from Paris, the commentators rushing their words, and the men sitting about with their beers, all together, not loud and cheering but desperately serious. It was some kind of championship; she never knew which. It was Switzerland against Greater Germany.

The game was over, there was a brief silence, then it was obvious: Switzerland won.

The men didn't cheer, even then. They were contract workers, signed up to show respect for a fee. They smiled, though, and they stood up like one man and toasted the victory with their half-liter glasses.

Müller used to read her the letters he got from home; his family all sent short, neat letters at regular intervals. After the game against Germany, they wrote, there was something like a riot in Basel, if you can imagine such a thing: streets full of whooping, shouting fans, glorying in the momentary downfall of the great Third Reich.

And when Hans Peter read that, he took Nicholas out into the garden, he told him what had happened, he took his boy's hands and together they danced a rapid, jerky jig.

A November night, quite cold. She was standing at the bedroom window and she was looking down the path to the road. There were no leaves or flowers. She could see the road very clearly.

She thought there was some kind of parade. Brown uniforms. It was dark, and they were quiet and they were keeping to the pavement: very orderly, unhurried, as though they were going to work. They didn't hide but they didn't have a band.

They almost all went past the end of the path. Two of them stopped. It was one in the morning and they were in uniforms and they were so quiet. They hadn't been drinking, obviously. They were under orders.

One of the boys—they all seemed like boys—stopped just opposite her window. She didn't know if he could see her. She thought not. He stood there and he stared in, as though he could see foreignness written all over the walls and the eaves of the house. He said something to the boy at his side, gestured at the house, seemed to point out Lucia at the window, and then they all went on.

The next morning the Jewish shop in town, the little haberdashers, was broken up. The windows had somehow dematerialized, but the street was stuck with glass. The silks and the bales had all been taken down and thrown around. It looked very lovely: all those colors shining in the sun. There were some of the boys in brown uniforms, SA, in and around the shop, and they were tugging out special things—lace things, silk things, embroidered handkerchiefs, rather elegant ties, and they were trying to present them to the passersby, like medals, like rewards. Most people walked by on the other side of the street.

She was never more conscious of being a dark redhead, a southerner, and very foreign. It suddenly made sense for Müller to go about alone in a town that was mad for blondes.

She knew there would be a war because of the ration cards. It was a brutal August day, hot and airless, and the policemen came to every house to announce that they couldn't buy anything much anymore without ration cards. There were seven different kinds, and the colors seemed all wrong, somehow: blue for meat, green for eggs, orange for bread.

Müller took note of the cards, but he didn't seem to register what they meant. "We're all in this together," he said, but he didn't seem convinced.

She watched the dust in the air: the still flecks of dust that did not catch the sun.

She waited without fear. Something had to happen; she simply did not know what would happen next. War must change everything, somehow.

She never expected that Müller would be called up by the Swiss army; he had never mentioned the possibility. Perhaps he thought it was entirely obvious, or perhaps he didn't expect to have to leave Germany.

He paid two months' rent and he left. He sent pictures. He looked fine in uniform, on a slope somewhere. He couldn't say where, of course.

She remembered the consoling pull of Nicholas's lips on her nipples. She had liked the sense of being absorbed in being essential to him. But he was a child now, not a baby. She had to think. She was in small-town Germany, her child could have German nationality but she couldn't, she didn't have much of an income because the Swiss army were meant to be voluntary heroes, and it didn't help being Swiss and Italian, which were two wrong nationalities as far as the butcher, the grocer, the baker, the laundry were concerned.

So the Herr Doktor Professor gave her some names and addresses in Berlin, and a little money and the tickets she'd need. It did occur to her that he might have wanted her out of the way.

THREE

He was six years old in the train. He sat under luggage like mountains, crags of leather, falls of belt. Everything smelt of other people instead of the outside.

A man was eating meat sandwiches out of greaseproof paper and his fingers shone. He was reading a newspaper. Nicholas wanted to show that he could read too, but Lucia kept him back.

Then they were in Berlin.

He remembered how open his eyes were, stitched open by sights. There were more people, more floors, more streets, more cars, more noise than he'd ever imagined could be in one place. He'd always been in a small town, his territory was a garden with geraniums; he could run down the street and be a shadow in the woods.

He knew this city was somehow his mother's place, not his. She held on to his hand.

There were flags everywhere, and people smelt strong. He might say, nowadays, that they smelt good, but he didn't know what expensive soap and French perfumes were meant to smell like at the end of a long day.

Their first apartment was not at all grand: five rooms. The kitchen wasn't clean. His pretty mother, who was always so careful, threw bleach around it and said something very rude about people who lived on fried food. She scrubbed until her hands were raw, and then she looked at her hands and shrugged and said they'd be having a maid, somehow.

Nicholas could see down into the courtyard from the kitchen, and into the street from the living room. He'd always been on the comforting flat before.

There was a corridor with doors, so he could play hide-and-seek. He could run from one room to another, arms out and dipping like a plane turning in the sky.

The fourth day, some men in uniform started hammering on a door across the courtyard. Lucia told him not to look, so of course he looked directly across the courtyard.

A window opened very wide. The men must have taken the glass off the sashes.

He saw the end of a piano on the windowsill. It was an upright piano, cheap, light wood, with some of the keys discolored.

The piano teetered on the sill. The men in uniform shoved it. It fell and splintered and the wires sprang about and sounded like a cat in the works. Nicholas looked down and he couldn't make out the particular shape of a piano anymore, just plywood, it seemed, and a bit of lovingly shined veneer on the stones, and the keys flung about like teeth.

Then there was a fountain of paper, pamphlets of music, that went up in the breeze and came slowly rustling down.

His mother pulled him inside and slapped him.

"Don't you look," she said.

Helen waited for him to come back to the apartment. She wanted to comfort him; she knew he wouldn't want to talk. She wanted him to sit in the kitchen while she assembled supper, wanted to share a glass of wine.

He didn't come. So he must have gone directly to his house, and he must be drowning in memories. He couldn't be remembering Hans Peter without the ghosts of all Lucia's notorious doings, and those ghosts parading through his mind.

He was not a witness. He only lived while things happened. He didn't have anything to say which he, and he alone, knew. If anything, he'd bring back the ridiculous details, like the toilet paper rough as wrapping paper, and the perpetual shortages, and the usefulness of all those fine paper propaganda leaflets that the British dropped.

He walked up the road to Sonnenberg. The sky was clean here, and the moon high. The snow was bright as mirrors on either side of the black line of road, shadows blue, fields evened out. Sometimes at the roadside the crust had broken on the snow and underneath that rough glass of ice he could see feathers of soft cold.

The house had been a farmhouse, once, when he and Nora found it: half solid stone, half the old brown wood of a barn. Geese straggled by the door. A small dog visited.

The world was brilliant as a picture in a lightbox. He could almost see clearly again: old eyes with ice for lenses. He would have stayed, if he could have done, outside in the cold, with the dog tasting his hand and the cat rubbing against him: an animate scarecrow, a passerby on his way to the high woods or perhaps to the next farm.

He didn't do what he had done every time he came home to Sonnenberg, didn't check the mailbox, didn't go to see if there were messages, somehow always expecting a message from Nora even if she was dead six years, which, to him, was only a detail.

He went to the barn instead. It seemed like a perfect replica of a barn that you read about in books: a strong wood shelter with logs stacked like art along one wall, with a lawnmower, a washing machine, shelves of jam and paint. It didn't seem to have a history of things breaking or falling at all. He looked out over the whiteness all around, and he thought for a moment the whole land had no terrible history, either: it was so easily reduced to its own bright, white, and shielding surface.

He loved to see the deer move against the woods, the branches of their legs and antlers. He wasn't even looking for them tonight.

He thought the process of fading, of leaving just a chalk mark in a bright white world, ought to produce some countervailing calm or resignation. That would be the proper order of things.

He had been sent to school at the Italian embassy in Berlin for a while. He knew he wasn't meant to be surprised, not by a great house that seemed all gold; only later did he suspect the railings were bronze. He saw doors of wood so black it had to be ancient, and seats taken out of churches, and the rooms were lit with a hundred cuts of light trapped by magic in glass. Now he would classify the magic: chandeliers from Venice.

He sat beside a boy called Luca, who seemed to think he should know about Italian things just because of his name. He explained that his father was Swiss, which was why he was also called Müller, and that Niccolo or Nicholas Müller-Rossi was born in Germany. Luca called him a "*Mischling*"—in German: a half-breed.

Nicholas didn't like the word. Then Luca realized that Nicholas's father was away, and in the wrong army. He didn't use the fact directly because everyone behaved in the class: little premature gentlemen of six and seven. But it was always the interesting fact about Nicholas: that his father was in the wrong army.

Nicholas started his childhood when the bombers came, when there was time and space to play at last.

That first summer was hot, unusually hot, everyone said. Everyone wanted to get to the water. Lucia took him down to Wannsee one August day to watch the powerboats whirling around out on the lake waters. She said he could swim.

They were with someone: one of Lucia's new friends, a man, of course, from the embassy. He was quite tall and he could play soccer well enough to impress a kid. He passed neatly, and Nicholas scored goal after goal between his jacket and the picnic basket.

He wanted to go out on one of the little sailboats. His mother looked up at the sky, which was part pewter and part a brilliant blue. Her friend shrugged. He thought it might be worth keeping Nicholas quiet and amused, and Nicholas was a persistent child.

They came away from the shore, and all of a sudden, there was a different kind of breeze. The boy felt wind across his whole skin. He saw his mother's hair, a fine red in those days, her own red, stroked out and flying in the wind. They were in a tiny sailboat, nothing at all, a walnut shell in between the motorboats further out, but it felt like they were exploring across whole oceans, that they had found somewhere wild at last. A few girls and soldiers, in rowboats, were laughing much too much.

Nicholas knelt up at the bows, staring out. The wind got brisk. There were pellets of rain and they beat back off the lake water. The sky blackened. There was a distant rumble of thunder.

His mother said: "It's beautiful out here."

Her friend said: "Look. We'd better get back. Lightning's no fun when you're out on the water like this. Exposed."

His mother stared at the horizon of green, tangled trees and she seemed to be willing the lightning to come. Out of the blue sky she brought white light, as though the sky had cracked open and shown the hot glare beyond. Out of the pewter sky, Nicholas truly believed this, she brought a different kind of lightning: red light, broad light, a tree of it.

Her friend stood, rocked the boat, took down the little sail he could no longer trust. "We have to go back," he said.

The wind flicked up ripples from the lake. They could see, looking away from the city, the rain starting in a curtain. Lucia's friend had the oars now.

She said: "It's beautiful."

Nicholas stayed at the bow, even though he had to hold on as the boat began to slip and turn, and his knees were marked and bloody when they got to shore.

His mother hugged him. She never bothered with that particular friend again.

He liked to think he remembered what was specific, what happened in front of him. So he knew the caretaker rattled pans when the air raids came. He'd come up out of the courtyard, two tin saucepans and a spoon in each that he worked like a clapper in a bell, and he'd run around, up and down all the stairs, insisting everyone go down to the shelter.

But children hear stories. They heard and believed that it wasn't always safe in the cellars. One whole building ran down, barricaded the doors, made sure the ceilings were propped with beams, settled to a glass of milk or schnapps or cold coffee; and then drowned, because the pipes burst and they couldn't get out in time.

There was nobody for Nicholas to believe. Things you knew seemed more real than things you were told. He sometimes thought he'd moved into a world from the comic strips.

He passed a butcher's shop and saw a sleeping donkey being carried inside. He thought it was asleep because the men were carrying it suspended from a pole, its hooves shining. Then he looked again and he saw the throat was slit.

So he relied on his mother, and she used to make things all right, one way or another. Sometimes, she took him to the Kurfürstendamm to make things all right. He'd wear a very stiff white shirt. It almost hurt, but he was proud to wear it: a badge of being a man. She wore new, shiny shoes. They ate kuchen with a lot of cream.

They took the subway home. They went one stop sitting in among the neat afternoon crowd, and the air raid siren went off: a noise that sounded as though it had to be wound up.

The train stopped in the next station. Everybody knew they had to get out, so everyone went to the doors. Everyone stood around.

A pudgy man, a silly man out of a cartoon book, started talking very loudly. Nicholas tapped his mother to make sure she saw him: a little walking joke. He was insisting on attention, but he couldn't speak properly. He kept stuttering over words. People didn't quite laugh at him, but they shifted about as he told them how to survive.

After a minute, when the crowd wanted to be somewhere else and showed it, he said: "Listen. I only took this job to get away from my wife. You'd want to get away from my wife."

He had the crowd silent.

"She's orders, orders, orders. I can't breathe at home without permission. So just give me a minute—"

The all-clear siren sounded out. Everyone stepped back into the train.

Lucia went out in the evenings, and cars came for her. She went out in a cloud of Chanel No. 5—Nicholas had time to read everything in the apartment after she'd gone at night, so he knew all the brands—and she left behind an expensive, perfect ghost of scent. Sometimes very late she'd bring back pasta in a box from some restaurant.

Nicholas understood he had to be out of sight if anyone called for her, although she never let anyone into the apartment. She made things up to him at weekends and when she could. In winter, especially, he loved the one bath night, Saturday or Sunday. The soap scratched, and it didn't lather much; in fact, it made scum on the water. But he loved the attention and he loved the sheer, luxuriating warmth. He was always wrapped up, but he only felt truly warm in the bath.

Other nights, Lucia would sit in the living room, alive but inside the pages of a book. She might as well have been a picture behind glass. Or she would be pacing about the apartment, and Nicholas would say something, and she would either ignore him, or at best say: "Not now." Other days, she was teaching him to dance, him so short, head fixed just above her belly button, counting under his breath to a waltz. He tried to hold back, to play the man properly, but his face always ended in the warmth of her belly on the turns.

She always tried to be home when the air raids came. He was sure of that.

She took him to the movies one evening, and the sirens went off just as they were coming out of the theater, and they had to get to a shelter. There was a vast new bunker by the zoo, all stuck about with flak guns. Its walls felt like all the rock in a mountain. You didn't believe anything could move them.

They were checked as they went in, and searched. Lucia's papers must have seemed a bit odd, being Italian married to a Swiss and living in Germany. It didn't usually matter. But it seemed that, at the entrance to the zoo bunker, she didn't know anybody.

The sound of the siren was winding up and up. There was a long line waiting to be safe.

She pushed another set of papers at the guards. They must have been Nicholas's papers: born in Germany. So he could go in, and she followed, smiling kindly, letting her bag be searched, letting the guard say that in that dress he hardly needed to search her. Being young, Nicholas still wondered if the guard disapproved or approved.

He heard gunfire. He heard the low, droning sound of air engines. He heard the sirens. He wanted to be behind those safe, thick walls.

People kept their hats on. There weren't many lights, but the few lights were bright like theater lights, and the hats made odd shadows on the pale brick walls, made middle-aged persons into pharaohs and Turks and general infidels. It took forever to climb up level by level through the press of people, who didn't want to move from the doors, who still at that time of the war had the old animal instinct to stay close to the ground and the air. When the anti-aircraft guns fired, the earth shook under them.

Later, Nicholas learned about air, how it masses together after bombs have fallen and comes through a city like a blind wave of force, throwing fire all around, taking down what the bombs themselves could not ruin. But at the time, he felt safe. He looked up at a man and a woman on the spiral stairs, curled around each other and playing with each other's fingers, and he felt safe.

On his bed at Sonnenberg, he dreamt of a man walking away: walking steadily, purposefully, and not stopping for a moment even when Nicholas was shouting, shouting, shouting. The man did not acknowledge him, not even by ignoring him.

He always hated the moments in magic shows where there's a flash, a puff of smoke, and someone disappears. The rest of the audience clapped, cheered, laughed. Nicholas wanted to cry.

He was good at imagining things, but he was still lonely. He couldn't, officially, go out after dark, and it was dark when school finished in wintertime. Lucia was often out. There weren't many children in the building. He heard a baby sometimes.

He wanted a cat.

He thought his mother would never agree, not even discuss such a thing. He sensed that it would be one last thing too many. Besides, she was not a sentimental woman.

He didn't know where to look for a cat, whether there were shops for cats. He didn't have money, anyway. He thought about leaving a saucer of milk by the door and leaving the door open at night, but the door had to be closed and locked.

The second winter in Berlin was very cold. The radiators knocked and rattled, and still sometimes ice formed on the inside of windows. He tried leaving a window slightly open in case a cat wanted to come in, but a knife of cold cut into the room and he had to close it again.

He had his own key when he turned eight. He had to have one, Lucia said, because he might need to go to the shelter before she came home, and she might have to spend the night out.

He never told her that he went out, too.

Those nights were like the dark in a movie house before the film starts, the same coughings and laughs from somewhere you couldn't quite place, the same sense of being crowded and of strangers on the move, feeling their way, one foot ahead of another, shuffling.

Cars went about with caution, with animal eyes: a slit of light through the felt that was fixed over their headlights.

He didn't want to be far away from home. He just wanted air, and the sight of other people. He watched the backs of the men going away, and sometimes he imagined he'd just missed his father.

Then he didn't know the way.

This was not his city. He hardly knew it by daylight. He was not sure which way he should turn. He couldn't call out because he knew it was always better not to be noticed.

He knew people must be moving around him. He didn't know who they were, or what they wanted. There were a very few torches, masked in red or blue, and people tap tapping along like the blind.

He saw a woman's legs: long, elegant, silky legs, just her legs, in the red light from a torch. He thought she might help him, so he tapped her on the back and she spun round, her torch catching faces in the black, and she said: "Well, kid?"

"I wanted—"

"Listen. I'm working."

And she gathered herself, and kept the light playing down on those long, silky legs.

He put his back against a wall.

Someone was shouting, not shouting but honking out loud so that people would know he was there.

He didn't know which uniform his father wore, so he didn't know which uniform to trust.

He heard a tram coming. That was good; there was a tramline in the street next to their street. He heard it rolling and shearing on its tracks, and he heard crackling in the air.

There was suddenly blue, bright lightning in the street, earthed to its wheels, shocks of light in the quiet dark. Nicholas, very still on the sidewalk, could make out the shape of the tramcars. He saw their windows where people sat in iced cold light, very faint, that made them look as though they were already dead and their faces had started to fade.

Then the dark came together where the electric flares had torn it.

Nicholas had seen the store at the corner of the street; he knew at last where he was. He listened to the tram going away.

He heard a kitten bawling under a pile of fallen stones. He pushed the stones away and picked it up and it squirmed in his hand and then settled. He put it under his coat and it peed on him.

He managed to hide the animal for a couple of days. He saved bits of meat from Sunday dinner. He cut little pieces of cheese. He wished Lucia would bring oysters, because there were always too many oysters, one of those curiosities of war, although he didn't know if cats ate oysters. He cleaned up after the kitten, and the kitten kept wonderfully quiet, except that it purred so loudly when it was lying warm against him that he thought the apartment would shake.

But then Lucia got a maid, like everyone else, and she had to know.

He sometimes made an inventory of what he must have known. He didn't know the proper rules of soccer, but he knew about fire, flares, bombs. He knew what they meant. He never learned to throw a ball, because ball games would have been disorderly on the streets, but he knew how to pitch a stone to bring down the plaster from a falling wall. He saw uniforms, and also dead people.

Lucia got herself a job out at the film studios, UFA, the Universum Film AG, taking the train out each day. He never discovered why she wasn't at the embassy anymore; he thought he would ask her one day. She told him her job was to make sure there were cartoons in the cinemas, which seemed like quite a good idea, except that he was never very impressed with all the kisses in *Snow White*. He said she should leave those bits out of her films.

The maid's name was Katya. She came from somewhere to the East. She didn't speak much German. She had a pudding face, she didn't smile. She had a wonderfully big bottom, an epic of solid flesh. She fascinated Nicholas when she sat down, or when she walked away.

She never seemed to have time off. She was allowed to go off for a few hours on Fridays, and he assumed she might go to the cinema, but when he asked if she was going to a film, she said: "*Verboten.*" He didn't ask again.

He found a name for the cat: Gattopardo. He'd much rather have given it the sort of name a friend might have had, but Katya took him to the zoo one afternoon—she always wanted to take him to the zoo, because it was an excuse to be out and see other people—and he saw an ocelot which had just the same markings as his cat. Katya pointed out the label and he asked his mother what it was, and she told him in Italian. So the cat became Gattopardo.

He watched Katya for the sake of watching some other person. She washed out the apartment with a mop, a soft, sluicing sound that he could follow from room to room. It didn't seem to make the apartment much cleaner. He remembered her food, heavy and with potatoes, always potatoes: potato dumplings, potato cakes, a dozen different thicknesses of potato soup.

One afternoon, when she was out, Lucia said Katya didn't know everything about potatoes. Lucia took three potatoes out of the store and she juggled them, then she peeled them and cut them and then she said, "Shhh, you must never tell anyone," and she took the iron out of the cupboard, heated it up, and put the cut potatoes on it. "Fried potatoes," she said, and she gave Nicholas one. It was a bit raw in the middle, but it was gold and it was perfect to him. "Remember that," she said.

Nicholas laughed more when his mother was around. He laughed more with her than he did with his friends from school, for he and his friends were about the immensely serious business of conquering the city, at least as far as legs and sometimes a train would carry them. He already knew Alexanderplatz. He knew what the whitewashed windows meant because a schoolfriend told him: gypsy families. He knew the florists' windows which ran with water in summer to cool the roses you could just see inside; floats of color. He liked to watch the turtles gliding in the tanks at the aquarium on Budapesterstrasse.

He was eight and a half so he was automatically in a kind of gang: six of them. They went about dressed sharp and neat: boy gentlemen. They smiled a lot. In any other city, they would have been ominous and unnatural, but in this Berlin they somehow seemed just another phenomenon on the frantic streets.

They decided to be explorers. They couldn't travel, so they explored where the bombs had fallen: it was a different place down there. They scrambled under fallen beams, cracked girders, in the new pits along what used to be decorous streets. They found treasure of sorts in the roots of a tree that had been torn half out of the earth; but the treasure was only an old cocoa tin with some boy's marbles inside. They played marbles for a while on the sidewalk, called it a championship, until somebody told them to move on.

They weren't afraid in daytime then. They learned to get thoughtful, then edgy, then breathless only when it was properly dark and the bombers came. All the rest of his life, when the sun went down, even in some solid, safe house in Switzerland, fires lit, dinner cooking, lights blazing, Nicholas trembled.

They saw one day a woman, old, dressed in black with a yellow star, carrying a canary in a cage. Nicholas followed her for a while, because people don't take birds for a walk, and the others followed him and she must have noticed them because she stopped suddenly. She turned to Nicholas, and he thought for a moment she was going to give him the cage and then he saw how tired and angry she was.

"What do you want?" she said, with the emphasis on the "you," as though everyone else had shadowed and hassled her, and now it was a gaggle of boy gentlemen in a line.

Nicholas said: "I never saw anyone take a bird for a walk."

"You like birds?"

"Yes. Yes, I do, but I have a cat."

"I have to get a certificate," she said.

"What certificate? To show the bird is healthy?"

She said: "I have to have a certificate that the bird is dead. We're not allowed pets anymore."

And then the bird began to sing.

He could never ask Lucia: not about practical things, physical things, much less moral things or things he saw in the street. He wanted a father to ask. But since Müller was away, doing his duty, like the German fathers of the German boys, he supposed, he was left to patch the real world together out of his random glimpses.

There was an older man downstairs who sometimes left his door open during the day. The apartments were big enough, but they were awkwardly built to exclude every possibility of breeze; Nicholas assumed that he needed the air.

But he was someone to ask, and Nicholas went down to see him often.

He had books. He said he knew Lucia well. He told Nicholas that Goethe and Schiller were great writers, that Bach and Beethoven were great musicians; he had a record with a scratch of the first Goldberg variations. He said these things as though Nicholas needed to be told them, but it wasn't entirely clear if he thought Nicholas was too foreign to have been taught them properly.

Once he asked Nicholas to run an errand, four streets away. He had to ring a doorbell three times, wait, and ring once more. The door still didn't open. He wanted to knock on it fiercely but the older man had told him not to.

An old woman opened after a while. "Tell him I can't find more," she said. "Tell him this is what I have, that I don't need." She gave Nicholas a little tin box, for throat lozenges, that rattled.

"What are they?"

She said: "Never you mind." Then she said: "We call them Jewish drops."

"But I'm not Jewish."

"Then you won't like them."

He carried the box back to Mr. Goldstein, who made the Jewish drops disappear into his hand like a conjurer does.

Nicholas told his mother about this. He wanted to discuss it, a little. She only said he shouldn't do such things. Then she went downstairs herself to talk to Mr. Goldstein, and from downstairs he heard music: and he knew it was Bach, the Brandenburg Concertos, and was proud to know the name, because Mr. Goldstein had told him.

"What's happening?" he asked his mother when she came back.

"Nothing," she said. "Nothing unusual." And she was right; the usual was accelerated, frantic, menacing, but it was usual.

A few days later, Katya complained about having to clean a rug that had suddenly appeared, a fine red and gold affair. Lucia said she'd sort that out. "It can go into storage," she said. He noticed there were a number of other new and fine things.

He always had the key in his pocket. He walked carefully, tiptoe, down the stairs. He half hoped Mr. Goldstein's door would still be open, although he knew that adults all locked up at night; he'd been careful to check the locks on his own door.

The stairs were still very clean, the paint washed, the light dull neon gray. He didn't like shadows at the time, and there were hardly any shadows because the lights were overhead. Sometimes he felt safer on the stairs than in the apartment.

On the next landing down, he stopped at Mr. Goldstein's door. He pushed it. It came open. It didn't seem he had opened it for the sake of the air, but it wasn't locked.

He ought to warn him, say something, but he didn't want to go any further in. But he could hear music, and if he shouted, Mr. Goldstein might not hear him.

The light was shut off in the corridor, but he could see some faint shine, like a candle, in the living room.

He knew he should stop there. He looked back and the door bounced on its hinges and swung shut.

He was still an adventurer. He knew Mr. Goldstein, and Mr. Goldstein would be glad to see him, surprised, but glad. He was an adventurer, brave and intrepid, and he ought to go walk on down the corridor.

He ought to turn back.

If someone moved on the staircase, that would explain why he lost his nerve. But there was no movement in his memory, no footsteps. All he remembered was suddenly starting to run toward that faint gold light at the end of the corridor and stopping short of the door and hearing the needle catch in the gramophone record.

Mr. Goldstein would now get up from his chair and correct the record. But Mr. Goldstein did not correct the record. The needle banged and fizzed on the groove.

Nicholas was more afraid to run back than to run forward. Ahead there was light, behind was a throat of darkness, ready to swallow him.

The light changed. The candle, which had been flickering in a glass at the level of a tabletop, was now down on the floor.

He opened the door. The candle caught papers on the floor which burned up in a little boiling of flame.

He knew what to do. He stamped on the flames. He picked up the candle and pinched it out between his fingers.

He had seen something in the light. He saw Mr. Goldstein, in his chair. But now he could see nothing at all.

This living room must be much like the living room upstairs, so it would have windows over to the left, with shutters inside. If he could get to the shutters and open them, there would be light from outside: the Christmas lights of a bombing raid, perhaps.

He felt his way across the room.

He said: "Mr. Goldstein. Mr. Goldstein. Are you asleep?"

He fumbled with the low catches on the shutters and opened them. He wasn't sure if he could reach the higher ones, but he did not need to. The shutters were off their hinges, and tumbled open by themselves.

Mr. Goldstein sat facing the street. He was dressed in a suit, the trousers creased, the jacket tucked about him neatly. He wore his medals. In his hands, he had a book, and Nicholas knew from the heft and the binding and the gold on the edges of the pages that it must be one of his volumes of Goethe.

The little box for throat lozenges sat on the table by his side, with a glass of water.

He backed away from Mr. Goldstein, from his stillness and his indifference to the odd sounds in the room and the smell of scorched paper on the carpet and he turned and ran into the corridor.

He ran downstairs, not upstairs. He just wanted to be somewhere else, to be out of the building.

He wanted to talk to his father, there and then. He wanted to be sure he was still alive.

It was cold outside. He fussed with the locks, which had never seemed difficult before, and he went upstairs to wait at the window for his mother. He didn't like to seem anxious; it only made her fret. She turned up in a tiny, silly car that night: a Topolino, a Fiat. He told her he wished they could have a Topolino. He couldn't find the words for anything else.

It was often six weeks between letters from his father. His father described mountains and rivers, but never said anything about the war. Nicholas didn't think it was interesting to write about the bombs, either. He didn't want to worry his father, who would be there if he could be but who had a duty somewhere else. Nicholas could not define duty, but he could feel how it must trap and pull a man.

Besides, what could he have said in those letters? He didn't have landscapes to discuss. He saw animals only in the zoo or the aquarium. He never did get used to the ground shaking under him. He found it strange how, with everything, from the conduct of the war to the troubles of the Jews to the price of coal, you knew and you did not know, all at once.

He didn't want his mother to know he could take the key and go down to the streets and be anywhere his legs would carry him, but she'd certainly read his letters before she found envelopes and stamps. And yet, for all his venturing, he was always aware that he was dependent on Lucia like something unweaned. If she didn't come home, he would die.

He did write in one letter how they kept bathfuls of water just to put out fires. The basement was reinforced with tree trunks. Someone loosened the bricks in a couple of walls so the fattest tenant could get out if the main doors were blocked. There were card tables, a radio. The basement somehow got organized into a set of rooms, one for each family. Everyone always kept a suitcase packed.

That letter got lost, or censored. In his next letter, his father complained there had been no answer to his last one.

As for the excitements, the diversions, it wasn't fair to tell his father.

They'd been out to dinner, mother and son, with a couple of men who must have been Swiss. She didn't touch them; Nicholas noticed that. He always noticed that. He remembered having oysters, but he wanted something called crawfish. They came, long, pink, and thin. Then he had venison because he was hungry for grown-up, show-off meat, and it arrived a little bloody in the middle. He was upset for a moment but, like a grown-up, he ate it.

On the street, there was a soldier standing. He was clean-shaven, but the uniform wasn't quite right, and he looked tired. He asked Lucia, very simply, if he could look at her pretty hands.

She was furious when the authorities banned perms. The big, glossy shops with truly expensive things had begun to close down, too; Nicholas had liked that old gold light they used to throw out even in the middle of the day. And there were no church bells anymore, because of the war effort, they said. He remembered the bells where he used to live, how they rolled and roared.

The outside world was now without fine things. It was entirely different inside the apartment. There were pots and plates and chairs—sometimes the chairs didn't have cushions and Nicholas asked why. There were some tapestries, a couple of pictures. And when they moved apartments, somehow all that stopped being clutter and there were a couple of rooms he didn't like at all because they were like a museum.

His father stopped writing—or, at least, his letters no longer arrived. It was wartime; Nicholas was told not to be disappointed, or even surprised. He began by waiting for his father and very soon he was angry with his father and then he put his father—the particular, complicated man, with his tics and skills—out of his mind completely. He thought he had his ration of parents: a mother who stayed with him.

He remembered life like some gallery, made up of exhibits and pictures that sometimes made sense and sometimes did not: little moments, little dramas, never connected because connection would be a reminder of how everyone was waiting, waiting, waiting. They waited for victories that didn't come. They waited for soldiers to come back triumphant from Russia, and they didn't come back at all.

They waited, most of all, for the bombers.

Just once, he saw a truck carrying people away: carrying Jews away, he knew later. He could see their feet under the tarpaulin sides of the truck, like a puppet show upside down: some of them in slippers, neat leather shoes, pretty shoes, one bound up with cloth as though the foot was broken.

The next day, maybe the next week, very soon anyway, he learned the rules of chess and saw there could be whole epics in the moves. He learned to sing. His mother was charmed, then infuriated. "*Aprile non c'è piu,*" he sang. "*È ritornato il Maggio al canto del cucù.*"

He learned about women's eyes from movie stills. The eyes were all important in those days: Zarah Leander giving things up, Luise Ullrich trying to get home, Ilse Werner with her girl's way of showing polite, devoted skepticism, and Marika Rökk, who was his favorite. He had that picture of her from *Kora Terry* where she's turned to the camera, arm bare, shoulder draped, the light brilliant on those perfect lips and those welcoming, understanding, and, above all, interested eyes.

Gattopardo grew sleek, too sleek, handfuls of belly fur and belly. Nicholas watched him wash, paws articulated and flexible and too complicated to map or draw; and his tongue going in and out between the toes.

Nobody told him how to put all this together into the kind of childhood you can remember when your father dies; or how to make a self from all these moments, or a moral code, or even a strategy for staying alive.

In February, he was coming home from school on an evening of black cold. He tried a different street for once. Katya would be waiting for him, but he didn't much like Katya, and his mother was still working. He had no reason to hurry, except the cold.

The trees were rattling; there must have been a high wind, enough to rush the blood along a little. The streetlights were already on, a violet haze. The windows of apartment buildings were blank, nobody home yet, and the balconies bare. You couldn't even dry anything; it would have frozen stiff.

He heard a soft wave of sound, like crying in the streets. He never heard crying. He heard shouts or orders or fights, or else silence, but not crying.

He turned the corner.

He saw a dozen women standing around the entrance to some undistinguished building. All of them looked young, younger than his mother. They had cloth coats and they had bare faces and they trembled with weeping.

He didn't know what to do. He thought perhaps he should comfort them, but he couldn't take the hands of all of them and he didn't know which hand he should take first. And he felt, perhaps knew, that nothing kind and personal could ever be enough. He saw loss itself standing in that street, plain as a monument.

There was nobody to stop him walking through the door of the building. He was a child, after all, and nobody expected a child to take an initiative so nobody made rules to stop him. And besides, this place was a school: a place for children.

The lights inside were all turned on. The first room had a few chairs, a few tables. It had cribs, a dozen of them. All empty. There were two medicine balls, comfortably battered, and some colored blocks, and on the wall, some drawings done by very small children: stick people in box houses by lollipop trees.

It was very quiet. In all his life he only heard the same kind of silence one other time, and that was during a full eclipse of the sun: when the light went wrong, when the life went out of the air, when everything fell silent and the shadow took away the sun.

Strollers stood in two neat half circles on the tiles. Outside noises broke in: trams grinding on metal, a car Klaxon.

March 1, 1943, was the first night the bombers got to the very heart of Berlin. It became a date he remembered, like a birthday, like a saint's day.

Until then, he could imagine there was an order in the world, a way to make sense of everything. It might be the order of prison, or the order of school with all its rules and bosses and communal rumors and fantasies, and also like being part of some great civilian army whether you liked it or not. But he imagined that the adults all walked down the street, carrying their assumption that the world made sense.

Of course, people sometimes saw too much, as stagehands step out of the dark between scenes at the opera. Ever since the Russian campaigns began, there were wounded people, on one leg, with one arm; there was a stump of a man, cut off at the waist, on a board with little wheels, who exercised each day in the courtyard, frantically pushing and pulling himself from side to side, getting nowhere. You also saw people with no particular purpose, when everyone was supposed to be part of the fatherland's machine, or people swapping rumors on a corner, or adults making jokes, or people who forgot to say Heil Hitler, ever.

Some schoolmate told Nicholas about the time Zarah Leander went to Hitler by special invitation to sing him a song. And the song was: "I Know a Miracle Will Happen Some Day."

Nicholas knew he was virtually a foreigner, so he decided not to laugh.

The caretaker came to take down the wooden shutters. Nicholas asked why, and he said: "Because they burn too easily." Nicholas said: "Why would they burn?"

There was a rush to patch up damage, put up flags, put up boards so nobody could see into the shell of buildings, put up notices to say that repairs were about to be done by someone about to be named.

Lucia asked Nicholas, quite abruptly, if he wouldn't rather go to school in Switzerland. He didn't know what she wanted him to say. He asked if he could be with his father. She said that wouldn't be possible, because he was still in the Swiss army and he was guarding some mountain pass somewhere. Nicholas wanted to know: "Who's he guarding it against?"

She said it was very nice in Switzerland, he'd like it. She'd always meant to take him. He said he liked it there, in Berlin, with her. She said there'd be more bombs. So he asked one more time: Would he be able to see his father? And she said he'd have to live in school. He asked if she would come to live in Switzerland, but she said she had things to do in Berlin. And it never once crossed his mind that he was at last old enough to be dismissed to school.

He told Lucia she could do whatever she wanted in Switzerland.

They could go to the mountains with Dad. Lucia said, again: "He's in the army."

Nicholas went back to the cardboard box with all his father's letters. He wanted clues, and there were none; a soldier writes carefully in a war. He was well. He was in the mountains. He said something about how much he admired the Finns when they tried to beat off the Russians. He told Nicholas when the blackout started in Switzerland, and about a movie they'd all been shown—about some innkeeper's daughter on the frontier in the First World War, who helps her lover get married to a girl from a much grander family. He said there was a song: "*C'est la petite Gilberte, Gilberte de Courgenay, elle connaît trois cent mille soldats et tous les officiers.*"

Nicholas woke up in his chair at Sonnenberg, old man as he was, with the kind of laugh that is part a cough, part a grumble. He thought: You couldn't sing that today, now could you?

Everything was backward and everybody knew it. Instead of crowds coming into Berlin for Hitler's birthday, for banners and parades and the Führer weather that sparkled in mid-April, everyone was leaving the city.

School was a bulletin board for rumors. Nicholas was the first to announce that you had to wrap a wet towel around your head when there were phosphorous bombs, or else your hair caught on fire and your brain fried. Gerhard asked why soldiers carried telephones when they were fighting a fire, and Nicholas said maybe to talk to the officers, and then that he didn't know. Gerhard said: There were soldiers fighting a fire and they got trapped in a building and they caught fire. So they needed the phone to ask someone to come and shoot them.

Then it was all zoo stories: how the crocodiles used to answer back the bombers, cold blood to cold blood, so it seemed.

The lilacs flowered as usual. The candles caught light on the chestnuts. All of the apparatus of spring was there, the prospect of getting out into the woods, onto the water; but Nicholas and his friends were preoccupied. Their little gang sensed that most other people also had gangs.

He'd seen a woman one afternoon in a gas mask, pushing a pram that was heaped up with blankets to keep the air from her baby. She was out for a stroll by the ruins of a movie house.

The year grew hotter and hotter.

Lucia said everyone was going away. The names stuck with Nicholas like a litany, which must be magic because you can't quite work out what it means: the Meinsdorps and the Edelstems, the Rocamurros, the della Portas and the Barros, the Furstenbergs were all going away.

On August 1, 1943, schools closed. Women, children, and the sick were told to leave the city. Nicholas's friend Gerhard was taken to the station, but it seemed nobody had told the railways about the crisis; so there were no trains.

The next day, a leaflet at the door: all women not doing war work, all children, to leave at once. The day after that: leaflets from the air, telling women and children to go. The temperature had slipped ruthlessly upward—90°, then 95°—and the heat met the crowds like a wall. They still butted and rushed their way to the railway stations.

Lucia was not leaving. Nicholas didn't understand. She knew so many important people, it seemed, so many names that must matter from the way she intoned them, so many diplomats and politicians and people who still had cars they could send to take her to dinner; she must have had a choice. She knew enough to want Nicholas in Switzerland, as soon as possible. But she didn't want to go herself.

She was still the whole world for Nicholas. What other world can you have when the sky goes red and streets start falling?

There were lines for flowers at the stalls on Frankfurter Allee. All these years later, he wondered what people expected from the flowers. A certain coolness, perhaps. Distinct colors, any colors, in a city turning the drab standard of soot. They were a reminder of a world of gardens and living things. Or perhaps they were subject to discipline and order: something you could arrange, when life was so manifestly out of control.

The radio was always playing dance music. Always.

He started to notice that things were broken, not just the ruins, although those had stopped being playgrounds because they were too obviously dangerous, great cairns of stone that could fall anytime. But people were nicer to each other, in a way. The formality, the starch, was also broken up.

He asked his mother why men had long hair now and women had short hair.

It was the right kind of night for catastrophe—cold, rainy, November, trees bare, world gone to mud.

Everyone felt safe under such heavy rain because the clouds would surely make the bombers' job short, and perhaps impossible. So Nicholas could see from the window the heavy leather curtain going back and forth on the bar across the street: people out, people in.

Gattopardo hated noise. He curled up against it. He ran frantic to escape it. But it was a quiet night to start with and he came to the window. Nicholas stroked him under his chin. He licked Nicholas's hand.

Lucia was out. She almost always had people to see.

Everyone knew, the way everyone does know things in wartime without being told, that nothing could happen after half past seven.

At half past seven exactly, the sirens roared.

The caretaker came around bellowing and ringing a bell he'd

found somewhere. Nicholas did not go down to the cellar. He didn't think the raids could be very long. And he wanted to see for himself.

He heard, first. He heard the bombers in the distance, like drums, then, unmistakably, engines rumbling, then roaring, then above his head. The sky filled up with noise. And that night, it did not come in waves. There seemed to be no intervals at all.

There was always a long moment between hearing the planes and the first damage. Gattopardo hid. Nicholas sat like a boy at a movie, with the curtains open. He thought at first the bombs were all duds, because sometimes there was no sound of impact you could make out through the roar of the engines and the pelting of the rain.

But first the marker bombs came down, slow as silk. Then the blast bombs: timpani and fire. Then the stick incendiaries, each opening in flames already, magically lit and consuming.

He saw light a few streets away: red light between the violet of the streetlights, a flash of a pale, poisoned green. He knew the blue was phosphorous fire. The sky was all neon, diffused by the rain still falling.

The planes did not stop. They shat fire on the city. On each pass, you could sense the earth a little less stable, the air less cool, the rain contaminated now with ash and cinder.

He did not move from the window. He could not make himself safe. The cellars would be barred now. He couldn't make anyone hear him through the appalling rumbling and thumping and roaring outside.

He was nine years old. He sat by a window and he watched a city die.

He felt a bizarre calm, a sense of distance even as the ground shook. From the trees on the street he could tell the wind was getting up. If the wind got up, it would tend and blow the fires. He thought that among the sounds of aircraft engines, of the air they displaced, of the houses spilling out their organized life onto the sidewalks in a mess of stone and wood and steel, there was also the sound of flames. You couldn't hear any one thing as definite as flames because of the hot pressure of the air.

The rain stopped.

There is that magical moment after rain when you can see forever. Nicholas could see too far.

A whole barrier to sight was falling away: a barrier that had been apartments and homes. One of the walls dissolved, just dissolved, as sand dissolves when water passes. Inside, he could see a chandelier hanging, a spreading affair of pink glass. He saw the chandelier rock and pitch, then fall to the floor. But there was no more floor, and the glass went on falling, catching the red flame light out of the sky and breaking it, down through room after room until he couldn't see it anymore.

The windows cracked. Glass fell around him. When the wind came in, and it was still a cold wind even with all the fires, the room changed with it: the room was stripped of life, naked like a dead thing, just objects on a platform of wood and rugs. The wind invaded, and he had no more home. It was like a kind of light that made things sinister or featureless or, mostly, alien.

He knew he had to shelter, but he didn't want to shelter. He wanted to stand out in the fire and shout. Other men tell you about the moment they think they became men, maybe in someone's bed, maybe in a moment of courage or epiphany. This was his moment: the certainty that he could not look away, let alone move away.

He was a hero. He also pissed himself.

He wanted to find Gattopardo, to comfort himself with something warm, living, subtle to hold. The cat saw him, and came for him, meaning harm. The sight of that madness helped keep Nicholas sane.

Gattopardo went for the window, for the glass.

Fire rained down close. There were sparks as pretty as Christmas toys.

Gattopardo went through the window with a fine grace. He seemed, in the blood light outside, to catch fire. He seemed to climb the sky, paws out as though he would rip it as he came down.

Nicholas, alone, was terrified. He wanted to get out of the apartment, but he felt responsible for the apartment. He wanted to find his mother, but she could find him only if he stayed where he was. He wanted to be held, to be given warm milk, to be talked into sleep.

The bombers had not yet stopped coming.

He saw the clock: a tall mahogany piece, gilt at the top, a pendulum that had not stopped all through the shivering of the city. It said: 8:25. He didn't know if it could possibly be right. It seemed the bombs had been falling for days.

He watched the clock. There had to be a last bomb, the diminishing roar of engines in retreat, soon, please, soon. He saw the minute hand of the clock twitch forward, the first time he ever noticed a minute being completed and recorded that way. He still liked to check his own watch rather than look at the clocks on Swiss railway stations, which also jerk forward on the minute.

At eight-thirty, the last bomber droned away, went from the sound of engines to the sound of drums and then to the sound of the rain starting again. All this time, the lights did not fail. But now they failed.

He wanted not to have to play his father's part anymore. He wanted his father there.

Lucia came home on foot, at eleven by the tall pendulum clock.

She came through the door and Nicholas, instead of wanting her to hold him, wanted to kick and thump and beat and bruise her. He was never so relieved, so furious, so happy, so wretchedly abandoned to every emotion he had known so far in a brief life.

She said: "I got down to the Adlon cellar. I couldn't get out, and I couldn't get to you."

Her shoes looked as though they had been cut.

"I never meant to leave you here, not when there was a raid—"

Nicholas showed no feeling.

"You know," she said, "people started dancing afterward. They danced in the streets."

Her hair, which had been gloriously red, was caked in soot and dust. Her eyes were tired, not bright at all. Her dress was intact but he noticed, as she walked away, that she was not wearing stockings. She had penciled the line of a stocking seam on the back of each calf, and the line had smudged.

She turned to Nicholas and said: "I do it all for you."

But he knew that could not be true.

He heard Berlin.

A bombed city creaks. The glass gets splintered, and it crashes often. There aren't any more old, solid verticals; they've all fallen. There are new verticals: water going up like a rope and falling in plumes against flaming walls, breaks in the road going up in orange fire where the gas mains broke, the roots of trees and the twists of melted cable in the air. Things rumble and predict trouble everywhere and anywhere at random. You go quickly in case the collapse begins while you're still in range of girders, doorjambs, flying lintels.

And the newspapers still came on time.

Then there's the sound of fire. It's never truly out. If you've ever seen peat fires, you'll know the kind of fire that burns just under the surface, that seems to smolder forever. Fire and dust together accounted for all the air.

The same night the bombs fall, the fires rear up and they run. As they run, they seem to press the air which is already dense with dirt and fire. The air itself becomes fire.

And the streets are all bright as in the daytime, brighter now because the November cloud and gloom are beaten back by this air which is fire. It never gets dark. You think it will never get dark again. But then day comes, and the smoke is so dense you think it will never be light again.

As soon as it seems nothing worse is going to come from the sky, people are out. They're slipping here, slipping there. They carry things. They have furniture on little carts. Lorries roll, maybe salvaging, maybe thieving. There's so much soot, you can't make out faces, and anyone might wear a mask.

He remembered a shop that sold antiques. It burned for days, and as it burned, the flames lit up the shine of brocades and silk inside, all red and gold.

As for the apartment, the windows were gone. The frames of the windows, something you always imagine as fixed and solid, now rattled and creaked. There were random doors. There was no heat, no light, no water, no gas. Someone had written on the side of the front door of the building, in chalk: "Lucia, where are you? We have room for you."

He went into his room and tried to close the door. It would not quite close.

He had a boy's world in that room, separate from all the prettiness and fussiness of his mother's rooms. He had pictures of machines on the walls, cut out from advertisements: cars and trucks, mostly. There were Ford cars parked in some medina under palm trees, Ford trucks in the shelter of a plane's propellers, Fords with wood-gas generators "for the home front." There were Mercedes roaring out of the horizon on caterpillar tracks, with bombers overhead like a guard of honor woven on a tapestry, and the cover of *Deutsche Kraftfahrt* for June 1939, with two pale cross-country Opels rambling over an open field; and a poster with an Opel rumbling over a slack wood bridge held up by railway sleepers.

All the shaking and settling had torn only one of them: a magazine page on the far wall, for Opel, "the dependable one." He liked that particular picture. Light beams cut a parallelogram out of the dark sky. Under that, two Opels stood, nose to nose, their headlight beams as solid as running water and on the same downward track. His father drove an Opel when he was in Bavaria, when he was a father still.

The emergency services were on the streets. They had cigarettes and coffee, which seemed astonishing, and they had liver sausage and buttered bread and soup. Lucia liked the cigarettes. She found chocolate, too, and an old salami in the cupboard which stank but which she insisted was still good.

There was another smell Nicholas could not place for a while among all the other smells that go with disorder. It tasted like the dead of winter at the back of the throat. It spoiled everyone's breathing, as though it could make the air too thick to breathe. Someone told him, later, it was the fires in every backyard, the coal supply of the whole city for the winter, all burning and all impossible to put out.

They couldn't even trust the bombers anymore. They'd come, and they'd drop nothing, and then they'd come over again. Sometimes they passed over three times before anything started to fall. It was because the Americans had reached Berlin at last, so Nicholas's friend said. And if the Americans could get here, they could come in tanks. And the Russians could come, too.

Lucia still had her job at the film company, but the studios were all flattened now. Two or three times, she took Nicholas to the Swiss consulate. It was the only building still standing in the diplomatic quarter.

One day she dyed her hair blond, a brittle, vicious kind of blond. She kept asking if he liked it, if he liked it at all.

The weather was going to be lovely, as usual, for Hitler's birth-day. Anyone who could go had already gone. The city was half empty. But everything was bright with low spring light.

A car came: a substantial, maybe official black car. Lucia wore trousers. She told Katya to help with the suitcases. Katya stood on the steps of the building while Lucia and Nicholas climbed into the back of the car.

Nicholas wanted to say "Good-bye" but his mother said to say nothing of the sort and he remembered that Katya was not to be told anything.

He did turn back as the car pulled away and looked at her where she still stood. He thought he caught her eye, and he thought he saw kindness there, which was not at all what he expected.

They came into a street that stood empty, except for the swastika flags of red, white, and black: still and silent and finished, except for the colors of the flags bristling and twinkling between stones, no windows left, balcony iron twisted about, stairs that went up two treads and stopped, the walls just fronts for pits and spaces where there were walls at all.

He'd gotten used to sidestepping the dung from the horses that drew carts around the city. So he was startled at the seven trucks parked along one side of the street in perfect order, large to small. He checked them like a collector: Opel Blitz, the kind that ran on gas and not diesel, and a square-cabbed Ford V3000S with a box behind the cab for firewood and a gas generator, and a Mercedes diesel with the huge insignia still, just, attached to the radiator grille.

They were unofficial trucks, going about under the remains of sundry paint jobs; the effect was like city camouflage. One looked ominously old, a canary-yellow square-backed tug, suitable for taking bread around a suburb. One looked fit to carry a whole life's worth of furniture. Two of them carried the names of household movers.

That morning, Nicholas met his mother for the first time: saw her operate. She commanded this whole convoy. She demanded. She checked and she bustled about. She wasn't the film clerk anymore, or the pretty woman who went out to dinner and came back late, or the mother who looked after her boy, when she could. She called the drivers together and made them listen while Nicholas fidgeted on the steps of a building which did not exist anymore.

She went inside each truck. The large one opened on newspaper and cloth and carpets, all wedged between wrapped things. The small yellow van carried boxes jammed together with blankets under and above them. Nicholas had no idea his mother had such possessions, or that they needed such protection.

When she came back from settling the drivers, she asked if he wanted to ride up front: first truck in the convoy, driver's cab. Of course he wanted to ride there. He would be the venturer, the explorer. He would be the guard and the intelligence man. He would gobble up the great roads.

He clambered into the cab, shook the hand of the driver who had one week's start on a fine wide moustache and smelled of tobacco and coffee. Lucia climbed up after him, and slammed the door.

The driver sounded his horn and kicked the starter button just above the gas pedal. Slowly, laboriously, the engine caught and the weight of the truck rolled forward, out of the dead street.

Nicholas saw a banner across the street: "Our walls are breaking. Not our hearts."

He saw a statue facing the wrong way into a wall.

He knew this was not the right day to be traveling. He thought they would certainly be stopped.

He had just seen all the furniture still in the apartment, Katya starting to wipe it. But the furniture wouldn't fill all these trucks, even if it had been loaded while he wasn't looking.

He wanted to see what was in the trucks. Then he understood that was the very last thing he should want. "Don't you look," his mother always said. "Don't you ask!"

They went slowly, in a cloud of black engine smoke, a faint smell of spilled fuel. They must have carried cans of fuel, because there was little chance of finding it along the way. Three of the trucks certainly worked on wood gas, so they had great hunchback stores and furnaces behind the driver's cab.

Nicholas studied the road ahead as though that was the map, and he was responsible.

He saw a wasted city, dust devils getting up among the ruins, the colors all wasted and buried, leaving only ghosts of concrete and brick.

He started to sing, the driver joined in, Lucia joined in.

Lucia watched the road in the side mirror. She shifted in her seat. She looked back again. Then she leaned across Nicholas and she grabbed the wheel and she said: "Stop now. What the hell is going on?"

The driver stopped, sat back, and said with a patronizing kind of patience: "You could have run us off the road."

"There are no trucks following us."

"All the trucks are following us."

"I can't see anything on the road."

"Listen," the driver said, "you want to look like a convoy from the air? It doesn't matter if we're civilian, not to the bombers. We're better off seven trucks, apart."

"I'm waiting here for the other trucks."

"We go down the autobahn, they kill us. Seven trucks together, they'd never believe we weren't military."

"I haven't gone to all this trouble," his mother said, "to give some fucking truck driver the profits."

And they waited until the trucks caught up, stopped behind, and the drivers each came out to ask what was happening.

After that, Lucia insisted the convoy stick together and stop often, and at each stop she'd get out and open each truck's doors and examine the cargo. The men had strong, cold coffee and beer, and bread and sausages.

They rolled south all day, skirting places. And they didn't travel down the autobahns, which had already been broken by bombing; they used old roads, side roads where they could.

Nicholas saw soldiers on horseback, soldiers sleeping in a ditch. He half expected lances and pikes and cannon out of some tapestry; he looked through the windows, and he looked back in time.

The driver said they were lucky it was spring. In winter, you had to warm up the engine with a blowtorch and then you had to rock the whole damn truck back and forth to get the pistons and the bearings moving. Nicholas listened to every detail. He had a small boy's fetish for the ways machines work, for figures and specifications: two-liter, six-cylinder, however many horsepower. He could hold the whole machine in his head, and somehow control its performance on these doubtful roads.

They kept moving at night, lights fixed down on the road, with the truck engines masking out the sounds of any planes above. Sometimes, they crossed other convoys that were on the move, shadows on the other side of valleys, great metal machines suddenly smoking out a wood: official, drab, purposeful convoys. At three in the morning, nobody could stay awake; so they parked off the road in the shelter of trees and Nicholas slept with his mother in the cab. The driver took a blanket down to the ground.

Before he slept, he propped stones under the front and back fenders. He said it would take the strain off the leaf springs and stop the truck rocking in the night.

Nicholas didn't sleep at first. He could check the trees through the window. He listened for engines, planes, wind in the branches, animals, birds, coughs and snoring from the drivers, and he watched for lights. But he must have fallen asleep, because there is nothing in his memories until the moment of waking up abruptly and staring into an unknown face, under a cap, with a uniform coat and its collar pulled high: the sort of face you see across counters, across desks.

Lucia also woke.

She did something so curious: she pouted and she half complained, as though she'd been caught underdressed by a man she quite liked. Nicholas didn't understand such things, but he saw the oddness of her reaction—no shock, not even surprise, just complete absorption in keeping the attention of the man at the window.

She told Nicholas to stay in the truck.

There were two cars parked on the road, long black cars: staff cars, Mercedes cabriolets, with great rolls of mudguard on either side of the high radiator and their enormous headlights blinded. Nicholas classified the cars, as usual. The first one looked like a 320, so it had to belong to someone important.

There were six men, standing by the cars in long leather coats. There must have been some light—moonlight, starlight—because he distinctly remembered glints on the coats as though they were polished. Lucia was arguing, gesturing.

He had to trust her so perfectly. They were out in the middle of a wood, nobody around, six men with guns in big, official, influential cars, and she had to explain how seven civilian trucks were on the move, how a woman came to be in charge, how an Italian and Swiss woman could have business here, how anybody could legitimately be heading for Switzerland; because Nicholas knew she could not tell a lie. There was no time or material for a lie.

The sky began to come back: like a pale cloth, then all suffused with pink, then bright.

The men seemed amused. Nicholas didn't know if that was good or not. They seemed to like to keep Lucia talking at the roadside, to alarm her, to make her flirt and chat and charm, to detain her.

Nicholas watched the sky turn red behind the trees.

Lucia shrugged her shoulders hugely. She came back to the truck and she picked up a thick envelope of papers for them to read.

One of the men, the oldest, considered the papers and clicked his heels and said: "Madame" in a parade-ground voice, as though he meant it. It was definitely "Madame"; he was trying to be respectful to a foreigner.

The sky was blue like a robin's egg is blue. Lucia smelt of sweat when she got back into the cab.

He should have asked her. But he wouldn't have known how to frame the questions: What are we carrying, why are we carrying it, why does it matter, why did they let us go? If he'd been able to ask those things, he would already have learned mistrust, and he still had to depend on Lucia.

Besides, he saw how serious she was. This was not the time for him to ask questions.

Much later, when he woke up in the long nights, eyes wide, brain stopped, and wondered how he could even be connected to such things, he had others to protect. He wanted wife and child, all the years, to live as they wanted and not to concern themselves with a convoy creeping down to the Alps. He didn't want to infect them with his doubts.

So the doubts grew until they stole his sleep. He was a realistic man, and knew he never had a choice—just a boy in a wood in a war—but he was sure he could never trust anyone who claimed that all morality was suspended for them because they had no choice. Year by year, he learned not to trust his own story, then not to trust himself.

———

The official cars droned away into the dawn. The drivers woke, complained, went off into the woods, and came back for cold coffee. One of them wanted to make a fire, but Lucia kicked wet leaves over the first flames and told him to get on.

They rolled around Magdeburg and Dessau and Weissenfels. They avoided Bayreuth and Nuremberg and Augsburg. They held to local roads, and then made dashes on the autobahns where they could, and then went back to the slow, narrow roads that they blocked for hours. Lucia muttered that she didn't know if it was worse to be bombed by the Allies or harangued by the peasants up ahead and behind them. She used a bad word before "peasants."

They saw the smoke coming up from Stuttgart.

Lucia argued with the driver; she wanted nothing to happen without her orders. She said they'd be faster crossing Lake Constance, which he insisted on calling the Bodensee. He said she was crazy to think the ferries would be running as usual. She said he lacked faith in the Reich. He said: "And you have so much faith you're moving to Switzerland?"

She said: "Then we'll go in by Thayngen and Schaffhausen."

Lucia never wanted to stop. The driver insisted. There was a cacophony of shouts and horns. When the truck rolled to a halt, and braking had begun to seem a long, slow, chancy process, they all looked back.

Five trucks followed. There should have been six.

"We lost one," said the driver, complacently.

Lucia kicked him once, hard, in the shins. He still had that soft, half-fancying look on his face, happy to be doing a job for this bright lady, but Nicholas wasn't sure his mother had done the right thing.

"Then find him," his mother said.

One of the other drivers, a man in late middle age carrying a lifetime of beer in front of him, came rolling up. "Went just off the road," he said. "We'll need a tow rope to get him out."

Lucia said: "Do it."

The heavy-bellied man checked the driver, just to see his reaction, just to know what to do. He couldn't tell because Lucia's manner and her accent were at war.

She sat on a wall. She watched the convoy, her particular convoy, turn back on the road. Nicholas never saw her face so bare, so tight and angry.

Nothing was safe until everything was safe across the border. And she wanted to be safe.

A black bird came down in the next meadow, then another. They could hear, over the gunning of engines half a mile back, sheep blathering in a field. They could hear the wind.

"It's nice here," Nicholas said, wanting something innocent to say. "Is it pretty like this in Switzerland?"

She rounded on him. "Pretty? Like this?" She spat. He never saw her spit before. "This is all," and she reached for a word violent enough, "landscape."

Nicholas said: "But the birds—"

"Some people," she said, "like birds. Some people like life."

"There's life here."

"What's living," she said, "is out there with its tail up shitting. That's all."

Nicholas stood up. "I like it," he said, obstinately.

She wouldn't answer. He could read a kind of contempt in her eyes: he had given up, he was not struggling on. He liked fields, and birds, and landscape; he did not value will, plans, organizing.

Breath knotted up in his stomach.

And she left him. She started walking down the road to where the men now had the lost truck grappled to a cable, and the largest truck was nudging it out of the roadside mud.

He didn't want to follow her. He sat back on the wall and he listened, harder than he ever listened before in his life. Every sound in the city pushed itself on you; here, you had to seek out sound and break its code.

He could hear a kind of whispering.

He turned. The whispering was just a roar at a distance, he realized. Across the valley, water was breaking out of the rock, falling like hard smoke, the spring melt busting out of its usual course and arcing out into the air.

Under his breath, he started to sing: "*Cucù, cucù, Aprile non c'è piu...*"

The largest of the trucks was struggling now, a sound so large it filled up the view and made the birds scatter. Then it stopped. He looked down the road, and he saw the convoy back in perfect line.

Lucia was shouting. Nicholas listened to the water. Lucia was gesticulating.

He clambered back into the cab of the truck, back in the convoy again, that little smoking particular of gas and wood fumes that stained the rosy, gilded sunset.

Two men in familiar brown shirts, rifles over shoulders, belts full of cartridges. Barbed wire across a bridge; it looked the way roses look in autumn, all bare and looped and thorny.

Men in procession, marching with shovels: no ease or enthusiasm, just taking used bodies home. They had a uniformed guard.

Across the bridge, men in Swiss uniforms under Swiss flags. There were white signs on trees and the posts that carried power lines: "Halt! Swiss territory! Crossing of the border forbidden. Violations of this order will be put down by armed force."

Lucia put on a hat.

One of the brownshirts and one of the Swiss guards from the other side came forward and talked to her. She kept saying: "Household goods." Then the brownshirt said it, and the Swiss said it and shook his head, and Lucia said, firmly: "Personal effects." Then she pulled out all of her papers.

The brownshirts saluted. Nicholas was not at all surprised. If she could turn away a line of predators in the forest, she could cope with these frontier pen pushers, whose guns were only ornament.

The Swiss asked for passports. Lucia produced hers, which was, by right of marriage, Swiss. One of the Swiss said, a little sharply: "Welcome home."

Then Lucia produced other papers, in a slim envelope. He consulted them, and was democratic with Lucia, but not sharp anymore.

There was a brief fuss about the drivers: whether they could be relied upon to go back. Lucia promised. The Swiss guards were not convinced. Lucia was welcome to cross; Nicholas was welcome to cross; there was no problem with the trucks, or their contents. But the drivers were another matter.

The bridge was at last a proper frontier, a place of suspicion and delays, of administration licking its fingers to turn the pages of passports and officials consulting each other out of earshot of the civilians on the road.

The drivers produced all the papers they had.

The Swiss soldiers had caps like turtle shells, rifles across their backs, sloppy trousers. One of them carried Lucia's bags across the bridge for her.

She did not seem happy to be across the border. She kept looking back to where the trucks, their engines now shut down, bulked frozen in the low evening light.

"We're here," Nicholas said, and then regretted saying something so empty. It certainly wasn't enough to take her eyes from the trucks.

She seemed to be willing their lights to catch, their engines to turn over, the whole convoy to roll over the bridge and into her brilliant future.

FOUR

He was all rusticity the next weekend, his memories stowed away: brown apron, pot belly, gray hair rampant, slipping peels off potatoes cooked two days ago for *Rösti*. The kitchen at Sonnenberg had always been Nicholas's territory; not even Nora disputed it.

He listened for Helen's car on the hill. The day was brisk, sky like a photograph, there must be a breeze: he hoped they could go for a walk. And Henry was coming, which would make it hard to find a corner for quiet talk.

The car stopped. Through the window he could see Henry and his stroller being unpacked at the roadside. The boy stared at the geese snapping about. The geese complained. Helen had a stuffed lion by the paw.

Henry, properly solemn, knocked at the door.

Nicholas smiled hugely, and he hugged Helen as though he needed to, and then he lifted up Henry, who said: "Geese," and wriggled.

Then he was putting butter in pans, taking up great scoops of the soft, light gold of potato. Helen was trying to take over the process, teasing to work the grater or the peeling knife, but he resisted. "I never have anyone to look after," he said.

Henry went upstairs to practice coming downstairs, which he had not quite mastered.

"I would have gone with you," Helen said.

"They didn't want you, either."

She so obviously wanted to ask how it had gone, what he had seen, if there had been any insults to add to the simple, miserable fact of his exclusion. But she could hear Henry bump, bumping on the stairs, coming down on his buttocks, and she went to see that he was all right and when she came back the moment for questions had passed.

There was liver with the *Rösti*, and a salad made from cabbage that had been sweetened by the frost all winter.

"It was a country funeral. Very simple. White flowers and a lunch afterward."

Henry contemplated eggs and what he could do with them: build castles of potato, throw, strain, squelch.

"I watched," Nicholas said.

"I never knew him."

"No," Nicholas said. "Nor did I, really."

He began to gather up the plates.

"There isn't anything to say," he said, firmly.

"It's not over. Look what happened to you yesterday."

"We're an embarrassment to a good Catholic family. An anomaly."

"You're not the embarrassment, Lucia is."

"They don't know anything about her. My father told them she was dead. She died in the bombing of Berlin."

"I don't know the whole story, either."

"I've told you everything I know."

She looked sharply at him. She did not like the idea that he might choose not to know things.

They listened to the quiet, which was a way of making sure that neither of them said things.

And then Henry was at the door, loud as a committee, demanding a snowman. They were both relieved; they both smiled great involuntary smiles; they went ambling out after the boy into the bright white garden.

Helen pitched snow at Nicholas, who dusted himself off and pitched back a packed, iced snowball which broke on the trunk of an apple tree. Nicholas worried out loud about goose shit in the snow, but he was still scrabbling under the crust where the downy stuff lay.

Henry labored on a great brick of snow, which he tried to throw, just throw away, but which fell back to the ground in a soft pile. So Helen made it the start of a snowman, scooped more snow onto the pile, firmed the soft stuff, packed it into a fat little body while Nicholas showed Henry how to roll a great head across the lawn.

Then Nicholas brought a wizened carrot out of the barn, and Henry brought little black stones for the buttons, and Helen put twigs to show the arms and hands.

They stood back, hot and grinning.

Henry began to kick the snowman down. He was shouting: "Snow Man! Big Man!"

Nicholas only laughed, but Helen was watchful. Henry was herded between them back to the warmth of the house, to the tile wall of the stove and the prospect of chocolate.

The geese barked and wailed. Down in the valley, a dog was complaining. Then the world went quiet outside.

Nicholas said, suddenly: "She cost me my father."

Then he said: "I shouldn't have said that."

"You never said it before."

"I couldn't change things, you see. All I could do was make a life for Nora and for you, and keep you safe."

She said: "You did that. You did all of that."

"It would be wonderful to resolve things," Nicholas said. "To have them over after all this time. I don't think it is possible."

"If there was a crime—"

"The law didn't solve anything in 1945. Why should it do any better now?"

Helen said: "Because all the circumstances are different. Because it's possible now."

"But who has the energy anymore?" Nicholas said.

She thought he must have slept badly again last night: panda eyes, watery and ringed with black. She wanted to hold him and let him rest; she wanted to force him into confession; she wanted justice and she wanted her father to sleep all at once. She invented an excuse for her confusion: that it was all about the healing force and use of bringing out secrets.

"I do want to know," she said. "I don't really know what you saved me from."

"You want everything acknowledged, I suppose? You want people to own their own past?"

"You don't think that would be comforting?"

"How could it be?" he said.

Henry had a helter-skelter, where the marbles could run this way, then the other way, down to a tray. He played carefully at first, watching the progress of one marble at a time. Then he scooped up handfuls of marbles, let them run crashing one after the other, made the wood channels rock. The noise of hard glass on wood was almost all they could hear.

But Nicholas did say, loudly: "I'm still going to the opera with Lucia. Even so."

He wanted the houselights down, the red curtains apart, the orchestra sounding out. He wanted to lose himself in the mass and swell of the music.

Lucia took her seat, parterre center, second row: the usual seat. She might be old, but she'd learned to be infinitely careful with her movements so that she took the stairs without undue effort, no unneeded pauses, took her seat a little early so she would not need to push past others. She expected a little attention, but she had expected that for three quarters of a century at least: her redhaired due.

He watched her attentively. He wondered always what others

could deduce from her careful appearance, what they thought of her if they only glimpsed her at some public moment like this. Perhaps she was heroic just for being old.

She'd suggested the opera four weeks ago, which was two weeks before he knew his father had died. He sent her a copy of the death notice, faxed it to the shop. If she saw it, she said nothing. He didn't expect her to take any interest in the funeral, since she'd abandoned Hans Peter Müller sixty years before, but he thought she might thank him for the information. Instead, she confirmed the opera, as though he would know now that he was perfectly obliged to her: his only point of origin.

Perhaps he was. He'd lost his wife. He'd lost his father. His daughter had her own life. What he had left, by the oddest of circumstances, was a mother who outlived almost all of them.

The velvet curtains opened. The whole high space of the proscenium was filled with a gray scrim, with a square cut out in which sat a man with a lyre: Tannhäuser, he assumed.

Lucia had brought him here as a boy, and he'd loved the size of the sound, and the rush of the music and the mad prettiness of the world on the stage: all harem girls and significant ghost ships and the singing Queen of Spades, fairy-tale stuff that a whole audience agreed to take seriously with a grand collective act of will. He wanted to be lost again in all that determined glory. He wanted distraction more than anything.

Until the orchestra came to order, his mind still worked on. The word he kept avoiding, and knew he kept avoiding, was "accomplice." A child could not be considered his mother's accomplice, not in law or morals, not without some particular evil intent of his own; and he knew he did not have that. He might have been implicated. He wasn't guilty. It was such an equivocal, intolerable position.

"Thank you for telling me about Hans Peter," Lucia said, very distinctly, just as the conductor raised his baton and there was nothing he could properly say.

She was smiling. It might be the prospect of the music or her clever little tactic or some memory that tickled a corner of her mind.

So she'd decided, again, there was nothing to be said.

Tannhäuser sat waiting for the overture to end.

He watched her in profile, radiant in the great brass blare of the first big tune: intent, not abstract like the old sometimes become, when their command of autobiography dissolves and with it their very self. So if Lucia was Lucia, so bright, so convincing, then by definition Lucia remembered. The idea made him shiver.

He wanted to think it was the strings, yearning energetically, stepping up to a great crescendo with an undertow of timpani and the bright, top amazements of cymbals and triangle. Everyone in the warm red circle of the auditorium, gilt still catching the dimming houselights, was being tugged into the music, sitting straighter in their chairs as the music wound upward and upward.

He still wasn't lost. He wasn't close to Venusberg at all. He was in polite, unassuming Zurich, which sometimes struck him as a much more alarming place.

For after Berlin, the city had amazed him. Houses still entire. Trees still in the ground. Pipes and cables in order under the sidewalks.

He kept waiting for trouble.

He'd go walking, looking for barbed wire, but there wasn't much. He saw boys fishing on the lakeside, and steamers taking off across the lake. He saw chocolate everywhere: it wasn't a secret or a privilege anymore.

Lucia had a magazine, a big, glossy paper, which she kept in the apartment those first few days across the border: *Die Schweiz*, the February issue. It was full of snow, of holidays, of trains with their windows open to catch the mountain air and laughing, joyful people on skis, on ox sleighs, in chalets, on open, shining mountains. There was a folkloric woman on the cover, in blue and red.

He remembered a crowd at a demolition, how every man wore a hat. It couldn't have been a very large house, just an unwanted element in between the new, rounded buildings that were smooth as medicine pills. It buckled inward and the crowds didn't trouble to stand back. The walls wrenched, and their clean, white plastered certainty twisted about, and you could see what made the whole thing stand: sand, shit, fiber. The crowd approved with an intake of breath. Someone clapped. Stairs fell slowly. The wall looked like new bread cut with a blunt knife. Wooden frames lost all their right angles.

In Zurich, when a building came down, walls failed, windows blew out, it was just a fairground show. Then the show was over and they built something new.

The sirens were whispering, a hidden chorus promising all manner of burning love. Tannhäuser was saying he'd had enough of Venusberg. And Nicholas still wasn't engaged. Sacred and profane love, he thought, was not exactly his problem. He'd never had to choose.

He invented himself, out of necessity. His father, very soon after the war, had a new wife, and was ready for a new life without Nicholas. His mother didn't know how to be Swiss, didn't care. She was not yet an anomaly in 1944 when she rolled into Zurich with her truckloads of stock, when women still ran businesses for their absent husbands; her antique shop was almost usual. But she was very curious indeed by 1946 when the women had all gone back to their homes. She wasn't even attached to a man, anymore. She was foreign, whatever her passport said.

So there was nobody around to teach Nicholas the ordinary

things: how to ski, the weather in the Alps, the wait for the proper job in a bank.

He grew fat quite young, just because he wasn't his athlete father; he did not want to win. He became a ragged-assed professor instead of a banker, and it was quite an effort to be a professor and wear corduroy in those days. Besides, he had no automatic coalition of people his own age doing exactly the same thing. He formed alliances laboriously: a shared taste for books, sometimes the same level of skill on a ski slope. He was never entirely sure of his friends because they did not, like friends from the same class and the same street and the same past, know everything about each other's lives already.

He fell in love just once. All the exploration lovers do out of enthusiasm, he did out of necessity. He needed to know. He needed Nora to know him, too.

He couldn't bear the notion that Nora was gone. He avoided it, constantly, never allowed it to cross his mind because that would be too much like celebrating the emptiness. He talked to her still.

He remembered her entirely. He couldn't always give single details of her because every detail was bound into the whole, and the whole was bound into his life. He had to think like a scholar to remember that at some point they met for the first time, began on a particular day at a particular place. He had been afraid to share all the need he carried with him, the confusion of a boy who knew war and a man who knew nothing, and Nora shared all of that at once.

She became the ruling principle of his entire life. He couldn't imagine a time before Nora, not a time that belonged to him, to Nicholas Müller-Rossi; which meant that he did not have to engage, day by day, with the fact of Lucia and her past. Nora absolved him.

He had not even been listening to the huge musical tussle onstage.

————

Tannhäuser was out on the mountain now. There was a soprano corseted to play a boy, a great chorus of old pilgrims, a crowd of hunters and nobles that arrived on a painter's scaffold dressed in gray-green. There were all too many vistas, lots of significance being wheeled about.

If he worried about general things, he'd worry why he ever needed Nora so much: if she was only an evasion, not all the reality he had ever known. He loved particulars instead.

Alpine meadows, for example: streams rushing, pretty troughs cut out of tree trunks for the soft, strong cattle, the dark trees, the clatter of ptarmigan coming up suddenly out of rowan at the side of a path, meadows woven with pale autumn crocus. He needed that sort of thing. Walking with Nora, he had the course of a stream, light broken in water, sudden shade, and a path over ground that was fallen needles and tiny cones. They still walked together when he dreamed.

They were both away in the mountains on one of those weeks when the Swiss dash up and down the Alps in pursuit of their souls: this was for postgraduate students, put out of their library stalls just to get the blood moving. They were bright, unconnected people, defined by work. They met, he knew, up by Glaubenberg.

On the first day, they went around in parties: bustling too much, sometimes singing. He wasn't given to outdoor singing. He saw Nora; Nora saw him. Nora knew him at once. He'd never had to tell her his story. It wasn't an issue. They sat together at dinner, both furiously hungry, forking down *Rösti* and sausage and chicory with too much vinegar on it. Nora said: "It's very brave of you." He said: "What do you mean?" She said: "All this Swiss business, when you don't really have to. It is an effort, isn't it?" And they looked at a dozen intellectuals in shorts, knees sunburned, and they were laughing out loud.

They separated a little from the group, went out one morning at nine and walked the ridge of the mountains around Glaubenberg, up military roads, over tussocky grass, down over meadows to the summer houses for the Alplers, through forest and rutted fields and down roads torn up by tractors and loads of timber. They were each other's breath all the way. By five in the evening, they were struggling up the last sharp slope to the *Berghotel* and they stopped short.

He couldn't breathe. She couldn't breathe. It had nothing to do with exhaustion, although that was close.

At the intermission, Lucia took a small gilt chair just outside the auditorium door. An usher hovered, trying to ask if there was anything she wanted, not able to finish the sentence.

She had, thought Nicholas, a perfectly self-contained look. She would engage with others, but she did not need to. "I have," she said, "seen better productions."

"At least it's simple," Nicholas said.

"It's always simple nowadays." And she began to complain about the grotto for Venus, which was a kind of sandbox, and the tenor rolling around with his bottom in the air.

He'd lost his way now in the milling chorus in evening dress that was filling up the blank bits of the stage, in the list of minstrels all about to sing. The music left his mind wandering.

Together, Nora and Nicholas. They waited to have a child. Occasionally, when he was in the middle of one of those therapeutic psychochats with a colleague in a café, he'd hear how children brought a couple together, saved a marriage. But that all seemed very alien. He and Nora had to learn how to separate just a little in order to have Helen. For years, they were a closed society, not ready even for a biological intruder.

Then Helen was born, and Helen was glorious, of course.

The three of them became provincials. Nicholas traveled to conferences, and he went with Nora on elaborate holidays; and Helen decided to take on the whole world; but these were all side issues in their lives. They belonged, Nora and Nicholas at least, to the province of an apartment and a garden and a study and a bed.

And Lucia did not. Lucia could be loved and respected. She kept a certain glamour, the glory of a woman sculpted or painted: a figurehead, a lovely fiction. She played with Helen, took her on expeditions into the city when she had time, supervised her taste, which was something she never tried with Nora. And Helen seemed fond of her, found her wonderful, but was also a little afraid of how she never seemed to become fragile with age, only stronger. Helen expected advantages, to be strong as Lucia grew weaker, lucid as her mind failed, but none of that had happened. Her sense of wonder, Nicholas thought, had turned to a mild pervasive anger.

He never saw his father. They had no reason to coincide, not in the same town, not in the same business; they couldn't be casual, so any meeting was draped with far too much significance. His father did not come to the wedding, although he did come alone to the party later in the day and said nothing at all to Lucia.

So Nicholas made up his father, as he made up himself, but with much less material. He made the man into a mean little cliché: conservative soul, started off good with his body but then turned steady, drab, persistent, and undistinguished in his work. It was a comfort when he so much missed the fact of a father.

And now the pilgrim's chorus was returning from Rome, and he managed at last to put away his thoughts. By the time the principals came through the red velvet for their curtain calls and their official bouquets, they seemed huge as though through a lens, lit from beneath as though by limelight, spectacularly alive. He got back, gratefully, his talent for being fooled.

The crowd milled under a great shining tortoise of umbrellas, went for cars and taxis and the trams. Lucia's car waited efficiently. Nicholas did not want a lift.

He had to stop thinking. He walked off into the rain along the Limmat.

He wasn't old enough to walk out of his own story. He wasn't so old he couldn't walk, couldn't reason, couldn't remember or stop remembering as a conscious act.

There had to be a way to escape the present city. It wasn't enough. It didn't hold Nora. It was slick and wet and shining, leftover cows on awnings from some old parade, chocolate shops and equally glossy pornographic cinemas in the new town, all packaged, all rich, and the squared-off corporate buildings with official art out front. He looked at the river through the rain, but not the clean, quick modern river: he saw the Limmat clogged with weirs and islands and mills and bridges and a prison, as it was when he was a boy. He passed some shops, bars, hotels on the front, but he had in mind the barbers where he had his hair cut as a boy, with its six machines for electric massage of the scalp and the smell of pomade and machine oil and talc. He rebuilt the power office that used to jut into the water, with the huge white outline of an electric bulb on the side; and even the fields of potatoes that had been ostentatiously planted in wartime where now there was snipped, rolled grass.

Rain caught his skin and left it briskly scoured. It didn't seem enough to shock him back to sense. He was still walking the wrong way, away from home.

What was he going to do, old man on a bad night? Get drunk, then stumble around the railway station in that odd, sooty, lifeless light of early morning? Get a woman, pay to lose himself for a minute or two; but he'd never done that.

He crossed the Limmat. He didn't have the training to handle so much memory. He couldn't do it alone.

When her housekeeper had gone, when she had drunk her warm milk with honey and a little Madeira, Lucia sat on the edge of her neat bed. It was a sleeping shelf, very plain.

She let every part of her clean face die. It was like an exercise: a relaxation of self. She retreated under the mask of her own features, where everything was consistent, where it was private and not uncomfortable and nobody asked questions.

Müller. So Müller died old. He must have been better stock than she thought. They'd kept their story alive a very long time, even so. And for all his virtue, his law, his authorized decency, she'd outlived the bastard. She had her little business; he had a plot and a stone.

She put on an eye mask. She didn't want it known if the pupils of her eyes were moving, making out faces while she dreamed.

·

Henry was off being socialized through play, at great expense, and the days were tricky. Henry was the occupation for which Helen had given up work; now he was starting his own separate life, she could almost fancy that work, the old, obsessive, fascinating kind, was something comfortable and enfolding, a structure to the days, a relief from all this coffee and waiting.

"Bullshit," Helen said, out loud. But she didn't want to be caught talking out loud.

They were better together, she and Jeremy. You couldn't say the same for all their friends. Besides, she careened about the world for years as though she was anxious without an air ticket. She'd worked for a bank, but not in a bank: she went about like a broker, now brutalizing some cable TV company, or flirting with the movies, or solemnizing a marriage between newspapers. She couldn't simply continue, not if she wanted a child.

So here she was, officially married, in love, with a lovely child. Everyone found it all too easy to accept the situation. Even her old colleagues didn't ask when she might come back; they said they envied her courage and her choice.

But Jeremy hadn't stopped moving. Jeremy was in New York, was in Los Angeles, was dining the money and trying to turn its taste to the pictures he happened to have in stock. He was flirting very studiously at cocktail parties, holding the attention of the buyers any way he could: performing much as she used to perform.

Nicholas once complained that Jeremy treated her like a novel he couldn't quite finish, but sometimes left lying around, forgetting where he put her. But it wasn't like that. They had separate orbits, which came together splendidly. They could hugely enjoy the game they played around the world, or at least the world's cities with money and major airports, and the knowledge that they chose and conspired in order to be together.

But now she had a fixed address: day in, day out. Everything was entirely satisfactory, but nothing more.

She didn't want to call someone, make a plan; it sounded too desperate.

She'd go to a couple of bookshops, why not. She was enrolled in the spending classes now: a rich wife. She could study shop windows like folk art, read each display like a museum piece.

She took the tram.

There was enough distraction for an afternoon, bookshops full of pink painted children, shops hot with red rugs, a window with a single stone Buddha lit so perfectly that nobody would dare buy or move him, a couple of shops full of souvenirs from a life nobody ever saw—tuned cowbells, pretty cow halters—and some with toys as intricate as jewels: a lake steamer, a funicular train, a machine for printing. There were shops a little below eye level on steep streets, full of immaculate bottles, or birdcages made from metal that had been beaten into lace, or paintings which were never quite strong enough to break through the brown varnish and get into the eye. There were shops so gorgeous you could never be lovely enough to go in, but plain people did.

Bankers sidled up to windows and ogled the chocolates. A tram passed, driven by someone's aunt in a two-piece. There was a window full of shining French horns, and another full of pretty pots, but she was not quite interested enough to see if they were jams or oils.

Among the steady people, in front of the parade of windows, a woman had stopped.

The wind was too bitter for anyone to stand still so long. The woman was looking into a shop window. She was very old, wrapped often and deeply in scarves and down.

She was crying.

She didn't touch her face. She let the tears run, and she held her shoulders straight, her body remembering the manners it had been taught.

Her face was neat with intelligence. Evidently, she was distraught, but evidently not because she had forgotten things, even forgotten forgetting, and did not know what to do next. She hadn't wandered off into the world and got lost like some ancient, humiliated child.

She was standing before Lucia's shop: the pretty plates, the welcoming lights.

She was crying, but other people all walked around her as though she was some inanimate obstacle, maybe not seeing her, maybe not wanting to see her. They seemed to understand that an old woman sobbing on a frosty street was something ominous. You stopped, you smiled, you helped, and you were bound to know her story, share her senses.

Helen stopped, though. She should not intrude. She should not embarrass this old woman, who didn't look as though she needed to be helped out of her tears. Much more, she needed to cry.

But she was frail, alone, cold; Helen felt a rush of responsibility. She had no other business to excuse indifference, after all. Her day was empty until Henry next came home.

So she said: "I'm sorry."

The woman didn't answer. Helen thought of raising her voice. But the woman walked a little closer to the great plate of the window. She'd set off alarms soon, for sure.

She stared inside. Helen wondered what exactly she was seeing: whether it was a splendor that she had lost, or sight itself she was losing, or some particular object which set off this flood of feeling.

The old woman said: "It was a table. A little table, with flowers in marquetry. Like a garden in the corner."

And then she noticed Helen, who said: "Can I take you for some tea?" She had to offer tea: something medicinal, something kind.

The old woman said: "I should be very glad to have some tea."

Helen offered her a handkerchief; she always had handkerchiefs, for Henry if he needed them. The woman blotted her eyes, once.

"I thought I would be angry," she said.

An assistant happened to come to the shop window, happened to flick at some intruding dust on the mirror shine of the woods.

The older woman walked so neatly and precisely nobody wanted to notice that her face was wet.

"I was so afraid someone would ask me what was wrong," she said.

Then, efficient like someone who's been at receptions and meetings and conferences all too often, she said: "I'm Sarah Freeman."

"Helen Garvey." Helen was helping, being kind, so she used her
married, wifely name.

"I don't suppose you know who owns that store?"

"Lucia Müller-Rossi. There's no mystery about it."

Sarah Freeman ordered coffee, after all; Helen asked for cakes.

"But that's not the name of the store."

"Mr. Harrod doesn't own Harrods anymore."

"She's still alive, Lucia Müller-Rossi?"

"Alive and in business. She's my grandmother."

Sarah Freeman said: "I'm sorry. I'm being a nuisance—"

"Not at all."

"I know the name. I mean, I knew her. Once. I shouldn't take up
your time. I ought to get back. Let me pay for the coffee—"

"You speak very good German," Helen said.

"It was my first language."

"You've been very kind. I shouldn't take up your time."

Helen said: "I'd be happy to take you home."

"I couldn't trouble you. I couldn't," Sarah Freeman said. "It's very
strange for me to sit at a table with the granddaughter of Lucia
Müller-Rossi. You have to understand that."

She stood up suddenly, and her small leather bag slipped out of
her lap and burst on the floor. Helen bent down to help her catch up
the papers, the purse. But Sarah Freeman swept the papers toward
her, covered them, and put them away quickly. A single credit card
receipt got away. Helen tried to pick it up, but Sarah snatched it.

"I want to help," Helen said. "I want to know."

Sarah said: "Everybody thinks they want to help, that they want to
know."

"I know something about Lucia. I'm not afraid to hear the rest."

"No," Sarah said. "You all have such courage. Now."

And then she said: "I'm being graceless. You were very kind. I don't mean—"

"It was a table? A little table with flowers?"

Sarah shrugged into her coat, so it was hard to tell if she meant the shrug to answer Helen's question.

"If I was sure I wanted to remember," she said, "then I wouldn't have been crying."

Helen couldn't stand around to watch which direction the taxi took. Between the shiny glass and the posters and the bent metal shelters, she couldn't even be sure Sarah Freeman even went to the stand or took a taxi, that the old woman hadn't disappeared into the railway station, to the suburban trains or the intercities.

She could be anywhere: the one witness who wasn't Lucia or Nicholas, who hadn't spent fifty years with memory packed away.

Helen ran down the steps among the underground shops, ran down to find a telephone directory. She looked up "Freeman"; perhaps Sarah was here with relatives, or living here.

There were seven Freemans. She went to a phone and called the first, asked to speak to Sarah. It was a misunderstanding; she had to apologize. She tried the second, and an American voice, a very tired and angry American voice, said there was no Sarah Freeman there, why would anyone called Freeman want to be there? Again, Helen apologized.

She wasn't a detective. She didn't know how to shortcut the process of examining every house in a city, every hotel and boarding house, in the half hope that somewhere there was a woman called Sarah Freeman. She had to assume that was, indeed, her name. She had to assume she'd check into a hotel using that name; Helen might be Müller-Rossi, or she might be Garvey. It took just a smidgen of social convention to fox the whole trail.

She spun around suddenly. She'd decided, like a children's game, that Sarah would be standing there. But Sarah was not: only the gentle waves of commuters, some with bread, some with lilies, some with briefcases locked with brass.

She could call all the other Freemans when she got home. And she ought to get home; Henry would soon be there.

She waited in line for the tram. When it came, when she was safely going home, she formed a very simple thought.

She could not pretend she never met Sarah Freeman. She could not easily find Sarah Freeman. But she did have some minimal clues: a woman who didn't know the shop, but did know Lucia as Müller-Rossi, a woman mourning a simple table, a woman whose first language was German. An old woman, too: perhaps not as old as Lucia, but going back to the years that Lucia never mentioned.

Sarah Freeman must have been in Berlin.

She wouldn't have been Freeman, though, which was far too English a name; Lucia might not know her as Sarah Freeman, if she remembered her in particular out of those years.

Whatever Sarah Freeman knew was more than Helen knew; and Helen wanted to know. Whatever it was could reduce an old woman to tears, which is not what fifty years of loss or mourning does; tears have to be tricked out of old eyes, by something that has just happened, or just been remembered or seen.

When she went back the next day to Lucia's shop, the windows had been changed.

Sarah Freeman sat down in the lobby of her kind, clean hotel. There were armchairs that were only ornamental, cushions too flat and orderly to have been used, set around a fire that never actually burned: a little tricked-up domesticity in a public place. Nobody ever sat there, except when they were waiting for a taxi to take them away. There was a basket of red, polished apples.

She liked it, she told herself. She didn't want, yet, to go to her room and be shut up. There wasn't any comfort in the room, even if it had a wing chair, a good bed. She didn't want to be enclosed. She'd have stayed in the street if she could. She wished she had the energy to go walking forever in the cold.

After all, there were no friends in her room, and she needed friends now. Here, in public, everyone was her friend: the waiter who brought a glass of Scotch and water, the girl behind the desk who was trying not to observe the old woman although it was her job to observe, the bright apartment manager, even the man sweeping the parking lot in the cold, working against the brisk wind.

The Scotch stung her mouth. Her eyes watered a little. Then she signed the bill, and added a few francs for the waiter. She thought she'd added too much. She needed friends, and yet something told her not to draw attention to herself: some memory, perhaps.

The hotel doors opened and shut. She felt the cold on her legs.

She'd been a journalist many years, trafficked in facts. Facts were supposed to heal and bring justice. The news levered up great static wrongs and pushed them headlong out of the way. But when it was a question of just one woman's history, a personal matter, a story she might not even want to tell out loud, then there were no headlines and column inches to instruct the world that this was a serious matter. She could tell the truth, and nobody need bother to believe her.

She put the Scotch down on a little round table. It wasn't helping.

A man stood just outside this circle of stuffed chairs, waiting perhaps: a trespasser. She'd acquired this public space, she reckoned.

"I'd like a drink," he said, "too."

She didn't want to invite him, and she didn't care to reject him. So he sat down.

She'd traveled beside him on the plane, he'd helped with the plastic around the knife and fork, and they'd grimaced together at the dry turkey and the sandy potatoes. His name was Peter Clarke.

But that was not an introduction, not enough. He'd said he was a tourist, on the same circuit—lakes and mountains off season, cities of Switzerland. He'd always wanted to travel, and now was going anywhere and everywhere, spending his days and his capital.

He had never picked up the useful habit of being alone, she thought. He might have just lost a wife of many, many years.

He sat, but with his hands on the arms of the chair.

He was not at all easy to place: white hair, a neat, unassertive chainstore tweed over shoulders that were only slightly stooped, a thin tie, his body in some kind of shape with the vague form of old muscles now working under too much skin. English, unmistakably: a small-town Englishman, perfectly preserved, maybe a rower in his time and perhaps a schoolmaster with a little extra money for coffee and cakes.

He liked her company, that was obvious; she liked his. She just wasn't sure if he was the one to whom she could tell all the things she needed to tell, who would do them justice.

"It's cold," he said. "Don't you think?" He seemed to mean all kinds of things by "cold."

She shivered. She hadn't meant to; she couldn't stop herself.

"It's hard to be a tourist in the cold," he said. " Your eyes water all the time."

So he'd noticed.

She remembered a party in London, 1940s, jiving on a tiny carpet, desperate wine, a man with a cigarette in a corner, talk about Thomas Mann: that kind of party. She remembered how she had wondered if the man with the cigarette would do.

She made herself smile. It had to be right to smile. It proved she was back in this moment.

She was grateful Peter Clarke wasn't the kind of man who launches into a whole life story all at once. She didn't need more stories. She needed an ally.

She liked him, too, she reminded herself.

Helen kept a list of numbers remembered from her other life: lawyers' numbers, friends' numbers, bank contacts, corporate persons. Usually, she kept the list in a file next to household insurance.

She called Georg Meier, she told herself, because he was a Zurich lawyer the bank once used. After she'd dialed the number, she half wanted to find it engaged or be brushed off by some bland assistant. She felt awkward that she was no longer Helen Müller-Rossi from the bank. She was only herself.

So she was a little grateful, dangerously so, that he took the call. They didn't know much about each other; they couldn't gossip through the last big deal they both handled; so they blustered for a moment about kids, weather, music.

Helen recovered herself.

"It's an absurd thing," she said. But she wouldn't have said that if she was still Helen Müller-Rossi of the bank. She started again. "Someone's turned up who used to know my grandmother. In Berlin, believe it or not. In Berlin, in the 1940s."

"The late 1940s?"

"No. No, it's not that easy."

"I see."

"I don't know all the story, but I just wanted to—I wanted to know if anything went through the courts in 1944 or 1945 or 1946, anything at all, where would the judgments be?"

"Bern, probably. Swiss Federal Archives, Archivstrasse."

"And if I just wanted to know whether a particular name came up?"

"This isn't business, is it?"

"No. No, it isn't exactly business."

"Then I could get a clerk to check this afternoon."

"You wouldn't do that if it was business?"

"No business could afford that kind of speed."

"The name," Helen said, "is Lucia Müller-Rossi."

"You want to know if your grandmother was in the courts?"

"Yes. As it happens."

"Best to check," the lawyer said. "People keep digging up the past. You might as well dig first."

"And if there was anything—"

"I'll get you a precis. Not overnight."

"Before the weekend?"

"Easily. Listen, you want to have a drink sometime—"

At dinner, Peter Clarke was all concern. He didn't fuss, though, only made it clear that he was entirely on her side.

"It's just," she said, "I saw something in a shop today."

She was still not sure he knew what it meant to be on her side.

"I saw something, and it disturbed me. Made me remember things."

He didn't ask. He knew very well that memory was a private thing; it took too much effort to explain it to others.

He said: "You don't want to be remembering all the time."

She changed the subject at once.

"I don't know," Nicholas said. "I have no idea."

"I thought of checking all the hotels," Helen said.

"All the hotels?"

"I was going to go to every one of them. With a letter for Sarah Freeman, to see if they'd accept it, and if they did, I'd have found her."

"And if she's staying with friends?"

"I don't know."

"And why? Why do all this?"

Helen thought she would have an answer all ready for him: something with slogans, bright and morally right. But she didn't.

"I suppose," Nicholas said, "the police probably know where she is. Don't foreigners fill in those forms at a hotel?"

"I don't know any policemen who would check for me."

"You could pretend it was some kind of emergency."

"But I'd have to lie—"

Nicholas said: "And you wouldn't lie?" He really wanted to know.

FIVE

Sarah Freeman sat at Peter Clarke's table in the breakfast room. She wondered, gleefully, what the furry old ladies and their stick-thin gents would think.

He wanted to talk about the lake. She said it was cold. She noticed that he poured coffee for her, automatically. He said it would be wonderful to be out on the water, in the mists, in the sun. She was a little surprised, but she knew the English could be romantic when it came to landscape.

She didn't trust the notion of finding allies by accident, let alone on the next airline seat and then in the same hotel; if someone was accidental all the time, they must be up to something. But she needed someone who would listen to her, consider her story, let her know if it convinced or not, if it was the right story to tell out loud.

So she tested him, coldly.

"Someone," she said, and she didn't specify, "was telling me about the Bührle collection. I wanted to see it for myself."

He'd studied the guidebook, but he didn't remember Bührle.

"It's open twice a week, I think," Sarah said. Then she said: "It's too cold to go for a walk, anyway."

He did like the idea of being taught by Sarah. He basked in her faint air of foreignness. If she couldn't quite put away her old suspicions of chance and strangers, that only made it more interesting: he had to convince her. He'd always been so well known, in such small places, he hardly ever had anybody to convince before.

He set off with her in a taxi into a sleek suburbia, all dark, shining shrubbery.

"It's supposed to be extraordinary," she said.

The Bührle house, when they reached it, was one more pile of discretion, wrapped up in ivy, with spiky irons along the roof.

He hesitated to lean on the door of such a grand suburban mansion. So Sarah pushed it.

They walked into a house, not the didactic order of a museum. The entrance hall was the way to a dining room or a bedroom: no bombast, no grandstanding. The stairs simply led up. The floors were squeaky parquet, and the windows looked onto winter lawns with the stucco of city snow.

Clarke bought the tickets.

Someone was calling loudly for "our driver." Someone else was talking, in German, about Venice.

Clarke realized he was nervous. Sarah, too, was sharply awake.

They turned together into the music room. They had it to themselves. For a moment, Clarke's eyes went to the grand piano, the view through the windows, anything but the paintings which were packed around the room in a tight, unbroken line, so many the eye could not easily choose one to see.

Sarah made him look. She walked him to the wall, and pointed, one by one.

She didn't know if he liked paintings, or if he bothered with galleries and names. But she would worry about an ally whose breath did not stop in this room.

There was a Lautrec tucked in the corner, a front-stage Messalina, a wicked woman in black, standing in limelight with hellfire red around her. In another corner, difficult to get to see behind a chair, a Gauguin: dying sunflowers, and a window looking out on a Tahitian beach. There was a van Gogh of chestnut blossoms, all riotously alive but in a space of peace and light and energy. There was more than one portrait by Cezanne, a glorious young girl by Renoir, a count and two daughters by Degas. Oh, and a field by Monet, a mournful sky, a pale pink-ocher village with tall dark columns of trees; but in front of that elegant drabness, a field bright with poppies, with tiny slashes of blue to make the red sing, with grass of green and yellow, a triumphant meadow with young girls flourishing bunches of flowers.

Two soft ladies in felt hats, eyes bright, talked about their need to see absolutely everything.

Sarah said: "There's much more. Come along."

All the names that Clarke knew seemed to be there. Canalettos: two. A Frans Hals that looked to him like something impressionist, a few brushstrokes for a portrait face. A Tiepolo with creamy bottoms. A Goya showing a procession. And two women lying together, Toulouse-Lautrec it said on the label, one bare-breasted and turning to her shorthaired, shirted friend whose hand was being attentive somewhere between her legs. And Picassos over the postcard desk, and Delacroix on the stairs and both horses and ballerinas from Degas, and a Braque and a Rembrandt and the lovely silvers of a Matisse scene of the Seine. And more, much more, the fact of so much only tolerable because each painting was so fine.

He could see the dizziness in Sarah's eyes. She stopped herself on the stairs. As for him, he looked closely, which had been his lifetime's job, but now he had the luxury of looking only for himself. He wasn't entirely sure what to feel, though. He was waiting for his heart to catch up with his eyes.

Sarah began to talk, softly. "I always wondered," she said, "what I would do to have one of these paintings. What I would do to have them all, all this."

"Yes." Then Clarke said: "I never thought I would own things."

"You know who Emil Georg Bührle was?"

"I never heard of him."

He was letting his eye play with a plump and underdressed harem girl standing in a shift, who seemed exotic until you realized from the calculated nipples and the accentuated bush that she was just a working girl in the costume that Manet ordered.

"When the Second World War started," Sarah said, with startling, teacherly clarity, "he was worth maybe a million Swiss francs. When the war ended, he was worth 170 million. Does that tell you anything?"

He didn't want to draw attention, so he walked, slowly, with Sarah talking in his ear.

"He had a machine tool company and he made weapons. And his best customers were in Germany. He made the 20 mm anti-aircraft gun, and it made him the richest man in Switzerland, richer than bankers, richer than dealers."

They turned into a room they had missed before, the Louis XVI room.

"That's her," Sarah said: the Degas portrait of Madame Camus at the piano.

Madame faced into the room, right hand picking at notes behind her back, a sheet of vivid Beethoven on the music stand standing out in the subdued light around her little, dark figure. The painted room was comfortable, predictable: a gilt mirror, a gilt lampholder on the wall, a cushion at Madame Camus's feet, a pile of scores to one side, the edge of a good rug.

Clarke knew the source of the light must have been somewhere behind the painter as he worked: lamplight, maybe, a single domestic source, catching the score on the piano and the woman's face. But it didn't seem like that. It seemed as though in this quiet, careful room, the music itself gave out light. It made a plain pink figurine throw the shadow of a winged angel. It caught the detail of a hand at the end of a long dark sleeve and brought it alive. It changed the dark, pretty face of Madame Camus into a kind of puzzle, because the proper doctor's wife was suffused by music as well as light. She seemed so muted and so fragile, but she had found and she was about to find again all the passion in the score.

He checked the catalogue in his hand. He didn't like to be without a book of other people's opinions; it put too much strain on his own eyes.

Sarah took the book from him.

"Provenance," she said. "Degas studio, of course. First sale, May 1918, Paris: catalogued. Sold for 32,000 francs. Then in the collection of Alphonse Kann, Saint Germain en Laye, from 1924 'until at least 1937.' Then: 'purchased by Bührle in 1951 from a private French collection.' You see?"

Clarke stared at Madame Camus.

"There's something missing. Fourteen years," she said. She sounded impatient.

Clarke could fall in love with Madame Camus. He had done so already.

"Of course," Sarah said. "Anyone could guess that Alphonse Kann was a Jew."

He tried to see grace and sheen in those studies for the woman's sleeves and hands: calm, too, and dexterity.

Sarah thought he was trying to slip past the real issue. So now she addressed the room, although it was empty except for Peter Clarke.

"Bührle bought this painting in February 1942," she said. "The Nazis were in Paris. They stole the great Jewish collections, they brought the pictures to the Fischer galleries in Lucerne. Then Fischer swapped them for the pictures the Nazis liked: the landscape, Cranach, Ruysdael, Rubens, anything with brown varnish. And then Fischer sold the modern stuff to men like Bührle."

Peter said: "But it was stolen."

"Ah, yes. Kann couldn't do anything; he was in London. And later the Swiss courts ruled that nobody could possibly have known the Nazis were behaving badly in Paris in 1942. Everybody, especially all the dealers, agreed on that. Apparently, nobody noticed there was a Nazi decree, from late 1940, that 'confiscated' all the art that the Jews had 'abandoned.' And nobody noticed that Bührle was in Paris himself in 1941, occupied Paris, doing business with a rather luckier Jewish dealer called Wildenstein. The courts agreed that Bührle couldn't possibly have known anything. He was much too rich to be guilty.

"But apparently he did know enough to consult a lawyer before he bought Madame Camus. He bought anyway. He went on buying, too. He bought his last stolen picture in 1944: a Picasso."

Peter Clarke said: "I was in a prisoner-of-war camp then."

He was already too much in love with the picture. Standing in this room, so close, he could sense the way the brush must have moved and the paint settled. Everything moral was suspended because of the fringe of the good rug in the foreground, the light, her eyes, the satin on her sleeves.

He might never have seen her if Bührle had not bought and shown her.

He never thought an art gallery could be a dangerous place. "Come on," he said. He wanted to get out of that polite house. He also wanted to stay in it forever, with those glorious pictures on the wall. He wondered if Bührle had somehow saved these pictures from the ruin of the war, been some other kind of moral hero.

On the stairs, they ran into an executive secretary type, fiftyish, so smart in her suit she could be sandblasted. She carried papers. It was as though somewhere in this house, the old man was still transacting business: guns, pictures, grabbing chances.

Sarah said: "He didn't sleep very well. It's interesting. When he was awake, he used to come to this house to sit all night among his pictures."

"I suppose it had to be the very best," Clarke said.

"Does it make it any better," Sarah said, "that he never killed anyone himself?"

Clarke insisted that they call a taxi. The afternoon was darker now, and colder. When the car came, and he had tucked Sarah into the back, he said: "So. The shop you mentioned. Is that the same kind of story?"

"You don't have to be concerned."

"I don't see how you can say that."

"You can't put things right," she said.

Later, at his table in the hotel, he studied the books he bought. He had so many clichés in mind: hard-faced men, did well out of war, merchants of death, all that. He wanted to see a specific face: Bührle with his huge teeth and his narrow, police eyes and the bone-cracking jaw.

Helen liked having a drink with Meier: a midday drink, almost like an assignation with office hours as an alibi. He was shiny-headed, blond, and strong. She kept wanting to sniff him to see if any human being could possibly be so clean.

"I haven't looked at this," he said, passing over a square brown envelope tied with string.

"Thank you."

"How's life now you don't have anything to do?" he asked.

But she hadn't practiced official, mannerly flirting for a while; she was rusty.

"Where's Jeremy these days?"

She took a taxi back to the house so as not to keep Henry waiting. She could still sense where Meier touched her shoulder as she was leaving the room.

She didn't wait to read the court papers: charges, testimonies, complaints. She knew she would either read them now, immediately, even if they were scattered around the room when Henry came back from nursery school, or else she would make excuses not ever to know.

They were photocopies. Somehow she'd expected documents

with age and taste. These had no archive smell, no suggestion that bits of other people's skin had settled on them over the years; the signatures just shadows without the pressure of a pen or the color of ink.

She felt a little like a judge, as though she was not connected to the name on every page: Lucia Müller-Rossi.

The woman couldn't be honest about anything at all, it seemed. When she loaded up the trucks to come to Zurich, she had the Italian ambassador's goods, too: porcelain with gold leaf, jewels and pictures. She sold the lot. They belonged to the Italian embassy in Berlin.

She thought: Lucia is a thief. Then she began to consider what the thought might mean. It was more than the statement that on some occasions Lucia had stolen things. It meant her very nature was to be a thief. And how can that be, how can the old lady at the Dolder, the subtle teacher of taste and manners, how can she be reduced to a single, criminal category?

Helen shuffled the papers.

Some people were ready to give evidence in 1946. Some, most of the others, were already dead; their families had to speak for them, if they knew what to say.

There was a woman who left her dowry with Lucia, and died in Theresienstadt. Another who left suitcases full of stuff, and then came back unexpectedly to find they'd been opened. A man who ended up in Sweden who said he never got back anything that he left with Lucia, and a woman who flew all the way from America to Switzerland—which was something, in 1946—to say that she recognized the property of her dead sister in Lucia's shop. And her sister died in Auschwitz. Then there was a man who gave evidence about his mother, who thought of Lucia as her very best friend. She handed her furniture to Lucia so buyers could see it and the authorities would not find it. She sold her pictures, and gave the money to Lucia to take to Switzerland; and suddenly the German office of foreign-exchange transactions knew enough to shoot her for having money in Switzerland.

All these stories, the documents said, tallied with Lucia's own file of names.

Helen finished the court judgment. Her Lucia was a "criminal prostitute," a phrase which amused her for a moment: maybe Zuricher gentlemen knew a nicer class of tart, who wouldn't do anything underhand or dubious, unless asked for and paid by Zuricher gentlemen.

They had considered charges of blackmail, extortion, and dealing in stolen goods. At the last minute, the charges had been withdrawn. Lucia left the court with a thirty-day suspended sentence for lying to Swiss customs.

So it was at least as bad as Helen had ever imagined, and this attempt to settle things, to name Lucia's actions and condemn them, had faded out.

She called Nicholas at once. Henry had a playgroup that evening, and she used the fact. She told Nicholas she had to see him, urgently. He couldn't imagine what particular circumstance made things urgent, but he was on edge and waiting and he knew what she would want to say.

She drove to Sonnenberg. He offered coffee, wine, cake. She said: "Have you ever seen this?"

She passed him the envelope, stuffed with the court papers, now a little disordered.

"Did you know about this?" she said.

"I don't know what you mean."

"Read it," she said. "I have to get home now."

"I'm not going to read this."

Helen said: "We're going to have to—"

Nicholas was round, kind, quiet; his form of anger was perfect stillness.

Helen said: "It's important—"

"You do not talk to me that way," Nicholas said. There was nothing at all in his voice except the words.

Helen stood up. "I met a woman called Sarah Freeman. I don't know why she was crying, except that she mentioned a table. A table just like everything else that came from Berlin."

Nicholas looked toward her, but not at her: she had become a gap in the light, nothing more.

Helen cleared her throat; she sounded almost nervous.

"Obviously," she said, "we have to do something."

He said, very softly: "Don't you think I have longed to do the right thing? Somehow?"

She slapped the papers against the table. He didn't react.

She bustled out of the house.

She drove back through a landscape ruled by the full moon, trick shadows, iced light. She didn't see that she had done anything but remind her father of a reality: of Lucia's past and actions. It was essential, obviously, to face all this: a matter of health. It was good, too: a matter of justice.

But her father opened his filing cabinets and put away the court papers at random, among the offprints and conference papers and thin carbon copies of old letters to colleagues. They had the bulk and faint gray of recycled papers; they were still obvious.

He poured himself cold water and sat down. Then he stood up again, and fetched a bottle of whisky and colored the water with it, a little oily gold settling in the glass.

He didn't even know where to begin.

Helen had to know it was not always comfortable, or even easy, to put knowledge away. Sometimes you had to do it, in order to live. He couldn't have spent fifty years being just the child of his mother's crimes.

He'd known very young that he had to separate himself from his mother. He had the oddest memory of Jelmoli's department store, a

New Look fashion show, a little theater made with pale screens in the corner of a floor. His mother took him: a boy of thirteen. He was dressed up; so many of his memories of his mother involved a collar that grazed his chin. There was a string quartet with varnished hair, potted palms, little round tables with economical lilies; and the women, stalwart, serious, and the men who particularly did not smile at the girls even when they came daintily down the steps, print frocks and tipped hats, seeming just for a moment to be in need of a little judicious help. One girl caught his eye and he blushed ruinously.

That was when he knew, as he remembered. His mother needed his presence, so she'd be accompanied and respectable, so she could pretend; and he must never know how much she needed that pretense. From that moment on, he separated from her.

He knew he had not moved far enough.

"I suppose we'll be the youngest," Sarah said. "Everyone else will be eating chopped salads. They'll be staring at the mountains and the mountains won't be able to get away."

So Peter Clarke was on his mettle, determined not to act unacceptably old.

He tried to see what she saw through the train windows. She let the city pass. She looked out at a fast river, without much interest. She saw the summerhouses put up at the end of allotments, little wood refuges each with curtains at its window, and her eyes stayed with the summerhouses as the train ran on.

She started to say something. She thought better of it.

They took the boat from Lucerne, drank coffee as it marked a zigzag across the black water, evaded a waiter projecting goodwill.

Clarke saw an eagle overhead. Sarah saw it, too, and frowned. She sensed all the grand romantic spirit she so much dreaded: bright air cut up with terrible crags, high meadows, dark woods, houses too high up and too far from other people for a proper social life. There were also stories of William Tell jumping overboard to escape old man Gessler, and walkways symbolical of Swiss identity: which, she thought, would probably be very well cleaned.

Clarke knew, somehow, he shouldn't point out the eagle. Instead, he said: "I can't tell what is rich and what is poor here. It's very upsetting for an Englishman. I can't even be a snob."

This raised faint interest; he was relieved.

"I mean: those chalets up in the mountains look so picturesque, but they're just for the men who stay with the cows all summer and make cheese. Then the streets, they all seem much the same. Some of them are more cramped, I suppose. Some of them have shops and trams, so I don't suppose the very rich want to live there. But those subtle differences, the ones I'm used to—"

"I know," Sarah said. She felt the need of absolutely anything that would sabotage the consensus, the perverse sense of flatness in among all these grand mountains.

"I talk too much," Clarke said.

She shrugged.

"You talk a lot when you think someone is obliged to listen. At our age. We tell people stories."

There was something she had to tell him if he was to be her ally. She owed him a duty of listening.

He said: "I could tell you a story. If you're interested."

He had settled himself like an old man in touristland, coat wrapped around him, looking out to the next stop: a rustic sort of halt, all wood. A bright gaggle of walkers disembarked.

Almost all his years, he'd gone walking: but it was always on the same paths, up, down, up, down, between the same rectangular patches of earth, one hundred yards or so one way, fifteen feet the other. He owned the ground with his feet.

"I was paid to look," he said. "It's called 'roguing.' You look for the variations—a pink patch on a yellow flower, doubles among singles, the dots on a plain flower. Things that are wrong, but that make them useful." He remembered, though, the colors: every break and variant in color that plants can provide. He watched them, he chose them, he checked off the valuable freaks with metal labels, which were always blank. "You lift them after a day or so," he said. "A fork in four places round the plant, so it comes up with a ball of root and soil. Then you take it away."

"I loved my garden in London," Sarah said. "I never spent enough time there."

"It was my life," Clarke said. "I was out there seven in the morning, seven at night in the summer. You just never know. You get little specks of dark on something brilliant, and in a year or so, you've got a flower nobody ever saw. You have to chase everything. There's a love-lies-bleeding," he said, "which came up a perfect dark Oxford blue, and we bred it true, and that's how we got a red. That's how it works. It was red like a ruby."

"All those colors," Sarah said. She shivered.

"It never made sense to people, really."

"I suppose your wife understood."

He said: "She got used to me."

Sarah, having other things to consider, calculated how long it would be before the boat docked in a town with a railway station.

"She was in the church choir," he said. "I was in the choir, too. And I rang bells. And so forth. I was always about the church. And Frances did know how to listen. And sometimes we'd be lying there in bed and her side against my side and we seemed like one body of warmth. One body."

Sarah said: "Why did you settle for that?"

"It's a long story."

They had the boat to themselves now, just peaks, black water, and the steady progress to the end of the lake.

"But I did go back to Frances. I always did."

They constituted a system, after all. Frances had kept the indoor plants, the pelargoniums, the amaryllis for Christmas carefully starved of water through the summer, the azaleas bent and tied into pyramids, the Easter cactus that flowered too late in glorious Technicolor red, the bulbs raised in a warm cupboard for church sales. Peter was in charge of a practical garden, nothing else. Every year, when autumn settled morosely on the flat land, he'd start to clean out the weak and the dead, cut back roses to stumps, take out annuals which still had flurries of pale flowers in order to plant onions, crocus, broad beans. Every year, Frances would be out in the garden at the same time, trying to save this plant which was still pretty, trying to stop the surgeon's work with secateurs and saw. She didn't want to argue out loud, so she followed him in silent disapproval. She hated bonfires, whose heavy smoke stayed in the air long after the last flowers had burned.

"Once she broke six plates while I was out," he said. "I never asked why."

Sarah asked how long it was to Flüeli. He looked at his watch and told her: a half hour.

"I came to London in 1945," she said. "I was Sarah Lindemann then."

"You don't have an accent."

"What accent was I supposed to have?"

She couldn't tell him what he most ought to know. She had to go sideways around the reality. She couldn't let some great horror, hooked and beaked, break into their talk, not two old tourists talking on a bright day.

"I remember 1945, too," he said.

But she went on talking.

London she wanted to like, even the heavy coal fogs in the night, even the ruins and the rationed food and the righteous drabness of the streets. She was, very likely, going to be there forever.

She was already not supposed to talk about the past. She could sense that. In London, the meaning of war was victory, and sometimes taking pride in having lived with pain; but mostly it was starting again, not remembering. She had nobody then who shared and understood what she knew. The pictures of the camps didn't help; they shocked people into silence.

She had a tiny room with some friends of friends of her husband. At night she slept on the floor so the bed and chairs would hem her in, and in the morning she scuffed up her bed to make it seem used. She had nightmares about being terrifyingly free to open doors.

Clarke was right to wonder about the accent. Sounding German didn't help. In some parts of London, they knew what it meant; but she took tea in a Corner House, with a lady's orchestra and a serve-yourself bar of mean cakes, and people fell away from her: the wrong kind of foreigner. She was cut, and tutted at, forcefully. She heard people calling her a German, Boche, Kraut, Hun, alien, and not even quite to her face.

She came back and she threw herself on the wife of the friend of friends: Marje, a woman of huge certainties, a taste for motherly organizing. Marje said she knew what had to be done.

Sarah Lindemann disappeared.

At first it was a matter of language. Marje made her listen to the radio, Women's Hour, Saturday Night Theater, a saturation of English, until the tight vowels and informal structures started to seem almost more natural than her German. In a sentence now she could get one word, two words as precisely right as someone on the BBC. Marje set exercises, had her sit at a little table to do them; Marje had a school at last. Marje stopped her when she slipped into a German construction or a turn of phrase or an order of words at table, and Marje's husband rolled his eyes, but Sarah listened hard.

Then it was checking. Marje had proofreading work for a publisher, and she handed some to Sarah and then checked it. Sarah had to spot the details of everything that was wrong in another language.

Then it was invisibility. Sarah thought she knew all about this: she had stayed alive only because she went out of sight for so long. But the English kind of invisibility turned out to be different from hiding; it was a matter of not asserting yourself even as you queued for bread, or a bus. Everybody hid from each other.

Then it was being who people expect you to be: being placed. The peculiarity of her story was slowly wiped away; instead, she had a presence that required no explanation at all. A war widow, on her own, needing work. Sometimes, she wanted to shout at Marje, wanted to tell her that she had lived through so many years of denial and anonymity and not being able to be what and who she was and that she would not go on this way.

Then she went on, because there was no choice.

She found a job, thanks to Marje's husband, in a tiny office in a little frock company off Oxford Street, where she pushed requisitions and reports into filing cabinets, and sometimes did a little typing. After a month, she was so used to the qwertyuiop keys that she asked Marje why she couldn't just stay in the needle trade: a useful, quiet life.

"Such a waste," Marje said.

"I don't mind," Sarah said.

"You're just tired."

"I'm going to be tired for the rest of my life."

Marje shook her head and again she turned on the radio.

Sarah came to realize that she was now a moral example, and she had to do as she was told if she wanted her little room, the company of friends, some comforting limits to the whole world she had to manage and fight. If she gave up, she would be alone. And although she was now undercover, a spy on the streets, not what she seemed, she could preserve what she knew: the books she had read, the music she heard, what she knew about Klimt and Picasso and Chagall.

She could do it. After all, she hid some things even from Marje: like the way she kept rehearsing in her mind, like a speech she'd one day have to give, her wish to die.

Peter Clarke said: "We were nobody when we came back."

"I knew Sarah Freeman. She could walk about London on her own. She knew where to go, and she went just where she was expected, and she did all the proper things. She wasn't work anymore. Some days, she was me."

"Yes," Clarke said, not quite understanding.

"And it didn't matter that I prayed at night, and didn't sleep well. I knew how to manage the days, you see. You learn that if you've been underground for a while. And to tell the truth, I never bothered to contradict all the men in suits all around me because at least I was in a comfortable trap. I knew more than they did, and I knew how much worse it could all be."

"What did you do?" Clarke asked.

She explained. She had gone to work on a Sunday paper, recommended as a literate, clever girl by Marje's publisher friends. Those were eight-page-edition days when everything was cut to fit, when the open columns belonged to gentlemen who had just dined at All Souls and belonged to more than two London clubs. She was the not-quite-pretty little thing among the suits.

She read the proofs. For that work, she came highly recommended. On Saturdays, she shut herself in a small cream-painted room with coffee and the smell of strong cigarettes still in the air, and she read half the paper on narrow, inky sheets, and she cut what seemed wrong or fatuous, too long or misspelt. She read, usually, the cultural and foreign half. People could not place her exactly, but they thought she would be more at home with the cultural and the foreign.

"I remember," Clarke said, abruptly. "Frances always used to read you." Then he worried for a moment, punctiliously, about the pronoun. "I mean, she used to read Sarah Freeman's articles, out loud. We never watched television very much, but she always read the column."

"There weren't many women on the paper then," Sarah said. "All suits. All ties. All clubs. But television was like movies, and movies were a woman's job like fashion. And I was a woman. QED."

"You were very funny."

The steamer settled by its last quay.

"I was a very good Sarah Freeman," she said. "I had my friends, even my lovers sometimes. I had my house and my garden. I had a perfectly occupied life."

She stood up, picked up her bag, took Clarke's arm down the steps to the wide main doors.

She said: "You see what it means, of course. I take an interest in this table, in this Lucia Müller-Rossi I used to know in Berlin, and I'm back to when I talked like a German. I worked so hard to be Sarah Freeman and now I can't be Sarah Freeman anymore." The doors opened on the gangplank. "Do you see?"

At teatime in Zurich, she was still distant. He tried small talk; she put on a perfectly adequate smile. He discussed the cakes, and she did not. She asked for one glass of water, and then another.

She let this empty busyness continue for a bit, and then she said: "You're angry."

He stared at her.

"I don't know why you're angry," she said.

He wanted to say he wasn't angry, not at all, but he didn't want to lie to her. He was furious at hearing stories about the choices other people made; he wanted to talk about his own choices. He wanted her to listen to his stories, as he listened to hers, to establish some equal seriousness between them, or else she was the only one whose life was all about war, loss, pain, change, and every huge matter of life and death.

He fussed with a napkin.

"It's that," he started. He started again. "It's not easy to say."

Sarah smiled: the smile of a thoughtful, but over-occupied, nurse.

"I had to make choices, too," Clarke said. "I knew a woman, saw her every so often. I was married. She lived at the other end of the country. She died, and I didn't know for five whole months that she was dead. I just missed her phone calls at work. Officially I didn't know her, so I couldn't mourn her, and then my wife died, and I was allowed to mourn at last and everyone got it wrong and nobody wanted an explanation. They all thought they knew."

"It can be easier that way," Sarah said.

Clarke said: "You don't have to patronize me."

He put his napkin down.

"What was your name before you were Sarah Freeman?" he asked.

"Before?"

"It isn't a very German name. And you were married. So either way, you must have had another name."

"An alias, you mean?"

"No. Just another name. My wife had another name before she was Mrs. Clarke."

Sarah said: "My name was Sarah Lindemann. I told you that. Before, it was Sarah Becker. I never had any other names."

Jeremy called from Los Angeles, full of business. He'd seen one minor, aspirational star at home, two directors, a studio executive who definitely had money and two who wanted to make it seem they did. He'd been interviewed by an agent, which he found odd. He'd been taken to lunch at a proper industry grill by a minor museum director who wanted to stage an Anselm Kiefer retrospective; they ate only vegetables.

"How are you? How's Henry?"

So she told him: disconcerted, alarmed, fretful, not quite sure what to do next. And Henry was perfectly fine. But she now had her own business, family business.

"You don't have to do anything," Jeremy was saying. "You have no legal obligation. I'm not even sure you have a moral obligation."

"But it's my story, too."

Jeremy said nothing for a moment. "Do you really want me to argue the point?" he said.

"You don't understand."

"You won't let me understand."

"I always felt uneasy."

"That's not true. She bought you cream cakes at the Dolder and you felt happy."

"I felt uneasy. Nobody talking. You go deaf with the silence in the end."

"You just have a hint. A suggestion."

"Someone from Berlin. A table that Lucia has, that's enough to reduce Sarah Freeman to tears. It's obvious enough."

"Not to me."

"Nothing ever gets resolved," she said. "Nothing. I'm going to call Georg Meier."

"You always liked Meier."

"Fuck you," Helen said.

Later that night, he sent a fax: a little scrawled short story, what a woman and a man might be doing by a lake, very pretty in its way. A cop came along and the man had to say he couldn't help himself, Officer, and nor could she.

She hugged the paper, then smoothed it out, and then she went to bed alone. The next day, which was the day Lucia did not go to the shop, she'd pay her a visit at home.

Helen allowed no settling, absolutely no ease: she circled in the room, considering a table, pacing in a state of mild embarrassment at how much aggression she exposed simply by moving and moving. She remembered this kind of physical language from negotiations, and how you had to remember at times to whisper with your body.

Lucia had posed herself on a neat, embroidered chair, by a table with a tasseled lamp, in front of tall, closed curtains.

Lucia said, loudly: "I suppose you'd like some coffee?"

"I don't think so. It's a little late."

"I'm an old woman. But I'm perfectly well organized. I can make coffee."

"I know that," Helen said.

Lucia, dismissively, flickered her fingers against the arms of the chair.

Silence again. Helen noticed for the first time that she was staring at a photograph of her own father: in plain, cheap silver, but in a prominent place.

She wondered if Lucia could sense that something had changed, something was going to happen: but the idea was absurd unless there were already lawyers involved. Lawyers always know when other lawyers are busy; they scent work on the wind.

If Lucia knew nothing, Helen must be discreet.

But she wanted confrontation. She wanted Lucia to change: not to be the lovely grandmother anymore, but to show herself as the woman in the indictments.

She organized cushions.

Lucia considered the trouble with being old: that you couldn't resist other people's kindness. They would always feel entitled to come back. Resist them too much, and they were sure resistance must be proof of decline, that you had something to hide. Resist at all, and you were only being selfless, trying not to trouble them too much.

Lucia said: "What is it that you can't bring yourself to say to me?"

Nothing. Helen said nothing and made a great, resounding statement out of it. Then:

"I met a woman called Sarah Freeman. She said her friends in Zurich love your shop," Helen said.

"They're very kind. Do I know them?"

"They always say you have such perfect taste. That you know how to find exactly what they like. That you always did."

Now it was Lucia's turn to make silence operate in the room. She did it by seeming to fade, her face vague as though it were dusty, her shoulders down, her eyes almost closed under the weight of fine eyelashes. Helen wondered about the sheer weight of her routines: about the fifty-five years of never going to the shop on a Thursday, the gap that all those Thursdays must make in a life.

"If you want to know things, I can tell you things," Lucia said, suddenly. "I do remember things, you know."

Helen shrugged. It was the gesture of a cross child who'd later regret refusing the offer of something sweet.

Silence. The two wills tussled: the will to make ordinary talk, the will not to listen to anything but a confession.

———

But once she was out of the apartment, Helen knew exactly what she had to do. It was only a couple of days since she met Sarah Freeman in the street. If the woman was in a hotel then, she might still be there. She couldn't do nothing when all those people doing nothing had allowed Lucia her rich, fine life.

She wrote a brief note. She said again that she was the granddaughter of Lucia Müller-Rossi, and that was why she was concerned for Sarah Freeman: that she would understand Sarah's suspicion, but she strongly believed that the wrongs of the last war had to be righted. They should have been righted at the time; that failure had to be undone.

She would like to offer help, the names of lawyers. She would do anything she could to support Sarah Freeman in any legitimate claim she might have. She realized the difficulties of dealing with a foreign legal system in an unfamiliar city. She offered, in effect, to be family.

So where would Sarah Freeman stay? She hadn't seemed grand, and she wasn't an age when ostentation was automatic. She hadn't seemed poor; if she was, she would hardly have chosen Zurich in autumn. She would probably not be up at the Dolder, and probably not down in the raucous streets of the Niederdorf. She would be in some decent, comfortable middle-class hotel.

Helen checked the phone book, and then she went out walking in a mean, faint rain. Her shoes were quickly wet; she thought that might make the hotel clerks suspicious as she walked in. People with messages come by car; they don't walk in from the rain all sodden, as though they're not quite sure where they're going.

So the wetness of her soles reminded her: you must be authoritative. She could do that, easily. She went to the desk and said she wanted to leave a message for—she'd have to say Mrs. Sarah Freeman, she supposed, not Miss.

The clerk checked a list, and apologized and went directly back to checking bills.

She set out for the next hotel and the next. Some of them were all chrome; some of them tried to look like drawing rooms; one had a basket of apples at the door. Some of them advertised their restaurant, trying to sell tourists on something "typical." Some were tucked back on pleasant, shrubby streets, but their parking lots gave them away.

Sarah Freeman wouldn't be at one of those anonymous, suburban towers: Helen already had a sense of the woman that could not involve staying in some businessman's shelter, a standard and padded pile. She had time in the rain to ask herself just why she was so sure, what notion of a woman like Sarah Freeman was ready in her mind before she even met her.

A hotel with a view of the lake, just. They were sorry. A hotel with a view of tramlines, and a lobby so narrow two people could hardly pass. They were sorry. A hotel flying the rainbow flag and proposing a discotheque. She didn't bother.

The rain was in her hair and in her bones: chill, wretched damp. She'd set out on a kind of pilgrimage and she was now a convincing pilgrim: determined, exhausted, cold, and manifestly, unarguably, magnificently sincere. Or so she hoped, so she hoped.

She didn't think, in her time with the bank, she'd ever been quite so self-conscious. But then she had mostly been selling a deal, a proposition, an abstraction, not asking a stranger to trust her at once, without papers to read or figures to scan.

A hotel close to the Kunsthaus: they thought they knew the name. A clerk took the letter. Then the clerk came back, shook his head, and said, no, that was a Miss Hermione Freeman.

Helen didn't turn away for a moment. Hermione was an absurd name; she could hear that. It was stuck between dowager and music hall. A Hermione might easily claim to be a Sarah. Or else Hermione Freeman might have thought it impolitic to give a Müller-Rossi her full name.

The clerk said, firmly: "Is there anything else I can do for you?"
She didn't respond.

"Would you like a taxi, Madame?"

So she shook her head and she did as she was told, so indirectly but so forcefully: she went away.

She kicked up rain from the sidewalks. She rushed along. She even ran for a few hundred meters. She stood at a street corner and she stretched for a moment. She thought of stopping for coffee, but she wanted to get on: to cover every possibility, check every hotel.

She walked across another forecourt, into another genteel lobby: no lifts, a desk tucked away to one side like an extra window.

She pulled the envelope out of her briefcase one more time.

"I'd like to leave this for Mrs. Sarah Freeman," she said.

The girl at the desk, who had one of those angelic faces as open as a calculating machine, said brightly: "I could tell her you're here. If you like."

Helen said: "Yes. Why don't you tell her there's a letter. Then if she wants to come down—"

"I could say she has to sign for it," the girl said. She had such nice, surprising country manners, not wanting to disappoint in any way.

Helen didn't like to sit on the pretty chintz, so she stood in the middle of the lobby, was considered by a waiter carrying a tray of *Birchermuesli,* shifted aside when two large Italians came by with aggressive luggage.

The girl was answering other phone calls. Perhaps she hadn't called Sarah Freeman, or Sarah Freeman did not want to come down, or this was the wrong Sarah Freeman.

Helen thought of hotel detectives: the moment they come to ask if they can help. The hotel was too decorous for that, she thought; and besides, she was waiting for a guest.

Water puddled around her feet.

She heard the elevator doors open.

"You have a letter for me," Sarah Freeman said to the desk girl.

The girl produced it. "It's from that lady over there," she said.

And Sarah Freeman turned to see Helen.

Helen smiled. Sarah didn't react. Instead, she asked for a letter opener, a silvery thing. She slit open the envelope. She held the paper away from her eyes; perhaps she should have brought her reading glasses, but was—was too vain, perhaps? Helen needed every possible clue.

Sarah read.

"I thought," she said to the girl, "I had to sign for this. That it was something important."

Helen said: "I would very much like to talk to you."

Now the girl at the desk was embarrassed by the possibility of a drama. She was absorbed in the pigeonholes for letters, able to hear, not needing to acknowledge.

Helen said: "I would like to help."

"You look half drowned."

"I didn't know where you were staying. I didn't know if you were still in Zurich. So I walked."

Sarah said: "You want me to trust you."

"I would like it. If you could trust me just enough."

"I don't understand why you care."

"If I don't make things right, who will?"

Sarah couldn't stand anymore the sight of a wet, sad girl: like a hopeful child. She said: "You have to dry off." She went to ask the desk clerk for towels, which required a call to housekeeping, and the sudden irruption of a waiter with a tray of bleached white cloth.

"She'll dry off in my room," Sarah said.

She sat like a child, legs at the edge of the bed: hair toweled, coat hung, frock by a radiator, in a white shift. But she was very aware that there was no simple exchange of roles, the carer suddenly needing care. Sarah Freeman was not the mother who brings warmth and hot drinks. She sat apart, at the desk, and she watched Helen intently; and Helen had to tolerate this, in case it was the price of trust.

"All this is about a table," Sarah said. "It's nothing important."

"I don't know the story," Helen said. "But I know the other stories. I think it's about something very important indeed."

"You don't understand. If it was truly important, I could never bring myself to trust you. I can trust you if it's about a table."

"I have a lawyer friend," Helen said.

"Yes, I expect you do." Sarah tried to act as if she was in a place of work, nothing as intimate as a small hotel bedroom with wet clothes; she even shuffled the papers on the desk, the tourist brochures and the menus and the giveaway magazines about expensive things, as though she might need to file them in a moment. "I suppose," she said, "you would like to know something about this table?"

Helen said: "Only if you want to tell me." But she didn't mean it.

"I'm only telling you this," Sarah said, "as a rehearsal. I suppose I shall have to tell it again."

Helen shivered. Her hair was still a little damp against her neck. But the shiver was for something quite different: the change that was about to happen. Sarah had been a cause, on which the moral issues were all clear, and she was about to become a particular person, and this was not a comfortable moment for either one of them—not for Sarah, who would have to acknowledge that she could so easily be generalized, nor for Helen, who would have to deal with all the floating strands of someone's history in order to keep her attitudes loud and clear.

"I was married once. To a man called Max Lindemann, in Berlin, in the war. He was a doctor. He was a proctologist, actually. He was a Jew, so he'd been expelled from the German medical association. He was," she said, "a remarkable man, very logical and precise. He found a lawyer and persuaded him that if he couldn't practice medicine, then he ought to get a refund on his subscription to the association. The lawyer went to court, and the court actually agreed. Dr. Lindemann won. You forget how perfectly ready people sometimes are to keep going in a straight line, even if they start from grotesque places.

"The association felt obliged to appeal, and the case was heard very quickly. They had a very simple argument: the details didn't matter because in law Lindemann was dead. All Jews in the Third Reich were legally dead. So he couldn't possibly be an active member of the association and he couldn't have any rights. I imagine their lawyer looked very sure of himself.

"Max loved telling the story. He'd tell it to everyone, because he didn't have any other victories to tell them. You see: he'd expected the association to argue the way they did. But he hadn't bargained for his own lawyer, who was a witty man and a dangerous one. He stood up and said that if Dr. Lindemann was dead, then I was due a pension: Mrs. Lindemann, Sarah. And what's more, the judge listened. He kept asking: How could a man be dead when he tried to practice medicine, but alive when his wife needed a pension?

"And Max was famous for this. He made sure he was famous for this. It didn't make the papers, of course, but the story went everywhere else, as stories do, where there are people to listen. This group and that group. The houses where Jews had to live."

She said: "You know about the houses, do you?"

Helen nodded.

"It's wonderful," Sarah said, "how people think they know already." She went into the bathroom for a glass of water. She kept talking. "His victory only worked on paper. And you can lose paper. Max couldn't practice medicine. He could advise, but he couldn't cure.

He could diagnose, he knew what was wrong, but he couldn't prescribe drugs and he couldn't operate, not even on Jews. He knew everything and he could do nothing at all to help. Poor Max.

"He started to believe that things had to change eventually. He couldn't have gone on if he didn't think that. All the wrecking and burning would be a memory and life would start up again, as it was."

Helen said: "And you knew my grandmother?"

"You're impatient. Impatient, already."

"I don't mean that. I was trying to connect things."

"We knew Lucia. I suppose she liked us, in her way. We'd lost a lot, sold things to keep going, like everyone else, but we still had some paintings that weren't all brown varnish and dark woodlands and heroes. We still had some records—some swing, some jazz, even some Al Jolson. There was a catalogue of degenerate music the Nazis put out in 1938, with a black saxophonist on the cover with the Star of David, and Max always kept it out. Nobody could object, really; it was an official catalogue. Nobody ever took it.

"Max liked Lucia. He used to puff up when she came in, back straight, chest out. I can't tell you how much I liked the fact that he liked her. She was lovely, and she was glossy and she was healthy and she made him come alive, just for an hour or so. And he'd talk and talk: opera in Milan, politics of La Scala, and she knew about Siennese painting and Max and I did, too. Not that it mattered much what I knew.

"She admired some of our things. She admired the table. I told her all about it, because I had time to get interested in all sorts of things in those days. We were prisoners, we had time. I told her it was made by a man called Pierre Fléchy, who had a taste for chinoiserie, and covering every part of a table with elegant vines that mysteriously carry the flowers of peonies. I may have taught Lucia about marquetry, but I'm not sure. She talked to so many other people.

"But she really wanted to talk to Max. And after a while, I'd see that he wasn't as straight-backed anymore, that she wasn't distracting him, and he was remembering that he couldn't go out anymore or go to the theater or keep his books and his pictures or help anyone at all. So I'd interrupt and say I was sorry we had nothing we could share for dinner, and thank you for the butter."

She spoke like a witness in court, like a good teacher: but then, Helen thought, she'd had five decades to remember the details, and to put them into one set of words and then another.

"They put Max to work," Sarah said. "He had his surgical skills, so they set him to making mercury fuses for bombs. It was delicate work, and the risks didn't matter because you can't poison a dead man. Am I telling you more than you want to know?"

Helen only looked at her.

"Of course I am. I should get to the point, shouldn't I? Is that what you think?"

Helen shook her head, but without vigor.

"To me," Sarah said, "all this is the point. My life, not just my grievance."

Helen said: "I understand." But she was trying so hard to stay on her own high and well-defended moral ground, the perfect wrongness of her grandmother, perhaps the perfect wrongness of the Swiss in tolerating her, that it was hard to listen with the proper humility.

"Anyway," Sarah said, "Max thought we'd been lucky, really. We'd lost money and jewels, of course. He said the Nazis seemed to think the only reason anyone would have a wedding ring was to smuggle gold out of Germany. As if, I said, we could ever leave Germany.

"Lucia stopped listening at that point. She looked distracted, then she concentrated, like a saleswoman concentrates on the house she's selling, or the day cream. She said she did, as it happened, have some spare room in her apartment, if we needed to use it, and she could probably find a van somehow. The embassy would have one. She asked if we wanted to sell, but Max just said nobody would bother to pay us. They just had to wait and steal things.

"I didn't want her to take anything. I wanted that table because it was like a little garden in the corner. It was my refuge, my place."

Helen knew she had to go. She dressed, and she smiled.

"I remember what I said to her, after all these years, because I wanted to change the subject. I said: 'You know, the stars. If you go out at night in the streetlamps, they don't look yellow at all.'"

In the hotel lobby, Sarah found Peter Clarke fussing for stamps for a postcard and directions to the Chinese Garden. "I imagine you'll be going back," she said.

"I don't have to go back."

"But your family—" She wanted him to leave her. If he didn't, he was different.

"I can go where I like. I can stay where I like, now." He spoke as though he had only just discovered the fact. "I can't leave you alone to deal with all this."

"But it's expensive to stay in Zurich."

"I have money."

"Of course you do. I meant—"

"I need to stay."

She looked at him with enormous curiosity. He spoke with such feeling you might imagine he was a lover making his pitch. But although that would be flattering, startling even, it could not be the whole story.

"I need to stay. I have to stay and make sure that—I have to stay."

She said: "You frighten me."

"They take this away from us when we get older," he said. "They won't let us be responsible. They won't let us care. I can't live like that."

She needed company. She was also nervous at a champion who seemed to need his role so absolutely.

"I don't mean to frighten you. If you'd let me explain—"

Sarah said: "You don't know my story." She imagined a man in whose life there had never been enough incident, enough feeling: a diligent life, paced out day by day on the seed grounds, which now could acquire all the glamour of horror simply by staying put. He could be righteous; she had to carry the scars; and she was annoyed.

"I can't just walk away," Peter Clarke said, leaving out "not this time."

He hated explanations. He decided to explain.

SIX

He was the youngest, so they let him ride up front where the bomb aimer usually rides: barred in with struts and spars and tubes in the breast of the plane, a gun in front of each eye. He was alone there, tense in place, the first into the air as the Lancaster climbed slowly off its huge truck wheels.

His bones shook. His ears stopped. He was fused to the lumbering machine that carried him. He couldn't hear a word from behind him.

He was dancing in the hydraulic seat, turning left, turning right, shouting out. He was bloody going home.

Up, the sky was full of light and no enemy. The green stopped and the sea started at a white line of shore waves. Below, there was an impossible space of water, channel leading on to sea, sea to ocean, ocean to ocean beyond that. He'd been in rooms so long, rooms with guards, in an old brick factory on the German border with a sick sense of order, officers to obey, functions to fulfill. He'd kept clean, kept fed, kept hoping. And now there was all this world, the color of spilled school ink with a shine like gun metal, and he was glorying in it, and he was terrified.

One morning there were suddenly no guards at the brick factory. So he had walked west with the others, blankets in his arms, chocolate and cigarettes stowed away, with a cart he half bargained, half stole from a farm. Everyone was walking west to get away from the Russians, old prisoners, old soldiers, following their own shadows in the morning and the dazzle of a red sun in the evening.

They slept one night in a hall of poplar trees. He was the first to wake, heard an engine, and went down to the road. Out of the plains came Americans in a jeep. He flagged them down, shouted for the others, bowled off along the straight roads to a camp. They gorged on steak and pie, all on one plate, and half apologized for being a nuisance. Then he flew in the belly of some great transport plane, benches tied to the walls and buckets down the middle. He waited again, and he had practice in waiting, until he and his mates were put out on an airfield in gangs and the bombers came roaring in to take them home.

Now everything below was water, kind water. He remembered wading: cold water in the shorts, body smacked down on the sea, sliding under the thick glass of the waves and feeling ribbons of weed around his arms.

He was not a number on a metal disk anymore: prisoner of war. Very soon, he could give up his army number, too. He was a man of twenty, that's all, which was all he had longed to be.

The sea stopped. The din of the Lancaster no longer mattered because the air itself seemed warm, seemed silent around him, and below him the country flowed by, pits and monuments and suburbs and towers all liquid and luminous like quicksilver. The green started again: creeping in among sand dunes, overpowering in the meadows. He knew everyone back in the belly of the plane was talking out a future, but he was hungry just for the green.

The Lancaster started to lose height. Through the smeared plastic of the windscreens, the lovely generality of the land was coming into focus now. The plane went low over gardens like the ones he used to know, broad beans just over, runner beans up their poles, boxed houses, lanes buried in trees. He could see particular houses where particular people lived. He had to imagine a life he could make: twenty, one of a great many young, official heroes, with no special appetite for a suit or a job, and no woman waiting, either. The war was over, but the war was what had shaped his world since he was a schoolboy of fourteen, his whole lifetime as a man.

He'd seen so many colors: blood, uniforms, unfamiliar woods and corridors and towns. Now, as the Lancaster lowered itself as slow as a cloth coming down to the ground, the colors were simple again, and glorious. There was the shine of grass, gold seed, bright growth, all stippled with dandelions. There was the deep white of hawthorn flowers, frothing in a case of green ground and blue sky, that filled the bombsights and the gun sights as the Lancaster bounced to the ground.

He hung on the glass for a moment. He had come home.

Everyone scrambled from the planes, the aircrew complacent as parents at a holiday. There were women with tea and sandwiches and English comfort, and order and patience enough to make the men into queues for rail warrants, cash, the coupons for six months of double rations. The trains were assigned. The men jostled to pack them out. This one was going to be a teacher, this one was going to make a million, this one was for Oxford, and this one was going to get into the sweet civilian civil service if it killed him, and build a new Jerusalem, rule by rule.

But the kid said nothing.

Working crowds parted for them. They understood that the men wanted to take off the prickling uniforms, undo the blanco and webbing and polish, and get started. They could not imagine there were some who were held together by uniforms, blanco, webbing, polish, rank, and orders; that this was all they had known.

On the train out of London, he looked out through dusty windows and he saw bits of London broken and torn down and boarded up, leaving gaps in the brick and endless fountains of buddleia and tall grass bristling on dead homes and factories. He remembered going to London for treats, seeing these same streets with their windows and gardens and the hints at the lives they contained, a whole maze of possibilities. But as the train jolted east, the tarmac of the streets was like a memorial to that old order. He saw a church tower marked with fire.

The smell of steam in the train, of old and half-clean clothes and worn seats, was comfortable: like the camp smells. He hadn't smelt the truly clean or open air for two long years. He stared at the pictures hanging above the seats opposite, a sepia countryside with a great church, a set of cliffs with people walking.

He looked out for the brick seed warehouses that came just before the village station, and the seed fields, assorted marigolds, godetias rampant, flocks of campanulas, a white tide of alyssum, but all marked out neatly into rectangles of brilliant color. His eyes came alive.

He opened the compartment door and stepped down on the platform. A fresh salt breeze shocked him. He straightened his back, and picked up his bag.

He walked by tiny brick houses opposite a slow river. He remembered seeing nets in the river, all full of cut parsley keeping fresh for the London train. Nothing now. People waved. A couple shook his hand, one after the other, eyes irritated with tears. The grocer's shop had the same dusty cans in the window, as though nobody needed them, not even in wartime. In the baker's window was a pinkish red, palish blue, sugar-white cake with a great "V" for "Victory" and a hand-lettered sign that said "Welcome Home Our Boys."

Everyone recognized him. "Peter Clarke, good to see you." "Peter, welcome home!" But he was not quite sure he was Peter Clarke anymore, not the same boy who used to defend the boundaries of the village at night with a .303 rifle, who knew to duck when the flying bombs stopped their whining note overhead and went silent.

He followed the river, which was full of bending weeds, past a Roman site where he once found a coin still deeply incised, and the mill with its rooms strung out across the water. The American planes dropped fuel tanks; you could make them into canoes; he remembered that. He came to a wood he helped his father plant: dark and tall now, but he still had in mind the small brushes of firs they set out at exact intervals, just before the war.

He slowed down. He noticed the verges, how they were full of thick green docks and plantains. He felt the lack of someone to come home to, a particular name and body and address which could be his future.

Now he was at the gate of his father's house. The rosemary bush by the door had grown huge in a couple of years, and it was stuck about with odd, papery flowers. He studied it. He held off knocking on his father's door.

He knocked, and his father opened the door immediately, as though he'd spent the morning standing ready.

The two men held each other.

"I'll show you," his father said. He went to the table, and pulled a wad of papers from the drawer and gave them to Peter, then went off to the kitchen and rattled drawers, slammed cupboard doors, and shouted back: "Just a minute."

Peter was left to stand and read. There was army form B 104-83: Peter Clarke "posted as missing," which "does not necessarily mean" he is dead. If his father heard anything, he was to send the post-card or the letter to the Record Office in Warwick. A little pamphlet explained that official lists of prisoners took time to compile— rooms of clerks laboring slowly—but "capture cards," filled in by prisoners after capture and sent to relatives, were "often the first news received in this country that a man is a prisoner of war."

He imagined he'd gone from the order of a regiment to the order of a prison camp, just changing numbers on the way. It was dis-concerting to find he'd gone missing from the record: on the first of July 1943.

Army form B 104-83A , dated the twenty-first of September 1943. The army number, his rank, then his name were there, with the news that he was a prisoner of war "at a camp not yet stated, Prisoner of War number not yet reported, details to be notified later."

Then the capture card must have come, and his father must have sent it to the Record Office. They thanked him, anchored Peter Clarke to a new number, and sent back the card. He was officially reconstituted: a case filed and sorted.

All this time, he had been in an old brick factory, in an office, at a wide desk with a German officer, some French and some British prisoners, all sorting and filing. He'd been an obvious choice for listing and organizing, because he was bright and he wrote neatly. He had worked in an office, then found himself fighting for a while, then he was back in an office.

He didn't think he had killed anyone. He'd fired bullets, but that was all.

His father should have been at work. He was always at work, except sometimes on Saturday afternoons. He nursed hothouse roses for a daily buttonhole, sat on steps for hours thinning grapes, pollinated nectarines with a lamb's tail on a stick, stoked the boilers, drove the cars, rode his bicycle down to the bank to cash the staff's wages, and came back to load guns on shooting days, or chase down swarms of bees and bottle their honey. He filled hothouses with bougainvillea. He put caps on flowers to make them meet a timetable for shows. He won prizes, too, but they came in the name of the owner of the house which he managed, decorated, fed, and even animated. He did all this with patience, and with kindness, maybe love.

He had brought back a bottle of whisky. "You're old enough now," he said. He handed out one glass, and sipped at the other. "It's good to see you," he said. He watched his son with the glass. "It's for drinking," he said. "Drink it."

"I'm not used to it."

"Enjoy it," he said. "It's time you enjoyed things."

"Nothing doing at the house?"

"Nothing to do," he said.

Peter considered what his father just said, and he could not make any sense of it.

"I made up your old room," his father said at last. "In the attic. You can stay as long as you want."

The cottage, after Peter's mother died, had come to seem low and small: whited walls under old thatch, a garden crowded thick with tomatoes and Michaelmas daisies and roses and bees and sage. It stood beside a one-track railway line, and at the side of the flint church. Somehow, it was never called a "house," let alone "the House"; the word didn't fit. A "house" was something like the great brick range you could glimpse down the road, the other side of a dark English shrubbery, with iron gates, a gravel drive, dells, and pauses in the wall of rhododendrons on the way to the front door. The house always seemed to shine, even on a drab day, after the sunlessness of the driveway.

"I thought I'd go for a walk," Peter said.

The sweat under his arms stained his khaki shirt, which did not seem proper for going up to the house. But a couple of kids came out from behind a hedge and cheered. An older woman smiled much too much, as though she was nervous of all the men coming home. He pulled himself through the dusty heat.

The gates were off their hinges. He saw that at once. The hinges had rusted, too. The driveway was rutted from heavy vehicles and the orderly shade of the shrubbery had become wilderness. It wasn't reasonable to be shocked, not in a countryside full of barbed wire and sentry boxes and tank traps and firing ranges, among people who wanted returning soldiers to see they, too, had been at war.

But he was still shocked: that his father thought he had nothing to do.

The lawns were torn, clods of black clay. The topiary by the kitchen garden, yew obelisks and privet globes, had new stems all defiantly waving out of order. There was glass missing from one of the drawing-room windows, and alongside it the wall was stained in the shape of a great dark funnel. One of the downpipes was clogged, obviously, and just as obviously nobody cared.

The main door, which was always ready to be opened, stood open already.

The house had been requisitioned for war use; all large houses were requisitioned for foreign troops or domestic training or intelligence. He knew that. But still he did not feel entirely comfortable swaggering in through the front door as thought it was now his communal, national property. It was not a question of deference, because that was all past now; he had become a registered hero, and probably the banker owner of the house had not. He only thought he might offend his father.

He walked to the back of the house, to the greenhouses where he remembered spikes of strelitzia, to the asparagus beds which his father said had to be salted once a month, to all the wonders and the order of his childhood. It might as well never have been.

War didn't change him. Peace did. He always knew the moment: when he stood behind that great house, saw a window open, and pushed through into the rooms as though he was thieving. There wasn't any more order to the world, or anything sure, and he might as well roam about room to room.

In the drawing room someone had written in red on the walls: a regimental tag, a Kilroy peering over a wall.

In the next small room, he remembered the paper on the wall: a zoo of gilded birds, peacocks and flamingos. The walls had been boarded over for safety. He pulled at one of the planks, just to bring back something of what he remembered: a room a child glimpsed once and then turned into a land for dreaming. The plank came away a little too easily, as though the nails had gone into soft plaster, or been disturbed already. He saw a narrow slice of wall, with peacocks on it.

Someone had cut all the gold eyes from their tails.

As he went back through the corridors he sensed their cool, damp outdoor smell, no longer safe and enclosed from the world, not smelling of burning coal and hot air as they once did at Christmas.

He asked his father for fruit from the garden. They picked apples together, the delicate skinned James Grieve with a sunrise of pink and gray on their skins. His father added some bread, a piece of cheese, and made sure Peter carried his papers.

He stood at the door for a while, watching his son go away. "Listen," he said. Peter stopped at the gate. "Listen, you live with it," he said. "You can live with it."

"It's not that."

"I missed you," his father said.

But Peter had already started walking, and he walked until he came to London again.

He tried to make a garden of his own. There were these great tears in the fabric of cities, where bombs had cracked up walls and houses and factories. He tried to fill one. He pulled at old brick to pile it out of the way, pushed aside beams that were fallen, found a pick and levered up the broken concrete of an old floor. He dislodged flourishes of herb Robert, the tight succulent whorls of saxifrage, and wires of pink convolvulus. He worked under fountains of lanky buddleia that were wonderfully alive with butterflies.

"There might be bombs," a boy said. "You know there might be bombs. My mum won't let me play here."

He hadn't thought of that. He only wanted to repair reality, to make it whole again, to make it blossom as his father used to do.

"You'd like my mum," the boy said.

"Could she lend me a spade? And a pick?"

From the chaos of tumbled spars and ragged brick he made a space marked out with stones. The iron cut into his hands, rusted and bloodied them. The brick he heaved into high, loose cairns, muscles tearing with the unfamiliar motion. He felt very strong until he had finished.

Then he tried to clean the earth, first pulling the weeds, then burning what was left, the smoke rising thinly between the gutted walls. He dug and dug again, turning over earth that had been tamped down ever since this great warehouse was first built. It was poor stuff, clay gone to powder. The more he opened it up to the light and air, the more it crumbled away. He knew already it would be far too alkaline for growth.

He would not give up. He needed water, manure, seeds.

He dug the ashes from burning into the ground. He couldn't find wasted stuff that would rot down; nobody was wasting anything. One night, he got into the backyards of houses where someone was keeping rabbits, seven of them, and he stole the dung. One of the does bit him, and the scar stayed with him, just under the thumb of his left hand.

In the seed shop, he ordered a half-pint of peas, a half-pint of runner beans. An old, cross man fussed with the little drawers of the seed cabinet and measured out ounces of carrot and cabbage seed. He kept an old seed catalogue on the counter, from 1937, with seed growers on the cover who looked just like Peter's father, and with luscious words for the flowers on which nobody now wasted space. It served to guarantee a future when he could again sell lovely, impractical things.

He scavenged the other bomb sites for seeds of fireweed, willow herb, so he could deliberately plant in lines and beds what would seed itself in time on any open space. He found lupins already gone to seed in a hot season, and planted them, too. He made a nursery out of a few wood planks, some jars for jam and for Marmite, some cans cut in half. He bought a tomato from a shop that wanted to give our boys a treat, cut it open, and dried it in the sun, under a hand-kerchief to keep the birds away; then he planted the seeds.

The warehouse had long ago been abandoned as a dangerous shell, nothing more, so the water was not connected. In places it looked as though the pipes had been ripped down for their copper, but perhaps that was damage the bombs did; it was hard to tell. At least the walls shaded the ground just enough to protect it from a vicious, browning summer.

He washed at the public bathhouse. He slept by the garden. Dogs came fooling around, and he chased them off.

It took a couple of weeks to bring back a kind of order to the space between the broken walls, and he worked as privately as he could, leaving boards in place at the old warehouse windows and slipping between them when he had to leave. He worked stripped to the waist, shirt bleaching over rocks in the hot sun.

He was being watched.

It wasn't the boy. He hardly noticed the boy, although he would be sad not to have the company. He thought at first it might be the Authorities, his father's compendium word for policemen, soldiers, taxmen, bureaucrats, the supervising classes. But there was just a shadow flickering where the boards were down on a high doorway.

He turned quickly.

The boy was there. He said, very earnestly: "This is my mum. You'll like my mum."

Her name was Grace, and she stepped out of the doorway like a kid on a stage. She was a short, pretty, soft-spoken woman, dark but with a bit of the flirt and the big, warm manners that he reckoned should properly be blonde.

He said: "I'm going to need water."

"I can see. Take some from my house," Grace said. "I've got buckets." He hesitated, and she said: "It's too far away for a hose. I'm sure it is."

"You live round here?"

"Of course we do." The boy was very sure of what he was doing.

"I like a garden," Grace said.

She gave him lunch every day. She wanted company, and she wanted to be grateful to someone that the war was all over, and she wanted a man who would take the place of the one who was so weak he left her to go and be a dutiful citizen and got himself killed. She lent him this other man's shirts and trousers from before the war, and his skinny, prisoner's body walked about inside them.

He carried buckets, back and forth. She watched him go, arms straining. She never asked anything in particular, why he was sleeping rough, why he was making the garden, why he was there, and why he was available.

She stood by the sink with her sleeves rolled up to the muscles of her arms, and her blouse slightly open on the soft folds of her breasts, she looked at him and she panicked. She pulled down her sleeves, buttoned her shirt. She said: "You're very young."

"I'm as young as you."

She put her hands in the soapy water and she flicked the suds at him. Then she said: "I'm sorry," as though she might scare him away. She wondered if he liked women, if he was okay. He didn't understand why she should be worrying and he went up and held her. She relaxed entirely, soft as a cat, molded on him.

He still wasn't sure. He didn't know these rules. He had a sense, walking west from the prison camp into the sun, of all the feeling that had been pent up for the war years and now was out free. He sensed all that fury in Grace, and it burnt him, but at the same time she was depending on him, holding him. His body wanted her, but his mind went cold; maybe she wanted just whatever he was growing, and, more to the point, the double rations that ex-prisoners could draw for six months: more cheese, more butter for the boy, the smell of bacon in the house again. Then he couldn't manage to be suspicious anymore.

They fucked in the afternoon, while the boy was out playing. She liked the energy he had, the gratitude; he loved the eiderdown softness of her body and the juicy, muscular need at the heart of it.

After that, she made him come in discreetly because of the neighbors. They mustn't know about the man she'd got, the strange man who did not sleep in the house. It was as though she understood that they had a license for a time, but at any moment it might be revoked.

He had not settled. He wouldn't concede that this consistent desire, the fact that the world made sense in her bed and that he felt whole there, had a meaning. He didn't have a history of conquests to compare.

"You play cricket," her boy said.

"I play cricket."

"You're a bowler. You bowl fast."

"I can bowl fast."

The kid seemed to take his presence for granted, as though he'd been the one to supply some gap in the house, to provision the place with a man.

Grace said one afternoon: "I don't know where you sleep. Don't you ever want to sleep with someone?"

"I like being alone. You couldn't be alone in the camp."

"Did you ever sleep with a woman? I mean, sleep?"

He didn't say anything.

"It isn't a promise," she said. "It's just keeping warm."

He might have moved in. He thought about it.

But one morning he went to the garden from washing at the bathhouse and he found the stones had been scattered.

He started walking again.

He truly loved walking. Each mile was a purpose in itself; he didn't need to imagine anything longer or grander. The camps had tightened him up like a screw, and now he was using his body again, feeling the blood come back to limbs which had a healthy sense of looseness.

And he was still in uniform, with a shirt from Grace so he could change clothes. He didn't need to explain anything, because everyone thought he must be on his way home. People were kind, perhaps a little alarmed. The uniform made him anonymous, too: one man in a million men all walking and driving and riding home.

He was vanishing. His father, he found out later, sat at home more afraid than he ever had been during the war. Then, he trusted a whole official machine to care for his son, but now he did not know if his son was to be trusted. He conjured up memories of trench war, mustard gas, exploded souls, and he wondered if his son had broken.

But his son was on a beach, trying to stay in the warm, salty moment. He thought of his garden, though, brown now with the summer, no rain and no watering. He thought of his father, how he should have let himself be welcomed home. He ran into the cold, gentle chop of the water, he washed himself, and he came out and lay on the shingle in the sun.

He could always cross the sea, he thought. There had to be a way.

He walked into Dover trying to look like the kind of man who carried the right papers. He was tired, scruffy, but so was everyone: the moment for parades was gone. He was a little dazed, so it seemed, uncertain of the way down to the marine station. Maybe people thought he'd been drinking, but they were in a forgiving mood for the moment.

To cross, he'd got to understand what was happening very precisely: which regiments, going where. He would not quite look right, but maybe he would not be checked. He walked down to the Dover marine station, Western Dock, to the platforms full of the smell of steam and heavy uniforms worn in summer and the occasional bonfire cigarette, and, just once, the sharp smell of coffee.

He saw the roof was broken up, the glass gone in jagged patches. He saw mobs bustling about, or just standing, waiting as though they had been waiting for hours, even days. All the precision of a railway, timetables and platforms and destinations, seemed suspended, overrun by men in khaki.

Down below the platforms was the dock itself, where three ships lay. One was open at the back to swallow a train. Two were smaller, as though they had come from smaller crossings. All of them had been stripped down, the comforts taken away, and all of them were painted gray to slip about in the careful anonymity of wartime.

He wanted to cross the Channel. But he could cross only as part of an army, on the terms and in the conditions made for wartime.

He wondered about sandbars. They couldn't have dredged the Channel, not during wartime. He wondered about mines, because the crossing must have been protected by both sides against both sides. There could be wrecks. He found himself edgy, worrying at the incurious stares of the waiting men, wondering when the marine police would notice that he was not properly attached to a group, wondering where he should go. He would need to report to someone. He knew that was the proper military way.

He clutched his stomach. He did feel a griping pain, but he was also scamming. He had to get off these platforms, get away from the ships, get away; he needed to organize himself. He thought he was going to throw up, wondering what the penalty might be for a soldier going the wrong way, disrupting orders he did not even know.

He did something right for once. He turned back.

He jumped down from the bus, as though he'd got the daily habit of coming home there, pushed past the little front garden that was all concrete and dandelions, and he knocked at Grace's door.

"Oh," Grace said. And then: "Oh. Good."

After he'd washed, and she'd given him dinner, he said: "I don't want to sleep on the bomb site anymore."

"I went to look at your garden. I tried watering it. Only I didn't know which plants to pull up and which to leave."

"I've only been gone a few days."

"I thought if you came back—it seemed a pity to waste it all. All that work."

He said: "Can I stay here?"

She started to put her fingers through his hair as though he was another child, but she stopped herself. The boy was watching, and he seemed tired, pale, anxious.

"Come on," she said.

Up in the bedroom, they were shadows in the great mirror of the wardrobe door. She'd lain back on the sheen of the eiderdown, feeling more naked than she ever had before. He was like a dog among the hollows and crevices of her body. She was sure for a moment; he was lost for a moment; and it came to the same thing, two bodies managing to charm each other. They settled into the horsehair mattress afterward as though they'd leave prints there for all time.

Outside the house, it wasn't so easy. She took out the ration coupons at the butcher's and he said something sarcastic about her needing steak, he supposed, and threw her some bits of boiling beef. She took him down to the pub and sat feeling very alone and conspicuous when he went off to order the drinks. One of the neighbors said: "Done very well for herself, she thinks. He's not from around here." "Talks nice," said another one, venomously.

He told her, bit by bit, where he used to live, what he used to do, how he got called up for a war and never quite entered it because he was a prisoner almost before he could fire a gun. She told him she was married, that he was killed, that sometimes at night she dreamed he'd come back in a rage, but she knew he never would.

"How do you know?" he asked.

"You just know things like that."

That night he lay awake, expecting to defend her against this stranger who would certainly come back.

She got up to check on the boy, who was tossing and turning and sweating under a sheet, whose breath came awkwardly as though he was forgetting sometimes to breathe, who cleared his throat like an old smoker. She came back and settled down beside Peter and said nothing at all. She was still not sure how much of a burden she could share with such a young man.

Since the pub was not friendly, and they didn't talk to people much at the café, they formed a closed circle of two, absorbed in each other so deeply that they didn't even have a private language that any outsider could hear. They didn't need the reminders of touch and graze because they knew that they owned each other.

The beans and the peas in the garden needed stakes. He didn't know where to get them. Grace opened the padlock on the boxy wood shed at the end of the garden and showed the old bamboos her husband used. Some were rotten, some were broken, and they smelled of damp, but there were enough to stake the peas.

He was working in the garden when he knew that something was wrong.

He threw the bamboos down crisscross on the ground. He went through the door and forgot to put the boards back. He ran down the street, knocked against a spinster, a vicar, a coalman on his way, skidded into the front garden, and realized he still did not have a key. He liked to ask to come in, usually, but this time he knew he had no time at all.

He knocked on the front door, on the wood, then on the frosted glass. He rang the doorbell. He ran around the side, through the second painted gate, and to the back door. He hammered on the green painted wood. He'd take a pick to the wood if he had one.

He shared Grace's terrified mood; it was his mood. In the minute he had to stand there, waiting for the door to open, he tried to start a story to explain his terror, but all he had was this instinct to be here and to save her.

The door opened suddenly. Grace said: "It's the boy."

He ran into the front parlor. It was a room like a waxworks, everything shining vaguely, an orange carpet, three chairs, and a table covered in a lace cloth. On this bright afternoon, the light cut into the floating dust from the old coal fire, and there was still the faint damp smell of smoke from the chimney. He noticed all this as though for the first time; he had not spent much time in the parlor.

The boy was on the floor, hiding his face. He made ratcheting sounds, as though he had gears in his lungs. He heard Clarke, and he looked up, his face blue and pinched.

"It just came on," Grace said. "He doesn't say anything."

The boy couldn't speak; that was clear. He couldn't cut the words out of his breathing.

"Get an ambulance," Peter said. He didn't know what else to do, except to get the boy out of the house, where there was nothing they could do for him. "Does anyone have a phone?"

"The woman next door. But she doesn't talk to me."

"She'll have to talk to you."

The boy couldn't stay still. He was trying to duck away from whatever was strangling him. His face ran with sweat that made the blue tinge in his lips, in the fine skin around his eyes, seem like a paint of some kind. But it wasn't on the surface anymore; it suffused the skin, poisoned it.

Grace went next door. The woman wouldn't answer for a moment. Grace shouted through the letterbox that she had to use the phone.

The woman crashed about in her kitchen, rattling bottles in a garbage pail so as not to hear. Grace shouted: "It's my boy. He's bloody dying."

The woman opened the door. "You should have thought of that," she said.

Grace could see the phone.

"There's a public phone two streets away."

"It can't wait."

The woman was like a bright, inflexible cutout of a shrew, a soft brown creature stiff with propriety.

"I'm very sorry to disturb you, Mrs. Rogers. I would be very glad if I could use the phone. Please."

Grace had performed. Mrs. Rogers allowed.

And the boy rocked back and forth airlessly. Peter felt for the child's ribs; they seemed to have great gaps between them with no flesh at all when the boy breathed, and then to fill out like a balloon when he struggled to pull in air. And the dust, from the fire and perhaps from the broken bits of the city, Peter could see that hanging in the air, a sample of what must have settled into the boy's lungs. Dust glints, he saw. It wasn't dull or inert at all; it was tiny blades.

"Nothing's happened," he said when Grace got back.

"He'll want a drink," Grace said. She brought in water, but it did not seem to help.

The ambulance arrived with bells. The whole street stood out of doors to see it, so she thought. The ambulance men put the boy on a stretcher, put the stretcher in the back, pulled Grace in afterward, and she wanted Peter to come, too. She shouted for him.

The boy rose up from the stretcher and hooted like a terrified owl: a grating sound, rough as sandpaper, that sent the neighbors back into their front rooms to watch between the curtains as the ambulance pulled away.

Peter followed. He followed, running. They'd never let him into the ambulance; he was just the mother's new bloke. But he could not fail to be with her; that was the point. He didn't know what he would do, any more than he knew what to do when the boy sat there looking like a bent paperclip with flesh on him, battling with something as ordinary as air.

He cut over a crossroads, by the Tube station, down a brick tunnel, along a street that somehow kept its plane trees even in the cold wartime winters, kept running until his breath caught up with him and he was running as though he was back on a track, running for glory.

He arrived sweating, awkward, falling over himself at the emergency room, and he found Grace at once.

"They took him," she said. "They just took him."

Both of them sat on wood chairs in the second row, in a low room painted white, with smells of antiseptic around them and cool, damp air coming from the door even though outside the sun was going down hot.

A nurse asked: "Has anything like this happened before?"

"He's coughed sometimes. And he does wheeze at night, I noticed. Of course, he's always seemed anxious, having grown up during the war, you're not surprised. Are you?"

The nurse said: "Has he seen a doctor about it?"

"He seemed well enough. I never thought about a doctor."

"We don't often see asthma here," the nurse said. "It's something you treat at home."

"But I didn't know—"

Grace wanted to be judged, he could see that, wanted to be told what she had done wrong so she could always be right in the future, and bring her boy back from whatever white, cold place now held him.

Instead, the nurse smiled. "He's going to be fine," she said. "Sometimes it does happen, out of the blue, like they say." Then she thought about the boy's cyanosed face and she stopped smiling. "They give him ephedrine," she said. "That controls the lungs. They may put him in an oxygen tent for a while, so he can breathe more easily. He'll be fine. You'll see."

They did not get home that night. They sat together, not touching. Once, Grace was asked to go forward and Peter was told he must wait. Grace went through the swinging doors. He thought he could hear her heels on the linoleum of the corridor floor. He tried to imagine what she would see.

"How is he?" he asked.

"I couldn't really see him," she said.

After a minute he asked: "What do you mean?"

"He's in a kind of hut. A sort of shelter. With oxygen."

He wanted to know exactly what she had seen, so he could share the sight and share her feelings. She couldn't say. Her heart was down there beating by the boy whose breaths were so desperate and forced.

At four in the morning, he went to fetch her tea in a thick, white cup. When she'd finished, he noticed that his cup was perfect, but the glaze on hers was crazed. He wished he'd taken the other cup.

A new nurse said: "You have to go home. There's nothing to do here. Take yourself home." She said to Peter: "Your brother will be fine—"

Grace said: "Thank you" before the nurse could say anything else.

Grace lay in bed like a plank, rigor mortis of the heart. She could not even cry. She was alert for news which would come to the door, like all the other news in her life had come: the death of her husband in a neat, official letter, the family letters before and after, but not many afterward when she had turned into an anomaly, a spare woman with a child. She would have liked a telegram saying that everything is now all right, and always will be. A telegram from the king.

He lay against her, flat against her, the skin of their hips and their shoulders touching and their bodies arching separately away in between. He wanted to share her warmth. He wanted her to share his warmth. It was a start. But the day was stark hot, a copper sun polishing the air, and she didn't want touch, either.

He couldn't bear this. Her pain touched him, but he couldn't touch her back. She wasn't just frightened for the boy in the next hours, the next days, he knew that. The boy had changed for her, become an unreliable body with frightening possibilities that she couldn't handle alone. She sighed very deeply, and sighed again, and again.

He asked if she wanted tea. He went to make some, anyway. He stood on the linoleum squares in the little kitchen, boiling a kettle on an electric ring. He looked at the soles of his feet, but they were clean; her floors were always clean because they were used. It was only the parlor that had dust through the air.

He made the tea, took down a can of condensed milk. Hot, sweet tea; he knew it was what she needed.

At eleven she got up, pulled on a church frock, said she was going to the hospital. He went with her. She visited the boy in his oxygen tent, and this time she saw his eyes open so wide they must be hurting him.

"They're looking after you, then?" she said, softly, just for the sake of his hearing her talk. "They're looking after you. Special tanks. Special injections. They'll make you good as new." Then her words speeded up. "Better, even, maybe," she said. "Better than new. You'll see. You'll be down playing football again. You'll see."

Peter Clarke sat on the hard seat outside. He wanted to help, somehow. He wanted to carry this burden that had suddenly fallen on Grace, and stop the boy hurting, too. He knew he had been ungenerous to his own father, that he had run away, and now he insisted on being quite magnificently kind.

She came out of the wards and she said: "They're doing everything they can."

The boy came home in an ambulance, but he walked out of the back. He smiled at the crew, who laughed back at him.

"What's for dinner," he said.

"Sausages," Grace said. "I got you sausages."

They sat in the kitchen. They spoke quietly, except for the boy, and they moved with care between the table and the cupboards.

Peter said: "You want to see the garden? Things are coming up now."

"You don't want to tire him," Grace said.

The boy stuck out his tongue. "I'm all right," he said.

"You have to rest," Grace said.

And for a week or so, it was almost all right. The boy sat at the window and he didn't seem to mind not rushing out to the other kids in the street; he was always a loner. He did visit the garden, but there was nothing much to see: a few broad-leaved sprouts above ground, the odd sight of weeds like willow herb all in pink formation.

Grace had the boy to sleep with her. She said she wanted to hear if his breathing changed during the night. She was supposed to listen for wheezing, she said, and if his breath came in pants or in long, slow sucks. Peter tried to sleep on the sofa in the parlor, which was not quite long enough for him.

Grace's concern was his concern. He was almost sure he did not become jealous.

The boy went to have a bath. He wouldn't let Grace go with him; he said he was old enough now. And she couldn't argue with him.

"He's fine," Peter said. He put out a hand. Grace said: "It's all right for you." He wanted to say: It's not all right at all for me. I know what you feel. I feel it, too. "He's never going to be all right," Grace said, suddenly.

She went to a drawer and pulled out a new white shirt. She had ironed and starched it meticulously. "I bought it for him," she said. "For later." She turned to Peter. "I want him to have a good white shirt. It makes all the difference. People look at you—"

They both heard a cough upstairs. "That bloody heater," she said. "It'll be the gas. It'll set off his asthma."

She slipped on the carpet near the top of the stairs, dropped back for a moment onto Peter, and then threw herself forward. The bathroom door wasn't locked; she wouldn't let the boy lock it.

He was standing naked by the bath. He was fighting to breathe and he was winning for the moment: a tenuous kind of victory that only emphasized the skinny pale ribs, the way his chest seemed to sink and to blow beyond what a boy's body ought to be able to do, the pallor of his tight face.

"I'm all right," he said. "Really."

All the boy had was a scrap of a life, enough to send Grace running for the terror and the ether smell of a casualty ward, enough to give her pain when he felt pain. There were going to be no miracles.

Peter Clarke had a sense of anger. This was a new bloody world, wasn't it? A new world of homes for all and a welfare state and maybe even medicine you didn't have to pay for, when pain would be somehow solved, when someone in authority would always know what to do.

So why don't they save the boy, then? Doesn't he matter in their grand overarching schemes? Doesn't Grace count?

The boy had been in bed for two days, Grace giving him drinks with sugar, making balsam in bowls for him to inhale from under a thick towel. She seemed to think this was like a summer cold. He lay in the double bed, curled up at the top on Grace's side, like a cat curls. She'd pushed a pillow under him where his back started to arch in spasms.

"Come and sit down," Peter said and led her out of the room for a minute. She did sit, but awkwardly; her flesh and her muscles seemed to hang from tired bones. She took a cup of tea, she finished it quickly, and she said: "He'll miss me."

"He'll be asleep."

"He'll miss me. He's my boy."

"I'll sit with him for a bit. You rest. Listen to the radio, put your feet up."

She glared at him as though she'd like to tell him he was wrong, all wrong. She couldn't. Instead, she said: "Just for a minute, then."

But the minute became an hour. He could hear her downstairs, not lying down sensibly but propped up in a chair and breathing awkwardly. He ought to have gone to cover her, but that would mean leaving the boy, who now lay still on his pillow in the crook of the big bed.

It's breath that will kill him. He'll fight for breath until his heart stops or the blood bursts in his brain. He'll die, anyway.

The boy was quiet. Peter moved closer. The boy curled into himself, and shook as though a whole other body was trying to get out through his mouth, and couldn't any longer stayed hunched down. He came up into Peter's face, his white, pinched face like winter in the hot room. His eyes were unfocused, almost blind.

Peter said: "It's all right."

The boy tried to swallow all the air in the room. His face had the blue-white edge of a carcass in a butcher's store, after the blood drains away.

His heart had stopped by the time the ambulance arrived, and the crew worked his fragile chest and blew air into him and still could not bring him back to life.

Grace came from the hospital and she could not speak. He tried to nurse her, but she did not notice. She sat in the kitchen, back straight, arms on the table so she did not even need to make the muscular effort to hold them up or down or out. She stayed like that for fourteen hours; he counted. Then he thought he heard her snuffling or whimpering, but she was trying to sing to herself, or perhaps to sing to the boy, something plangent and sentimental and now without tune or rhythm: "Danny boy, the pipes, the pipes are calling . . ."

Then she said: "I did it all for him, you know."

He didn't expect her to make sense, not in these circumstances. He was just glad she could speak to him again.

"You have to eat something. Drink something."

"I'd like a gin," she said.

"You don't drink gin."

"How would you know?"

She was right; he didn't know anything about her tastes except for what she had given away in the past few weeks.

"Do you have gin in the house?"

She laughed. "You been looking for it?"

"You said you wanted it—"

"I said I'd like it. I'd like to sit in the pub and have a good glass of gin. I would. I might as well. I don't do anyone any good sitting here like a statue, do I?"

He knew this was a trap. He just hadn't lived long enough to see how the trap worked and when it would spring.

"That's what you think, isn't it? You want me to cry. I won't cry. I won't do it."

She stood up without due care, and the long sitting made her unsteady. "I thought I could make the fire in the parlor, just lay it, not light it. Then again I could wash the floors." She looked around her, as though the house now puzzled her. "What do you want me to do?"

He said: "He's at rest now."

"You expect me to be grateful?"

"It's kinder. He's with God."

"You don't bloody want me to thank God, do you?"

He didn't know how to react. She could almost be accusing him, but he was almost sure she had no grounds. The boy's death was officially natural, a matter of dirty air and ruined airways. Anything he did, if he did anything, he did to spare her pain.

But now she was in full, fierce spate. "I did it all for him," she said. "Had you in. Had you to live here. It was all so he'd have a man about, and so we could get more food, so I could look after him and make a life for him and there'd be someone else to care for him. You needn't fancy yourself."

He said: "Listen, I don't have to stay—"

"No," she said. "No, you don't."

He'd been told, down the years, in the worried tones of a house full of men, about women's moods and hysterias and how they blow out as suddenly as they appear. He thought she might think again after a night, after a week, and need him again.

"I'll sleep in the garden," he said. He took only the uniform he was wearing when he first came, nothing else. To find it, he had to clear drawers. He saw the starched white shirt she bought for the boy out of her hopes for him. He handled it as carefully as he would handle the boy himself.

He lay down on the dry ground between neglected rows of peas and beans, using his jacket for a pillow.

He wanted a sign that he should go back. He was almost sure he should go back. But she couldn't phone him, couldn't smile at the window when he went past; he felt too self-conscious just to walk in her street, anyway. She'd have to come to the garden to find him, and he knew in his heart that she would never do that because she was not the one in the wrong. Even if what he did was right, and drastic enough to be truly kind, he knew he could not claim to be in the right.

Three mornings later, the stubble itching on his face, sandy dirt ground into his khakis, he climbed onto a train and went back to his father's house.

SEVEN

He never did like being left out. People were meeting. People were talking, not to mention hints and glances. Sarah's story was being drafted and polished where he couldn't see, couldn't read it.

He had sort of a right to know.

He'd already changed the whole city into a puzzle, and his occupation. He read the dullest corner carefully. Show him a pleasant bakery, with strong women eating cake, and he tried to work out their wartime stories. He contemplated crime encoded on the discreet facades of private banks. The process was a mad, solipsistic kind of politics: anything might require action, so everything was charged with drama, even the tram slinking into town or the girl selling vitamins in the pharmacy or the damp, high inner halls of a flowershop full of tulips and palms or the ticket line at the Hauptbahnhof.

He began to eat lunch alertly. He fussed about Sarah, in case she was just waiting for the right time to explain things.

He strolled past the bookshops on either side of Lucia's shop. He considered maps, prints, volumes of Max Frisch carefully bound, some Goethe and some Rilke. He waited for someone to go into Lucia's shop, someone to come out.

He wondered if this Lucia would simply talk to him. He was almost in her country of the very old; she would trust him. They were fellow conspirators against time and the young.

But he could not quite imagine how he would make a social half hour with her, and then how he would put his questions.

He tapped his fingers on his thigh. He pinched the cloth.

He longed for the familiar precision of his fields, his seedbeds, the sight of rogue colors, rogue shapes. He longed to know where he was down to the last row of the last cultivar because, here in this polite city, he seemed to live in the middle of an abstraction: faces in whose business he had no business, streets like the idea of streets, not specific, not dirtied, not full of particular and demanding faces, and landscapes hanging like postcards at the end of those streets.

Helen had control of the kitchen for the day: and Sarah sat across the table from her, looking quizzically at the carrots being shredded, the chicory being grilled, as though these were museum things you don't see every day.

She had insisted on bringing Peter Clarke. She saw him as a safety device, something to open up the closed and explosive possibilities of Helen, Nicholas, and Sarah at a table, even if they both insisted they only wanted to help Sarah, to make things right. She wondered why they didn't simply go to Lucia; but if Lucia had not, in fifty years, shown signs of remorse or guilt or even anxiety, then going to Lucia would never be enough.

"Why don't you work?" she asked Helen abruptly.

Helen said: "I wanted to have a baby."

"You don't have a baby anymore. You have a child, and he's gone off to nursery school."

"I wanted to be there when he comes home. I didn't want to have to tell him I was going off around the world and I'd send him a postcard."

"Men do that all the time."

"So," Helen said. "I'm not a man."

"Lucia never stopped working, I don't think. Not in Berlin. And she's had the shop ever since, you tell me."

"I make my own decisions."

Helen had chicken breasts in her hands. She smoothed them

out, spread the fillet out from the meat, and slapped each one of them, very hard. The sound of the slaps cut the air in the room in two, between her and Sarah.

"This Meier," Sarah said. "He's a friend of yours?"

It was all accident, this accuracy. She said what was obvious, what she wanted to know; she had no special and magical insight into what Helen was feeling. And yet she was accurate, and it stung.

"He was a colleague."

"In the same office?"

"He was a lawyer we consulted sometimes."

"So what does he know about restitution?"

"He's interested."

"Good," Sarah said. And then she said: "I feel I should be helping., I feel I should be having a drink, too, but maybe I'd better not before Meier. Better to be as sharp as an old, old woman can be."

Two old men going briskly through the snow. Nicholas Müller-Rossi, round as he was, was surprisingly efficient. Peter Clarke swung ahead. They formed a conspiracy that cut along the cleared black lanes.

Nicholas was glad of Clarke. He was company. He was an ally for Sarah. But most of all, he was something new. Nicholas didn't like colleagues his own age, retired, who now felt cut off from work, their whole meaning left behind in some university office. He didn't always want to go into town and organize a meeting with his older friends. He wanted strangers, who did not assume all the things that he was supposed to assume.

As for Clarke, he surprised himself. He wanted so much to be the champion, Sarah's protector, but he fell easily into this brisk walking chat with Nicholas. He even had time to feel a slight resentment: the notion that old men were safe and therefore automatic allies.

Two Englishmen, two Swiss men, could not have been as direct.

Clarke said to Nicholas: "I don't meet many professors. I avoided the geneticists. They didn't understand what I did."

And Nicholas, with a certain generosity: "I've never met anyone who did anything as lovely as breed a flower. A new kind of flower. I wish we could look at the garden afterward, and you could tell me if there's anything here that you bred."

Clarke smiled, grateful even for the carefully plotted overture. Evidently, he had already been researched, or perhaps explained; which meant that Sarah talked about him.

"All I can do," Nicholas said, "is point to a couple of books."

"It's lovely here," Clarke said.

They did not want to slow on the last rise of the hill, neither one of them. They wanted a view to see when they reached the top, though, which would allow them time to breathe.

They'd been walking in a brilliant landscape, with helpful signposts giving the minutes to the next summit, with the blue-white shine of snow; but now they came to a wood, a wall of trees. The branches painted out the light: dead, thick, and black. The snow stopped exactly where the trees started.

Nicholas pointed to a view of white fields; Clarke looked with him.

There was a noise between tearing and a crash. The two men were very still.

Out of the lifeless wood came a young deer, legs splayed, eyes wild, frantic at the end of its cover and alone. Its sides were scratched where it had forced through nets of thorn. It barely noticed the men, because it ran directly for them, as though it had a single idea of direction and could not change, or perhaps the sudden bright light was blinding. It took to the path, then looked back, then broke away down over the fields, at once quick and uncertain, legs skittering on ice.

It was gone in a minute: just tracks in the white.

Nicholas said: "Well."

Clarke smiled. He also said: "Aren't they a problem, the deer?"

By the time they began to circle back to the house, they had sorted out other things in common. Since they had known the same war, they both knew how parachute flares come down soft and bright as Christmas lights, the cone a searchlight makes as it rakes about the sky, how the cone glints at its apex when it catches on a plane; and then the dot dot dot of fire from the ground, and the silvery machine transfigured first into a mirror light, then into a torch flaring and falling out of the sky. They both knew bombs whistle as they come down.

All that they could share with a few words of history: Nicholas in Berlin, Peter Clarke close to London before he was taken off to war.

But Clarke wasn't happy with the notion that such shared knowledge made them equivalent; that was clear. He wanted to listen, but he knew those were his planes, his side raining bombs down on Berlin, for all the right reasons; and those were alien machines in the sky over his village, murderers with wings.

Nicholas sensed that, or perhaps he only expected it. He was used to the general sense that no experience out of Nazi Germany—not being in love, not eating a bratwurst—could ever count as entirely human.

He even told Clarke what Clarke was bound to think of the wartime Swiss. He expected the world to be angry. He said he'd sometimes tried to explain that there really had been rationing, that cats out at night sometimes ended in pies, but the Swiss never rationed what foreigners ate: so foreigners, most of them, reckoned they were in a land of milk and honey and potatoes. But then the foreigners just compared black acorn bread with chocolate, ersatz honey (just add sugar) with cheese from the Alps. The Swiss had not suffered properly.

"I don't make excuses," Nicholas said, "and I'm not boasting."

Peter Clarke said: "And Lucia?"

Nicholas knew he'd have to answer. "People knew, nobody could do anything," he said. "I asked my father once why nothing was done and he said it nearly was, but still nothing happened.

"Nothing happened. I mean, nothing that mattered. There was a trial. My mother had difficulties. I remember she grew thin, so I tried to reason out why that was happening. Children do that when things are going wrong. I lay and I thought. It couldn't be the rations, which were far more reliable than in Berlin, and far more generous as well. We saw eleven liters of milk a month, and a hundred grams of raw bacon, two hundred of butter, and half a kilo of sugar; we even saw meat, coffee, chocolate, and sweets. Nothing that happened had to do with lack.

"She could be ill. But she didn't seem ill. She had a kind of shining, polished shell that never opened; and if she was ill, it would surely have started to break. Her eyes were very fierce. She was concentrated on the world as if it was a chess game, although she would never be the kind to play chess."

He stopped, and stamped on the road.

Gray flirts they were at lunch: Nicholas and Peter, chivying each other out of the way for Sarah's attention. It was a reflex action, a little absurd, but it filled the huge silence left by the person who couldn't be mentioned and the subject that couldn't be raised.

Peter talked about gardens, and Sarah had a garden in London. Then Nicholas talked about some production of *Pericles* he had seen, and the translation; Sarah knew about it. Peter suggested another lake trip.

Sarah said to Nicholas, suddenly: "You had a cat called Gattopardo."

"I did."

"A tiger."

"Yes, I did. In Berlin, when I was very young."

Sarah smiled, and then she started to cough as though she was choking and she had to be helped from her chair and given water.

Clarke watched her as closely as any lover or any policeman. And in doing so, he noticed very clearly who else was watching: Helen. He couldn't be sure if she felt protective of her grandmother, or concerned with Sarah. He was suspicious, he realized.

Nicholas and Peter heard the car go away, taking Helen and Sarah down into Zurich to the lawyer's office. The geese complained quietly. No dog barked.

"What if it's better not to remember?" Nicholas said.

Neither one of them could cope with the question.

"People expect the English to talk about their schooldays," Nicholas said. Then he thought he had made a mistake, blundered into the thickets of English issues of class, and Clarke did not go to the kind of school that makes for polite conversation. Or maybe he was wrong about the English.

Either way, it was too late. He had to confess, or else he would have to listen to the huge white silence.

"I liked school when I went in September," he said. "It was very separate, up above the lakes and the mists. It had walls and customs, so you could always dream of breaking out or breaking rules, and the air was brilliant. A huddle of tall, blocky chalets, some single conifers, in the middle of unbuildable ground that was, inevitably, known as the park. The chapel, which looked as though it had been stolen from a village, painted a subversive yellow. After that, there were Alps.

"I found, to my surprise, that I liked books. I liked being away from home. I liked both so much I didn't mind being told about my character, about the glories of being far above cities and fogs, about the importance of whatever faith I might happen to have brought with me. The easiest ploy was to claim a Catholicism my mother had never mentioned much.

"I got into a fight in the first snows, which were wet and blinding and soft. I was out between the chapel and the dormitory and so was one of the German kids: a soft-spoken, angry boy called Helmut.

" 'You let us down,' he said. He could shout into the new snow with little chance of being heard.

" 'What do you mean?' I really didn't know.

" 'You Italians. Wouldn't fight. Couldn't fight.'

"Whatever I was, I knew I could be even more German than Helmut, having seen much more of Germany being burnt and broken.

" 'You can't fight, can you?' He had come up very close to me on the path, both of us wrapped against the cold.

"I backed a little, slipped a little. I didn't want trouble.

"He was determined, I could see. My feet tricked me on the new wet snow. I wasn't sure I could hold a position if I had to.

" 'You don't fight. Do you?'

"He was bulked out with coats and pigeon-chested to begin with, so he looked like a top-heavy burgermeister on the pathway. But out of him came a boy's unbroken voice, a flute where there should have been a growl.

"I started to laugh.

"He pushed my shoulder.

"I didn't stop laughing.

" 'You Italian,' he said. He piped the words.

"I stopped, I picked up new snow, I threw it over his head so it broke and fell around his shoulders like wet dust.

" 'You can't even fight fair,' he said.

"This time, I grabbed both his arms. I wrenched them behind his back and I went on pushing them up and up until his face was forced forward. He was howling, but the noise meant nothing in the snow and the wind.

"I felt something snap.

"He was crying now, big hot tears between the soft flakes of snow on his face. I let him go and he went down to the ground, and one of his arms seemed to hang at his side.

"He said: 'You've done it now.'

"I heard a master say: 'Get in, boys.' I waited for Helmut to make his complaint, but he just said, when he had pulled off his boots in the main building: 'My arm's gone funny.'

"In the sanitarium he said it was an accident, because he could never say he had been beaten by an Italian. And then I was the violent Italian, which helped." Nicholas smiled.

Sarah Freeman concentrated, but now like a child at an exam, like someone trying to see past the horizon. Georg Meier made a note of this.

"I saw the table in a Christie's catalogue," Sarah said. "In London. I knew it at once. It was on consignment from a shop in Zurich, and I rang Christie's to ask if I could see it, but they told me it had been withdrawn very suddenly. The shop belongs to Mrs. Müller-Rossi, but of course I didn't know that."

Helen said: "And you saw it in the window?"

Sarah said: "Oh, no. I didn't see any one thing in Lucia's window. I recognized everything. It was like seeing a world that died, all on show."

"You do know what they will do?" Meier said, quickly.

Sarah took in the round, small eyeglasses, the neat brush-cut hair, the expensively modest suit, the immaculate skin: a man with a profession, but no experience of his own.

"Mrs. Freeman?"

She said: "I have some idea."

"They will point to your age. They will ask for your medical records. If there is any suggestion of a stroke, of odd behavior, of the first signs of dementia—"

"I don't think so."

"They may simply point out that you are trying to recall events from sixty years ago."

"I am not trying to recall them. I am remembering them."

Helen said: "Is it necessary to be so aggressive, Dr. Meier?" She gave his doctorate its full defensive force.

"I could be kind," the lawyer said, "but then Mrs. Freeman would be entirely unprepared for what may come. Do you want that?"

Helen said: "If I wanted that, I would never have suggested she talk to you."

"I know this is not a pleasant process," Sarah said. "I've seen worse." She grinned, and grinned even more at the disconcerted quiet in the room.

The lawyer cleared his throat. Old men do that, pompous men in clubs, judges on benches; and he could not be more than—what— thirty-five? She wanted to laugh at her worry that she was losing her skills at placing men.

"Very well," he said. "There is a rather exact list of questions I have to ask. Who made the table? Is it known?"

"Pierre Fléchy. *Maître ebéniste.* Born 1715. His work is very valuable."

"There's no title, of course, no subject. The date, can you say?"

"I don't know. 1760, maybe."

"And the country of origin?"

"France."

"Type of object. Well, that's obvious enough. The medium, now."

"Wood. Marquetry. Lacquer."

It had been her garden when she could no longer walk freely out-side: a single object that proved she and Max had not yet been destroyed, that they still had eyes and hearts.

"And the measurements?"

"I never measured it. It was the last nice thing we kept in the apartment, in a corner. I suppose I could guess."

"Better not to guess. If you're wrong, it looks like proof you've misidentified the piece."

"Oh," Sarah said. "Oh, yes."

The table had stood surrounded by piles of books. She remembered the rough edges of the pages, like stacks of leaves. She imagined the titles on the top. Max kept rereading Balzac at the time, but he read magical Balzac, *La Peau de Chagrin.*

"Now," Dr. Meier said. "Is the piece signed?"

"It's stamped. The stamp was still attached when we had it."

"And dated?"

"I told you."

"Any edition, any number? Inscriptions? Any special marks—did you ever have it repaired?"

She had polished the table even when she couldn't get polish, had saved it from the faintest scratch of dust. Thinking now, all that care simply puzzled her.

"It wasn't repaired while we had it," Sarah said.

"And the present location? Or the last known location?"

"In a shop in Zurich. You know that."

"Any other description?"

She wondered how the table would look to anybody else. She didn't know. So she shook her head, gently. Then she said: "It's chinoiserie. That's what Fléchy was known for."

"Photograph?" She shook her head again. "Insured, I suppose?"

She said: "Max would have handled that. He'd be the policyholder. I don't even know the company and I don't know which city and I don't know the number of the policy." She thought she might have to explain so she said: "I have no papers. Nothing from that time."

"Next," said Dr. Meier, making a copperplate note. "Circumstantial information. Was the victim present at the seizure of the object?"

Sarah said: "Yes."

"Ah. Then we don't need to ask if he fled his home."

"He did. He knew what was happening and he went into hiding. We used to call people like him the 'divers.'"

"But he was present when the object was seized?"

"It wasn't seized. I handed it to Lucia for safekeeping."

"Now," Dr. Meier said. He tapped his pencil on the perfect stone shine of his table. "What if Frau Müller-Rossi says that your husband gave her the table? Gave it to her without entail?"

"Why should he do such a thing?"

"You admit you entrusted her with the table. And he expected at any moment—"

"He expected to be killed."

"Frau Müller-Rossi was an attractive woman?"

"She was—bright. And redheaded. And she had a vast smile. And she had good legs. Yes, she was an attractive woman, I suppose. A professionally attractive woman."

"And your husband might have been susceptible to such a woman?"

"You mean, did they have an affair?"

"I mean, could your husband have been persuaded, by her attractions or his feelings, to make her a gift of the table?"

Sarah stared at the shining man. She, too, thought she never saw anyone so clean.

"I know he did not."

"Do you know everything about your husband?"

"How could I not know? We couldn't go out at night. We couldn't go to the movies or go to a concert. We had to shop at special hours."

Dr. Meier waited. It was not entirely a kind waiting.

"We spent every day, all day, in our apartment, in each other's company. You didn't lose sight of people, Dr. Meier. If you lost sight of them you might never see them again."

"Memory is very odd, isn't it?"

Nicholas sneezed, abruptly.

"I remember I walked too fast when I was in Zurich. You walked fast in Berlin so you spent less time at each point a bomb might fall so you had more chance of living. But in Zurich, there just wasn't enough city to walk fast."

He opened a new bottle of wine.

"I remember once, when my mother was out, opening her wardrobe, which was more like a small room. It smelt like roses and old wine and a little like a dry-cleaning shop. There were so many clothes. Some of them, a few, had her initials. Some of them had monograms like ERK and SL and MH. I counted sixteen different monograms and I couldn't count anymore.

"So I ran away. I went down to the lake. There were swans plodding around. A hot-chestnut vendor on the waterside. The smoke hung about, sociably. There was ice everywhere, creeping out over the water."

He didn't say that the ice was starting to break into great gray-white plates, each big enough to be a boat that could push out from the river walls and tack back if the current seemed too lively. Boys were out on the ice boats, punting them with long poles, edgily balanced. Their adventure couldn't last: the ice would soon melt or crack or capsize.

In any case, he had to get home. In any case, they didn't know him and wouldn't ask him to join them. He went home crying for friends.

———

"I know what Max told me," Sarah said.

"Max always told the truth?" Georg Meier treated interrogation like plainsong; he didn't like to miss his cue.

"He told no more lies than most men."

"You realize a court would expect a widow might be ignorant of her husband's little affairs? Or that a widow might deny they ever happened, in order to keep a memory entirely for herself?"

"I only want Lucia Müller-Rossi to acknowledge that she stole that table."

Meier said: "One last set of questions. Can you document the piece? Appraisals, maybe? Transport records or maybe a storage bill? Did anyone ever put your table in a magazine?"

"I'm afraid not. It was just furniture."

"And you are absolutely sure there could be no piece like it?"

"I am going to swear an oath. I am going to tell the truth that I know. What else do you want me to do? You want papers and—"

"It's absolutely true that an invoice for the table when you first bought it—"

"Does everyone have to prove their whole lives? I thought an identity card was enough."

"Not," Dr. Meier said, "with the power you have to harm Frau Müller-Rossi. She'd be out of business, out of Zurich if you won. In the present atmosphere. So the court will sit and it will think—How much do we need to know in order to do this terrible thing?"

"This," Sarah said, "is a terrible thing? A little justice is worse than the crime?"

Helen said: "Sarah, if you don't want to go on?"

Meier said: "One last thing. Is there anything in the medical record which could suggest impaired memory? Anything at all?"

Helen said: "I don't think so."

"Who was the foreign minister of Britain in 1947?"

Sarah said: "Bevin."

"What's the church behind the Berlin Opera House?"

"It's a cathedral. St. Hedwig."

"Who painted the *Demoiselles d'Avignon*?"

"Picasso," Sarah said. And then: "Pablo Ruiz Picasso," just for emphasis.

"This is general knowledge," Helen said.

"Yes, it is," Dr. Meier said. "It matters, because we would have to show that Mrs. Freeman knows enough about art and the world, and remembers it clearly enough, to identify that particular table. There are many pretty tables."

"I know when I don't know, too," Sarah said.

All Sarah could see was his shine, as though he was bottled and the light was on the glass.

"I imagine my medical records could be found. I had cancer once, but they caught it very early. Cancer of the breast. I have had no mental problems, unless, of course," and again she tried to make him smile, "I've forgotten them."

For a moment, she had the oddest sense of slipping into one of Max's fantasies. He loved English whodunits, loved their sense of order and propriety and the moral certainties that you could comfortably expect in the last ten pages; and now she, too, would like a pleasant, written world out of English novels, where death had proper witnesses, was documented and proved, where there were priests and doctors and wills read out aloud to family gatherings at long polished tables, and lawyers to tot up what was left and assign it with all the nice pedantry of the makers of great dictionaries, or phone books.

Dr. Meier then asked, as though the question was social and casual: "What did you have for breakfast this morning, Mrs. Freeman?"

"I had coffee, and a *Gipfli*. I had raspberry jam with the *Gipfli*. I did not have butter."

"And where did you have it?"

"In my room."

"I mean: at what address?"

"I beg your pardon?"

"At what address? What number, what street?"

Sarah Freeman said: "Ninety-seven. Hotel Grindelwald."

"And the street?"

"My short-term memory still functions, Dr. Meier. I know where the bathroom is. I know how to catch a bus in London when I need one."

"The street?"

Helen said: "I'm not sure we need to go any further today."

"We'll need to go much further," Meier said. "Any hesitation, any pattern of hesitation, any tendency to fluster or be unsure, anything like that will tend to discredit you. And it will be used. Perhaps not in a court, but when the lawyers discuss whether to bring a case, and when Müller-Rossi's lawyers argue among themselves. If all this had been solved in 1945—"

"We're here precisely because it was not," Helen said.

"Of course," Meier said. "But if we had witnesses—"

"I have one enormous advantage as a witness," Sarah Freeman said. "I am alive."

Meier smiled for the first time.

Sarah stood up. "I had breakfast on Tiefenaustrasse this morning," she said. "Number ninety-seven Tiefenaustrasse."

Helen smiled at Meier on the way out, but she wouldn't stay to talk. She was afraid of all the wonderful possibilities of a clean, mechanical, biddable lover.

"My mother has absolutely no talent for worrying," Nicholas said.

"They should have rung by now," Clarke said.

"She thought it a kind of failure, an admission that she could not reason her way out of trouble. I could tell something must be wrong, I wanted to help. I wanted to be there. But I'd head back to school and after the train and the funicular, and the bus, after settling into the dormitory again with the same official friends, after the first games of tennis and the first failures with irregular neuter nouns of the fourth declension, she faded in my mind. I read, and I played, and I hardly noticed what everyone was saying.

"Schools work like that, I think. Everyone knows something, long before the person affected has the slightest clue. Everyone knew that I might be leaving, but I smashed balls back across the tennis court and I knew nothing at all.

"I did notice that other boys began to be kind, in a rather slippery way. Even the 'slaves,' which I regret to say is what we called the cleaning women, seemed ominously sympathetic, and smiled if I wanted more coffee at breakfast.

"I used to watch the woods and the driveway to the school from our dormitory window. I liked the flicker of birds on the boundaries of the woods. I liked the random order of the vans and cars that made their way to the door: meat, priests, bread, parents, fruit.

"I saw a taxi come to the door. I saw my own mother.

"She'd said nothing at all to me about coming to the school. She wasn't supposed to be there. You hate the unusual when you're a junior boy.

"I saw the door of the main building close behind her.

"I sat at my window with a book in my hand, a full half hour. It was Shakespeare and it was *Hamlet*. I didn't look at the pages, but they were my excuse for not looking at the door of the main building.

"Which opened, opened violently as I remember, and my mother came raging out with her coats swirling. She ran on the gravel path to the dormitory. She stood at the foot of the stairs and shouted my name.

"I seriously thought of not going down. In fact, I sat away from the window.

"I heard her on the stairs, and I went to the door of my room, just to avoid a scene.

" 'Come along,' she said. 'Come along. We'll send for your stuff later.'

"She tugged me down the stairs. I didn't want to go. At the door, she said: 'This school has insulted your mother. It is not possible for you to stay here.'

"I said: 'But it's not half-term yet.'

"On the driveway I said: 'But how are we going to get home?' Then I said: 'I ought to get my books' and I tried to dash back but she stopped me."

For Clarke all this remembrance was random, not a considered confession. But he was polite and took another glass of wine. He would remember things himself, for Sarah.

"They'd frozen her bank accounts. Stopped her selling things, so she couldn't find the school fees. They knew perfectly well what she was. They just couldn't find a way to deal with her, or perhaps they lacked the will to do it. Then it was 1946 and nobody wanted to say anything, or admit anything, and the case was dropped."

He went to the file cabinet. "Helen gave me these," he said. "I'm ashamed to say I never did ask for them myself." He opened the packet. "I'm sorry," he said. "You don't read German."

"No," Clarke said.

"They found a file of letters from Americans, you know," Nicholas said. "People trying to get visas for their parents left in Germany. Jews, of course. They thought Lucia might help."

For a moment, Sarah Freeman panicked.

"I'm not the right one," she said to Helen.

She was standing by the newspaper kiosk, by the tram stop, opposite the Kunsthaus, bundled against the cold that seemed to blow up from every side, and she began to shiver. Nobody would particularly believe her, they would all suspect her motives, she wouldn't be the proper and decently forgiving victim, she'd be wrong and Lucia would be right just because Lucia had gone on so long beyond her crimes. She'd be bringing down a grand old lady for the sake of a bit of marquetry with nicely turned legs.

Worse, if they believed her, they wouldn't think it mattered: not a table, not something so easily put right.

She looked around her at the serious faces, the blank eyes, the well-wrapped persons all waiting for the same tram.

"You think you're right, don't you? That'll carry you through. But I'm tired and I'm cold. I'm an old woman. And you expect me to be brave every day, all the time, until all this is resolved."

She realized she had raised her voice.

She did not want people to watch her. It was always better to slip about unnoticed, better in Berlin, better in London, better here. When she'd been almost famous for decades, her wit and writing tossed about the fireplace on Sundays in a million middle-class homes, that was a disguise of sorts, a trade, a performance in which she did not need to involve herself. Nobody saw her in the act of writing.

People were looking at her now. Well, she'd ignore them.

"I know you want to be right," Sarah said, very quietly. "I know you haven't had much chance."

The tram came and waited an extra second for her to notice and to board. She didn't move.

The driver frowned.

Then she climbed aboard and left Helen standing in the cold.

———

"My father died, you know," Nicholas said. "Just the other day. I never really knew him and I missed him so much when he was alive and I can't work out if I miss him more now he's dead." He could feel the wine softening his tongue, making it inaccurate sometimes.

Peter Clarke could not remember the moment of losing his father. He thought it half indecent that Nicholas lived with such a fresh memory.

"She always talked about him as this great athlete. I remembered him that way: the great football player. Then he was a soldier on a mountain pass. But when I saw him after the war, I saw a banker. No, I just saw the bank. He was a clerk, a face for the bank, in a drab black suit with a neat tie, all of him perfectly brushed and polished. He always sat on the edge of the chair as though he had no right to be with us, or didn't want to stay.

"He did take me skiing once. We went on one of the ski express buses, with the skis sticking out of the back like a cigarette pack. He said I was going to be good, but then he dashed away from me and he was much more quick. I was still a boy.

"When he visited, they always had something for me to do, something outside the house. But I heard them. Their voices were so tight you expected them to snap, but they never raised their voices.

"They argued about the Jews, a couple of times. He'd say there weren't enough of them in Switzerland to be a problem. She'd say he was anti-Semitic like all the rest. She was very proud, this is the oddest thing, of not being anti-Semitic.

"Then the war ended. He didn't want to see her anymore, but he did come to see me at school a few times.

"I heard the Swiss boys talking about the Soviets on the borders, about the revolution that was coming like it almost came in 1918, about the way we all had to hold together; and I heard them talking about the *'faux suisses.'* I thought: That's my mother. That's me. No wonder my father doesn't come to see us anymore. We're the false ones, the ones who don't know just what we're doing."

He gulped his wine, got up a little unsteadily, and went for a new bottle.

"I couldn't find him for a while. Too many Müllers in the phone book. Besides, I thought he might be doing more army service. I thought about the railway station. Everyone, sometime, had to catch a train. I looked out for groups of soldiers.

"My mother didn't like me in the shop, so I was supposed to be a man and go about on my own."

The new bottle was exactly like the old, from a dozen crates out in the barn: a carload from the Valais.

"One night, I remember it was cold. There was ice, and it cracked like sugar brittle round the boats. It was properly dark, winter dark, and all the darker because of the extra lights and colors for Christmas.

"The bakeries had shut down for the night, so there were no more spices and sugar on the air, only beer and the smell of frying, the smells that meant the men had taken over the town. I thought I might see my father. I went out to see him.

"I was in an alley with the snow piled in the middle, and the footprints of days on either side. The trees were paper white. The air was silent. I expected the smell of beer to start the snow melting and falling.

"At the end of the alley people were standing still. I didn't expect that, not on a cold night in the town. If people were standing still, they must be expecting someone.

"I heard bells, heavy bells.

"I got down to the bottom of the alley and I stood up on a doorstep.

"The next alley was narrow, too, a cobbled slip that broadened out down the hill, I suppose. I saw lights moving. The bells clattered, their sound a little muffled because they were carried by hand.

"Men in white were coming. They wore hats full of candles, and they had bells. They wore masks.

"From a distance, their faces were blank, full of straight lines. They walked two abreast down the hill, and they seemed to fill out the whole line of the alley.

"They came close, and their faces were terrible. This one's nose was a triangle of card, that one had a letterbox mouth. Some faces were rounded out, some had hats cut out with deer, stars, flowers. The blankness, the prettiness of the candlelights, was suddenly alarming. They were bringing peace and happiness, whether you wanted it or not.

"I wanted to think that one of them was my father. But he was in an Advent procession. So he couldn't possibly talk to me."

Clarke's head began to hurt, with the wine, with the fumes from the fire in a closed room, with the endless parade of human fact that Nicholas could marshal before him.

He so much wanted to be on Sarah's side, to do something that was impeccably right and just and good after a whole long life of equivocation. He didn't want the issues to turn subtle on him. He wanted to keep his great advantage over these people who had been in Berlin in the war. And each anecdote was spoiling his certainty: of being on one side, of opposing the other. It reminded him of that Christian burden of forgiveness. It loaded his mind with questions that gave the enemy enough time to get away: questions like, What would I have done in their place?

"I'll walk to the station," he said. "They must be finished with the lawyer by now. Sarah will be back in the hotel."

"But there's so much else," Nicholas said.

"I know. And I'm not listening anymore. I have other things to do."

"You think it's a waste of time to know what happened."

Clarke thought for a minute. "Yes," he said. "Yes. You know as well as I do that you've told me nothing that could help. Nothing that could help make things right."

"You can't repair history."

"You can face up to it."

"And what exactly would that mean?"

Clarke was silent.

"You think you faced up to history? All those nights the bombs were raining down on Berlin?"

"I was bombed as a boy. Then I was on a battlefield. Then I was in a prisoner-of-war camp."

"You mean you had an alibi?"

"As you did?"

Nicholas said: "I thought you'd want to know. Who else is going to listen?"

"I sometimes think," Clarke said, "that if we go on talking long enough then nobody will be responsible for anything any longer. No more juvenile delinquents, just cases of social exclusion. No more wickedness, just underprivilege and failure to thrive morally. No more Nazis, only victims of totalitarianism. Is that what you think?"

Nicholas was standing now, not steadily, head down. "I didn't want to remember," he said. "I put all this away so I could make a life for myself."

"Remember. Don't remember. It makes no difference."

And Clarke tugged on his coat, flicked his scarf around his neck. He walked briskly away, too briskly for Nicholas, even though he was younger, to have a chance of catching him. Only at the first fork in the road did he remember that he was not sure of the way.

He was still pushed on by anger when he got to Zurich, anger and wine. He'd made up a scheme as he walked, as he waited for the train. He would confront Lucia Müller-Rossi himself. He would take back the table.

By the Hauptbahnhof, he no longer saw himself raiding the shop like a bailiff. He'd be subtler. He'd ask after the table in the shop, express great interest, then drop some hint about title to the piece. He'd ask her about provenance.

He sailed to the door. Then the process of security, the ringing of the bell, the door buzzed open, slowed him. Then he found that there was no old lady to be seen, only perfectly smoothed-down people in black who seemed a little disconcerted by this older man, as though he might at any minute bump into something fragile.

"I'm looking for a table," he said.

"Yes," said a girl.

"Marquetry. Flowers. Eighteenth-century." He couldn't quite remember the name of the man who made it. He couldn't be exact enough to be suspicious; which was annoying, since the whole point was to worry the old monster by his knowledge, his policeman's concern. Then it occurred to him that he was being vain. He was much too old to be a policeman.

He stood, flustered for a moment.

The girl said: "We do have a piece that you might like to see." She came between him and anything of value, he noticed.

She pointed to a small table: flowers gilded onto black lacquer, vines everywhere.

"Would you ask," he said, "where this comes from?"

"I'm afraid we wouldn't have that information."

"It's very important," he said. Then, as he turned to leave, he said: "Please ask Mrs. Müller-Rossi for me."

So her man, a round creature with huge exophthalmic eyes, sat in the small room usually reserved for privileged customers, at the back of Lucia's shop: a white, plain room for looking carefully at things.

In the nature of things, it was her lawyers who came to Lucia, out of deference to age and standing, but also discretion: all kinds of questions were being raised about people like Lucia Müller-Rossi, and it might be better if she did not visit the office until all that virtuous high pressure had gusted away.

Lucia said: "I hope none of this will be necessary."

The lawyer nodded.

"And I think I probably know the law as well as you do."

He said: "Of course, Frau Müller-Rossi. It is your business." He smiled, and she wondered if there was a minimal innuendo: that she'd have to have known the law really well so as not to fall foul of it.

"Oh for God's sake," Lucia said. "I may be over ninety, and I may have a lot of money, but I could still be wrong."

Her man looked at his notes. "Article 933," he said, "protects you if you received the goods in good faith. Article 934 says that if you received goods that had been taken from their rightful owner against her or his will, then the rightful owner has five years to claim. No claim, no recovery. If you bought them at auction, or from another merchant, you can be told to surrender the object, but you have to get back the price you paid for it. And Article 936," he said, "provides that if you received goods in bad faith, they can be taken from you at any time."

"So the issue is my good faith."

"Precisely. And I'm sure any court would notice the fifty years, more, you've been in business here, and so forth. However, there are other issues. If property was stolen in occupied territory, by military or civilian organizations, armed forces, or occupying forces, between September 1, 1939, and May 8, 1945—"

"And if the property changed hands in Germany?"

"Oh, then the normal laws apply. Anything that happened in Germany was normal."

Lucia tasted the words.

"Could you say," the lawyer asked, "why you think this issue might be raised?"

"It's fashionable."

"But is there any other reason?"

Lucia did not explain that she sensed a coldness, an activity, a curiosity in her family which she did not like, nor that some old man, not a plausible customer, had been asking the wrong questions in a loud voice. She said only: "I gather there is some question about a table. I had it for some time, sold it in the 1950s, bought it back—for sentimental reasons, I suppose. Then I consigned it for sale in London. Then I decided I would not send the table to the sale."

The lawyer said: "For sentimental reasons?" He seemed surprised.

"Someone evidently saw it," Lucia said. "I think it was a woman who calls herself Sarah Freeman."

"Calls herself Freeman?"

"When I knew her, she was Sarah Lindemann. Married to a man called Max Lindemann."

"She would be the complainant in this case?" the lawyer asked, hoping to anchor himself on a date, a name, a writ.

"Poor Max," Lucia said, distracted. "Such a lively man. Sarah simply retreated to their apartment and she sat there, like an animal that's been marked out. Hands clinging to the chair so nobody could make her get up. Eyes wide open, and not bothering to see anything. Poor woman. Poor man."

"And you came to know Herr and Frau Lindemann in Berlin?"

"Max just wanted to live until he had to die. He liked his friends, he liked music, he liked paintings. He was the only man I've ever known who could talk in an interesting way about wine—not just adjectives."

"The table was his property?"

"I never did go to bed with Max," Lucia said. "I don't suppose that matters now. But just for the record, we couldn't have managed. It was too complicated for him to leave the house after dark, and I worked all day."

The lawyer wanted her to start to be discreet again, as soon as possible, before she handed over some incriminating scrap that he should never know; for he did assume there would be something incriminating. He also wondered if the old woman now regretted her virtue with Max.

"I remember the evening they gave me the table," Lucia said.

He pulled his legal pad toward him, American yellow foolscap, his affectation.

"I was working at UFA. The movie studios, you know? You do know?" The lawyer nodded. "It was the night we'd seen the first movie with my name up there on the screen, in very small letters—by 'we' I mean just the people at the studio—and I went to the Lindemanns with a bottle of *spumante* I'd cadged from the Italian embassy and a bundle of asparagus. Max loved asparagus. You know it was an Aryan vegetable." Lucia made a face. "Nothing much made sense in those days.

"Anyway. Max opened the wine. I explained the movie. I thought they'd find it ridiculous, just like I did: it had cute frogs, neat caterpillars, a bee buzzing around a meadow and finding a gramophone and playing the records with its sting. That sort of thing. But Max didn't laugh at all. Instead, he panicked.

"His calm had always surprised me. He was being buried alive very slowly, like all the others. But there was Sarah putting out the glasses, and plates for the asparagus, and chatting all very proper and mechanical, and there was Max saying: 'It's not going to end, is it? It's never going to end.' I didn't say anything. I didn't have anything to say. So he said: 'Why don't you ever say what you think?' "

The lawyer was reluctant to nudge such a venerable client along. But he did say: "And the issue of the table?"

"I don't remember whose idea it was," Lucia said. "I wish I did, it would be very convenient, but I don't. Maybe it was Sarah who asked if I could just look after some things. Or maybe it was Max, who did want to have the best things put away so the party functionaries wouldn't steal them. Or maybe I said they could leave things with me, for safety. At any rate, nobody ever claimed the table."

"Ah," the lawyer said.

"Max meant to give it to me," Lucia said.

The lawyer did not for a moment show that he was alarmed. He could see that memory was now an indulgence for Lucia, a little drink for the mind.

EIGHT

She sat on her embroidered chair, the housekeeper working the parquet floors in the hall with a cloth under her feet, the shop due to open in a half hour. She liked polish in the air: beeswax, a little rosemary. The driver would collect her in a few minutes, in seven minutes, to be precise.

The authority of Lucia Müller-Rossi rested on stillness, like a monument, and this morning her hand shook once or twice. This would not do. The business was an obligation every day, and in return, it sustained her, gave her a position, someone to be each day.

She did not like having even seven minutes without anything to do.

The housekeeper jarred the bucket along the wood.

She wondered what it meant to fight for your life when you were already ninety-two.

The driver rang the bell.

She would like company. Helen judged her, and was finishing with her. She didn't really know that husband of hers, the wandering dealer. Nicholas was distant, and thought that was loving enough.

The driver was at the door. He was a short, slim Turk, in his fifties perhaps, his trousers immaculate and cheap, nicely pressed by a wife, no doubt.

In the car, she said: "I want to buy chocolate."

The Turk asked where she would like to buy chocolate. She realized she had never known his full name.

"Sprüngli," she said, "of course."

At eleven in the morning, there was a considerable line. The Turk said he would be happy to bring her whatever she wanted, but she wanted, most of all, to go stand in a line and buy chocolate.

At ninety-two, being ordinary is hard. Just being is remarkable enough. So the crowd parted for her, and she rather enjoyed that. The assistants brought her, with proper solemnity, slices of bitter orange dipped in white chocolate, and arranged them in a neat box. She paid, as she always paid, with cash; it was nobody else's business what she bought.

And in the car, like a schoolgirl, she dipped into the box and ate.

The shop lights went up over lacquer and porcelain, ormolu and inlays, over warm rosewood and the shine of tables, vases, chairs, and desks, all polishing the air around them.

She sat at her table. She listened to an assistant reciting her messages. She was prepared to examine, she said, the porcelain Handkiss Group, Meissen, 1730s, that was on offer: which, the assistant said, looked a little odd since the lady was holding an oversized coffee bowl. "Probably the whole arm," Lucia said. The assistant looked inquiring. "If the arm got broken, they'd have to replace the bowl as well. The bowl itself doesn't break that way." The assistant said: "And the man's lips don't touch the hand." "That," Lucia said, "doesn't mean anything. Things vary. They just mustn't be wrong."

Lucia didn't have to look up to know there was a customer at the door. She knew, in the same way dogs anticipate a shot.

She was hardly ever the one who spoke first. She liked the customers to have the notion that a conversation with Lucia Müller-Rossi was a privilege to which you were admitted, the promise of a glorious deal. Should she be a little absent, which was a natural sign of her age, the customers worked all the harder for her attention.

The assistant smiled too much, she thought. Customers have first to buy respect before they buy anything else.

"I've seen something very much like it," the woman, an angular person, was saying.

"Yes. Yes," her bloodless husband said.

"Very much like it," the woman said. "This must," she said, "be the original."

Lucia Müller-Rossi did not enjoy ignorance, but she was not above making a profit out of it.

The anteroom of Georg Meier's office was designer sparse: the carpet was gray, the chairs gray, the receptionist's desk all glass and chrome, the phones immaculate on shining surfaces.

Sarah Freeman should have made an appointment so as not to be out of place in such a considered room. Instead, she turned up like some eccentric old person who could no longer cope with diaries or even dates and times.

The receptionist had called the secretary. The secretary had taken matters under advisement. There was a pause in which, so Sarah Freeman thought, her significance to Georg Meier was weighed and tested, then balanced against whatever else he had to do that day, tending a client, pruning or mulching a contract.

Perhaps the secretary would not even mention her to Dr. Meier. But then how would they devise a mannerly way to get rid of her, since she was old? Sarah still had the journalist's instinct for when she was likely to be received and answered, and when not, and she was fretting.

She had put herself here to be humiliated. That was what she expected, after all. She was no more than a hobby for a corporate lawyer like Dr. Meier.

She longed for the simple, ordinary distractions of house and garden at home. She found it hard to tolerate these long minutes with nothing in particular to think, in the anxious, impatient, rigorously polite atmosphere of some doctor's waiting room.

A door flapped open. A woman came through, acknowledged

Sarah briefly—just in case, Sarah thought, in case I matter—and left the office.

Anyone else sitting here, with a proper appointment, would have brought papers in a briefcase, would make a call on a mobile phone, would disguise the fact of waiting. She couldn't. She was old; waiting was her talent, obviously.

After ten minutes, she asked again if she could see Dr. Georg Meier. The receptionist called the secretary. The secretary listened, and put the phone down. Sarah thought she heard the moment of disconnection, the cut.

She deserved to be angry.

She'd worked half a lifetime to avoid anger, always thinking that anger would rope her up and leave her helpless, as loud and ludicrous as a heroine tied to the railway tracks. She'd been angry only once to memorable effect, and she found the memory shameful. It was the day Churchill died, and some shiny, radical child in the office, an intern of sorts, had said: "Good riddance." She had stared at him, then crossed the office, then slapped him across the face twice.

She could remember the feel of hitting the man, and then how quickly anger died away and left her sick on adrenaline. Remembering it all, she could now imagine a whole bill of indictment for Churchill; but he had fought against the people who were trying to kill her, and at that moment she couldn't bear the notion that this bright, dumb baby intellectual had forgotten the fact.

The phones rang. The receptionist coped.

And then Meier scrambled out of the corridor, drying his hands, like a rushed surgeon.

"I didn't know you wanted to see me today," he said.

"I just wanted to tell you that I am going back to England."

Meier said: "Will you come and talk to me? In my office?"

"That's why I came," Sarah said.

He sat her down, ordered coffee. "You weren't angry, were you?" he asked.

She knew at once that he wanted proof that she could be angry. And since she knew, he had to apologize. "I didn't mean to annoy you," he said.

She said: "I'm a little old for that kind of game."

"Do you want to go ahead with this case?"

"I'm going home."

"You don't have the energy? You're not angry enough?"

She wanted to say she didn't need anger, didn't need to be fueled by anything except a cold sense of justice.

"I'm angry enough," Georg Meier said, quite unexpectedly. "I'm angry for all the members of my family who died. When it's the anniversary of Kristallnacht, I want to get out there with a baseball bat and I want to beat in the windows of the stores the Germans own and I want to wear a placard on my back that says—'Happy Kristallnacht.' "

She stared at him.

"But," he said, "you see that I can be quite perfectly calm when I need to be. If that works better."

She wanted to say: What right have you to all the strong emotions that we had to set aside in order to have lives?

"Do you want to think about it?" he said.

She took a taxi to the hotel. She found herself remembering a man, a filmmaker she once knew who was never angry at all, put up with any casual idiotic remarks, as when some French actress talked about the Mediterranean as "that Jewish sea," was kind to the world even when it was indifferent. She knew one other thing about him: he was among the troops who first entered Dachau at the end of the war. She concluded—assumed, really—he exhausted all the possibilities of anger in that moment.

"I have my ticket," she told Peter Clarke. "It's perfectly simple. I already called the airline."

"You didn't meet Lucia. You didn't even go into the shop," he said.

"I don't have the time."

"Without you," Peter Clarke said, "nothing happens. I mean, nothing happens to Lucia."

"Nothing changes then. It's always easier when nothing changes."

"I'll come with you to the airport."

"I'll take a taxi. It's easier."

"I'd like to come with you."

Sarah laid down her knife and fork. "You tell me. Why does everybody think I need them?"

Clarke was crestfallen.

"I don't mean to be unkind. I came here for a silly reason, and I've done all I want to do."

She seemed to be willing him to agree.

"I can't do any more," she said.

"But—"

"Have you any idea what I dream?"

Clarke looked at her, old eyes wide. They were in the Kunsthaus restaurant, big square tables far apart, couples and quartets being sociably loud, and yet he thought the question hung around for a moment, suspended on silence.

Then the forks clattered, the talk swelled again.

"I'm sorry," Sarah said. Then she ate very quickly, as though she regretted what she had said, and she said: "I don't know how she got away with it, all these years."

"You have to tell me what she did."

Sarah shrugged. "I only know what happened to me."

"Then you have to tell me—"

"People never grasp it. They say they understand, but they never do."

"Try me."

"I lived in a shed," Sarah said. "The sheds they had on allotments, on the summer gardens. A wooden shed with curtains, two meters by three. I lived there for a year.

"It was very full. Rakes, spades, forks, hoes, brooms. Raffia and drawers and nails and dust. Seeds drying. A pile of old magazines to read in summer. There were tools hanging on the walls, and sometimes I caught myself on them and I sucked at the cut to try to stop infection.

"The shed belonged to friend, a baker. He brought food every day, almost every day, and took away the waste in an old bucket. He said he walked backward over his tracks so it wouldn't be clear where he was going so often. I don't know what good that did.

"We couldn't move much, two meters by three, and there were two of us: me, and a boy. The boy had stayed on to do cemetery work and then it was too late to get away and he had to hide, too. In winter, sometimes the rats got the cloth we used to block the drafts.

"Lucia doesn't know all this. I'm sure she doesn't."

"She ought to know," Peter Clarke said, "if it's her responsibility." Sarah spoke rather quietly.

"Our friend couldn't carry water every day because it would be too conspicuous. We couldn't wash and drink, both. So we washed when it rained and I could move some of the planks in the roof and then it was hard to put the planks back so the water puddled on the floor, and we slept there. And I had to move the planks silently. We coughed silently. We shat silently. I wasn't private, not for a moment, for a year.

"The boy lay there and I wanted to sing to him, tell him stories, but we had to keep as silent as we could. And all the day and all the night I wondered what was left outside our box. There were old curtains at the window. I didn't look through because I was afraid I would find someone looking back."

Peter wanted to hold her hand. He thought of ghost stories: of white moon faces seen through dirty glass.

"I am," Sarah said, "another one of those terrible stories. They get so familiar with time. I do have another history: my history as Sarah Freeman. I'm not going to give that up just to be angry again."

Clarke said: "I'll get you your table. I'll—"

"It's never just about an object. It's about the whole past."

"Sometimes I envy you," Clarke said. "Being able to claim back the past."

"Envy?" said Sarah Freeman.

The remains of the meal lay heavy on the table. The waiter who came to see if everything was all right, to move the plates and make the usual offers, stayed away.

"It went on for so long I stopped imagining things. I couldn't imagine the feel of a chair, hot food, a bed. Anything."

"Then there were three whole days," Sarah said. "Nobody came. I remember the boy's skin: it was as thin and as blue as watered milk. And it was quiet at night, too. I'd been in Berlin all through the war, and quiet was the one thing I couldn't stand—no engines, no bombs, just fire and wind, hissing and whispering out there where I couldn't see.

"I had this absurd idea I should change things. But I couldn't change things outside the shed, so I thought I'd get up and change the tools around. The rake for the spade. The fork for the hoe. I'd make the shed change, and it wouldn't seem like a prison anymore. But I didn't have the strength. You know what it's like to be impossibly weak, where your legs don't answer you when you try to stand up? And besides, if I changed things, then we could never get about safely at night. I couldn't drop anything, hit anything; there must be no noise at all. And besides, I was hungry and I knew I couldn't waste my strength.

"I so much wanted it to rain."

The restaurant room, cool already, seemed to lose its last colors. Clarke wanted her to go on, and he wanted her to stop, wanted to spare her the pain of telling him, wanted her to tell him everything so that he could—could somehow become her equal in pain, perhaps, or simply find a cause, a wrong to right. He would not have been able to separate the two.

"I was sure he'd come, my friend. He always came. I couldn't hear anything at all when he came, I couldn't look out, I just had to trust. Then the latch would flick up suddenly, and I had to learn to trust all over again. There was nowhere to hide.

"But he hadn't come, and I was empty. I kept rubbing my fingers together, to keep them from going to sleep. I have to do that now I'm very old, but this was fifty years ago. More than fifty years.

"And then I started to think: I could move. I could go outside. Probably there wouldn't be anyone there. But I'd been shut up so long, curled up, always wrestling for a bit of space the boy didn't want. We might as well have been married.

"The third day came. It didn't rain, so there wasn't any water. It was still very quiet. I thought my friend—my good, good friend—must be dead. Or maybe they caught him, in which case we had to get out of there quickly.

"I remember feeling flushed as though I was exhausted, and then touching the metal of an old, rusted spade which seemed very cold indeed.

"And then I was truly angry. I'd come through so much, the boy was still breathing, too. We couldn't waste all the year we'd been concentrating on staying alive.

"So I prized the door open. Very slightly. I pushed at the door and it began to slip open, rotting on its hinges. The hinges were quiet; my friend always kept them oiled. I put all my weight on my legs. I hadn't done that for a long time.

"And I looked out. The whole world seemed so huge."

Clarke said: "It was like that when the guards weren't there any-more. At the prisoner-of-war camp. You couldn't really imagine going for a walk and not being stopped by a wall." Then he regretted what he said. Perhaps she needed the uniqueness of what had hap-pened to her much more than any companionable sense of things shared. Perhaps she didn't need to know what he recognized.

"I'd been imagining what was happening outside, all those months. You do, you know. You hear the sounds and you make a panorama out of them. You hear the thunder and the blasts and you sometimes see the colors of fire when you open the roof for the rain. And now, I looked out and I saw—I saw it was all over.

"The boy pretended he could stand, but he couldn't, not even with his hands braced against the sides of the shed door. I told him he'd have to walk, I couldn't help him. He took his hands off the sides of the door, and he teetered for a moment. All bones and angles. Then his legs folded up and he was down on the threshold of the hut.

"I was furious with him, of course. I didn't have the strength to help, and I knew I had to help. I kept wiping my hands on my skirt. I wasn't even surprised—a growing boy, a whole year keeping still, with not enough food. I couldn't leave him there, because if my friend hadn't come, then something must be terribly wrong.

"I kept thinking it was the quiet that was wrong."

She took her napkin and folded it exactly. "I am telling you my dream," she said. "It happened once, and now that I think about Lucia, it happens again and again and again."

She summoned the waiter. "I'll tell you the rest," she said. "I just need a little walk."

There was a fine fountain of gray stone, water very clear and hardly moving. Sarah looked into it for a moment, composed herself, and talked again: walking with Clarke as though with a school class.

"There was a cart," she said. "It hadn't been used for years. The wheels were set with rust. I remember I had a bit of stone, and I banged on the wheels and the rust came off in red flakes. Then the wheels screamed.

"I thought perhaps I could loosen the wheels. I ought to find oil. But now the door was wide open, and the shed was full of air and there was a brilliant moon and we might have been seen. And the boy kept saying he didn't know, didn't know about his legs and arms and he couldn't quite bring himself to ask out loud not to be left there.

"I was thinking: We move, with the cart, and there will be tracks. So we have to have somewhere to go, or else we'll be caught in the streets. Our being alive will be treason.

"I pushed that damned cart. I don't know how. I got it to move a bit through all the grass and weeds, but then it rolled back. I tried pulling it, and I slipped over and I took the skin off my knee and I was almost relieved that I could feel the pain.

"The boy helped. He slung himself so the cart would tip up and move on its front wheels. And I started to push."

She said: "You never tell me I can stop. You never let me stop."

"I don't think you want to."

"I will always have it in my mind: the boy all flaccid, and the scream of the wheels and the jolt of the rough ground and the big high moon and the appalling quiet. The boy was crying at first, but he tried to do it quietly.

"I saw the city at the end of the allotment fields. There wasn't much to see. First there were the cabbages and the old brown stems. Then there was rubble, stone and ruins. It looked very old indeed, as though there'd been time already for wind and water to weather it down. There was nothing sharp or jagged.

"I saw a statue facing the wrong way. I remember.

"I stopped in the doorway of some building. I suppose it was an apartment building once, and I suppose I once lived somewhere like it. Only it wasn't a building anymore. There was a sketch of steps, some chunks of wall, a couple of rather elegant window frames that rocked in the wind. And above it, stars and quiet.

"I had to have water. But there wasn't water, only rust from the tap: a bit of red powder, then nothing. So I went on. There wasn't anything to do except go on.

"And now, I don't know what happens if I tell this story out loud. I never told anyone before. I thought if I gave you details, you'd want more, and more. You'd want to know about the ulcers on the boy's legs. You'd want my hands slipping on the handles with blood. They did, but I never wanted to have to say that just to make people believe.

"I can't tell you anything else."

Clarke said: "I wanted to know."

"You don't know anything. It was a year, and you know just one night."

"I can try," Clarke said. "I didn't live your life, but I can at least try."

"The boy was dead," she said. "So I didn't need the cart anymore."

She packed with a precision that made her laugh, as though she had decided she could lock everything away and go back to England. She could lose the suitcase, and all her memories with it. She could leave it in this room; but they'd send it on with mechanical decency.

She went for a drink of water.

Since her ticket home was open, she thought she would simply take the train to Kloten and take the first available flight. She didn't want to book, because that might hold her up and what she most wanted was to be on her way. Then the prickling self-consciousness took over: perhaps she did not truly want to go, to be committed to a window seat on a twelve o'clock plane. Perhaps she was waiting to be stopped.

But the bellboy had the cases in reception, and she had paid her bill, and nobody stopped her.

Peter Clarke ought to be here. Helen should be here. Nicholas, perhaps. She'd let it be known that she was going.

They didn't care, either.

It was such a spoiled girl's complaint; she was shocked at herself. Obviously they were concerned. It could be the perfect evidence of concern that they were letting her go now that she wanted to go.

The taxi arrived. She stepped through the awkward revolving door.

The cases were in the back of the taxi. Nobody came for her.

The taxi cleared the city, went into a tunnel, emerged in another city, and headed to the airport. The driver loaded her bags onto a trolley, and she struggled to check in.

She didn't have the will to stay, not in her muscles, not in her mind.

She put herself in the line. There were six people ahead of her, including the inevitable couple with passport trouble who had too much luggage and wanted it all checked through to somewhere in South America with an airline nobody knew.

She heard her own name on the air: Sarah Freeman, to go to airport information.

Peter Clarke called the hotel room, but the voice was unfamiliar: Danish, perhaps, trying to be polite in English to this odd old man.

She'd gone.

And why shouldn't she walk away from memory, from this duty that everyone wanted to impose on her? He was beginning to be clear now: that the duty lay on others to resolve things.

He called Helen. But she was not at home. He called Nicholas, who said he hadn't heard anything. Clarke tried to read his voice, whether he was glad, relieved, or disappointed that Sarah Freeman was going home, but he could not: Nicholas spoke to a beat he couldn't interpret, an arbitrary lilt.

He called the airport.

"I didn't get a chance to say good-bye properly," he said.

"I have a plane to catch."

"Have you checked in?"

God, she thought: he's such a regular person that he'd worry if she wasted the ticket.

"If you haven't checked in," he said, "please come back. I wish you'd come back."

"Can you give me one good reason?"

"I like you very much," Peter Clarke said. "I want to make things right."

"I'm tired and I want to go home."

She was standing in the rush of people, at one of the three phones on the information desk, blocking the anxious relatives, the ones who needed to find the office of baggage irregularities, the nurse, the police, the insurance-company shop. She felt like some teenager being summoned back by a lover, if teenagers still loved melodrama, if they didn't just shrug and let go.

She was damned if she'd go back just for Peter Clarke.

"Helen wanted you to meet Lucia again," Clarke said.

It couldn't be true, she thought acutely.

"I asked them to find you a new room," he said.

She never had confronted Lucia, not in that earlier life, not in this one. She wanted legal process at most, which meant keeping her distance. She wasn't at all sure what would happen, face to face: wasn't sure what she had felt about Lucia then, and how it would spoil her nice clean fury now.

Lucia would know things. But she knew worse.

She put the phone down, and Clarke knew what that meant. He called Helen to say she should be at the hotel when Sarah returned.

"She might admit it," Sarah said.

Helen had her arm looped through Sarah's arm as they walked, slowly, along the lakeshore.

"It worries me," Sarah said. "She might admit it and say it was an unfortunate misunderstanding, and why didn't I come forward before? She might simply give it back to me."

Helen said: "She won't do that. If she did that, she'd be admitting all the other possible claims on her."

"But she could say it was impossible to find me. That I was in London, that I changed my name, that I might be just a little famous but my picture was never in the paper and why should she be reading the Sunday papers from London in any case?"

"She didn't want to know." Helen took a deep breath. "She assumed you were dead."

"You don't know that. I don't know that."

Sarah tugged her arm from Helen's grasp, and she started to fidget in her handbag, scrabbling under a mirror, a Chapstick, some cards and money.

"I do know that," she said. "You're right, I do. Besides, why should I be the only one who isn't entitled to know everything about someone else all at once? Everyone in Berlin knew everything about me because I was a Jew." She tipped the bag, pushed the papers to one end. "They didn't have to prove anything. Why do I have to prove everything?"

Out of the new disorder in her bag she pulled half of a *Gipfli*, which flaked in her hands.

Helen said: "We could continue this later."

Sarah tore the croissant and threw it for the swans that had been fussing out on the water with a show of elegant indifference and now turned with great power into shore.

"Does it worry you," she said, talking out to the water and the white birds, "that I'm not the perfect and civilized victim? Not always brave and always sure?" She turned to Helen. "I'm a lousy touchstone, aren't I?"

"All this can wait."

"I won't live long enough to wait. They're going to ask me why I waited so long, aren't they?"

"You couldn't have known where Müller-Rossi went."

Sarah turned to Helen. "Call her Lucia," she said, "or Frau Müller-Rossi. She is your grandmother."

"You couldn't have known that she was in business, or where she was in business, or guessed that she got the table out of Berlin, even. It isn't likely that any single table survived the ruin of Berlin."

"You think that will work in a courtroom?"

"We're not looking for devices."

"But we have to. We have to look for what works."

"Besides," Helen said, "nobody thinks like that anymore."

"Anymore?"

"I used to think that way. It was all too late and too awkward. This house was stolen, that's a fact, but there have been five owners since then and do you throw out the man who bought the house in good faith and could barely afford it and needs somewhere for his family? And suppose there's a business that was stolen; in fifty years, it's been nationalized and privatized and globalized and probably now it's been downsized. And suppose it's a masterpiece of some kind which is maybe in a national museum where I'd want it to be. And suppose it's money. You leave cash alone for long enough, it's anonymous again, it's like buried treasure."

Sarah brushed the crumbs from her fingers. "You think this?"

"I used to think all this," Helen said.

"And now?" Sarah said.

"I know it is theft. It has to be put right."

"And punished?"

Sarah waited. The swan in by the shore, Helen with her fierce certainty, the swan in its perfect pose, Helen standing there: they rhymed, she could see.

"You don't have a lot of patience with history, do you? Your father's history or your grandmother's history."

"They can't expect us to care about the details now. They left them out for so many years."

"And you don't think it is all too late? That we have to move on?"

"No," Helen said. "I know it took sixty years for people to listen. As it did in Britain, and in Holland, and America and everywhere else."

"Good," Sarah said.

"And that is why any court will want to throw out your case," Helen said. "Because they tried it once before and they couldn't get a conviction, and then they didn't do anything even though they knew all about Lucia. They had their one chance to be moral and superior, and they threw it away, and now they're defensive."

"You see things very clearly."

"It doesn't mean I'm right."

Helen handed her a tissue to clean her fingers. Sarah thanked her like a child. Helen took Sarah's arm again, seemed to direct her along the path.

Sarah said: "I'm wasting the bit of life I've got left. I'm wasting it on a woman I almost forgot for fifty years."

Then she said: "When can I meet her?"

Nicholas went to see Lucia when the shop had closed. He felt he had no honorable alternative: if he couldn't even talk to her, then he was just an accomplice in her silence.

It was the big change as you got older: you knew you were implicated. Only the young could protest and boycott and go out masked in the streets and burn cars and stone the police and think that made them right and pure.

But when he sat down with his little brandy, he didn't know exactly how to start with Lucia. He rather envied the police, who start with uniforms to say who they are, and warrants to say what they are allowed to want.

He nudged the subject, said it was extraordinary how everyone— the newspapers in particular, he said—was talking about the 1940s. He said even younger people seemed to be interested, as they had never been interested before; because, he said, it seemed a moral issue now.

He waited for Lucia. She didn't help. She wondered if he would come to the opera next month: something French, she said, Massenet. She said Massenet was underrated.

There was a blunt fuss of a sound: the apartment bell.

Lucia looked up. Nicholas waited for her to say who it might be, who was expected. Lucia said nothing. Nicholas supposed he would have to go to answer the door.

The bell rang again.

It was not the moment for strangers, but it was not possible to ignore the unsocial, unnecessary noise.

The intercom fizzed. "Delivery," a voice said.

Nicholas never questioned deliveries. He could hear the elevator trundling and rising.

But he should have asked Lucia, he thought.

He heard the elevator doors open. There was a knock on the apartment door.

He felt absurd squinting through the spyhole. He knew nothing more when he saw the faces outside.

There were three of them: two squat, purposeful men and a young man in a very careful jacket. He thought they had a faintly deferential air, so he opened the door.

The young man said: "Is Frau Müller-Rossi at home?"

"I'll tell her."

Lucia said she had no idea what anyone would be delivering to her. She could not guess.

"It's not roses," Nicholas said. "It took two men."

"I don't expect roses at my time of life. Lilies, possibly."

The two men carried their parcel into the living room. The young man followed.

He didn't seem to know what to say, so he spoke very quickly. "We thought," he said, "you might prefer to have this in the apartment. In the circumstances."

"Do you want it unwrapped?" the older man said.

Lucia, in her chair, glared at them all. She was not prepared for company, her hair a little wild, her skin all too present through the paint. She said: "You may as well."

The men didn't want to look at her with her bare face. They began to strip away paper and card and tape and string. The parcel had legs, it seemed, and a flat top. It had the shape of a desk. Inside the brown card and paper there was tissue paper lying against the wood. The two men lifted the tissue paper away, without tearing it.

The desk was covered in huge open flowers, all in light wood cut into the darker wood, with gilded corners and gilded handles for the drawer. It was a little carved garden in a corner.

Lucia seemed to want to protest, but she wanted even more to stay entirely in command of the moment, which meant she had to pretend she knew what was happening.

"Thank you," she said.

"Just for the time being," the young man said. "It seemed better, in the circumstances."

"I shall be back in the shop tomorrow morning," she said, too clear and too emphatic.

And when they were gone, she said to Nicholas: "Everyone is suddenly so interested in my little business."

"Someone has to tell the story."

"I suppose so. I always assumed you didn't want to know."

"It's a fine table."

"I sold it once. Bought it back. I couldn't bring myself to sell it again. But it was in the shop where anyone could see it. I'm becoming careless. Or I'm becoming frank. Or just very old indeed."

Nicholas, who had so much wanted to be the interrogator, now wanted to stroke the worn fabric of her face. He thought, wrongly, this was a sign of weakness.

The housekeeper called at eight and said Lucia was asking for Helen.

Helen asked why Lucia did not make the call herself, but Lucia's housekeepers were not expected to consider questions beginning with "why." The housekeeper did say, though, that she was leaving early that evening. She'd be gone when Helen arrived. Frau Müller-Rossi would want an egg, and some Madeira.

So Helen walked, not wanting the old woman's imperious ways to be rewarded. She was grateful for the first specks of hard rain.

She rang the doorbell, but Lucia did not bother to answer. Usually, Helen did not use her own key to the apartment, never challenged Lucia's autonomy, but this time she did.

The inner doors all seemed to be open, but there were no lights. Helen could hear music: the pilgrims' chorus from *Tannhäuser*, the pilgrims coming from far away and cresting some stage hill. She stood quite still for a moment, wondering whether to call out.

She realized one door was shut. There was enough light from the streetlamps, pale bluish light, to let her pick her way through the treasures of the hall. She pushed the closed door.

Candles burned. The light was steady and gold. In a circle of light, Lucia sat, the music bawling at her now. Helen fretted at once about the neighbors. Then she saw that Lucia's straightness was carefully supported, that it did not necessarily mean she was alert and awake. Helen wanted to turn down the music so it would be possible to talk, but she kicked against one of the candles, which spilled a little spoiling pool of wax which stayed alight for a moment on the rug. She snuffed it out.

Lucia was smiling.

Helen found the volume control. "Lucia," she said. Lucia said nothing. "Lucia," she said, "this is dangerous."

Lucia slipped out of her chair and onto the floor.

A pair of candles lit her shawl for a moment, and there was a stench of burning. Helen stamped on the fire. She held Lucia under the arms and dragged her up from the floor. She felt the slackness in Lucia's body, the will that had relaxed and died.

She thought Lucia might be dead.

Softly, the pilgrims' chorus repeated itself.

She stashed Lucia in a chair. Lucia's mouth drew back from a smile into a gawp, as though she was drunk. Lucia's teeth, a few on a plate, slipped in her mouth. Lucia's features slacked like old cloth over her bones.

She had been reading Goethe. She'd even marked a page:

Ich besass es doch einmal
Was so köstlich ist!
Dass man doch zu seiner Qual
Nimmer es vergisst . . .

And Helen was not confused, not frightened, not unsure anymore. She was angry. She was a fury in a drawing room. She grabbed at Lucia's hair, half afraid the old woman wore a wig, and she slapped Lucia's cheeks, a little powder coming away all pink on her hands, and she shook the woman. She was no longer afraid that a touch would break a bone.

She was tackled and winded by sheer, sudden fury. Her father had told her about Goldstein's suicide, about the body between the candles, about the volume of Goethe. She knew exactly what Lucia was doing: she was stealing Goldstein's death.

I once possessed it
The thing that is so precious
To one's torment
One never forgets it.

She couldn't have it. If this was Goldstein's death, then she'd used barbiturates. Then, if she was drunk on barbiturates, she had to be made to move. Helen would walk her, up and around the drawing room, even if her slack hands knocked down the pretty porcelain, even if she left behind a trail of broken things. That was what Lucia had always done to others, after all.

She dragged Lucia to the window and pushed her out into the air for a moment, into the cold sting of the rain, which fussed in rivulets on Lucia's powdered face. She shook the old woman's fine dyed hair like cloth in the streetlights.

She wanted the world to see.

NINE

Lucia woke surprised. She often wore earplugs so she could listen to her own heart; any shocks and bumps would come from the workings of her own body and not from the outside world. So it was not the quiet that alarmed her.

She opened her eyes. She could see white walls, which were not her white walls. The bed was smaller, tighter than she liked: the wrong bed.

They'd put her in a hospital.

It was just a charade, she thought. She took a few pills to get to sleep when the world upset her; she had not, of course, taken a reliable dose.

She wanted to throw off the bedclothes in one grand gesture, a test of will and muscles, but they were so tightly folded that she had to tug at them. When she was free, she could see the plain cotton gown that was scratching against her skin, with a faded pattern of blue flowers.

There was no machinery in this hospital, no tubes, cranks, screens, or ventilators. The room had a window, but the blinds were down.

It was not an ordinary hospital, then.

She did not want to try the door. They would not have humiliated her by locking the door.

She had invented a little moment of romance, and she had not intended anyone to see it; being old was not a state of being reduced to the practical. She was entitled to poems, candles, music. Perhaps, since she was old, they would believe she was praying.

Under her breath she rehearsed speaking for a moment, wanting to get it right, and then she shouted: "Service! *Servizio!*"

She was mortally afraid of the time when nobody even thinks of listening to you, when all your reasons are obviously unreasonable and you struggle to say what you think and people comfort you instead of listening.

She must be haunted; everyone would think that. And now it mattered what they thought, because that would be the condition of her leaving this clean, brutal place.

For there was nothing delicate or particular in the room that she could see: nothing painted, nothing shaped, only unkind angles and crisp sheets and plain whites and the closed blinds. They had not left a book, no patch of color, and she could not make out where her spectacles lay. They must have left her spectacles, surely? They had not put a picture on the walls: she supposed that images might confuse the other images that were supposed to race inside her mind and tell them all about her.

She was not available to be understood.

She had performed this charade once before, when she was much younger, for a set of three judges in a Zurich courtroom: a gentle subservience to investigation, followed by a proper measure of self-righteousness, all notions of anger carefully put away.

She could remember how to do it. But all these years later, she couldn't be quite sure she had the strength or elasticity or concentration. She'd hesitate at the wrong moment, and lose everything. She'd be angry, or even guilty.

She closed her eyes.

She could summon such terrible images: fires and deaths, treacheries and murders, a city dying before her eyes. They didn't come. She only imagined her entire person was, at that very moment, being dissolved by a committee of doctors and concerned relatives.

She would only surrender if struggle was out of the question, she told herself. Then she thought: Perhaps it is. Perhaps if I struggle, I will crack bones that never mend, open cuts that I do not have the blood to heal.

"I am old," she said out loud, and then she thought she had better not say anything out loud while she was alone and being watched.

"I left her there," Helen said. "I had to leave her there."

Peter Clarke had gone to make tea, and now he put the cup beside her. She had Henry's train in her lap and her hands: a red and yellow engine, two generous carriages. The track ran in an oval in the corner of the room.

"They said she's physically all right," Helen said. "And then I had to leave her. I can call the clinic at ten."

He thought of Lucia in the clinic, which meant he thought of how he would be in a clinic, in a place whose official name was a "home," in a world come down to four square walls and sometimes a view of the prints of landscapes in the corridor on the way to piss.

"I told Jeremy last night," Helen said. "He's still in New York."

"She'll be fine," Clarke said.

Helen attached the carriage to the carriage, and the carriages to the engine; all of it connected. She'd been dreaming of a train, she was a passenger, everything was traveling on the train or connected to the train, everything, and she couldn't get off. The train stopped, and the doors stayed locked. Then the train didn't stop at all.

Clarke said: "But he'll be home soon."

Helen smiled.

"And Lucia will be fine," he said.

"You think she will be?"

He wished he could give her the reassurance she needed, but he had only words, not touch, not love; so he would have to get the words right. He might slip and make things worse.

"Maybe she's warning us. If she really is—depressed, I mean, ill, then I suppose the whole business has to stop here. You can't drag some frail old madwoman into court."

"She was sane a very long time."

"The candles, the music, the Goethe: it was like a play. I always loved the show of her—the clothes and the glamour. She lit those candles as though she was parodying herself."

Clarke wanted to go back to his own bright-colored memories, to a small enclosed world of family, seed grounds, fields of brilliance, trips to the sea. He knew what was right and what was wrong there; it seemed more a matter of custom and rules than judgment. You knew your side, and kept its laws.

And Helen kept traveling on the train she remembered from her dream. So she broke apart the carriages and engine in her lap, and set them down by her cup.

"I've no idea what makes her do things," she said.

Peter Clarke said: "Sarah wanted to be here."

"I know." And Helen folded her hands.

"I don't think it can be stopped now," Nicholas said. "I don't want it to stop."

"Helen's worried," Clarke said. "She worries people will think it's a way of evading the moral issues if Lucia is sick. Avoiding what you want and she wants."

"Helen wants a full accounting. It's not a question of a lawsuit, or a settlement, or publicity or anything like that." He sighed. "It's me, having to go back over a story that I put away a long time ago."

"You were only a boy in Berlin."

"Helen," Nicholas said, obscurely, "feels very Swiss. I suppose I taught her that."

"I don't know what you mean."

"You're Swiss because you come from the place. It's not a question of language, because we have too many, and it can't be religion, except that we're all insistent Christians. It isn't blood, either. It isn't race. It's to do with those bloody mountains. The glaciers. The passes. The lakes. You know other people teach their children history at school to make them patriotic; we take them into the mountains for a week."

"You're what you're born," Clarke said, with a defiant show of common sense. "I'm English. You're—" and then he realized that Nicholas must have had some kind of choice, being born in Germany, one parent Italian, one Swiss.

"The thing about being really good at natural wonders," said Nicholas, "is that we're incompetent at history. We lose the plot, because it doesn't interest us. We're obsessed with that one big statement: that we come from the Alps, that we're somehow a separate people."

"Yes, yes."

"I'm sorry if I don't make sense. It's just that Helen somehow feels all this. She loves the place. And when the place is contaminated by its history, she's—she's disoriented. She wants to put things right, but more than that, she wants to put things back. She won't stop."

"Quite right. Something was stolen. Something has to be handed back. You didn't see Sarah crying—"

It was always so particular, Nicholas thought; Clarke's kind of history was a list of particulars, with no big thought to turn them into a story or a philosophy. He only wanted to know things. He wanted things to be right. And all the other human circumstances, muddled as usual, simply did not count.

The doctor was a wonderfully social man, without exactly being ingratiating, affable without ever for a second losing concentration.

He wore a peculiarly good suit, very tight-waisted, and he smelled of a London aftershave.

He said: "It would be wise to make some tests. Some assessments."

Helen listened brightly. Just as the doctor was playing a doctor impeccably, she would play the grateful, intelligent listener.

"It's possible that your grandmother suffers from depression. There may be something physically wrong. It's also possible she is not entirely as capable as she was. And it's possible she simply dozed off with candles burning, which I suppose any of us could do." But he could never do such a thing, because it would imply that for one moment he had closed his cold assessing eyes.

Helen said: "I'd like to talk to her. Is that possible?"

"Of course. We want her to be comfortable."

"Then perhaps—"

"She only has her hospital gown to wear."

"I brought clothes."

Lucia came to the doctor's rooms in her hospital gown, with a white robe over that, with a nurse just behind her. She'd never before shown Helen her maculate self, warm brown marks on the face; without powder and lights, she was stained by age.

She took the comfortable chair across from the doctor, as of right.

"I know," the doctor said to Lucia, his eyes still on Helen, "how distressing this has been. We simply want to make sure that there are no underlying issues. Problems, that is."

Lucia sat silent.

"As the brain ages," the doctor said, "the gray matter undergoes progressive synaptic and neuronal loss. Happens to everybody. Sometimes it's noticeable at forty. But after the age of eighty-five, it's something we have to think about very carefully."

Helen found herself nodding, smiling, making small gestures as a doctor's audience is meant to do. Lucia, for the moment, sat quite still: horrified, it seemed, at the insult of his talk.

"So. There are a number of things we can do. We can take a history, your granddaughter can help us. We can eliminate a good many things—check the drugs you take, check your thyroid, that sort of thing. Check for malnutrition. There are one or two tests we normally do that I'm sure aren't needed, but they're part of the routine."

Helen said: "What do you mean?"

"We test for tertiary syphilis," the doctor said.

He still would not look directly at Lucia. She was an impressive ruin: hair still red and wild, features elegantly sharp, but she willed herself into a certain blankness. If the damned doctor chose to think her incompetent, she would wait and prove him wrong in one considered action.

In the meantime, she wanted him to look at her. Her authority lay in her eyes.

"There is," the doctor was saying, "a very simple preliminary test. Frau Müller-Rossi, perhaps you could answer a few questions."

She waited patiently like a good child.

"Do you know the date—the day, the month, the year?"

She couldn't speak for a moment, dust of anxiety in the throat. She had to speak clearly, get the language right; they noticed language. Then she told him.

"And the day of the week? The name of this place? Your telephone number?"

She said: "At the shop or at my apartment?"

"How old are you now? When were you born? What was your mother's maiden name?"

She answered. Helen thought she was a little slow, as if shocked. But Lucia was only being careful. It didn't matter if this man considered her old, but it mattered very much if he considered her sickly old.

"Will you please count backward from twenty? By threes?"

Helen watched Lucia's face, thought she saw a flick of impatience there. The old woman thought she would win, somehow: either come back to her life, or escape all responsibility for it, and make it seem her moralistic family preferred some medical compromise to the truth.

Lucia said: "Twenty. Seventeen. Fourteen. Eleven. Eight. Five. Two."

The doctor said, encouragingly: "Very good."

Lucia's face barely changed. She knew, because she had acquaintances who had been old and put on trial by doctors, that she must not seem angry at this patronizing tone. The doctor would consider her anger inappropriate. He would call her demented.

"Well-educated people always do well on that test," the doctor said, to Helen.

She wasn't safe yet.

"Tell me," the doctor asked Helen, "about your grandmother's apartment. She has a housekeeper, I suppose?"

"Of course."

"It's sometimes difficult if there's a loyal housekeeper. They cover up the little incidents, the forgetfulness about washing, the fits of temper. The family just don't know."

Lucia held the arms of the chair. She'd learned that trick in front of the judges: anchor yourself, and then you can hurt yourself if you have to, just to distract from the questions.

Lucia thought: I am old, and therefore he knows what I am. But he does not know who I am.

The doctor said: "Tell me. Are you basically satisfied with your life?"

Now how would she answer that one? She liked the taste of tea, the smell of freesias, the delicacy of a Chinese tree picked out in blue on a porcelain plate; these things were not unsatisfactory. But how could anyone be satisfied to move awkwardly, to speak indistinctly, to have hair that is white and brittle and a face that has been etched away with lines?

". . . that your life is empty?"

Her little business occupied her. He might guess that her care to maintain her name was an occupation which had never ended. Besides, she would never dare have a life that was truly empty; she would have to open up memory like a locked storeroom and visit it closely.

". . . are you bothered by thoughts you can't get out of your head?"

These must be standard questions; he was taking them, she could see, from a printed list. He would not want her to list the thoughts that refused to dissolve, unlike so many thoughts now simply dissolved into forgetfulness. He wanted only a "yes" or a "no."

But if he expected her to confess to conscience, she would not.

Helen felt uneasy in her stomach, annoyed at the process which made Lucia, her grandmother, into a parcel of flesh to be analyzed.

"Are you afraid that something bad is going to happen to you?" the doctor said.

Lucia particularly did not look at Helen. She didn't want to see what was in Helen's eyes: whether the girl wanted her healthy and sane in order to ruin her.

". . . worry about the future?"

". . . do you think it is wonderful to be alive now?"

And then: "Do you worry a lot about the past?"

She thought: Not unless the world decides to worry a lot about my past.

"Do you feel that your situation is hopeless?"

She wanted to laugh. She had an extraordinary possibility at this very moment: she could choose to be an old woman. She could subside into pleasant rooms and constant care. She could outgrow responsibility.

"Do you know where you are?" the doctor asked her, abruptly.

And the temptation passed. She would be very exact.

"I am in the hospital," Lucia said, "in a doctor's consulting room because I seem to have alarmed people. I am so sorry, Helen. I some-times have difficulty sleeping at night—"

"Very often?" the doctor said. He wouldn't stop concentrating.

"You will notice, Doctor, that I am not at a loss for words."

The doctor nodded. "Later on," he said to Helen, as though Lucia was wearing a cloak of invisibility instead of a hospital dressing gown, "you'll find a certain withdrawal from life—a lack of interest. Anger, which is only natural, and depression because memory is fading. No care about appearance or actions." And here he looked at Lucia after a hospital night. "Manners go. Sometimes they misplace things and then insist and insist they were stolen."

"I talked to her housekeeper," Helen said, not wanting all these obligatory tests to turn into trouble. "My grandmother is meticu-lous about lights and fires. She's always alone when she goes to bed because the housekeeper leaves after dinner, and there's never been anything out of place."

"So what do you think happened last night?"

Helen said: "I think you should ask Lucia."

"I've been rather tired," Lucia said. "A business—issue, as you would say. I organized some candles, some music, a book of poems that I like, and I tried to relax. I took a sleeping pill, and it took effect faster than I expected."

"She did all this," Helen said, pointedly, "while the housekeeper was still in the apartment."

The doctor said: "You don't think this—accident—might be some kind of aggression?"

In front of this neat, scented, impassive man, Lucia was no more than her dossier said: which mostly was "very old."

"I really think," Helen said, "my grandmother would be better at home."

"It will be on your responsibility, Helen. We can't be absolutely sure she has not had a stroke."

"I think," Helen said, "those tests could be run quite quickly. And then perhaps late today my grandmother could be released?"

This talk did not make Lucia entirely comfortable; she hadn't expected Helen as such an ally.

"What is this?" the doctor said directly to Lucia, holding up a computer mouse.

Lucia thought for a moment that she had truly forgotten the word. It was not a word of her generation. She knew she couldn't hesitate too much, couldn't seem to stammer, must produce a perfect sentence. "That, Doctor," she said—and she worried at the word, the "switch," the "key," the "rat," in French the "*truc*," in English the "thing"—"is the mouse for a computer." She must not on any account show the relief she felt.

The doctor said: "I don't think it would do any harm if she rested at home. For a while."

Helen, as very nearly next of kin, thanked the clinic for their discretion, made Lucia's health sound like the kind of business secret that is almost sacred in Swiss law, and paid the bill at once. She thought she caught blame in the senior nurse's eye, as though this should never have been allowed to happen.

Lucia was dressed again, and slightly painted with the makeup Helen thought to bring.

"I don't understand," she said, "why it was necessary to take me to that place."

"Would you rather we'd taken you to the cantonal hospital? With sirens blaring?"

Lucia said: "I took some pills to sleep. That's all."

Helen said: "And you made a whole play out of it."

"I had appointments the next day. I would never have missed them."

The Turk drove too slowly. Lucia was irritated by his care; she waved her hands.

"I have been a proper, respectable businesswoman in this city for almost sixty years," she said. "Nobody has to worry about my checks. Nobody worries about their husbands. What I sell is what I say it is, and it is fine. I do not draw attention to myself, only to the shop and what I sell, and I sell under another name, as I always have done. I am a private person and I do not wish to be made public. Do you understand that?"

She was hunched as the Turk helped her out of the car, and across the sidewalk and into the building, and into the shiny metal box of the elevator. But then she saw herself in the mirror of the walls. She straightened herself.

"I hope you can afford your morals," she said to Helen. "I always had the morals I could afford."

She used her own key to open the apartment door. She pushed it hard, and she swept into the hall.

The living room had not been touched.

Lucia said: "That woman. She's not here?"

There were porcelain bits on the carpet, and candlewax, and damp. Lucia's chair had shifted from its usual place. A table was overturned.

"This is intolerable," Lucia said. "I shall fire her."

Helen watched the old woman pick her way about the room, checking and inspecting how the damp had darkened the carpet by the open window, and the rain left faint stains on the pale curtains.

"I might as well have been burgled," she said.

Helen said: "You said nothing happened."

"The woman should have cleared things up."

"I told her not to."

"You told her?"

"I wanted you to see all this."

Lucia sat down very cautiously.

"I made a mistake," she said.

"And the candles?"

Lucia said nothing. For a moment, Helen fancied she might mean a mistake in the past, something terrible. But then Lucia said: "You never had a chance to do wrong. You should be grateful."

"I don't want excuses," Helen said.

"There might be explanations."

"I couldn't stand them," Helen said.

Lucia said: "So you have one point of weakness?" She rubbed her hands together out of necessity because they were dying on her. "Such a strong girl," she said, furiously.

Sarah had the power to alarm him, make the quiet, decent Peter Clarke terribly aware that nothing was going to be simple ever again.

"Purpose," Sarah said. "They want bloody purpose. They all want me to be their bloody purpose because it's easy for them and they know I am right." She spilled gin on her skirt, looked up defiantly. "Easy. Easy. Easy."

Clarke said: "You think it's easy to think these things of a mother or a grandmother?"

"What the hell else do they have except bad thoughts about the past? The past is a bad thought in itself. They've grown out of politics, they've grown out of nations, they just want a good time and a nice car and a quiet life and a winter holiday in the damned Maldives. There's nothing left to connect them to history except what their family remembers, and that's not entirely real to them. Hegel," she said.

"I expect so."

"Hegel. They really believe they have come to the end of history, and the end of politics, and from now on they just need managers to cope with a few fiscal questions. They don't need morals anymore, so they find them interesting and amusing and diverting and—like a game. They play at condemning, they play at pardoning. They play at it all. They don't understand what it means to the rest of us."

Clarke said: "I'm sometimes glad I didn't read too much."

"What do you mean? You mean you're glad you don't have to doubt and worry?"

"I doubt," Clarke said. "I doubt if my legs will carry me through the day. I doubt if my heart will still work tomorrow. I don't worry, that's true. But I doubt."

"That's different."

"Yes. It is. It's fundamental."

"I don't know why I talk to you," Sarah said. She slammed her glass down on a glass table.

"You have to talk to someone," Clarke said. Later, he came to think he'd come dangerously close to a declaration with those words.

"I suppose so," she said; which was the answer he wanted.

And they sat, old, stiff, opposite each other.

"If she asked me to forgive her," Sarah said, "I wouldn't hear her. If I hear her, I have to deal with her as an equal. She asks, I give."

"She won't ask."

"I'm not equal to her. She is wrong. She did wrong."

"Nowadays," Clarke said, very carefully, "people don't seem to think about doing wrong. It's all psychology and excuses."

"They like an absolute wrong that comes along with dramas and spotlights and horrors. That, they like. And in time, they'll explain that, as well." She sat forward. "And if I just coexist with the woman, not challenging her, not prosecuting her, not throwing a rock through her lovely windows—what's that except forgetfulness, pardon in disguise? And if I do anything, if I do anything—"

"We used to say you shouldn't bring yourself down to the other person's level."

"Exactly," Sarah said. "It's in the moral philosophers, and it's in your common sense, both. It's a question of where you stand—remember that? And whether you're entitled to look down on someone. A question of level."

"Nobody else is up there with you. Nobody else is still alive."

He saw that her eyes were watering, but out of anger.

He shouldn't say anything more. He should start to repair the afternoon, fill it up with a gentle walk, the sight of the lake, the prospect of cakes and coffee; whatever it would take. But he said, even so: "You think she can forgive herself?"

He was startled, even alarmed, to see that her face was suddenly easy and loose, not bent in with feeling as it had been.

"Nobody can do that," Sarah said. "Nobody. You pardon someone, you make yourself equal with them, but she's always more concerned with what she did than with forgiving it. Crime traps you that way."

She smiled. She'd managed now to push away the image of an old Lucia, a sad Lucia, sitting under the influence of a pill in the middle of flames. She needn't bother with pity. She seemed to relax back into the chair, no longer tense on the edge of it.

"You know," she said, "you forgive, you give. It's like in French: *pardonner* is close to *donner*. *Geben* to *vergeben*. *Dono* to *perdono*. Pardon is a gift, and I won't think of giving it, any more than I would give her my table."

"I only thought—"

"You're a good Christian. It's not the only kind of goodness. And when it forces people into forgiving the ones who sin against them, it's a mistake. It makes the virtuous just the same as the wicked: two terms in the same equation."

"I'm afraid to stand on the high ground. I'm afraid I would be lonely."

"Would you rather be down with Lucia?"

Clarke didn't show that he needed to think about that.

Nicholas came, all solicitude, all pity. Lucia suspected him at once. He thought she was weak, thought she was panicking. She much regretted her taste for Goethe and candles.

And he chattered, as though the substance of what he said didn't matter, only the sound, as though he was soothing a child or a cat.

"You remember the milkmen?" he said. "Those metal cans. Those carts with huge wheels. Those first few days in Zurich, I used to look at all the washing in the sun on the roof terraces and I thought the whole city was cleaning itself—washed, polished, and bleached on the line."

"Yes," Lucia said.

"And the food in the windows. Caviar. Bananas in a silvery light. Cakes that looked like hats. Hats that looked like stars on a net, or a butterfly. There was a couple on a bicycle, with a trailer behind and a sofa on it. There was that lottery seller on Bahnhofstrasse, in a metal drum, with a metal hood to keep her dry. And the men went shopping in the market as well as the women. Great tentacles of carrots, like something underwater. And—"

"I sometimes think you're older than I am," she said.

Nicholas said: "Just because I remember things?"

"I remember Berlin. I had a life in Berlin."

"We'd go out of the city sometimes, on a train with wood seats," Nicholas said. "We never went anywhere from Berlin. At least, I didn't. I was quite alarmed at how easy it was to go somewhere else when we got to Zurich."

"You were old enough to have tastes. You seemed to like flowers and open air and mountains."

"We used to eat in village places. You remember? With wooden walls, and those grand tiled ovens for warmth and wrestling pictures on the wall, enormous square men hurling each other."

Lucia said: "It was good for you. I expect."

"I remember," Nicholas said, and Lucia could already tell from his bright eyes that this was not going to be an innocent memory, "one place with little windows and lots of geraniums. A big, generous woman serving. There was a younger man in the corner and she asked if he'd like something 'special' in his omelette. He wasn't a friend; she called him 'Mein Herr.' You were listening, and when you ordered, you asked for something special, too.

"But I suppose the woman didn't feel like doing favors for someone foreign and glamorous with a child in tow. The omelettes came back plain, but with a bunch of parsley on one side. So you inspected the young man's plate, as best you could, and you thought there was a whole meal hidden in between the folds of egg: bacon, perhaps, certainly liver. All that was rationed at the time.

"The woman brought the bill and you'd been charged for two 'special' omelettes. Do you remember?"

Lucia fussed with a little stone deer, head pressed back against its flank, a piece too sentimental for her usual tastes. "Do you remember this?" she said.

Nicholas wouldn't stop. "You wouldn't pay for 'special' omelettes, but the woman kept saying they were special. You said there was nothing in them, and the woman said of course there wasn't; there was a war on. You said: 'But that young man had liver. Perhaps bacon. He had to use a knife and a fork.'

"The woman blocked the way. 'You may not know it, Madame,' she said, and you could tell she never said 'Madame' in a friendly way, 'but here in Switzerland food is rationed.' You said: 'The bill was wrong.' She said: 'Are you going to pay?' And there you both were like statues on a fountain: righteousness and righteousness, head to head.

"Then the woman said: 'If you think I'm breaking the law, I'll call the police.'

"And then you gave her the money, full payment and a small tip. The woman said: 'Ah. Must have been a misunderstanding. It's so easy, with all the different languages. Madame.' "

Nicholas beamed. "It was the first time I ever saw you defeated," he said.

Lucia dropped the stone deer onto the carpet. She looked down at it for a moment and said: "You used to like that fawn."

Nicholas scooped it up and put it back in place. His face was now close down to Lucia's face, but for all his anger, he could not quite bring himself to be unmannerly. He pulled back.

So she was not going to discuss the first years in Zurich. And he was not going to go away without bringing something into the open.

She thought it had better be Berlin.

He said: "It must have been difficult with a child, and on your own."

He did not want to ask out loud: "And were you ever on your own?"

"You, Niccolo. Like having a lover you couldn't mention. I'd have to go out, and I'd have to leave you, but some nights I'd get a lift from a few streets away just so I could come back with a squeal of brakes and you'd know I hurried."

He thought: She is going to say that every fakery was kindness, because she wants every kindness to be suspect.

"It was a lively city," she said. "Until the bombing got worse. I came alive in Berlin. I'd been in a small town so long. I was so glad," she said, "to be back in a big city. Glamour and spectacle and gray and black and ceremonial red. All that history. Great shows, although you could hardly get tickets. You could always get pasta, oysters, and game because they weren't rationed. And there were men.

"All the soldiers. All the men in the ministries," she said. "The diplomatic corps. There were so many young bachelors and so few women. You never sat down to a table with even numbers."

He said: "You must have enjoyed yourself."

She paused. She would have liked him to see her as she had been: the sumptuous breasts, those long silken legs, of course, but also the way she challenged men. She had a real taste for sexual pleasure, but she had always seemed at one remove; a man had to make her real before he could love her. She had to be brought down.

She could tell him these things; that was the threat that lay between them. She could make him listen to what he did not want to know. She could explain, and perhaps her nice monogamous child needed the explanation, that when she was calling out and her eyes had gone to glass and her whole body turned on the axis of the man inside her, that man was still not quite sure she was not acting again. So he had to go on testing and proving and hoping.

"To war," she said, raising a glass. She had measured her irony exactly. "Sometimes it's fun.

"I always tried to get things for you. I brought you oysters one night, two dozen of them. I'd forgotten you had never seen them before. I thought they were a great treat, and I don't know what you thought—organs, I suppose, all gray-green and slippery. I said they were good, and good for you, and ate one. You looked at them and said you could see things moving inside.

"I really thought you were just being difficult. Childish. You said you wanted salami. I said you can't always have what you want. You said you'd like me to stay home more. I told you I had things to do. I told you at least you were safe, and oysters were just as good as meat. So you said you wanted meat. I told you I did what I could. And I was so annoyed I held your nose, and I poured an oyster into your mouth."

He hadn't remembered until then: not being able to breathe, this sliding, lively thing in his mouth, and his mother's huge eyes.

"We stepped around the broken glass," Lucia said. "We had straw shoes about that time: chic and shining, but they were made of straw. We couldn't get fish, so we ate oysters."

Nicholas said: "You went dancing."

Lucia shrugged.

"But you were there."

"You saw more women in black after the Russian front. Men without legs. They started reserving seats on the trams and the buses for men wounded in the war. I even saw some communist slogans once, on a wall near the Roman restaurant. I wondered how long they'd last. Hours, not more."

"You can't say you didn't know things, guess things. See things."

"Of course."

"How could you carry on—?"

"Life doesn't stop just because history is going on all around you. People fall in love. They trick each other. They get hangovers, and they change flats, and they go swimming."

"You could have left."

"Could I? Müller was in the army, no money. Besides, I didn't want to see him. It might have been safer in Switzerland, but it didn't seem that way at the time. The Swiss all talked about retreating to the mountains and fighting to the last man, although they didn't seem clear about who exactly they'd be fighting. And they left the women down in the plains.

"Besides," she said, "I was having a good time. People have a good time in wars, you know. It happens. Ask your friends about the blackout in London and the things they'd never have done if the lights were on."

She thought she was almost safe.

"They rationed clothes. So we fussed about hats." Lucia said: "You'd expect me to remember that, wouldn't you? Well, I do. Why shouldn't I remember? I needed my looks. My looks brought my contacts, and my contacts made my life better, and I did it all for you."

"I really don't know anything about hats," Nicholas said.

"And there was nothing, nothing I could do."

"About hats?"

"Nothing I could do about what was happening."

"But they were your friends?"

"Max Lindemann was, among others. I met a lot of others through Max."

She was waiting in a café window the next morning, the room full of hot still air, view of breezes catching at bare gray trees.

She hadn't waited for a man in forty years, not Sarah Freeman.

The froth on the coffee looked all constructed, maintained. Laws of gravity, laws of entropy, weren't enough to make it die. Carefully, she began to spoon it into the saucer.

Someone at the next table noticed, and made a point of looking away sharply so she would know he'd noticed, and she didn't give a damn.

She had the surface of the coffee bare now. It was a beige surface. She added two, then three spoonfuls of sugar. Then she added one more. If it wasn't going to be coffee, it could be a kind of sweet.

The mumble of the bells sounded out like a great machine, the chimes flying off like sparks.

You don't get patient as you get older, she thought. You get resigned.

He'd better bloody come, Müller-Rossi. And he better not think she had any kind of absolution to offer, or even help.

She sipped the coffee.

She had thought very hard about not coming back at all.

The bells stopped. She thought she could hear the water running in a stone fountain by the window. She didn't want to order another cup of the coffee. She thought about tea, instead, but she knew it would be hot water and packaged herbs.

She tried to remember who said *"Tout comprendre, c'est tout pardonner."* She knew it was Madame de Staël who said *"Tout comprendre rend très indulgent."*

The door flapped open and Peter Clarke came romping into the café like a big dog. Since he wouldn't wear his glasses, he paused a moment before he found her. He sat down at the table and looked at her saucer full of froth.

"I hate the coffee here too," he said.

"Good morning."

"I'd have brought you a paper, but I suppose you could read the Swiss papers."

She shrugged.

"Or we could go somewhere else," he said.

"What about Nicholas?"

"Oh," he said. "Nicholas. Yes. Well, I called his house. No answer. No answering machine, either."

"But he didn't say anything about not coming, did he?"

Clarke sucked his teeth. "He didn't say anything," he said, trying to be pedantic. "He doesn't say much. But I'm sure he'll come."

"I suppose the Swiss haven't changed, have they?" she said. "They're always on time?"

Nicholas went one last time to see his mother. He never had a key to her apartment: not being on such casual terms, and Lucia being a woman—ancient but independent—who would have resented any suggestion that she might have emergencies.

Helen had another key, but then she knew so much less.

He carried the court papers with him, in a torn envelope, no briefcase, as though they were something newly delivered into his life: a revelation.

But he'd always known. He'd known as you know the weather from a pain in the bones or a pressure in the head: not consciously, but thoroughly. He knew the money had been frozen, there was a prosecution; he heard these things in his father's voice on his occasional visits, the peculiar embarrassment of a banking man who finds his wife is a storybook villain, a headline of crime. He'd once been taken to the courthouse with Lucia, as though she wanted to show him off: her claim on motherhood and honesty. She implicated him.

His father also made sure he knew the terrible charges, extortion, dealing in stolen goods, blackmail, and he remembered how they were suddenly abandoned even though there were living witnesses prepared to come into court. His mother had been convicted, one month suspended, for misleading Swiss customs: declaring the contents of those seven trucks as her own household goods.

Being silent, he did not just obscure the facts. He diminished them. Lucia herself would soon be able to do the same: anyone would believe that, ancient as she was, she had lost her memory of those years. Together, they were fading history until it could no longer be read. He was almost sure he never meant to do that, but Lucia was old, she could tighten her mind at will, she must have some residual sense of shame even if it was buried under a fluent justification of every damned thing she had done.

He'd trigger her. He'd remind her about Zurich as the war ended, about the barbed wire coming down and the GIs taking "Switzerland Leave Tours I, II, III, IV," staring at every scintillating thing in shop windows, the sudden free flow of Coca-Cola and the chewing gum which shockingly stuck to your heels on the pristine length of Bahnhofstrasse.

Then she'd remember how she was always more frantic than before, more occupied, reckoning out each hour and each day. She expected things to go wrong.

But he would show her again how that summer shone: shone

with sun off the lake waters, with the white trousers of the sailors on their small boats, with the glittering hair of the girls on the steamers. The days were full of flowers, of fishing and swimming and sailing.

He'd gone with her once to the tea dance in a rose garden at the Hotel Baur au Lac. They did the foxtrot together as a stiff and distant dance, which amused the other people. He was so proud of her, and glad that nobody approached her, tried to talk or dance with her; but he also knew she hated to be ignored.

An American wanted to ask her to dance. She was disposed to get up with him. But one of his friends called him back, and he smiled apologetically, and he never tried again.

He watched the couples turning in the afternoon sun, and he was happy with the cakes, too, mysteriously aware that he was a child and not a child at the same time: in a limbo of sun and perfume and sugar.

He mustn't get lost in his own memories. They were just little levers to open her own past. He could remind her how at home she lay for what seemed like hours in the bath. He'd fretted at the door.

He'd even wondered, just for a wishful moment, if she had arranged to meet his father that time at the Baur au Lac, and if she was angry that he had not been there.

She had to tell him. There was nobody else who could demand that, and nobody else who had a chance of succeeding. He was marching to her door like a priest in search of confessions, for the sake of souls, and not simply for the law.

Then he ran out of street, and he ran out of memories, and he was standing, wrapped up, at her door. He felt the cold of the wind off the lake.

"It's me," he said through the intercom, under the eye of the video camera.

"Nicco," she said. "I was just going out."

But where would she go on a cold Sunday morning? She had no

appetite for Mass, was still a little annoyed that funerals were not in Latin.

"It's very urgent."

"Why couldn't you have phoned?"

He wondered why she didn't simply let him into the apartment, whether there was something she did not want him to see: disorder, maybe she wasn't feeling well.

"I have the court judgment," he said. "May 26, 1946."

The intercom worked only when she held the switch down. He thought she'd released the switch for a moment, a faint insect noise through the speaker. He didn't want to shout on the street, it would have been absurd: a man in his sixties bawling "Mother, Mother" into a machine.

The intercom clicked again.

"Go home," she said.

"I have to talk to you."

He tried to argue, but he was arguing with a silence and a nest of wires and a dead bell.

He caught the shine of the camera lens above his head and its little black snout. He wondered if she was still watching him.

"Of course you have to go to him," Sarah said. And Peter Clarke, too, said: "He must be very upset."

The phone was a body, dead and heavy, in Helen's hands.

Nicholas was not in Zurich. He always called before coming to Zurich. But there was no answer at the house, either. Clarke was alarmed by that; you always answer the phone on a Sunday, hoping for a family call, to be remembered.

Helen said Nicholas might be outside among the trees, gone for a walk, tending the geese. He never liked to have an answering machine in the mountains; it seemed incongruous, somehow.

Both Sarah and Clarke were angry on her behalf at Jeremy, whom they'd never met, for not being there.

Helen was beginning to know things. She should never have handed him the court papers, "in the matter of Lucia Müller-Rossi." In that righteous moment, she hadn't understood that she was disrupting the balance in his life, which now depended on not quite knowing and ignoring things. He couldn't ever again bear reality.

He was wired to be on time. She'd seen him once, through a crack between curtains, standing in the utter cold outside their house waiting for precisely eight o'clock to ring the bell.

She'd have to find him.

Little Henry came in, solemn, with his Lego train to mend. Sarah took it from him.

Helen pulled on her coat, only smiled at Henry, slammed the door. She threw herself into the car, started the engine with a roar.

Clarke said: "She'll find him."

Sarah went to talk to Henry. It was serious business, although she found bending down difficult.

Helen didn't want to knock at the door of the old farmhouse. It would seem absurd, this concern, if it was at all misplaced. It would be as though she expected some melodramatic consequence from the simple act of reminding a man of truths he already knew. She shouldn't be so arrogant.

She found it hard to tell if the house was alive or not. There were no lights, except where the low sun blazed back out of window glass. There might or might not be a faint haze of fumes coming up from the chimney, but it would only be the oil central heating even if he was at home; he'd lost the habit of lighting a fire. He used to light the fire for her mother, Nora, he said.

The barn doors were shut. There was no car in the road. But there was snow in the air, so he'd have the car put away.

She had her key.

She shouldn't burst in on him like this, unannounced. What if he'd run to pick up the phone, and missed her call and was worried and waiting now for the next call.

She sat in the car and pulled out her mobile phone. She ought to go see him, and talk to him face to face; she knew that. But instead she dialed.

She thought she could hear the phone ringing inside the solid walls of the house: ringing in the clean kitchen, among the low, deep chairs of the living room, in the bedroom to the left at the top of the stairs. She imagined the sound seeking him out.

A thought: if she slipped the car out of gear, let it run down the road without engaging the engine, then if he answered she wouldn't be embarrassed and have to say she was calling from the front doorstep.

There was still no answer.

She sat back in her seat. She certainly couldn't use her key now; she'd been told, by the unanswered ringing in the house, that Nicholas was not there, not available, or did not want to be disturbed.

Now she was like a detective, up out of the car, trying not to walk in the tracks around the house, seeing footprints that led to the door and led back, seeing prints sunk down into inches of snow that must be old evidence, looking through the windows where the shutters were not closed.

He'd been there. He was gone.

So she tried again the usual methods: she tried calling the apartment. No answer.

She felt entirely cold. It was a curious sensation, not at all like the cold you feel in your skin, in your eyes, on your teeth; it was a pervasive cold, in the bones.

She walked to the barn doors. They were closed with a strong wood latch that she could easily move.

The car was there.

She looked around the horizon, trying to read every detail, every smudge of dark under a tree that could be a man walking, every faint line in the snow that could be tracks, every place where the bright, white fields disappeared into the dark of woods.

She saw him walking toward her with a frozen, snowy cabbage in his hands.

"I am glad to see you," he said. "I have things to tell you."

She looked at his smile as though it was a document that needed study.

"I've picked a cabbage. For salad."

"You're all right?"

"I'm all right."

But he wasn't. He tried to cut the cabbage while it was still solid, the great sharp blade glancing off ice. Then he said: "We could have cheese."

Helen said: "But it's Sunday."

"But I'm here on my own," he said.

They ate at the kitchen table, quickly, as though they were going somewhere.

"I wanted to tell you that I love you," Nicholas said.

The words amazed Helen, and then horrified her: not their meaning, of course.

"I used to be so afraid we wouldn't make a home for you," he said. "Because of my own mother and father. Because of the divorce and then—then everything that kept us separate."

"But you did."

"I've been remembering," Nicholas said. "I've been remembering much too much. All the old women and men are remembering, and we're talking, and it sounds like thunder but it's really just snoring and farting and growling and complaining. There are some things I wanted to tell you I remember.

"There was the time my father took me to lunch to tell me about the divorce. He didn't say why and neither did Lucia. But he'd become very straight, very proper in the war years; he'd learned his place, in a way. Lucia did not fit. Lucia was suspect. Lucia was being investigated. Lucia was a false Swiss. I think he had to disown her just to hold on to his own new sense of place.

"Anyway. We ate in one of the guild house restaurants, high ceilings, wood walls, gilt and starch. I had, I remember, a Wienerschnitzel. I don't remember what he said, only his very careful kindness. I left him at the door of the restaurant.

"I remember feeling that my face was set on that day. I would never be able to change."

He tried to smile, but it didn't work.

"I knew my father was leaving me. I had some sudden rush of warmth for my mother. I wanted to kiss her. I wanted her to know I loved her, and I thought it was urgent she should know.

"I ran to the shop. The doors were always open in those days, everyone trusted everyone. I ran right up to her and I threw my arms around her.

"I felt her stiffen. So I pulled back, I thought I had done wrong, I thought I was inappropriate or unmannerly or unmanly. I pulled back, coughed, made my body straight.

"Then, only then, she unbent.

" 'Don't you love me anymore?' she said."

Helen shivered. She said: "You've decided something, haven't you? Tell me what you've decided."

He washed the dishes when she had gone, wiped them, and put them neatly away. He wrapped the cheese and put the bread into a basket. He put out food for the cat: dry food that would last for a while. He also put out the garbage into the cold.

He sat down to write a letter to Lucia. He had such extreme things to say that the first draft turned out pompous and the second was unclear, and he didn't get it right until the fifth draft. But he went on because he would not allow her to misunderstand him.

He thought of writing other letters, but all that mattered was that Lucia would know.

Then he drove to the mailbox, and then he drove up the mountain roads toward Glaubenberg. Close to the very top, at one of the cowherds' houses on the road, he left the car and went for his walk.

It was afternoon already, and the dark was rising as a tide rises. The cold came with it, black branches held in a glass of ice.

Nicholas had stopped shivering. The cold held him in ways he associated with warmth: the warmth of a bed, a coat, a blanket, a coat somewhere in an army or a nursery.

Then the cold slipped between Nicholas and his skin, so he could hardly feel it anymore.

He could smell damp on the air, which is just as distinct as smoke. When he walked into the woods, he'd seen the mountains closing in on him, which is what they always do when there will soon be snow.

He had a sense that people were stealing away from him, somewhere at the edges of his eyes, all of them trying hard not to let him see them go.

Such a kind man, he remembered being. Then he couldn't remember how he used to regret not remembering things, when a word got away from him, when a face lost its place.

He was stumbling, not over tree roots, but over his own slowness. He was alarmed. He stood quite still between the trees. It was so warm, he thought, and he was tangled up in clothes. He threw off his jacket, his sweater, his shirt. He was a man made for good suits, gartered socks, silk ties, in padded civic dining rooms, in company, and he was blundering out here in his shining skin.

Eyes opened wide. He did not want to be startled by anything in the half-dark.

He now knew the meaning of the word "alone." Even the word "alone" was too weak, for this was certainly not the trivial aloneness of a night in his own house, a bowl of soup, a book; he could repair that loneliness with a phone call, a walk to the bar, just waiting for the next morning.

He missed small noises behind walls, or down streets, or the closeness of a telephone. He missed the other people who could remind him who he was. He even missed, in a way, his criminal mother.

He could hear nothing except a slight wind polishing the snow.

He could let go now.

He didn't have strong glasses. So the distant Alp was a pink smear on the sky, and he was surrounded by slipshod, charcoal verticals that must be tree trunks, and a sheen on the ground which was like a painting of the color white and not the color itself.

He was surprised to be on his knees.

There was a small kerfuffle of splashing snow, a black splutter of feathers moving up to his shoulder. He didn't know birds moved at night.

The bird was at his left eye. He couldn't defend himself, but he thought of it. He felt what must be his very self retreating inside big tendons and bones and curling there like a scared creature.

Another bird stirred.

He sank down. His head fell back, like a hanged man. He tried to get breath into his lungs; he couldn't help himself. He even tried to scream, but he could produce only a rattle in the throat.

He sucked such bitter air that his chest seemed to freeze from the inside. He couldn't help himself: he wanted to break out of the sharp, knifing ice that held him.

He shouted, briefly.

The bird flew off, startled, but only to a close branch.

No blood was flowing from his eye. So he knew his heart was abandoning him.

But he could hear something, movement at a distance, something between a rumble and a crack, a world of snow and rock now starting on the move. He thought his howl must have set off some fresh, deep snow that lay on the old frozen mirror of snow. He knew all about that. He heard the new snow moving, gathering itself, rushing like water. It was working at the trees, gouging out small rocks, building its own boulders out of ice and spray and stone.

He knew what to do in an avalanche. You spit or you piss to work out which way is down. Then you swim up through the soft crystals, like fine iron filings with their own brilliance, and with luck you may live. Then again, snow will keep you warm if it doesn't drown you. He knew all this, had known it since he was a child. It was second nature.

He thought for a moment he'd saved himself: involuntary virtue. So he was laughing when he died.

TEN

The shop opened at the usual time. Assistants fussed with the single bunch of bright, heavy keys, then spread about the painted rooms, and seemed to fade away.

Lucia, too, was on time. The assistants had the door open for her, and a brisk mannerly set of "Good mornings" in appropriate accents.

She took her usual chair. She was fussing with an assistant over a pretty little Meissen group, showing how the flesh was only very slightly tinted: "Like sugar," she said, "the same faint pink you find on a sugar pig. And the hair: just look at the hair. You see the shape is molded, but there's hardly any color. Just fine threads of brown. It looks almost like gilding." Her interest seemed to dim briefly; "Eighteenth century," she said flatly.

The assistants clustered about, papers and files in hand, asking minor questions, reporting details, watching for tips on their immediate future. They knew Frau Müller-Rossi did not usually waste her time in teaching.

"We're glad you're well again," the favored assistant said.

It was an obvious impropriety; all the others knew that.

"I'm always well on business days," Lucia said.

The assistants dispersed, back to their natural shadow state.

The little red light flickered on her phone. Lucia answered. There was a brief silence on the line, as though someone was waiting for breath.

"This is the police," a voice said.

Three hunters, an operatic little party: boots, grays, greens, wool trousers, and felt hats. They found Nicholas hanging like butcher's meat in the crotch of a silver birch. He was laughing so freshly they imagined for a moment he was alive.

They stashed their guns and bags against trees, and trudged into the deep snow. They discussed for a moment the propriety and legality of touching the body, and then they pulled it down until it fell and cracked like glass.

They knew that people often pull off their clothes while dying in the cold; it seems a man gets impatient to die. So all three decided not to be surprised by the gray, loose bareness of the body.

They thought to look around for clothes. There was a down jacket and a wallet inside, so that identification was easy: Herr Professor Niccolo, sometime Nicholas, Müller-Rossi, a known name, distinguished by a careful book on Shakespeare's early tragedies.

Since there was no sign of coercion, his car was parked at the pass, there were no other tracks in the snow, and the hunters were very proud of making sure of this, there was an official story at once. He was an old man who had an accident while walking in the woods, and died of hypothermia.

The local police looked about for next of kin. They called Helen first, because that was the kind of call they were used to making: reporting the death of a beloved father. They felt able to tell her everything.

Helen said: "I'll call Lucia."

The inspector said: "I'm sorry. Lucia?"

"My father's mother," Helen said. "I'll tell her."

The inspector blurted: "She's still alive?"

"Obviously. You'll find her at her shop, but let me call first."

"She's in business?"

"Yes," said Helen, sharply, "under another name."

Two senior, polished city policemen called ahead to Lucia. The question of dress, and whether they should take an unmarked car, was considered at a high level. If they went in uniform, Lucia Müller-Rossi might think they were investigators, accusing her in some way. Given her standing, and her record, there could easily be a misunderstanding.

So they went in civilian clothes, and an unmarked car.

"He was Swiss," the inspector was saying on the way. "Lived in the same canton most of his life. Son of a man from the place where he died. He knew perfectly well you don't go walking at night in the Alps on your own at this time of year. He must have known what he was doing."

"He was sixty-six," the driver said, a handsome blank stamped out on a farm somewhere. "What possible reason could anyone have to kill themselves at sixty-six?"

They parked just behind the long shopping show of Bahnhofstrasse and edged into the rush.

"His skin was all white with hoarfrost," the driver said.

"I'm not going to go into details."

The inspector, alone, rang the bell to be allowed in.

Across the whole glittering distance of the shop, Frau Müller-Rossi considered him.

The buzzer sounded. The inspector entered. Frau Müller-Rossi said: "*Grüetzi.* Welcome."

She sat alone.

"*Grüetzi,*" the policeman said, politely.

He walked across the shop, between the lovely things all lit to seem immaculate. He came very close to Lucia.

He had never in his life been so close to somebody so old, he thought. He knew that her face must be an illusion, and he worried that a change of lights might take away the skin, the blood, the color in the eyes.

"I am sorry I come with bad news," the inspector said.

"I know," the old woman said.

He stood by a table very close to her chair, which held objects she did not want out of her sight, devices really: a pair of halved metal balls, one topped with a kind of heart shape, the other with a rod and a screw; a fine wood frame, like one end of a suspension bridge, with channels where the cables ought to be, and a wooden carriage with huge wheels and no top. There was a fine, inlaid, gilded, and painted screw that he recognized: Archimedes' screw, for drawing water out of a pool.

"Archimedes," he said.

"And the Magdeburg hemispheres. And a device for showing the trajectory of different objects in movement." She picked up a cylinder that was covered in polished metal, and ended in a kind of tit. "Look," she said. She drew out a box of papers, painted with circles like eyes and pupils; outside the circles were bright distorted scenes, stretched for an anamorph. She found one which was all black and gray, with a pink streak. She set the cylinder on the paper, and in the reflection he saw a bearded man in black. "Not that one," she said. She put down a paper with a curious, square-angled pig figure tucked into a swirl of sideways draperies. "Now look," she said. The angles resolved themselves in the mirror, the pig-pink became soft and flexible, and he was looking at a naked woman climbing into bed.

The old woman said: "My son liked that one. But he never said so."

He said: "It's charming."

"And much more than you could afford."

"Madame," he said, "I regret to have to tell you that your son has been found dead."

She said: "I'm closing now."

"We wanted to inform you personally—" He tried to sound official, nothing more, but that was because of a muddle in his mind between compassion for an old woman who's lost her only son, deference to a substantial citizen, deference to her grand age, and a sense that Lucia Müller-Rossi used all these things to stop questions before they could be formed.

"He was an old man, wasn't he?"

"I suppose so."

"And he died of natural causes?"

"He did."

"I'm very grateful," she said, "that you troubled to come and tell me this." She had, almost within reach, a phone, fax, computer, a terminal for taking credit cards, and still she held the room as if it were her private drawing room. "These are private matters, you will understand."

"If there is anything—"

"I don't think I need to know any more, not at present."

The policeman had never been a servant, but he knew very well he had been dismissed.

He let the cold of the night into the shop as he left. He hoped the door would lock open and blow the old woman away like dust.

Helen took responsibility because there was nobody else. Jeremy said he'd come back early from Boston, of course. It was no business of Sarah Freeman or Peter Clarke, although now they stayed around her as though they were a kind of family, trying hard not to make any claims, just to help. And she would not talk to Lucia, not yet.

"The priest is bound to know," she told Jeremy.

But he didn't seem to see the point. They had all this world in common, deals, timing, airports, but at the root they were so entirely different her words went past him.

"Because," she said, annoyed that Jeremy made her say it out loud, "he can't be buried in consecrated ground if he killed himself. So he can't be buried with my mother."

She wanted him to acknowledge sentiment. She understood he

was in a practical Marriott room somewhere, far away, maybe the bathroom TV still on CNN, drapes shut, air conditioning high, two empty water bottles out of the minibar, but she still wanted feeling.

"The whole thing's ambiguous," Jeremy was saying, reasonably. "It could be an accident."

"I don't think so. Nobody thinks so. He knew the mountains."

"There's no suicide note, is there? You don't have to say anything."

"I have to tell the priest it was an accident. He'll want to be told."

"Say what you can."

"He has to be buried with Mother," Helen said. "I couldn't keep them apart."

Then he said: "I'll fly back today. I'll talk to the priest."

It was, they both thought, a start.

Now Nicholas's absence was as loud in the house as his presence had ever been, enough to subdue them all.

Sarah Freeman wanted to know everything, then she wanted the interpretations and the explanations, and she had to have them now.

"I don't understand where they found him."

"In the mountains up by Glaubenberg," Helen said. "He must have gone for a walk in the woods and gotten lost. Or he didn't notice the time. I suppose."

Henry walked about solemnly. He asked once where Jeremy was; he called his father "Jeremy." Helen, who was always so agile and loose, now held her hands so she could touch her sides when she needed reassurance.

"You think he could truly have made a mistake?"

Helen shrugged.

Sarah raised her voice. "I didn't mean him any harm."

"Of course you didn't," Helen said. "It has nothing to do with you."

"How can anyone freeze to death? Don't you try to walk away from the cold?"

Clarke said: "I think once you're really chilled, you give up. I think. I'll make you some tea."

"Please don't bother," Sarah said. "I just want to know."

The doorbell rang once, and Clarke broke away, gratefully. He wanted Helen to cry for a while. He wanted Sarah to be quiet. He wanted everything to be appropriate, which did not happen. So he straightened his cuffs because he never felt quite formal enough for the Swiss, not even for a Swiss delivery man.

Someone had sent flowers: a mass of green-white tuberoses with a chapel smell.

He walked back slowly. He saw how every surface shone in this kitchen. Everything was in its proper place.

He decided Helen might not want the flowers just yet. He laid them in water in the sink.

Then he thought: It won't do. A sin like suicide cannot answer Lucia's crimes. The answer has to have its own moral worth. We're being distracted.

He sat down at the table and he walked his mind into a church. It was a trick he'd learned when he was much younger as a way of memorizing things, stacking words and ideas around an imaginary building: a greenhouse, a warehouse, a church. Now he could pass between instructions and morals on the walls, step around the facts he was supposed to confront.

He was still as muddled as the rest of them. A hundred sermons told him Lucia might be redeemed; he wanted her punished. He was supposed to forgive, he knew. He kept remembering this, like a phrase out of catechism. He did not think he had the right to be magnanimous, though, because it would involve setting aside the crimes she had done to others. He was not the one who could forgive.

Their attention should be turned, exact as a knife, on Lucia. Nicholas's death occupied the whole house with sorrow when they should have been busy with anger.

He had startled himself.

He'd always imagined that his deep moral sense was a fragile, flexible thing. He was very sure of his own weakness. He'd never talked about Grace, kept her as his particular secret. He'd run away from Grace, whom he loved, and then from the death of her child, because he was afraid he could not summon a grand enough sympathy to remain with them. He remembered, too, the temptation of going away from Frances.

He should find a vase for the tuberoses. They were such a particular, heavy flower he was not sure Helen would want them at all. Then he thought: But it was always the gardeners, the men, who organized the flowers in our house.

The night Jeremy came home, nobody slept well.

Helen fought with the sheets, then fought with Jeremy, then woke up with her eyes wide. Jeremy watched her through the night. Once she woke up and shivered with tears; she had dreamt that everything canceled itself out, that everyone was neutral, that no wrong could be redressed in the tangle of everybody's rights. Once she sat up and began to argue soundlessly, her hands talking. She never allowed herself to dissolve into sorrow; there were still things to be done.

Peter Clarke, in his hotel room, was reading, but not reading properly, only glancing down lines of type. He grumbled out loud at the bedside lights, which were never strong enough. He was thinking about the past, which was the subject he shared with Nicholas.

They had talked about Shakespeare's past, and sometimes their own. Sometimes it was an image of the war through which they'd both lived, but they did not need to go into detail; it was enough that each shared the memory and knowledge of a war.

So later they could talk about comfortable things: parades; the taste of apples; particular tin toys, a MitEuropa train with passengers and lights, a few tin soldiers in a wooden box carved out to serve as a fort; birthdays; bodies of water in which to swim, a lawn and a lake with swans for Nicholas, violent birds, and a slim black river with weeds and unctuous mud for Peter. Nicholas loaned Peter his book on Shakespeare's early tragedies, which he thought was written like a careful pastiche of English; Peter, in a public park, pointed out a bed of tall lupins and explained that they were his, that he had spotted, chosen, bred, and selected them until they constituted a fixed category, a cultivar.

Clarke did wonder if Nicholas had simply walked away from Lucia into the snow. He was used to leaving her, being sent away while his mother was going through her trials—to school, a couple of weeks in Piedmont with a cousin, a *Berghotel* once to walk himself out of worrying. But then he thought: I am the one who walks away. He began to sweat.

And Sarah Freeman, in her room, looked at her little case, set against the wall with its airline tags. She'd unpacked and let all those demons loose.

She couldn't bear the idea of kind, thoughtful Nicholas out in the cold woods, and Nicholas dead. He should not have died. He had nothing to do with it.

Then she had a thought of which she was half ashamed. If Nicholas killed himself, he still hadn't made any reparation. He hadn't, even now, suffered as she did. So he was not entitled to eclipse her story and her pain or, worse yet, annex it and insist on being mourned.

Finally, like the others, she slept in the shallows. She did dream, but it seemed like what she could remember of another dream: that she was in a rich, fine house with a great open aquarium as one whole wall, with weeds and a reef. She sat and watched the fish, in her dream, all turning at once, all blue, green, and gray, all flickering and shimmering: not clown fish, lionfish, sergeants, and exotic parrots, but plain, shining herring.

Lucia had Nicholas's letter. She thought of not opening it at all: making it a dead letter. She opened it with her fingers, which she hardly ever did; there was a perfectly good silver blade on her desk.

She looked at the torn envelope for a moment. She liked the roughness of the edges. This was not an ordinary letter, which she would pull directly from a neatly cut envelope. This was something particular, and not safe.

Her fingers were not swollen or broken, but they were not quick anymore. So in taking out the letter, she tore the envelope down its seams. She let it fall to the floor.

And she read the two sides of cream notepaper, written neatly, as though he'd thought long and hard and made several copies until he had the fairest fair copy of them all.

She set the letter on her desk.

So he couldn't bear it. So he couldn't live with it all. So he couldn't thank her for having known and borne all there was to know, and lived with it, too. He seemed to think he'd protected Helen, but he didn't think that she, too, had protected him.

There was nothing proven. The charges had been dropped.

They thought Berlin was a city, operating like a city, when really it was all of it a kind of underworld, the parts any sensible citizen would avoid, if she could. People went around with soot on their faces like robbers, and gas masks, and it wasn't enough just to be who you were; nobody could see. Everybody needed protection. Somebody important had to know your name and your fate, and to care. And even then, you worried. Ambassadors worried. Ministers at the Swiss embassy worried. You could die tomorrow and yet you still had to act as though the world made some kind of sense.

She picked up the phone to call Helen. Nicholas had saved her from the story; Lucia would make her hear it all.

But then, what story was she to tell? There had never been any evidence against her, none that made the slightest sense, how could there be? There was envy and there was spite. Who was she, a foreigner, to turn up with beautiful things? Who was this newcomer who wouldn't be provincial, wouldn't dress down and keep quiet and go home? Somehow it was fine for the banks to be legalistic, to demand death certificates for people from the camps, and account numbers and proper papers before they'd even think of parting with what the dead clearly owned; but if she was left with other people's property, if other people could no longer claim it, she was somehow a thief.

She had nothing to confess.

And those terrible others, who didn't care at all. She remembered how disgusted she had been with the friend from the studio who said it was odd to see Germans wandering around with sacks in their hands, like you used to see the Jews.

As for Helen, she was desperate for occupation, anything that would stop her seeing her father's body all bright with frost, or save her from circling the issue of what it could possibly mean to bring such an ancient woman to justice. Lucia couldn't be deprived of goods, life, freedom; she had such a short lease on any of them.

So Helen went immediately to sort out Nicholas's possessions, to turn the house and his memory into a dead estate. She went like a detective, or a pathologist, someone for whom the papers were all evidence: the file cabinets of letters on paper with curious seals, black-bound notebooks, conference agendas, offprints, postcards with the names of books, sometimes proofs, sometimes manuscripts rolling up under the pressure of the rubber bands at their waists.

She sorted as best she could: the ones that would be part of the Müller-Rossi gift to some university library, the ones that were clearly private, the ones that a biographer would need if ever her father had a biographer.

He wouldn't, of course, unless there was some polite notice in an academic quarterly. He would end up dusty as those papers. A thousand memories of kindness weren't enough to keep him alive, although the shadow of a crime might give him a certain notoriety.

She organized books by size and not by subject, and she slammed them into packers' boxes for someone else to use. It was like an autopsy of the mind, this process: or something geologic, layer by layer of old thought and knowledge now made orderly and put away.

She heard the geese complaining in the snow.

She went into the kitchen to make coffee. There was an over-serious espresso machine, one with a handle to pull and a tendency to shower the room with hot grounds, and she left it well alone. She made coffee in a pot.

It was the snow that made for quiet. The house was never noisy; but in summer there was not this sense of stilled life. She longed for spring.

She sat down at the kitchen table.

She thought that Nicholas was not supposed to die. He was only supposed to know, and that was supposed to change things. His death was unreasonable.

The phone rang.

For a minimal second, she remembered calling the house from outside the house. She'd pick up the phone; she'd hear her own voice, nervous, sheepish.

Everyone knew Nicholas was dead. His death led to obituaries, and comments on Alpine danger, and a little bit of tabloid sensation since he had been naked.

The phone still cut up the quiet, three separate tones: from kitchen, living room, and bedroom.

She put the white mug down on a marble surface, hard. The cup held, and then cracked, and the last of the coffee pooled out onto red-white stone.

She'd have to clean it now. She ought to answer the phone.

She reached for the phone and it slipped out of her hands, hanging from the wall. She heard a voice saying: "Professor Müller-Rossi? Doctor? Professor?"

She got hold of the receiver. "Yes," she said.

The voice at the other end was secretarial and peevish. "Will you please tell Professor Müller-Rossi that the seminar has been rescheduled—"

She was the one who killed Nicholas.

She put the phone down on the corncrake voice, blotted up the coffee with a paper towel, and went back to the papers. She was hoping for a pardon on a spare sheet of A4, some explanation that would take away the knowledge that she had caused her father to die.

She started laughing at the notion: causing someone to die. It sounded like a subclause of a fine, gothic contract, a euphemism, something you want to stop someone doing, but don't dare suggest they might ever try. She was also guiltily aware that she was denying her father his own decisions.

It was as cold as the day he died. She wondered how he could be sure enough to walk into that wood in the cold. He must have meant it as a statement: to Lucia, when all else failed. He was too good to bear the information. But how could he derive such an instinct for good from Lucia when it was she herself, all his childhood, who had been wrong?

For the first time, and in thinking about a suicide, it crossed her mind that there might be such a thing as innate good.

It must have been the quiet.

The phone rang again. She ignored it. She thought it might be some other secretary or a salesman.

She thought she heard a car on the road, heard it stop, a door close quietly. Then it was as though the house door opened, a cold shaft of air, something moving in the hallway: a coat put on the side, perhaps.

She stood staring out of the window. She didn't want to see an intruder. She thought it might be a cleaning lady, but Nicholas did not have one, or else a neighbor curious about the lights. It might be something worse.

Her mind was full of ghosts, cold ghosts.

She felt hands at her waist, warm and utterly familiar hands: Jeremy.

"I closed the gallery," he said. "I've come to help."

And the fit of his body made her smile.

The funeral Mass would be at Glaubenberg, at the small chapel there; and the burial in the graveyard of the small town down by the lake, where Nora already lay. Helen made the arrangements, organized a priest to go up the mountain from the small town by the lake, ordered the flowers, talked to the *Berghotel* by the pass about the lunch. Then she invited Sarah Freeman, and of course Peter Clarke. Then she went to see Lucia.

"I've made all the arrangements," she said.

Lucia seemed to take that for granted. She was not a woman to make uninteresting arrangements for herself.

"I have," Helen said, "invited Sarah Freeman. Because she was a friend of my father's." Even now she wondered if she should have said "of Nicholas's," if she was being too possessive and cutting Lucia away from her son.

Lucia said: "My dear."

Helen made a gesture like dusting her hands.

"You think that's appropriate?" Lucia said.

Helen said nothing.

"It is because of that woman," Lucia said, "that my son is dead." She, too, would not say "Nicholas." She, too, insisted that the man was hers.

Helen put a sheet of paper by her side, with the times for the burial and the Mass.

Lucia did not tolerate her silence. She seemed like a player again, an operatic lady who can rehearse a story and turn it into recitative, and expect to be heard with attention.

"There is so much I could tell you," she said. "If you were prepared to listen."

Helen examined her, the look security guards give a stranger. She knew this would come: the telling of stories after all these years. But she was not sure if Lucia would burden her with every terrible thing, would make sure that she, like Nicholas, lived in the shadow of this old woman's career; or if this was the moment when she would justify herself, try to make an accomplice out of Helen.

So Helen did not want to listen and could not leave.

"I never minded how separate Nicholas became," she said. "I could still see him. I could see you. I was an observer. I could help out. At least he wasn't absent from my life."

A long, ingrained habit of decorousness stopped her from going on like that; she had no way to show her loss. She was not the kind of woman you expect to show great feeling. She'd lived such a considered, businesslike life that such a show would seem like sudden madness. And yet it might seem madder to talk reasonably and politely about the fact that you are more than ninety and you will still outlive your child.

She had work to do. Out of calculation, she attacked.

"You gave him the court papers, I think? You were the one who brought all this up again."

But Helen was proof against that accusation; she'd made it too often to herself.

"It was," Lucia said, "disgraceful. I only helped people. I moved money out to Switzerland, and they could have it whenever they arrived in Zurich. I charged a commission. So do banks. But banks wouldn't do it for Jews. You had to find someone like me, who would take a risk, who knew people at the Swiss embassy. And I tried to protect all the beautiful things that people had. They weren't just objects, or names like Meissen and Gobelin, or things to trade. They were people's lives, the point of people's lives. I stored a Breughel once and it broke my heart that somebody would have to live apart from it.

"I did my best. And then when Berlin was falling apart, when the Russians were coming, when the Americans were bombing and bombing, I got out. It took some ingenuity, but it meant I had all that evidence of all those lives, safe in Switzerland. I was keeping the owners alive, in my way."

Helen said: "If you don't feel well enough to come to the funeral, everyone will understand."

"You will not talk to me like that," Lucia said. And then she subsided, smiled, almost simpered. "I loved Nicholas," she said.

And if that was true? Helen thought. What difference did it make if the woman was capable of the most perfect and selfless maternal love? Helen knew, from having Henry, there was gratification involved, too, and a life that filled the gaps in your life: a constant person.

"They kept questioning me when we got to Zurich," Lucia said. "You may as well know all this. Nicholas must have known it."

Helen wanted to defend her father, but Lucia was a lawyer working for her own life.

"They just keep on questioning me," she said. "Again and again. First it was money. How much did I take to Germany in 1932, and of course it was nothing much; how much did I bring out of Germany in 1944, and of course it was more. Then all the customs people, and the people who had to track down German goods in Switzerland, they turned up. I told them I had brought only household goods. But they keep coming to the apartment. I know these people, little people, they have no idea at all how people live. It's as though they were chanting under their breath 'But those are Meissen, those are pictures, that is tapestry, that is silver, that is old, that is lovely.' "

Helen heard the change to the present tense, but she set it aside because Lucia was still lucid, fluent, loud.

"They spend whole days counting things in my apartment. Everything in my apartment. I can see it just makes them angry. They keep asking: Where does this come from? I'm like the art teacher. I'm always explaining. I tell them most of it is from Italy, because it is, you know, it's the goods I used to have when I was a child, it's the house in Milan with the great copper bees, it's what I know. I have to explain who the Rossis are; can you imagine?" Helen wondered if she was acting, if this rush of words was considered rather than compulsive, if she was simply trying to make sure nobody could spoil her story. "I do buy things as well, I buy from my partner in the shop, the name over the door. And they go to the damned bank and the bank tells them I'm overdrawn and I never had the money to buy anything. So they say. And they talk about Swiss secrecy."

It was vivid to her, obviously; but Helen could not quite tell if it was vivid like yesterday, or vivid like this very moment.

"You know they went to Müller. Such a proper man, such an orderly man. He kept an inventory of every little thing we owned when we were in love, and he gave it to the authorities.

"I really don't know what to do. I have Nicholas, of course, I have to care for him. He has to go to a good school. I can't open my own little shop, it's always under somebody else's name. I make some money but it's simply not enough. Not enough. I am poor. I can't be poor. I have no talent for being poor."

The present tense, the present threat.

"The divorce doesn't help. Müller hinted at all kinds of things, and the court seemed to care about them, too; I truly believe they wanted to call me a 'loose woman.' " She stood up. "This is such a small town, this is such a clean country.

"They keep asking for proof." She was not addressing Helen in particular. She seemed, so the odd gentleness in the voice, the deferential swoop of the body, suggested, to be addressing someone of influence. "They say I sold goods from the Italian embassy in Berlin. But the Italian ambassador himself gave me those things to sell. Am I supposed to call him a liar?

"I did tell them that I bought some of the goods. But what else could I say? They seemed to think Berlin was like Zurich: an orderly place.

"It's supposed to be safe here. Everyone comes here to be safe. I want to be safe. But I'm an Italian woman, with a child, alone in Switzerland. The Swiss have their doubts about the Italians, you know. They have doubts about foreigners. They want to keep all their secrets."

Helen said: "The funeral is tomorrow." She wanted to see if the word "funeral" would shock Lucia back from this historic present.

Lucia said: "And then these people called Bernstein started claiming some quite nice Meissen plates they said they'd left with me: gold-bronze on white, I remember. They wouldn't go away. They kept insisting. And I was just an Italian woman, with a child, alone in Switzerland, when the Swiss were looking out for all the fake Swiss to throw out.

"So I gave them money. They could never have brought a case into court, they didn't have papers or anything. The Swiss wouldn't touch anything that happened in Germany. They didn't have the law on their side, and the plates were mine, now, but I had to give them money. It was," she said, "outrageous."

So now it was memory again, not the pressing reality. It seemed to slip back and forth in Lucia's mind. She might have found it all easier if she had been some kind of believer, with a grand idea to defend instead of this catalogue of little actions, each one subject to being picked open by the law. She didn't have a life; she had details, and she couldn't lose even one of them.

"They're going to auction my property," she said. "They're going to sell everything I have. If they can find a way. I think they'd break the law to do it. I can't use any of my bank accounts, all blocked, even the ones at Müller's bank. I have no business. I have no money. It's the middle of term and now I have to go to Nicholas at school and take him away because there isn't the money to pay the fees. Taking him away from his friends, from his books. From his life."

Then, abruptly, she was back on the day before a funeral, back remembering: "Sometimes," she said, "I think that's why he was so lonely later on: they made me cut him off."

She seemed to realize that something was odd about her telling of the story, because now she fussed for sympathy, for some warm reaction from Helen in particular.

"My health suffered. I told the court that. I had creditors at the door. Even my lawyer walked out on me because he said my stories didn't add up. Then he said there were rumors he was having an affair with me." She snorted. "You see how they thought of me? They couldn't even be honest about wanting me.

"Besides," and now she was singing her case, "other people did things. They didn't do such constructive things.

"I was never close enough to tell Nicholas the whole story," she said, "like this. I didn't want to burden him. I didn't want him to turn against the money that was buying his degrees and his comfort." She was testing Helen with her eyes. "If I'd been alone, I could have saved myself without all the dealing. I'm sure of that. But with Nicholas, I had no choice."

She was shivering a little; Helen put a shawl around her shoulders. "I see their faces," Lucia said. "Sometimes. So full of hate and suspicion. I see Eva, who got fat in America. I see Richard, who said I was the immediate cause of his mother's death. I see them all lining up to take advantage. I was sick, I was out of business, I was exhausted. These wretched people in the clearinghouse, who were supposed to go after all the Nazi property in Switzerland, came after me instead. But they didn't have the papers. And even then, they didn't acquit me. They just let me go and they never mentioned the case again."

The trade respected Lucia too much to call and offer her, say, a fine piece of red Böttger stoneware on such a difficult day.

The staff couldn't find things to say to her. In their eyes, the son was old enough to die, and the mother too old to mourn him. They left her in the warm golden light at the front of the shop, until the car came at ten. And then one girl offered to close down the shop out of respect; and Lucia asked why she imagined that might be necessary or appropriate. The girl stood back.

"This is a business," Lucia said.

She was alone on her way to the funeral. The Turk, driving neatly, did not count.

She looked at gray-green landscapes passing fast: at neatness, cleanness, precision, and squared corners. I'm guilty of not settling for all this, she thought. I don't settle. I've always dealt in glamorous, lovely things. She saw immaculate green, some snow, clear roads of houses hunkering down, the gilded onion dome on the church, the brilliant white of the church walls, all through the smoked glass of the car windows.

She was going to see Sarah Lindemann again. Like old times, like old and present times. She rehearsed her repertoire of polite, minimal gestures, little statements. She thought there would be no disruption of the moment, out of respect for Nicholas, and perhaps a little respect for her as a bereaved mother, too.

The shop must stay open, she thought; that was obvious. The business had nothing to do with her personal story, facts, or feelings. She had insisted on that for fifty years.

She must not be angry with Sarah Lindemann, she told herself. Poor Sarah had come too late. Sarah was the brown mouse in the corner, her hands always passing one over the other, a spineless, lifeless little thing. Max Lindemann always puffed up when Lucia came to visit; without her, he was a deflated thing. And Sarah never went out.

Lucia kept her talent for resentment through all her cushioned, organized life. She revived it easily. She couldn't trust her family, never could. She was ominously quick and clever and visible for a grandmother, and they wanted to find the fault in her so they could be kind to her and make her ordinary. They loved Sarah because of her accusations, not in spite of them.

Perhaps Sarah Lindemann wouldn't come. Perhaps she didn't like Christian funerals.

All the others, the family, the friends, the older colleagues from a long working life, had gathered by the small chapel in the graveyard, had left their cards of condolence in the stone bowl, had gone in processions of one past the coffin on the cart and seen the face of Nicholas Müller-Rossi for the last time. The cold light shone off the white flowers matted on the coffin: autumnal chrysanthemums, asters in wreaths.

And once they had done what was always done, they were left waiting for Lucia. Their love for Nicholas, their memories of tutorials, dinners, afternoons on mountains, their desire to remember his kindness, goodness, cleverness, were all vitiated by this nervous anticipation: of a single old woman, who was determined to arrive very exactly on time.

Sarah Freeman stood by Peter Clarke. She had thought she was ready for this moment: she now knew she was not. Lucia would be close to her, close enough to touch, to hit. Lucia might speak; she would speak back.

It was eleven o'clock, precisely.

Sarah thought she must not take away their moment of saying good-bye. But it was as though Helen was offering her this moment, as a sacrifice, some kind of recompense. You can do that to gods, Sarah thought, but not to old ladies. We don't know how to take such gifts.

Lucia stepped out of her car. Helen thought to go forward and help the old woman. But Lucia did not want help, did not need it, would not accept it; and did not deserve it. All these things went through Helen's mind. She held gratefully to Jeremy's hand, the two of them standing so close the others could hardly see that particular contact, skin to skin.

Lucia walked without self-consciousness. She was in black, and veiled discreetly: another mourner in the crowd. But she knew very well that nobody could take their eyes from her.

Sarah Freeman saw her as she might see the remains of a story: something picturesque and old. Then she remembered everything in a second, a roar in the ears and the eyes and the mind. She tasted a Berlin street on the wind: the horses, the wood fumes, the coal fires.

The priest came forward. "Frau Müller-Rossi," he said.

Helen waited to see who would answer: the Lucia with the shop still open on Bahnhofstrasse, or the one who was beginning to live in her history. This old woman in black, almost stately on her small feet, might be either one.

She only bowed her head and took her place, a mother mourning for her son.

Sarah turned away a little and followed the cart by Peter Clarke's side to the black ditch cut between the older graves.

Lucia went first, but alone. She was the first to asperge the grave with holy water, the first to throw her bundle of white flowers into the hole. She watched the workmen lower the remains of Nicholas into the place which had been prepared, five years earlier, for his wife, Nora.

She didn't cry. She was kept charged by the anger in the other mourners.

She crossed herself twice. She did not do it out of respect; she wanted protection against all the dead.

She had an impression of the others around the grave; she chose not to look too carefully. Their faces were solemn and white, coats dark, their talk very low but still echoing across the odd acoustics of the snow. They stood as a block, which made her think of them as a conspiracy.

But the priest was very gentle with her age and her loss. He went with her, in the car, up to the mountain chapel for the Mass.

Behind her, on the long way up the mountain, Jeremy drove Helen and Sarah and Peter, all of them anxious in their ways, Sarah that she was going to a remote place with only a few people and would now, surely, have to talk to Lucia; Peter Clarke that he would not know how to protect Sarah and make it all end right; Helen, in a vein of melodrama that was most unusual, thinking that her father had died to shout out from the dead about Lucia's crimes, and nobody at all was listening.

Lucia and the priest arrived first. The chapel was tiny, a whitened box with a high reredos at one end, some pale and solid wood pews, some stained glass in small windows. There was a door to one side of the altar leading to a sacristy; the priest left her alone.

Lucia turned around. Against the far wall, where the door opened onto the road, there were a hundred bright and tiny colored images on board. Here, a cow who was cured, white and black; here, a woman who came through childbirth alive; all saved by prayer and recorded in paint. She used to delight in such portable beauty.

She tried to compose herself for the Mass. It would be in German. She was not in a state of grace, she could hardly take Communion; she remembered all that.

"Lord in your mercy, hear our prayer. We pray to the Lord, Lord, hear our prayer." But she heard it in Latin in her mind.

She didn't understand why the chapel should seem so much more intimate than the crowd around the grave, why she should be suddenly afraid. It had nothing to do with sin; this was a place for absolution. It was not the judgment of others, because she had already faced that down, and there was little or nothing Sarah Freeman could do to her now. As for God, she was not in the habit of thinking about abstract nouns.

But she remembered a phrase from the Mass: "Dying, you destroyed our death."

She could not go on forever. She couldn't do it now.

Sarah said: "I'm not the perfect victim. I shouldn't be the one. I can't confront her at a time like this."

"You have to explain," Jeremy said.

"It ought to be someone else," Sarah said. "There are so many others."

"We're going to celebrate Nicholas," Peter Clarke said, quietly.

Helen was surprised at the certainty in his voice, the authority of a believer of some kind.

They walked up the steps of the little chapel, and pushed open the double door.

Peripheral vision goes with age, Lucia knew that very well indeed, and yet now she sensed someone coming up behind her. She thought it would be Nicholas. Nicholas would give her an explanation for this bizarre rumor of his death. He would be the orderly, sensible, professorial Nicholas, and not this romantic suicide who walked into the snows. He wouldn't be at all judgmental. Everything would go on as before, and she would be allowed to continue until death, which could not be so very long delayed, as long as she maintained the perfect front. She would stay sealed in this hermetic privacy that she had endured so long.

For the moment, Lucia made herself stand as straight as old bones, properly maintained, allow. She would not give the slightest advantage to this Sarah Freeman. She would hold the space of the chapel as her territory.

She turned. She had to turn: she had to know.

She saw Sarah Freeman dip and make the sign of the cross.

She stared. She had meant to seem uninterested in the woman and her doings; but this was entirely unexpected. Perhaps the crusader had compromised just a little, somewhere along the road. Perhaps she had just seen weakness.

She straightened up.

Sarah Freeman took her time over the uneven floor stones.

There was no music in the small chapel, no sound from the sacristy, and as yet there was nobody else for the service. A bit of birdsong sparkled outside. Nothing now could save the two women from meeting.

So Lucia, to keep her advantage, stepped to the end of the row of pews. "Frau Lindemann," she said, thinking to honor her. "Sarah."

Sarah smiled. Lucia was infuriated.

"Sarah Freeman," Lucia said.

Sarah sat down in a pew, arranged her skirt.

Lucia wanted her to say something. Anything she said might somehow go wrong, be spoiled, be equivocal. It would help tell Lucia what she must do.

Helen and Jeremy stood at the back. Clarke stood close to Sarah, but on the side. The quiet weighed on them all.

Lucia said: "I didn't have a choice, Frau Lindemann."

Sarah looked interested, but as though she thought Lucia could do better.

"I had no choice," Lucia said. "And the table is yours, if you want it now."

Sarah's silence was perfectly composed.

Lucia was shouting now. "I had no choice," she said. "It was Berlin. The Gestapo. The—"

Sarah stood. "I know you had a choice," she said.

She seemed a proper grandmotherly figure now, small and quiet and patient: someone intervening in a meeting, being reasonable.

"I know," Sarah said, "because even I had a choice."

Lucia stared at her.

"I didn't have to be a Jew," she said. "I didn't have to live in the Jewish houses or eat Jewish rations or go away to do hard labor until I could be murdered. I didn't have to live one whole year in a wooden shed, with a boy who atrophied alongside me. I made a choice."

Lucia did not have to say that she did not understand. Her eyes were shocked open.

"The Nazis had a calculus of race. I had only one great-grandmother who was Jewish. But I had Max Lindemann and I would not leave him."

Lucia had the doubts of any habitual mistress about the loyalty of wives, but she knew she had to be quiet.

"My race was an administrative mistake," Sarah said. "A clerk could have corrected it, would have been happy to correct it. Would have apologized, I expect."

And then Lucia ran out of her defenses. She said, very loudly although she had not meant to shout: "I had no choice."

Sarah Freeman was on her knees for a moment, quite composed. The doors flew open on the next worshippers. The priest came in hurriedly.

Lucia sat through the service. She did not go to her knees, or rise for the responses, or go forward for Communion. She watched Sarah Freeman do all that.

And then she ordered her car at once. She thought the others might have a free, open day, but she had work to do.

Peter Clarke had always loved walking. Each mile was a purpose in itself; he didn't need to imagine anything longer or grander. Walking gave a rhythm to his life. He was glad, relieved as well, to use his body again and feel the blood come back to limbs which had a healthy sense of looseness.

He was far above the others now as they stood, heads bowed. Everything was quiet, the air cool and damp, the cold white of the enclosing mountains beginning to warm with a little faint pink from the falling sun. It would be time to go back soon.

But for the moment he stood in the smell of woods and listened hard. He heard nothing discordant. There was not even the echo of a war. He had not left things undone, he thought, not this time.

He hung on the great comfort of silence. He knew that he must be very close to coming home.

Behind him, Sarah had run out of breath and stopped to sit on a dry wood trough. She pretended to care very much about the view.

"There are so many others," she said to Helen, "who ought to be here, who ought to have spoken against Lucia. And it had to be me. And I was not even a proper Jew in the Nazis' terms, which were all about blood and race. I do have a great-grandmother who was Jewish, although she was so much determined to be German I doubt if she would have told you that. I'm not even a '*Mischling* of the first degree,' as they used to say."

She frowned. "It was all absurd, of course. That was why it was so powerful; you couldn't test it against reality. It was arbitrary, too, not everything worked. They used to collect the ration cards for everyone in the Jewish houses, all at once. People liked to have Aryan cards; there was less trouble buying things. And eating. But my card came, and it was stamped with a 'J' and I didn't complain."

"Why wouldn't you?" Helen said.

Sarah remembered for a moment the evenings, around eight, after curfew, sitting with Max in their single room, wanting a book they had been forbidden, wanting to be out, wanting to eat some Aryan vegetable like asparagus.

"I have to tell you," she said, "that I married Max for love. I just didn't go on loving him. It happens. But it isn't supposed to happen in a war, in a nightmare. I know that.

"I'd much rather tell you almost anything else. I always used to remember the order in which things happened. When we were told we couldn't drive for fun, then we couldn't drive, then we couldn't sit down on a tram. No cigarettes. No clothing coupons. Our books checked and edited and burned. The move from the apartment to a house we had to share, then we had to scrap and negotiate to keep even our two rooms. The new taxes. I learned it all like a litany so I could always recite it in perfect order.

"And this," she said, "is easier to remember than Max."

She put out her hand to Helen, asking something: a share in her certainty, perhaps. "I should have saved his typewriter," she said.

"They took away typewriters after a while. But he was writing his story. So many people were writing their stories. They wanted to live on paper, to have a record of what they'd been and who they were and we all knew the only record would be the taxes and confiscations and—whatever was going to happen afterward, when we didn't have enough life left to live."

She saw Jeremy's sympathy, which he was subtle enough not to pantomime. She wondered, being with these practical people busy about a new world, if there was any more point in telling the stories or if she was damned to sainthood in perpetuity: everything particular about her erased because she had suffered, nothing but a survivor. Then she thought: But I can go on trying.

"We were always together in a single room," she said. "We had a kind of truce. You can have a truce in a war, so why not in a marriage? I was always loyal. He was always there.

"How could I leave him? How could I walk away? I was meant to love him.

"No cigarettes, no movies, shopping at fixed hours in fixed places for a few of the things that everyone else could have; all that. You can't imagine how life shut down around us, until the simplest things were part of the prison. And we never brazened it out, as the younger men often did, just went walking, just bought tickets to a show; we had known what it was to be citizens, you see. They never did."

She closed her eyes for a moment, but when she opened them again, she was still among the mountains, still dressed in black, still looking down on a stream full of winter water.

"We applied for thread. We applied for trousers. I had to apply three times, beg in the end, so Max could be given new carpet slippers. I owed him that much."

She had begun to rock a little.

"People were taken, people were accused, people vanished. Food short. Turnips and lettuce. Medicine was impossible. There were people sick, people we knew, and Max could do nothing, nothing at all, except that sometimes a diagnosis comforted them—that it wasn't even worse than they thought. And they kept us moving."

Jeremy said: "I thank God you survived."

"I don't," Sarah said. "Not every day."

He didn't want to press her, but he did want to know.

"The damned card came. I could have refused it, but I took it. You know why? Because I wanted to suffer with Max if I couldn't love him anymore. I thought it was the least I could do. I didn't want the shame of simply going off. I certainly wasn't going to make a new life while he was losing his. I couldn't just make the officials check my record and go away, maybe marry some blond and breed some boys for the fatherland.

"I stayed with my life and with my husband. I chose. In the nature of things, a bureaucracy likes everything to be consistent. So all my cards now carried the letter 'J.' "

She said: "The other people in the house didn't know I had a choice to make. But Max never questioned me, and he knew. He never said he was grateful."

She wondered for a moment if Max could hear her, nagging him after sixty years.

"I did not make the right choice," she said. "If I'd refused the card, you see, I could have saved Max. Other gentile wives did that. They fought for their men. There were all those women who went down to Rosenstrasse in 1943, when their men were arrested, and just would not go away until they were free. The Gestapo couldn't fight a street full of furious women. And there were other men who got through the war somehow because they were married to gentiles."

Sarah's whole body ached with memory, like broken bones.

"But I couldn't," she said. "And because of that Max died.

"I played patience all day," she said. "I didn't read or talk. I turned those cards and shuffled them and turned them over again. That's what happens. First you die, and then you're just bored."

Driving back to Zurich, Helen saw things because her eyes were not entirely trustworthy.

The pile of ration cards in their odd colors. The ones marked with a "J." Waiting on a hall table, perhaps, to be collected by each household from each room. A matter of routine, because the notion of marking people out and cutting them out of the world had become routine.

The cards that Sarah shuffled, day by day, so she had occupation, something to hold while her mind turned over and over the same incidents, moments, facts.

A fancy: that Sarah turned up the Queen of Spades.

When Sarah and Peter Clarke had gone, she took Jeremy's hand and they went to bed to remember, as quickly as they could, how much their bodies knew and loved each other. The rest, they could settle later.

For their last night in Zurich, Jeremy arranged tickets for the opera, and sent Sarah Freeman and Peter Clarke off to be together without having to talk too much. Helen loved his blunt kind of thoughtfulness.

There was in the Opera House the usual faint smell of good wool, good skin, good perfume everywhere, the unostentatious ether that money lets loose in the air. When one woman was on crutches, a man's face was bone-thin, it was shocking in a whole house full of such well-being.

Clarke saw Lucia Müller-Rossi.

He wondered how well Sarah could see her without the glasses she would wear for the performance, and he held her elbow tightly, and Sarah felt the new pressure.

She looked at him, but she did not ask.

"Look," Clarke said. "Over there."

Sarah held fiercely to her small, shining bag.

They could see only Lucia's head, sometimes the crowd parting as she sailed through them under authority: as the doyenne, as the grande dame of her business, the one with the shop that tourists passed with a sense of awe at all the money in the world, and Zurich in particular.

She was alone, not even an escort of convenience, Sarah saw. But her hair was the red of a wine with light coming through it, and she was in elegant black.

"I remember now," Sarah said.

Nobody spoke to Lucia. Nobody cut her, but nobody acknowledged her, either, except by making room for her progress up the stairs to the parterre, and by maintaining those faint smiles they were all at once directing somewhere else.

Clarke wanted to say that he was shocked. The death of Lucia's only son was known in the papers: distinguished scholar, accidental death. In Peter Clarke's world, people would speculate, hesitate, make up a story and hold on to it; they would be curious. They would read the obituary several times to work out its true meaning. They would want to commiserate and sympathize. But here, they spared her any embarrassment, or any sentiment at all. Each frock and shawl, each smart suit, each veil of perfume, insulated them carefully from the possibility that she might in public show any pain or loss.

"Nicholas used to bring her here," Clarke said. "Helen told me."

Lucia allowed herself to be seen, head up, back straight.

She must have worked out the seats long ago: not the public spectacle of a box by the stage, but the center of the parterre, with a view down on the crowd in the stalls and the protection of the balcony overhanging her head, and the sense of being properly private but among friends.

On the eighth step, going up, she tripped a little. She stopped.

The people around, even the older people, the ones who should have understood, drew in their breath very slightly. She had broken the rule of invisibility. They might now be obliged to steady her, encourage her, touch her, and help her.

Lucia continued. But the memory of her little slip seemed to stay on the stairs like a shadow.

At the shank end of the evening, when her housekeeper had gone away, Lucia sat very still on the edge of her neat bed.

Age had immunized her against the thought of loss; she was not prepared for the real thing. Besides, this death was a gesture, a slogan. It was vulgar in intent, and terrible in fact; and it was meant to insult her, not move her.

She was rehearsed in every other move of all her life, but not this one.

Now it was done, she did not know how she had endured the hour's drive into the mountains, the walk in the village where Nicholas had chosen to live, the minutes at the graveside in her nice dark coat. She knew the techniques that she used to defend herself: the quiet, the watchfulness, waiting for people to come to her. But she also knew, as she stood there, that this time she was allowed nothing else. She was obliged to be an old woman; all strong feeling was improper and not possible at her great age.

She could, of course, have chosen. She knew that. She simply could not bear to know it. It disorganized her mind.

She wished Mr. Müller had been alive to hear the news. He would have had to cry.

She sat on the bed. She stared at the wall. Without her glasses, the wall became, as in a camera obscura, as flexible as a surface of water. It must be a wide expanse of water, she thought, but it was trapped, still water, with sometimes the tiny surface vortex of a fish gobbling air. It seemed not to be deep.

Her mind was emptying out, day by day, like the warehouse of a business that's starting to fail.

There had been seven messages on the answering machine that Sunday: "Mother, I must talk to you." Seven times she'd failed to pick up the phone, even to say she couldn't talk just then. She resented thinking that the number seven somehow mattered.

But in memory, around the edges of the water, there were tall and brilliant yellow flowers. She didn't know their names. Some of them were dense and stinking, some of them open and elegant. They grew up out of rubble, and they masked the rotted undersides of skeletal, torched cars.

She remembered running by this stretch of water. She was running, and she was looking for someone or something. She looked up, and she saw, just beyond this new dark lake, the remains of the Reichstag.

There were three children out on the water. One of them was Nicholas.

When he froze alive, he was telling her to remember. She did remember. She did.

He would have been nine.

The children drifted in the silver light off the water, their raft bobbing if they tried very carefully and nervously to change position, water sluicing over the planks and wetting and staining their shoes. They had rigged up a shirt as a sail. Nicholas was shirtless in the sun.

She didn't want him to swim. There could be anything at all in the water, poison, explosives, knives, the dirt flooding back up out of the sewers. She wanted him to be covered and protected. She saw the raft and it seemed to be very far out at sea; but if it came back to shore, there were only these bright yellow weeds all clamoring with color and life, weeds that were hostile and swallowing the remains of a city, and the old cars rusted up and smoke stained, and the huge broken mass of the walls of the Reichstag.

She stood at the borders of the lake. She had to listen very hard to make sure she was not shouting still.

Then she shouted out loud in her room. She was afraid for Nicholas. She had to save him.

And after that, there was no more wall between memory and living.

ELEVEN

She's anonymous again: nobody more anonymous than a mother with a clinging child, with a brace of fat suitcases, in a cloth coat, in the steam and the sweat of all the women and the men busy about her on the platform. She slips into Berlin. The trains hiss and shout.

She will not be anonymous one minute longer. She swears it.

This must be Berlin, she thought. She was almost sure. It might again be Paris, she might be high on her father's shoulders, but she thought she was now in Berlin.

Nobody helps her get a taxi. Bad sign. But then she's a mother, just a young mother, and all that red hair doesn't count. She'll make it count later. In the taxi, she wonders which of her names she should keep, and in what order.

She has a reassuring bundle of little notes written on thick card, addresses and phone numbers and who wants what. The Herr Professor Doktor certainly knows people. She has someone to call out at the UFA movie studios and someone else in Himmler's private office. She has someone in the Italian embassy who says she might be able to give Italian lessons to German speakers, since her accent is perfect social Milan, and her family is a known family.

She winds down the taxi window. She breathes the city like other people breathe forests or the sea; soap, exhaust, and the lights go directly to her blood, brighten her eyes. When later she walks down the street and she takes in the glances of men she doesn't know, never will know, she loiters in their looks. She sits at a café table and everyone sitting around her is a character in the story she is starting.

But when she goes to the Italian embassy, she's just this Italian woman, married out to a Swiss, abandoned perhaps in Germany and struggling with a very young son in Berlin. She braces herself, makes herself shine, in case she faces the easy disrespect of some functionary in a bad suit.

She uses a side door. She waits a while. But the men look at her, the women look at her, and she cannot be ignored. Her looks are her introduction. And the invitations start to arrive, and she never quite knows who inspired them, but why should she care as long as the invitations keep coming?

One night: it's some air attaché in a tiny Topolino, Ciro's, champagne. She likes the fact of French champagne, not some *Sekt* or *spumante* or worse. She sits at a starched table, relying on bright eyes and fine legs, and it works: she is buoyed up constantly by looks. She likes the formality, the music, the wine.

She wants to dance, but public dancing is forbidden. Just when the wine shakes her loose, and the laughter rises all around her, and she truly wants to be up, wants the air attaché touching her, wants to sweep about to the music, she knows she has to hold herself down to her proper place. She fidgets on the neat, painted chair. All around her is a sea of bachelor faces, young men with ranks, missions, embassies, all bright and immaculate and shining, and she wants to be noticed by them all, to check the field, why not?

She is dancing, though. It must be San Martino's. She can't quite explain what San Martino's was. Or perhaps it is the Chilean embassy, they had fine dances.

She's dancing, dancing.

Nicholas is asleep when she gets home. She loves him so much. He's protecting her, in his way, although he may not even know it: by being asleep, by not upsetting her evening plans, he gives her a life. The two of them are true conspirators, breathing together.

Tonight: cocktails with the witty Swedes. Tomorrow: supper at Roma, because you don't need coupons for pasta and you can meet the Italian press corps, hear the latest. Then: the moments of absurd obligation, like the little party where she joins a row of Italian women, some chic, some resigned, none of them domestic, all knitting bootees and jumpers for Goering's new baby.

She teaches: how to sing a sentence properly, the use of *benzi* with the subjunctive, irregular plurals, and the different kinds of pasta. She likes these daily trips into the embassy, the sense of privilege stepping off the streets into a private, guarded enclave, footmen around, flowers in the corners, chandeliers of pink Venetian glass: of being where she ought to be, without any of the encumbrances of her own family and background. She looks at the paintings and sometimes wonders if she might have inherited them from someone, if things were different.

Old Mr. Goldstein, neighbor downstairs, at the door. He can't have a private phone anymore, he explains, and he does not find it comfortable using the public ones.

She's dreaming what she'll dream again in sixty more years: the scattered memories of nights at parties, bring your own bottle, of balls with an endless supply of blond, clean officers, the schemes to get to the theater when tickets were reserved for soldiers on leave. A show about a female pig, which Hitler much enjoyed; she didn't.

She sometimes takes something from the embassy to her new Jewish friends, the ones with whom she could really talk, who had nothing to think about except paintings, music, books, and the end of the world. She took jam, chocolate once, butter, toilet paper, a salami, and sometimes vegetables from the kitchen, and she felt like a heroine: a gracious person, charitable to the unfortunate who are forever moving from a small apartment to a smaller one, then into rooms in a Jews' House, leaving behind their domesticity and their peace.

This has to do with Max Lindemann, somehow. Max Lindemann isn't dead yet.

Lucia, the doctor said, would fret when she was awake, like a sleeper who is dreaming, cat's paws working away on the air. She had started to ask for the lipsticks she knew in Berlin, 1940, and a powder she used to like; and she didn't understand at all that she couldn't any longer have such things.

She believes what she's told, but on principle: because nothing is unbelievable anymore. Some officer tells her, over coffee at the embassy, how everyone used to think all the phones were tapped all the time ("and now," he says, "we know that's true") and wouldn't even talk close to a phone still down on the hook, just in case. "The Poles," he says, "used to keep a tea cozy over all their phones." She has to ask what a "tea cozy" is, and then she starts to laugh. "No, no," the officer says, but he is laughing, too. "It's perfectly true. Ask anyone."

She doesn't believe the war will go on. But Churchill becomes prime minister in London, and there is soon to be a new Italian ambassador in Berlin, and while she is out trying to buy a second jar of jam for April, which is only worth doing because it is not entirely legal, she believes in the war all at once. There will be no easy retreat, not to Switzerland, certainly not to Milan, not to any kind of normality. She has to live on the swings.

One of the embassy cleaners tries to talk to her. She doesn't much like this, doesn't encourage any notion that teacher and cleaner should be on equal terms, but the cleaner is boiling with a story. It has to do with being down by the old Jewish cemetery in Weissensee, and looking in through the gates and seeing children playing there: hide-and-seek around the marble mausoleums, firing finger guns around stones, running and shouting in a vast walled city of the dead. She could hear their voices echoing off all the great graveyard houses.

"They have no respect at all," the cleaner says. "Dirty Jews."

Lucia has nothing amusing to do that night. She sits with Nicholas until he goes to bed, and then, as she sits in the armchair by the tiled stove, she starts a kind of fever dream: Nicholas, playing in among the dead, dancing on a stone, pelting a friend with snow or water and writing in the dirt on monuments, pacing slowly in a street of tombs, ducking, looking side to side, waiting for an ambush that never comes.

She woke up, aware that she was remembering a dream about a dream. She was confused for a moment. She did not like confusion at all. She preferred the certainty of the ever-present past.

The embassy is fizzing with anticipation, but careful to maintain an indifferent facade, as though its ways were so settled that no new ambassador could possibly upset them. The new man gives his first reception. Lucia, in a city without women, is invited as a matter of course. She holds the invitation in her mind: and so she knows the date, May 22, 1940.

This ambassador is a solid man, not tall, not short, a muscular average, dressed in all the perpetual power of the Grand Fascist Council, so he feels no need to strut or preen unduly on his own account. She likes the fact that he can stand still.

A few days later, one of the military attachés takes her to the movies, to see a bit of rococo called *Hotel Sacher,* a long sugared memory of Hapsburg Vienna, of moustaches, uniforms, parades, and ballrooms. Both she and the military attaché hate the film. She half expects this particular attaché to make his move, but instead he mentions that the new ambassador would really like to meet Lucia.

"And his wife?"

"Probably not his wife."

"But he's not alone."

"You're alone," the attaché says. "That's the point."

Girls in the wet, hot garden by the lake; roses; great blue balls of aga-panthus; music out of speakers; a lawn full of skirts rising high like theater gauzes on long, bare dancers' legs; then the soft rain growing harder; then everyone turning on the wet grass, all aware they might slip any moment but nobody slipping, everyone fast, everyone graceful, everyone singing.

Men in uniform like maypoles, women dancing attendance around them. Uniforms crusted with gilt and brass, shining in the rain. The rain suddenly ferocious.

Lucia shouting: "We might as well swim!"

The girls in costumes, the men bare-chested, all running for the water. The rain spluttering on the lake.

The men conspiring without talking. The boats tied at the foot of the lawns. Everyone jumping aboard.

The racket, the smoke, the false-started engines. The boats roar-ing out onto the lake, cutting great white circles out of the waters, some of the women clinging now to the men just as the men had expected: the women exhilarated, alarmed, ecstatic at the rush of the air and the bucking, roaring motion of the boats; the men enchanted with their thoughtful risks.

There was some kind of memorial service that day: a marshal killed in an air crash over North Africa. Then, this "quiet swim," held in honor of Foreign Minister Ciano: a diplomatic afternoon full of pretty girls and music, at the Italian ambassador's house by the Wannsee.

And after the swimming and the boating, skin baked warm and dry by the sun, a drawing room in the ambassador's house with the curtains closed. Ciano is there, and a woman. The ambassador is there, and Lucia. Outside, it is still a bright, splashing afternoon, but the two couples turn together very closely, pressed together, as though it was the last half hour of the social morning in some night-club they all once knew.

A knock at the apartment door, gentle but repeated. A couple in their sixties, pleasant in appearance, the man almost military, the woman's hair solid as a helmet.

"Mr. Goldstein sent us," the man said.

The woman adds, quickly: "Your downstairs neighbor. You know."

They sit perfectly still in Lucia's living room, as though they didn't want to claim unneeded space.

"I don't quite know where to begin," the man says. "You know how things are. To be honest, we can't even know if we ought to trust you."

"Mr. Goldstein said you were a good person. He said you knew people. You're Italian, aren't you?"

"And Swiss," Lucia says.

"So you're not German? We're German. It doesn't seem to be doing us much good."

"The thing is," her husband says, "we have to make some kind of arrangement. We can't stay here waiting. Since you're Swiss, I suppose you're allowed to send things across the border, aren't you?"

"I suppose so."

"And you're Italian, too," the woman says. "I used to love Florence."

"There's some money, for visas," the man said. "And a few things that are worth something. So we have money if we manage to leave. We can't carry anything, of course, they'd take that from us."

"They'll take it soon, anyway," his wife says. "I didn't want to ask you, I know how difficult it must be, but Mr. Goldstein said you were a good person and we don't have time anymore."

"I can see what I can do—"

"If there was anything at all," the wife says. "Of course we'd make it worth your while."

"Some friends of ours put money with the Swiss embassy, and they sent it to Switzerland, and they collected some of it later."

Lucia says: "I have to think about it."

"Mr. Goldstein said you cared about music, and pictures," the man says, standing now like a soldier stands, precisely straight. "Sometimes I go outside and I wish I was blind."

His wife studies Lucia. "I'm sure Frau Müller-Rossi doesn't want to hear—"

"I understand," Lucia says, filling the word up with all the meaning her guests could need.

"We have some jewelry. It's nothing much, but there is one good diamond. There's gold: the wedding ring. We have some furniture, now we have to move again into a smaller place there's no point in keeping it. It's worth something. People still seem to want furniture, don't they, if it's old and it's French?"

"But I can't sell this. People would want to know where I got it."

The wife says: "You have such good friends."

So Mr. Goldstein must have noticed the long black cars that sometimes bring her home.

Through a car window: lake waters crowded as any city street, stuck with bare bodies, families and couples overlapping and entangling in the shining continuum. There is a slide wet with water, a mass of men around it. She can see a plain girl in a swimming cap on the slide, shoulders like a porter, arms thrown back and forward like a foursquare dancer, dazzled by the sun and the laughter, herself smiling wildly, not wanting ever to reach the water, wanting always to fly on all the shouts and cheers.

The love of a good ambassador involves the resentment, at the very least, of his wife. Lucia starts to feel very slightly under threat in the embassy, as you do when being buffeted by a theater crowd; uncomfortable, no need to look out for the knives just yet. So she starts to call on all those other names that the Herr Doktor Professor kept mentioning in his letters, in between the high-flown stuff about the nation's soul and future, and what he'd do to her between the bears in a corner of the Berlin Zoo.

She knows a man in the Ecuadorean embassy who is good for a passport, cash down, for people who might need one, and a counselor at the Swiss embassy who would help move money, and the Italians, when it comes to anything practical, are still downright deferential; but she needs German friends. She sits in a café on the Kurfürstendamm, lit by great white globes: coffee and a cake with the man from Himmler's office, nothing definite, a noncommittal start.

"He taught me, too," the man from Himmler's office says, meaning the Herr Doktor Professor. Lucia, just for a moment, imagines him being taught as she was.

"He's a remarkable man," Lucia says, because that seems safe.

They prattle a bit. The official, named Hans, says he is proud to work for such an honest servant of the Reich, a man whose ambition is to die poor. Lucia can't see the point of that, but she keeps quiet.

"Such an honest man," Hans insists. "He has laid out the exact vitamins and calories required for every person in a concentration camp. Unfortunately, it is not always possible to ensure the local people do as they're told. Some of them are not," and he pauses a moment, wondering if this could be counted as obscurely disloyal, "entirely honest," he says.

Lucia says: "No." Hans, she can tell, expects to be overheard.

"And he works all the time. Less than an hour for lunch, just soup and some fish. A quick supper, just one glass of red wine. Then he works until two or three in the morning."

"I'm lucky you could get away."

And she sings her own little aria: how much she loves Berlin, the excitement of it all, the sense of being at the heart of history; and she uses exactly that phrase.

Then she says: "Sometimes it's difficult being a foreigner."

"In what way?"

She doesn't have to say anything more. Even now, she knows she could make some general point, express polite and social regret at not herself being born German.

Instead, she says: "People ask the most extraordinary things. A couple came to me last week and asked me to help them get money out of Germany. I mean, I know I have foreign passports, but I would never think—"

"Jews, I suppose."

"Yes. Yes, I suppose they were."

"You have their names?"

She always remembers names: she was raised politely.

Mr. Goldstein is at the apartment door.

"I shouldn't have sent my friends," he says. "I didn't know what to do. You seem like a good person and you know everybody—"

"I had coffee today with one of Himmler's assistants." But she doesn't need to boast.

"You know everybody, Frau Müller-Rossi." He takes his hands out of his jacket pockets for a moment. "You know, I saw Herr Himmler once. I was in the street, outside a movie house, and he was there with his fat little wife. They had no bodyguard, no protection. They were going to see *Broadway Melody*."

"Everybody loves the movies."

"I used to," Mr. Goldstein says.

A small, sealed van arrives that day, and unloads a pendulum clock, some good Meissen plates, some gold rings, a silver coffee service which looks English, a few austere chairs, and an unexpected daybed which cries out for odalisques.

And now—time seemed to be rushing her—Mr. Goldstein is waiting at his door when she comes home. He's sorry, but there's no point in her doing anything now, because his friends have been taken away. They must have tried something foolish, because there was talk in the building about currency offenses, which are a hanging matter.

"I'll always be grateful," Mr. Goldstein says. He sighs. "Grateful for what you were going to do."

Lucia turns up the stairs, not wanting to seem hurried.

The violinist comes in daylight on Sunday, and leaves his violin. He says he can't use it anymore, and he can't bear the idea of it being broken for firewood. Perhaps Lucia would be very kind, perhaps she would keep it for him? He will play for her one day.

He doesn't have the right to call again, but he does. October, already cold, and he says he just wants to tell one other person, someone who isn't a Jew. He has to pack for a work detail: two socks, two shirts, two underpants, two wool blankets, one sweater, some bed linen. He has to sign over his bank account in return for his board and keep.

"It has to be hard labor," he says to Lucia. "Doesn't it?"

Then days pass, and she's on a tram. There are a half-dozen people with suitcases. She almost falls over a case that blocks the aisle. All the people with suitcases wear yellow stars.

On Levetzowstrasse, they all get off. They walk into the burned remains of the synagogue.

She hears a baby crying in a cardboard suitcase.

The violinist does not acknowledge Lucia. Probably he does not want to get her into trouble, or perhaps he is obscurely ashamed. She sees he is not a young man anymore.

She almost remembered, for a moment, what it was to remember.

Here's a nice puzzle, for which she has the mind: the perpetual present invaded by a sense of perspective that could only come from the past.

She knows, now, as she knew then, that so many people wanted to trust her. She knew about passports, even after America entered the war and there was no more hope in waiting for a U.S. quota number. She understood the preciousness of things, their market value and their emotional price. There was sometimes a misunderstanding— someone who came back to find their suitcases had been opened— but it was rare for people to come back.

She knew how much silver could be exported, what area of carpet, before the authorities wanted their share; and she was happy to cope with what could not be taken abroad. She was entirely help- ful in this.

She once saved a Jewish woman from deportation, and her repu- tation was burnished by the fact. One woman, who got out to Switzerland, sent money every month because she couldn't see how Lucia, civilized Lucia, could get by in Berlin.

She knew, too, how to shuffle money through the banks in coun- try towns, into her own accounts and out into the Swiss embassy; and then into Switzerland where, at a discount, its rightful owners would claim it, if they could. Gentiles, too, were interested; the most surprising people seemed to have the private kind of Swiss account.

Indeed, so many people trusted her that their trust became a practical problem.

She remembers all this: and then she can't stay remembering anymore. She's there.

Her skirt is dull and long, arms covered, and she has a head scarf: the uniform of a serious woman, a mother. She's in a stopped train, which does not move for hour after hour, but nobody dares to leave it in case the next is worse. There is nothing to be seen through the windows. People no longer try to keep themselves separate and respectable. They pile like cats or little dogs.

She is going back to Berlin. She thought she could throw herself on the mercy of holy women, that they were bound to help her great work of charity; for it could have been that, she thinks. It could have been that.

So she came out to the sandy lands just south of the city, to a new and practical convent, devoid of fine monastic touches, just walls for prayer. She has not made an appointment; she assumes the nuns will have mercy. She walks over the gravel drive as though she's crossing a church to light candles.

The porteress has a face that laughs, although she's a singularly skinny woman. A gun goes off somewhere close, Lucia startles, the porteress says it's just Father Gerhard out after squirrels. And her face laughs again, silently.

Lucia waits in a corridor. It could be a sanitarium, a cheap hotel, even a barracks, except for the black crucifixes on the wall.

Finally, the abbess sees her. Lucia's unannounced appearance is so odd that it requires the attention of someone senior. There is always the possibility of some kind of trap.

Yet Lucia hasn't thought this out. She doesn't think the nuns will be suspicious of the outside world. She expects them to accept. They're beyond the world, so they should be accomplices in the world without guilt.

The abbess is a formidable woman when she chooses to be still: a face of hard, durable virtue.

Lucia is a little girl, a flirt, a worthy mother, a citizen more troubled by her virtue than her sins, one after the other. The abbess stays still.

Lucia is saying that she has household goods that she needs to put into storage for friends, for Jewish friends, and perhaps the Mother Superior could help her?

The abbess says: "These are difficult times."

Lucia says she is trying to help these people, but she can no longer find the space.

The more Lucia talks, the more she feels obliged to work her arms and smile too much and sometimes mention a saint.

"I'm afraid," the abbess says, "you will have a long and uncomfortable journey back to Berlin."

She makes no argument against Lucia, does not justify the empty cellars that a new nunnery must have; she only offers a sandwich of cold pork for the journey back. And then she says: "People come here because they are pursued by their sins. It's not usual that someone comes here because they've done too much good." And Lucia doesn't know whether to read judgment on that alabaster face.

But on the train, she knows. She wonders what the nuns are up to, what they're hiding; they must be hiding something. They've forgotten all their Christian duty, their duty to her.

All this she seems to remember while she's still brushing off some sailor, some clerk, some weekend athlete who's breathing too close to her on the still unmoving, jam-packed train.

Oddly, she remembered the rest like a memory, although it happened after her visit to the convent. She knew if she couldn't beg space, she'd have to find it some other way, and, with her limited resources, best to fuck it out of someone. The ambassador had this odd little Dutch cottage out toward Potsdam; it was the house he didn't mention. There were cellars under the cottage. She was there with him once, went down into the storerooms with a candle, saw a whole empire of red brick caves just waiting for a purpose: her purpose.

She pleasured him in a corner with the candle flickering. He was happy to give her keys to the cellars.

She filled the first rooms with simple wood to screen off the rest because she knew the Gestapo liked their share of any prizes going, and she was not prepared to pay very much for their protection. But once through the first rooms, she had more than objects in her store; she had her childhood, her entitlement to gilt and marble and show. Sometimes, at the weekends, she'd go down to her storerooms and walk around with a flashlight, picking out a shine of glass here, a brass molding there, marble or silver or sometimes even gold. She felt protected by so many things.

She needs a new, official job. The ambassador's attentions are perfectly fine at teatime at Wannsee, sometimes in a booth at Horcher's restaurant, anywhere you care to name that is not the embassy, where his wife sees and hears and also imagines everything. Lucia needs to be able to come and go at the embassy, but not to work there every day.

The Herr Doktor Professor, in a letter of odd tenderness which for once made not a single pornographic suggestion, reminded her about UFA. "In wartime," he wrote sententiously, "the *Volk* must be amused."

UFA: her first day. She walks in through the studio gates with all the authority of a star because nobody knows she is nobody in particular, and she wants them all to think she will matter.

The second day is harder. She has a place assigned, an office and a rank. She's supposed to know where she's going, no need to stop and ask a passing man, and she has a job to do at a fixed time. It is nobody's business to recognize her or look after her.

She loves to get lost, when she can. She reckons if she doesn't matter, she won't be challenged. She slips inside hangars of gypsy frocks and hussars' coats and a whole stand of showgirls' headdresses, of spats and toe shoes and furs. There is dust on the more diaphanous costumes. Neglect is puritan, it seems. There are the remains of Africa in a corner. And fairy tales, imperial worlds, all organized by size of collar, waist, and foot.

She's challenged once. She apologizes and walks briskly on.

Armies pass her, peasants off giggling with airmen, dozens of Bohemians, a new species for Lucia, all tousled, wild, and paint-stained, all loafing until someone snaps: "Action!" Everyone is some-one else, like a factory for Carnival. In the hot spring sunshine, she passes streets and bridges in a world that stops the very moment it can no longer be seen by the whirring cameras which, around here, are God. She passes great bunkers and huge tanks full of water.

Nicholas knows something about this. He's decided they have live lions out at UFA, and a black man, and a model train. But she can't take her child to her work, however much he wants to be with her and wants to see the lions.

On a Sunday, he says: "You couldn't just stay here for the day? One day?"

"I have to work."

"A Sunday. All day."

"I have to do things."

"We could go sailing. You could bring your friends and I could bring my friends."

"We'll go out to dinner."

The maid Katya puts a huge dish of boiled potatoes onto the table, and a bowl of yogurt. Lucia says: "Is that all we have?"

Katya shrugs.

"I like it," Nicholas says. He wants to be reassuring. Or maybe he's gone over to Katya's side, because she's always available. "It's good."

"But you ought to have meat, and cheese, and pasta, and fish, and chocolate—"

"I don't like chocolate."

"But you do like chocolate."

"No," Nicholas says. He runs out of the room.

She frowns for a moment. She says to Katya: "I'll be out tonight."

Lucia on the hospital terrace, eyes open on something two meters away; but there was nothing there. Helen spoke her name, very quietly. Lucia pushed at the air. Helen said: "Lucia. It's me."

Lucia's eyes snapped open.

"It's me," Helen said. "I'm real."

She could read a clash on Lucia's face. She expected the hand to come out to test her.

But instead, Lucia reared up out of her chair, stood firm, and shouted: "You're real. What a wonder. You're real and you think it matters."

Helen stepped back. The nurses, by reflex, formed a cordon.

"What's so wonderful about what's real?" Lucia said, a little quieter now, but clipping out her words. "We got butter from coal. We got leather from fish skin. We got frocks out of wood pulp. You call those things real?" She reached out to cuff Helen, like a child who needs direction. It didn't seem to matter that she missed.

"The whole city was illusion. You saw it. All the open spaces, they built plywood streets like a movie set. You couldn't tell the difference from the air. They put netting over the avenues so they looked like parks. They turned the lampposts into fir trees. They filled the lakes up with scaffolding and tarpaulin and painted it all to look like houses.

"The bombers came and they had firemen ready, and their job was to start proper fires and keep them burning and burning. You know all this. You think real things would have saved your life?"

Helen knew she was talking, now, to Nicholas. She was softening her voice. She forgave him for whatever he had made her remember. And she sat down.

"You remember the advertisements," Lucia was saying. "There was one at the cinema with such pretty kangaroos, and a bull in a fine shiny smoking jacket and a cow, with horns shaped just like a lyre. I don't remember anything about what they were selling."

Helen wondered if Lucia noticed her reactions, and simply transposed them to Nicholas: and if Nicholas was a boy now, or a man, or a cold white carcass. She would react if it would help the old woman; she owed her a duty of kindness. But she was glad not to be recognized, glad that none of this had to do with Helen in particular. The distance made it bearable.

"The kangaroos were dancing," she said. "They looked rather *moderne*. Art Deco, I mean. I think they must have been selling shoes."

Lucia might be addressing the dead, but at least she knew she was dealing in memory.

"Me," Lucia said, "I knew about cartoons."

She composed herself. They could watch the process: the face controlled, the back straightened, the hands in positions that could be sustained.

"They really didn't want people to have things to miss. There was a war on, and they were all half pretending that civilian life was all just the same. The bombs came down and the cinemas needed—I don't know. Cute frogs and grasshoppers. Stories about silly geese. You couldn't film reality anymore. Then the Americans came into the war, and there was no more Walt Disney so they needed Wicked Huntsmen and Evil Queens and Handsome Aryan Princes.

"So they ordered the animators to Berlin, and they didn't have a choice, but when they arrived they turned out to be solitary and thoughtful and slow. That wouldn't do. There was a crisis, and the studio had to be seen to respond. So they built offices, allocated space, promoted executives who were supposed to animate the animators. And they hired unnecessary people, like me.

"I wrote scenarios. I went to an office, between Berlin and Potsdam, and sometimes I went out to the UFA studios at Babelsberg. They'd brought in some cartoonist from a newspaper, and I worked with him. Then we sent the stories off to Herr and Frau So-and-So who were making the films."

She smiled. "Herr and Frau So-and-So acknowledged receipt very politely, and filed the stuff. We got paid, and we got ignored."

Helen imagined Lucia, cigarettes burning out all around her, making jokes to distract all Germany from the dead people walking in its streets. That was not unimportant work.

She said: "It was a shock when I first saw one of our films. I remember it very well. They had these small screening rooms, hard leather chairs. Someone smoked a cigar, someone sitting at the back. So it's dark, and then there's a flicker of white light, and then the screen fills up with numbers and then. Well, then. They had a bee, an ordinary bee, that flew down out of the sky and through the flowers and the grass, and then past particular stems and particular blossoms. Very close, very real. Then the bee was circling this record player on the ground. Then the bee uses its sting as the gramophone needle."

Helen said: "Clever," not meaning it.

"Here's the bee, the record, the needle, and then there's the music. It was a song about the week being nothing without the weekend. It was swing." She looked ahead triumphantly. "Don't you see? Swing was illegal."

She could not sense reaction.

"It was illegal in Germany," she said. "The song kept going on and on about nature being a good thing, which was almost all right. Blood and soil and getting back to the land. But then it kept saying that a whole week serving the fatherland was no use at all without time off. And this was wartime, with production targets and women working. It was very nearly subversive."

Did Lucia any longer even need her audience? Perhaps it was a kindness for others to sit and listen, to license Lucia's unstoppable flow of memory.

She certainly wouldn't be interrupted. "You could see there were the remains of a picnic, and beside it a garter. A garter someone had lost. With a lucky clover growing through it. We were all so decent and proper, that was the official line. No good German girl ever lost a garter."

"I never saw that film," Helen said. She wondered if Nicholas had seen it.

"It was lost, after the war," Lucia said.

Helen thought, without saying it: Then how can we know it existed at all?

Around this time, she loses touch with Max Lindemann. A mutual friend says he's moved to Riga or one of those Baltic towns, but it's only a hint of a story, not even a rumor, produced for the sake of seeming to know and having something to say.

She takes Nicholas to the aquarium because he's bound to like that. It turns out he's been there before. She is a little annoyed, but she still loves to watch as he watches the turtles glide and turn in the water.

She sees Sarah Lindemann on the way home, who nods, but not in her direction, as though she doesn't like to do anything so definite anymore.

Lucia crosses the road.

"How's Max," she says, falling in alongside Frau Lindemann, who scuttles forward.

"Max isn't, I mean, isn't."

"You mean he's left Berlin?"

"It's very difficult. I shouldn't be seen talking to foreigners."

"But you and Max—"

Sarah Lindemann so much wants her not to be there, to leave her alone. "Max is so obstinate," she says, very softly, smiling at strangers, pretending interest in a window, "and so he thought it would be better—"

"You're alone?"

"It's better if you're not at home. They go away if you're not at home."

"But you're on your own?"

"Not exactly. There isn't room anymore to be on your own."

"He's well?"

"It's very hard to get soap. He just can't keep clean." She ducks and shakes her head as though she was talking to everyone else except this obvious foreign woman and her child.

"But he had such lovely clean hands," Lucia says. "Could you tell him from me—"

"That's all over. All over. Now let me get along."

She darts across the road, startling drivers, and leaves Lucia and Nicholas standing still on the sidewalk.

But then she telephones after dark, which means she must be staying with gentile friends who still have a legal phone.

"I went downstairs," she says, "and they've been already. Already. They've taken the nameplate down from Frau Bernstein's apartment."

"They do that," Lucia says.

"Lucia," says Frau Lindemann, and Lucia can hear the effort the words are costing, "I would be very grateful—"

"Yes?"

"If you could collect some things. Like the table Max wanted you to keep for us. Just some things that have come to matter."

"Of course," Lucia says. She has a talent for this: nothing in her answer smacks of the businesswoman.

"Some Meissen."

"How lovely."

"If you could keep it until things are better. Then I'll come for it."

"But this apartment might get bombed, too."

"I don't think the Gestapo will come so close to you."

"I wish I could get some things to Max—"

"Come for coffee, on the Ku-damm," Frau Lindemann says. "I'll pass by and you can come and talk to me."

And there, between the globe lights and the starched white tables, she gives Lucia the name of someone who might find Max and pass on a message. She also gives Lucia a little shopping bag, very tightly packed with paper and solid things.

"I'll bring the rest," Sarah Lindemann says.

"Thank you."

"They call them divers, you know," Sarah Lindemann says. "The ones who hide."

Lucia says: "I didn't know."

"I went down by the Bernsteins'. They were holding an auction. And you know," Sarah Lindemann says, "there were cups still on the table. They still had tea in them."

Helen came from the hospital with so many questions; she tested Sarah's tolerance again and again. Each sensible question dug out an appalling memory.

"But why did you tell her anything?" Helen said. "Why did you trust her?"

Sarah said: "It wasn't a question of trust."

"I don't understand."

"There wasn't anybody to trust. You did deals, that's all. Everybody did. Didn't anyone ever tell you about the special trains that ran from Belgium into France, with the ceilings hollowed out to smuggle cigarettes? Or the railway station at Prague, and the tens of thousands of dollars that were changed there every day? Or the money that went to the Ecuadorean embassy to get passports or—"

"You dealt with Lucia."

"There was nobody to deal with except one kind of thug or another. Some of them were in the government and some weren't. I sometimes think," and she carefully did not look at Helen directly, "you have too much respect for the Nazis. Their crimes were enormous. They were the first truly modern killers and thieves. They staged gigantic shows. But they were small-time criminals, all the same, a protection racket on a continental scale. They had no great vision, only clichés: searchlights and Teutonic giants and all that rubbish. Even the Holocaust was a failure of imagination. They couldn't imagine their new world for themselves, so they had to make it new by taking away some defining fact about the old world."

Helen said: "How could you phone her? How could you talk on the phone? They must have tapped phones."

"I suppose I already knew nothing would happen to Lucia," Sarah said.

All she can hear is dance music, but she doesn't hum along or step to the rhythm. She can hear dance music coming from every radio station; that's all there is. Wherever she turns, whenever she has the radio on, she knows there is morale in grave need of boosting.

Lucia, the old lady, knew there was something she did not want to know. She could not quite seize the order of things, and the connection between them, so she was always afraid there would quite suddenly be something she did not want to live again; and she would be living it. She would be behind this managed face, made immaculate with powder, and she would be living an intolerable thing.

She was suspicious of the ease with which she remembered UFA.

She's on the cafeteria line, edging forward, considering the list for the day: stonefish patties. She never did know what a stonefish was, but ground up and thinned out it is not at all a glorious dish. There is red cabbage, white cabbage, and potatoes. There is vanilla pudding, as always.

Someone she half knew, an assistant director's assistant who'd seen her eating here, says: "I've got something to show you."

She could still ask herself why she was in this particular moment, looking at a plate of pale green and purple-blue cabbages. Something shadowed the memory, all memory, all that she saw and knew.

"We're making a man fly to the moon by balloon—live, in front of you," the man was saying. "And he rides a cannonball and he turns invisible and—"

"And everything," says Lucia.

"I'll show you how it's done," the assistant assistant director says.

He's eager, even though he's fortyish and his hair is sparse and the lenses in his glasses are impressively thick and maybe explain why he is not in a uniform. He is working very hard at being charming.

She says: "I have to get back to the office."

"They don't even notice if you're there. How could they miss you?"

They stroll to the tall fortress towers of the sound studios, the distance between the two of them becoming more of an issue at every step: he getting closer. They slip between two huge sliding metal doors, along the line of the sliver of sunlight from the gap.

Inside, the space is dark until it becomes brilliant with arc lights, dusty and full of piled struts and angled flats until it turns into the skin of a palace or a garden.

They are under a gigantic wooden gallows, up to the ceiling, lit by naked lightbulbs, with ladders rising up to a perch for the camera. The gallows allow the camera to look down on a great drum, hanging on its side between scaffolding. It smells of paint, turpentine, and new cut wood.

"You see," the man says.

Lucia, old in the sun, did not think she remembered what had happened next. But that did not stop it happening again: vividly, and now.

The man clambers up ladders to the side of the drum. He tells Lucia to climb up to the camera's perch, which she does with difficulty in a long skirt; and he watches every step.

"You'll like this," he says, almost plaintive.

She sits dizzyingly high. She wonders when all the other members of the crew will come back. Her legs dangle in the air, no support, and her back is pressed hard onto the cameraman's seat. She is afraid to move in case the high scaffold might move and rock underneath her.

She's not fascinated enough to lose her anxiety. And this anxiety rhymed precisely with her sense, sitting in a hospital chair, that she did not want to be in this place a second time.

Below, in front of her, the man puts his shoulder to the huge drum and he begins to turn it.

"Look through the camera," he says.

She looks. She loses the world for a moment: she sees only a glass square and the guidelines inside it.

"Just look," he says.

And through the camera she makes out a road. She could be flying along it. There is a landscape all painted on the skin of the great drum and then the walls of a palace that rises up in pink sugar with guns on the battlements, a tower that goes up in monumental layers to meet its own painted shadow on a painted sky.

The drum stops moving, so the palace is still. It is in full view of the camera.

"Now imagine—"

She is very aware of eyes.

"—that you're flying, flying, and suddenly you collide with the top of the palace—"

Down below, around the square wood scaffolding, men have assembled silently. She didn't see them come; she was busy with a fantastic palace that shivered a little while the assistant assistant director talked. She can feel the presence of the men, though. She has to get down among them. She has to get through them.

The palace moves again. It comes steadily toward her, closer and larger, only the steadiness of its motion to tell her she is not truly flying into a painted world.

"And *kerboom!*"

She wants to tug down her skirt, to cover herself, but she is straddling the cameraman's perch and she can only study the great drum ahead of her and try to imagine she is still almost alone. She doesn't want to struggle for the ladder, and come sashaying down and down in front of this random lot of stagehands and gaffers. She sits, motionless.

"*Kerboom!*" The man's shout is a challenge. She has to be stirred and impressed. She can't just freeze.

She grips the cold metal of the camera. She thinks she can hear, far away, the faint whistling of a falling bomb; but she tells herself that is impossible, that the soundstages are sealed against the outside world. She might as well be sitting in a vacuum. Then she can't hear the whistling anymore. The bomb has landed.

She sees the light between the soundstage doors.

The scaffold shifts under her, like a chair no longer braced doesn't just stop being solid; it stops being a chair.

She sits up in the dead, still air, under the wide saucer lights in the roof, and she feels cold sweat going very slowly down her spine.

She hears the flat sound of an explosion. She can hear everything through the gap between the doors.

She hopes for a moment that the sound and the impact may be movie tricks, that maybe the men down below are nudging the scaffold and making it sway, worrying her, disconcerting her, and someone with a drum and a blanket is making the sound as an effect. But if that's true, she needs even more to get away briskly.

She swings herself over to the top of the ladder, going down backward, not knowing who's waiting down below.

The men shift forward, an audience to every curl and bend of her haunches as she clambers down.

She can't move.

She is only halfway down, arms and legs apart so she can flatten herself against the ladder, and she can move neither up nor down. And she has to be out of there, to be somewhere else.

She feels the men's eyes.

She can see, through the rungs of the ladder, that her new friend is still standing by the drum, holding it steady, waiting for it to lock back into place.

She edges one foot down. A man cheers. She slips a little.

She moves her hands down first, and then her legs. She wants to be close to the ground so they can all support and hold her and protect her. But she doesn't want them to touch her at all.

She reaches the ground, eyes back in her head, as unpredictable as any animal that is alarmed.

The men part for her, but not much. So she pushes them apart.

Lucia tells the office she is taking the afternoon off. The director, who seems to be amused at the notion of Lucia needing to ask to do nothing for a while, says she can take his car.

The old woman fretted in her bed, side to side, tugging the sheets out of place, talking politely as though at some social gathering.

The doctors decided there was no value in giving her a sedative. There would come a time when she needed them much more.

A paper in her pocket: the address that Sarah Lindemann gave her, in tight writing. She tells the driver to take her there.

She tells herself all she wants is a little sane conversation, and to be among other outsiders who don't simply want to fuck her or to stare at her, who don't live in a romance and do allow her to think out loud. She's hungry for difference in a world full of normal horrors.

The driver takes her to streets she doesn't know: each block lined with five featureless stories of apartments, each range of dark homes with another, smaller block inside it, squares within squares, broken only by tunnels of archways and entrances. There is a little bar on the corner, hung at the door with heavy leather curtains for the blackout.

She tells the driver to wait.

Max can't be here. This must be someone who might know someone who might pass on a message from a friend who knows people, who might even help.

She goes out of the sun and into one of the tunnels. The air changes. The tunnel is broken, five times, with a line of dim light where one court backs onto another. It smells of soot, of sewers not working well, of machine oil and ersatz soap, sometimes beer, once rotten meat. She looks down to see where her neat straw shoes were walking: on a rat-run of grime, old paper, old dirt.

She has never been to such a place. It isn't at all like the back-streets of Milan, which were old and familiar and open even when they were hung with washing and full of children; this is exotic as a souk. She worries about who might be ahead, behind her, whether the children pick pockets. But she worries even more that the smell will stay forever on her skin: the smell of people who have nothing at all, not even the cleaning and bleaching sunlight, to lose.

Max Lindemann can't be here. This place cannot be in Berlin.

She walks carefully, but she tries not to walk delicately: not to look different, even rich.

She finds the proper door, knocks and knocks again, waits and knocks again. She wants it to seem that she knows a code, which means she knows a code is necessary.

She thinks there may be someone behind the door: a child, dog, or idiot, she doesn't care anymore.

"Is Max here?" she asks through the door.

No answer.

"Can I leave a message?"

No answer.

She shouts: "Max! Max! Are you there?" And her voice doubles in the narrow tunnel and comes back from the far courts crisscrossing on itself.

"Max!"

He infuriates her with his discretion. He's supposed to come forward and show his face for her, risk anything for her.

Her driver leaves the car for a moment and says, quietly: "Signora. Perhaps if we left now—"

An official car stops at the end of the tunnel.

"Max!" Lucia shouts.

Three men in black step out of the car. Lucia walks toward them, incensed that Max is not eager to see her, that the people behind the door do not trust her. She is also instinctively, carefully aware that three men with guns and warrants are walking toward her.

When Frau Lindemann comes with the other dishes and pots and vases she wants to save, she says she has not heard from Max for a week. Nobody has heard from Max.

Berlin is shutting down around Lucia. They've closed Horchers, and the Quartier Latin, the Neva Grill and Peltzer's Atelier and Tuskulum; so she doesn't know, this evening, next evening, where to go for all that venison, wild pig, chicken, the meat that does not require coupons, to be eaten with the tide of red wine that still floods in grand Berlin cellars.

She's seen the art trade, too, being shut down, at least the official trade: so shops stay shut, but the prices roar along. Brown, varnished pictures: prices up a third at least. Her friend in Himmler's office, who expects to get out of the war in good shape, says there was one picture at Lange's auction house that he knew for a fact was worth only four thousand Reichmarks, that Lange's put up for sale at twenty-five thousand, which was already pushing it, and which sold to a Munich dealer for sixty-four thousand; "and God knows what he'll sell it on for."

So she asks him about furniture. "Anything Louis XV, Louis XIV," he says. "Lots of it coming in from Paris, but the prices don't go down. They always lose the cushions, though, and it's difficult to match them now all the good shops are closing."

She thanks him politely.

She hears the bombs coming closer. You can't trust anyone anymore: they wait for the bombs to break open buildings, and they steal whatever they see. The Gestapo take away a woman on a stretcher. The city is either ruined by heat or frozen white: two seasons, equally bleak.

She's thinking, always wide-eyed on the world for every possibility.

Everyone who hasn't left is about to leave: fussing about getting the silver safely to a bank, the children to the country, throwing out clothes they don't need, getting the furniture somewhere safe before the bombs hit at home. Even her diplomat friends have no more magical answers. They can still dance, they can still travel a little, but they're squabbling now about the supply of country houses still standing. Italian officers turn up to find their landlady has given the lease to Romanians; so the landlady, the officers smugly say, is now in jail.

She takes in every rumor, every fact and sight, so she can calculate her survival, which she begins to think will mean her escape.

She tells herself she did not denounce Max Lindemann. People do disappear. They disappear all the time.

She has her little business, her storage service; that's how she sees things. Everyone has a second job nowadays.

She does this to protect Nicholas. She likes the warm, kindly feeling in other people when they see a mother protecting her child. She's going to get out of here, and Nicholas too.

But she isn't with Nicholas. She's out socializing. She goes out for her little business, her means of leaving Berlin, of keeping Nicholas safe. But she likes the parties, too.

She likes the Spanish diplomats, Federico Díaz in particular. He has proper drink in a proper house. And he has presents, too, and she likes presents.

Lovely lights. There is mariachi music, and she loves the blare and attack of the tunes. She wonders where Díaz found Mexican musicians in Berlin, but then she's seen black actors on the set in Neubabelsberg; there are all sorts fitted into the corners of the great white Reich.

She wants very much to dance.

There's no ambassador, of course. This is the kind of event at which he'd probably appear with his wife, which nowadays means he'd rather not appear at all.

"Every few weeks," a bright little woman is saying of a friend. "She goes to Switzerland every few weeks. I think that's very brave. You never know about the roads."

"Why does she go?" Lucia asks, having not quite caught any of the names.

"She's lady-in-waiting to the Infanta, when she can get there."

"How extraordinary," Lucia says.

"I see nothing extraordinary about it," the woman says, and turns away.

These people should be her friends. She's fazed by how many have seen her, know her for an associate of the Italian ambassador, but also know all too clearly what kind of associate. That woman's a Furstenberg; they should be friends. There is a Henschel; they're always at the same parties.

She talks for a while with a minister from the Swiss embassy. She takes one more drink.

She is the daughter of a distinguished Milano banker, after all; she might yet be near the start of a dynasty. She has a worth like the worth of all these women, and it is fired up now with the brandy that Díaz had brought from his vineyards in Jerez.

She pauses at double doors that lead into a study. She sees a gun pointing at her.

"*Pop!*" says a Furstenberg, smiling furiously.

She wonders if the woman is sober; if she knows about the safety catch; if she does, what she has done about it.

"*Bang!*" says the Furstenberg, now annoyed that Lucia is not performing the proper smile. The safety catch clicks off.

Lucia says: "*Prego.*"

"Oh, really," the Furstenberg says, and turns about half-circle. She has the gun pointed now at a pretty writing desk across the room, at an odd white figurine of a cat-whiskered dwarf.

She fires.

The bullet tracks over the desk, lodges in the wall.

"Bugger," she says.

She tries to pass the gun to Lucia, to pull her in. Lucia, flattered, steps forward.

Federico Díaz says: "First one to hit gets scent. Or stockings."

He has them ranged now: seven women, good names, fine ways, all waiting their turn.

Lucia aims, closes her eyes, fires, and looks up. She can't tell where the bullet has gone. Díaz is rubbing his elbow, with pantomimed irony. The other women laugh.

They are firing at a perfectly fine little Böttger piece, early eighteenth century; she knows what will be the usefulness of such objects in an emergency, like the emergency of losing a war.

"I'll get a target," Díaz says.

He won't talk about politics with her. The ambassador, truth to tell, doesn't care to talk very much at all. Talk implies the kind of social life that he gets at home.

But she can't miss some things. Here is Mussolini talking to Hitler, and nothing coming of it, not even a grand formal pronouncement. That is bad. The English and the Americans are in Sicily. Then the great northern towns of Italy shiver and burn under raiding bombers.

The ambassador comes to her, for once. He says: "There are some papers, some money. Some silver, some plates. I know you know people. You could get them to Switzerland."

She wants to shout and laugh. She's depended on him for parties, for her odd and equivocal place among the diplomats. Now he depends on her for half his life.

Then the ambassador buggers off, which is his phrase, not hers, and it seems he's going to some Grand Council session in Rome.

She waits. What else can she do? Even the ambassador can no longer figure with precision his chances of survival and usefulness.

He did once say to her, as they disentangled on a single bed in a servants' room at the official residence: "I wonder what would happen if Italy changed sides."

She blinked at him. First of all, she was annoyed that he was thinking politics just seconds after he had come; wasn't she occupying him enough? Second, she didn't understand what he said. Italy and Germany were allies, surely, and it was unthinkable either should change sides.

He muttered something about the workers in Turin. She said she didn't understand, and drew a sheet around her, which was difficult since he was lying on the other half of it. He said the workers in Turin were on strike again and in Milan, too, and maybe there'd be a revolution. It would be better to lose the war than see a revolution.

She wondered at the time why he had spelled out his pillow thoughts just this once: better to be always discreet, or always talkative. She understands when he quits Berlin suddenly; he has simply been telling her that it is time for him to go.

The heat crushes her. Agreeable ambassadorial lawns are closed to her. She does take Nicholas to the public beaches, where he's her escort and her protection. She's so absorbed in her boy that nobody ogles or bothers her. She can walk the boardwalk among soldiers still in uniform, cross the city of wicker cabanas on the beach, and she does so as a mother, no temptation to any of them.

It was the mothers who sent the soldiers off with pride. Perhaps the soldiers hated mothers.

Women and children are to leave Berlin. Schools shut down as of August 1. She worries about leaving, but she can't leave, not with the cellars out at Potsdam and everything stored there.

A railway station, not even a main railway station, besieged by women in head scarves and children wrapped up warm despite the smothering heat and all carrying cases. They won't find a seat on a train. In any case, there are no trains.

Phone call from the Swiss legation. They've been told to leave Berlin by August 15. Her friend the minister says: "But I do know you have your own resources. It's entirely your decision whether you go or not." Then he adds: "We can't advise you to go." And then: "But it might be as well to be ready."

She notices the lines for flowers in the Frankfurter Allee: women and men wanting tokens of summer life.

She hears that many of the South American diplomats are leaving, at last. She imagines them packing up parties and dances in their trunks, music and all, a whole social life ready to be unwrapped and remade in some other city.

She also hears about the political realities in Italy, fragment by fragment, sometimes from chatter in the embassy itself. There has been a meeting of the Grand Fascist Council, her ambassador present. Nineteen to seven, the council asked the king of Italy "to assume command of the armed forces and the fullness of his constitutional powers." Mussolini was not present. When he went to see the king the next afternoon, he was much surprised to hear that his resignation had already been accepted. As he left, he was bundled into an ambulance and taken off to a city barracks.

She is alone.

She's done so well, for a woman in Berlin. She's been a brilliant kind of neutral, on absolutely all the right sides. She is Swiss, which used to be at least a comfortable nationality, and Italian, which used to make her an ally, and with a child born in Germany, which gave her a certain claim on the authorities in an emergency.

But now Italian is an insult. Her Italian allies are on the wrong side. Italy is divided up between the Allies advancing in the South and the Germans in possession of the North. As for the comfortable Swiss, she hears stories that they boo the German newsreels off the screen.

She's telling Nicholas it's time he got out. The embassy staffers will soon have to leave, she's sure. She can't establish their exact moving day, but they are the fascists who repudiated Mussolini, and Mussolini is the man the Germans just rescued from custody and put back in charge of a shrunken little stub of a Republic.

She walks to the embassy. It's a cold day in a tattered city: leaves down on the ground, streets bare.

She turns the last corner, and the whole street is cluttered with parked cars. The embassy is besieged this morning, as it used to be on the nights of grand receptions; but in daylight she can see a couple of ambulances standing by.

On the steps, women who once snubbed her. They wear their heaviest coats, like armor. Men who know vaguely who she is, or rather what she was to the ambassador, aren't sure if they should acknowledge her or not. Some nod. Some find themselves looking another way, any other way. All of them have that lifeless, helpless air of people with nothing to do but wait, and all of them have suitcases at their sides.

"They'll beat us up, of course," says one of the military attachés. "They're bound to beat us. But then they'll have other things to worry about."

Lucia asks: "You know where you're going?"

"Holidays," the attaché says. "We're all going to the Alps."

"Really?" Lucia says. "You know where?" She has visions of some nighttime crossing into Switzerland, maybe into the arms of her lost husband, she can imagine all kinds of safety, at the very least into the protective comfort of his nationality.

"Garmisch," the attaché says. "Isn't that a joke? We'd all have killed to go to Garmisch for the winter. We'd all take skis but we're not sure they'll have room on the train."

"That's not close to Switzerland, is it?"

The attaché says, shrewdly: "Not close enough, Lucia."

And she walks on. She sees that a bomb has twisted some of the grand bronze and old timbers, shivered the gilt off cherubim and brought down the great glass chandeliers; what's left does not quite add up to the old splendor. Against the occasional Old Master, the black stained wood from churches, the marble and the double painted doors, there are people squatting, fussing, suitcases tucked under their arms or used as seats, like refugees already. All their heads are down.

As she's leaving by the main front door, one woman, a sharp-faced secretary bird with fingernails still long and painted, says: "This is for all the Italians, you know. All the Italians have to go."

And Lucia says: "My dear. I'm so sorry. I am Swiss."

"I mentioned the shop," Helen said. "She didn't even seem to process the idea. And then she was angry. You could tell she knew there was something she ought to remember, but she couldn't. That's half a century, gone."

"I don't want to know," Sarah said.

"She's always angry, the doctors say. She's worried by something, something she has to do. She keeps very quiet, though."

"We all got used to that."

"You think she thinks she's in Berlin?"

Sarah said: "You know how frightened I am of being like Lucia? Of losing the present time entirely, all the possibilities, all the scents and tastes and—and hopes. How can you hope if you're on an endless loop of time, past time, time you've lived already? You know how it turns out."

"She sometimes seems to be discussing with a child," Helen said.

"Then she's gone back," Sarah said.

But Lucia woke in a hospital room again. She'd woken there before. She was acutely aware of the smell of the place.

She couldn't quite remember how she knew things: but she knew very well that the ambassador was sneaking off to Switzerland, asked the Swiss to save his family's life and find him some quiet place in a discreet canton, for preference German-speaking. He liked Zug.

She knew things. She heard rumors out of Garmisch that things were terrible: so bad that nobody cared who took power or who lost it.

She is walking on a street by railway tracks. She hears Italian being spoken in a cattle car. Prisoners of war, obviously. A cold, frosty morning.

Suddenly, she's grateful for the Swiss.

The doctor visited. She said: "I feel very tired. It's extraordinary, don't you find, the way your resources are suddenly gone. You can't lift that arm or speak that word. You just can't."

"I'm glad to find you so lucid," the doctor said.

"I really think I need to rest." It was better to rest than find herself sodden with regret and ready to make apologies and amends for all kinds of crime.

So she decided the doctor was Nicholas. She roused herself for a moment to be a mother: a loving look, determined and rather knowing, an order given with the eyes.

There were no crimes, only circumstances. She was sure of that.

All the art dealers lost their stock, except for old man Grosse in the Esplanade Hotel, and he was just lucky. You saw people tugging bits of furniture down the street and you never knew if it was their furniture they were saving or furniture they just found. They tugged mattresses sometimes. When they bombed the zoo, there were snakes in the hedges and tigers in the cake shops and crocodiles in the canals, so they said. And the colors: it was like fairground neon, but all the time, phosphorous blue and flame red and sometimes an unnatural acidic green.

There was no possibility of an orderly deal in this disordered city. The courts waited until the war was over to demand "orderly deals."

She was trying to hold on to that justifying thought, but it wouldn't stay with her. She stared at it as though it was written, or a solid object, but she couldn't see. Then she couldn't remember. Then . . .

The Hotel Adlon, an odd island of business in a wrecked city. Food on plastic plates, which no longer seems a scandal. It is a sign of privilege, though, a scandal in the eyes of the unlucky, if you manage to get a table.

And how smart people look, how uniforms hold in all disarray like they hold in a spreading gut, how a briefcase of the right leather makes a man look useful and a pair of slacks on a woman who cares about her face and her body will suggest she's useful, too, that she has been cleaning house or cleaning a city and deserves her drink.

She's alone, cold, without a useful nationality, in a city surrounded by invaders. She knows she's losing. She wants to know the forfeit.

It comes briskly, without fuss. Her friend Hans from Himmler's office introduces her to a woman called Magrit Huber, who knew everyone at the Swiss legation. Lucia has friends there, but not enough.

Magrit is waiting in the Adlon, at a table. Hans is with her.

"My dear," Magrit says. "Things must be difficult."

Lucia is perfectly presented, entirely calm. She can't agree. But then she might need this woman, so she can't call her a liar, either.

"When the ambassador left," Magrit says, "there was some trouble about the cellars in Potsdam. So I've been paying the rent."

Lucia wonders if this could be true, and, if it is true, how much it can matter. The owners were bombed out and long gone, in no position to insist on payment.

"So I have the keys," Magrit said.

Lucia sees her storehouse emptied out by some improvident bitch who happens to have the lease. But she smiles.

"You have a remarkable collection," Magrit says. She's a very tall woman: a stork. "Too remarkable to remain safely in Berlin, I'm afraid."

So she's taken it already: shipped away everything. But Lucia smiles.

"Don't be alarmed," Magrit says. "Hans and I were discussing your problems, and we want to help. I have a shop in Zurich, a little gallery. The stock would be so much safer there. There are people with money who can buy."

Lucia's smile isn't calm anymore; it's just unmoving.

"Naturally, you would have an interest. You would be in the little shop all the time. You'd take a percentage of the sales."

Lucia knows an interest is easily dissolved. Contracts don't stand like they used to stand. So she starts to talk. She makes Magrit understand what she knows about Meissen: details, marks, what's fake and what is not, what it means when something looks wrong which sometimes means it's right but badly mended.

She concentrates. She never concentrated like this before, not on love, not on Nicholas. She spins expertise out of the air, golden names, lovely things, all set in a hierarchy of time and value. She makes Magrit want the knowledge of these things as well as the things themselves. She explains why there is never an AR mark on a love scene, how apprentices got to paint the sword marks so you never know which is which. Which thrower and which molder marked their work with four dots and which with two stars. All exquisite, intricate knowledge which turns those exquisite, intricate objects into the stuff of a shop and a sale.

And so the deal changes. Clearly Lucia is not just a woman with a talent for acquiring things.

"We'll be partners," Magrit said, brightly. "You can sell things. I can't. You can be out front."

Lucia thinks: She's grateful for this little holiday while I talk, no bombs, no burning, no dead, just the shine of luxury.

"I can't imagine being a shopkeeper," Lucia said.

Magrit frowns. "You'll survive it."

"You didn't earn those goods. You did nothing for them."

"Thank God," Magrit says.

Lucia won't be judged, but she can't afford to complain. So she's quiet. But Magrit goes on: "Hans may have something to say to you about that."

Hans says: "One or two things. You can come to see me at the office."

The room very slightly rocks. The bombers come just then, without a pause, roaring abominably, pressing the air overhead into a blind wall. There have been raids before, but none when the planes did not stop coming.

She's thinking of Nicholas back in the apartment, of what is left in the apartment, too. She can't get back now, not through the fire and rain that's falling. She has to wait among the gentlemen with briefcases, and wonder what business they found to do anymore, and these women in neat slacks, smiling, whose business still thrived, and some bright girls shouting about oysters and a very few men in uniform who did not look deadly tired.

She says, out loud: "Nicholas."

"Who's that?" Magrit asks, sharply. "A friend of yours?"

Lucia says: "Yes."

"A good friend?"

"Yes. I'm worried about him."

"Listen," Magrit says, "we all take our chances."

The roaring always came in waves before, but tonight it is merciless and continuous.

"He is my son," Lucia says.

Magrit glares at her. "Are you coming to the shelter or not?"

In the tight rooms of the deep shelter, the diplomats' shelter under thirty feet of concrete with its own special entrance, Magrit stays very close to Lucia. "Just don't think," she says. "Don't think. Dear."

Lucia looks down at her legs. She had no stockings that morning, so she'd charcoaled the line of a seam on the back of both legs, and now Magrit has smudged it.

She'd rather have no place, no time, than this place and this time. Her memory seemed to run forward as well as backward, to encompass what would happen next even as she seemed to live the closeness in the deep shelter, Magrit's bony concern, the taste of breath on the air. She is breathing Magrit's breath.

Their alliance did not last. When the Berlin goods were selling, and Magrit sensed trouble from the law, she sidled out of the business, let Lucia take the blame. Magrit was now entirely respectable, had her share of the capital from the Berlin goods and an annual rent for the use of the shop and her name over the door. Lucia could never challenge what Magrit demanded, however much it taxed her own life; she could only wait for her to die, which she did quite suddenly in 1956.

Memory inside memory now. How in the shelter, she is trying to be somewhere else. How surprised she was to inherit the shop, as though Magrit once had cared for her; and how glad to have independence at last. How Magrit loved to think about touching.

Frau Bartels is out of the ground floor at four in the morning, off to collect the newspapers she'll push at people's doors by six or seven. Nothing stops her.

Lucia is watching from the apartment window.

Frau Bartels picks her way between fires and ruins. She can afford not to notice the wreckage around her. She has her little business.

There are window frames loose from the walls, doors gone. Trees have their roots in the air, solid and bizarre. Where gas pipes have broken, there is perpetual fire, like a cinema effect.

Nicholas wakes up. He asks for Gattopardo. She hasn't seen the damned cat. He asks again. Then he says he saw Gattopardo climbing the sky. She tells him not to be silly.

She didn't want to wake him sleeping so warmly, so deeply, but now she reckons it is time to get down to the street when the emergency services arrive. She picks up bread, butter, sausage, thick soup, and coffee. She's no idea why suddenly there's enough for ordinary people; maybe there was always enough, and she never needed all the schemes and concentration.

She takes the cigarettes, even though she does not smoke, because she will need things to trade, and she wants things to carry, that she does not have to store, that Magrit and Hans cannot take from her.

Nicholas was there. Nicholas is with her. And now she has spun off in time, not anchored to her present hospital room or to that Berlin street, but sitting in some drawing room with Nicholas.

She did it all for him, she wanted to say. She couldn't ever tell him that; he would have gone away at once. She pleaded sixty cold years of perfect front and never taking credit: her first punishment.

She could never have done what she did without him. There would have been no point. He was, in a certain sense, her accomplice, whether he liked it or not.

But, no. He was dead. He was gone.

Then she'd thank God she never told him the whole truth. Perhaps he had not, after all, been so important to her.

She started to notice the darkness at the edges of the room, not the lights anymore.

Time rushed her, wouldn't let her stop for comfort. Berlin has gone wrong. It has energy, but the energy of a machine spitting and ratcheting over its own gears. And the lights, which used to be everywhere: bright, pretty lights on department stores, glamorous lights on plain facades, pillars and discs and towers of light, even a tower which said *"Licht ist Leben,"* light is life, not to mention the white globes by the café terraces on Kurfürstendamm. Now entire streets are dark. The theater of the city has shut down; there's no more show.

The studio is stymied: an hour or so to work each morning before the start of the raids, and often the shots were lost because of the strain on the actors' faces. Work is being shipped out to the countryside where it seems less dangerous, and then to the Bavarian Alps, and to Pomerania, East Prussia, Mecklenburg, anywhere far away.

But she can't go. She works for animators, and animators stay by their drawing boards; they have no excuses for showing strain or filming in safer places. Her boss reckons that the Allies will not bother with Babelsberg again. It is already ruined, and what's left is far too fragile to assemble the stories and dreams it once contained.

She goes to one last screening at the UFA building in town: a cartoon, with her name on it in small letters. She settles in the dark.

She sees a very young goose in love with the city and the chance to wear gaudy feathers, to go close dancing, and to meet exotic beasts. The goose makes herself finery out of anything she can steal: pig's bristles for her eyelashes, a spider's web for a veil. She turns down a steady kind of gander, and she lights out for town; and there she meets a slicked-back fox, in a fine gray uniform with spit-polished boots and long black cars at his disposal. She falls. She pines. She even goes home with him. And when she does, she sees his lair: sees geese caged ready for slaughter, sees the menagerie of slaves and bones.

Lucia knows it is all over if this film can be shown.

She is at her desk, writing a letter on a piece of good paper, embassy stock. She is writing to Himmler to ask for his help with a question of papers. She will send the letter by way of Hans.

She's off to dinner with some Swedish envoys, who have lobster and copies of *Vogue*. She's off to see the new Italian ambassador, since she's still an Italian citizen, but she never gets past the outer offices, among minor paper pushers hot to give the impression they personally have a war to manage and a nation's soul to save.

Hans calls. He says Himmler is most interested in her case, and remembers her from various parties. But he says Himmler likes blondes.

She can't check the story. It sounds right. Perhaps Hans is humiliating her, perhaps he is helping, but either way, she can't do without him.

She tries a hairdresser. The hairdresser laughs. "I can pour a kettle over your head, if you like," she says. "I can't even heat the water. You want color, you're on your own."

She walks back to the apartment. On the way, she sees a house gone crazy like something in an old fairground, beams slanted, door askew. That doesn't frighten her anymore.

She shakes the bottle of hydrogen peroxide. She doesn't like the sour chemical smell that comes out of the little bottle. She doesn't like the notion that she is treating her hair like a wound.

She'll never again be a contingent person, dependent on others. Never. She'll get out of Berlin, and then they'll have the devil's job to prove who owns that cellar full of riches. She'll play along with Magrit while she has to, and then she'll make a business of her own.

There isn't enough chemical. She's never done this before, but she knows it will not be enough.

She goes to neighbors, to the stiff, proper couple who took over Mr. Goldstein's apartment and filled it up with a bronze relief of Hitler and a number of little flags. They do not have hydrogen peroxide. Antiseptic would imply imperfections in their world, an unpatriotic thought.

So she tries the caretaker. She tells him Nicholas has a deep cut, and the caretaker says Nicholas was all right when he left the house to go to lessons. The caretaker produces a medicine bottle, almost empty. "You could use brandy," he says. "Or whisky, or grappa. You people always get something. I know."

She still isn't sure she has enough. She tries Frau Werner, on the ground-floor landing. Frau Werner is always nervous about reality, and in her nervousness, she'll surely have provisioned, years ahead, for all imaginable catastrophes. And she does have old aspirin in a tea caddy, bandages and gauze laid out in what was once her husband's tool box, and the hydrogen peroxide stashed at the back of a cupboard, behind a row of drinks that have grown a sugar crust with neglect.

Lucia smiles. Lucia begs.

Frau Werner says she's seen all these people who weren't prepared for the worst, and look what happened to them.

Lucia says: "I'll pay."

Frau Werner says: "That's fair."

Back in the bathroom, facing a clear mirror, Lucia douses her hair in the chemicals and water. She knows she has to wait. She doesn't know how long.

She wonders what it would be like to need to go to parties wearing glasses, or to wear false teeth and explain them to a lover, or to dye her hair in order not to seem gray and superannuated. She has to provide for all these coming times.

Breakfast time, she has a mass of brittle, yellow hair, persuaded into shape.

Nicholas looks shocked. She's furious. She's given up the very look of herself.

"They say," Clarke said, "you get trapped in a moment. You stay there. You don't have any more past or present."

"You don't have any more biography," Sarah said. "Autobiography, I should say—the story you tell yourself. And you have no more self, because of that."

"Is she still there, even?"

She is there, alert, exact, attentive. In the office of Henrich Himmler, she expects to use charm as usual; but immediately, everything is business.

"Magrit will make sure you can take the goods into Switzerland," Hans says. "But you will need papers to take the goods out of Germany."

"I see." She envisions dinners, quickies in a cot.

"Your information has been very useful at times."

Lucia does not see herself as an informer. She sees herself as a dealer in information.

"We'd like just a little more. We can pick up the male Jews easily enough because every decent German male is in a uniform, so the ones who aren't get checked on the street. We can't pick up the women so easily."

Hans has an envelope, a thick envelope on his desk. "A *laisser passer* and an authorization for fuel and trucks. You help us, we help you."

Lucia says: "I came to see Herr Himmler."

Hans says: "He's such an honest man," meaning he is too honest to have time for Lucia.

She has no tactics left. She tugs on her gloves.

She hears him shouting after her: "Remember. We would appreciate your help."

Outside his door, there's a long, polished corridor, with a bustle of men coming at her, and in between them a little man absurdly crucified on the shoulders of his burly minders, his muscles all tense, face wounded with pain, his pince-nez trailing from his neck. The man's face is round, and almost Asiatic under the grimace. He is struggling with his dignity and the hurt in his gut.

The scrum passes.

"Herr Himmler," says Hans, through the door. "You have now seen Herr Himmler."

Outside, people stare. She knows exactly why: such crude blond hair can only be some kind of disguise.

Sixty years in a decorous town: sixty years of dealing, most of it honest, and proper and timely payments of tax, passing on beautiful objects to people who truly desired them, sitting in the middle of the glint and shine of what was inessential but often perfect.

But sixty years, also, without memory, so that she could not be herself all those sixty long years. She was alone even with lovers.

She walks out into the street. She's infected already with this loss. People see it in her eyes. But they think, in the circumstances, that what they see is death, and they think it will not be Lucia's death.

She's not going to give up now. It will take only a few more sins.

She is walking the wrong street. It isn't the kind of place she would like to be found, much less spend all her waking time: it's a broken place, a gap between things left standing.

She always meets Sarah Lindemann, always sees that her dress is torn but mended.

Sarah doesn't see her as a friend. She sees just a wild card, a slight variation in circumstances which might help when nothing else can.

Sarah says: "They keep telling me there aren't any more ration cards. Not for me, anyway. You know people, don't you? You know who could help?"

The two women on a street, for a second that will not ever end. Then Sarah always looks into Lucia's eyes, sees the coldness of morgues and storerooms, and a passion for such things.

Lucia's hand is out. "Come with me," she says. But Sarah always breaks away, running zigzag in the traffic, arms and legs everywhere, always through the same corner shop with a door on two streets. She won't stand still to be delivered. She is running for her life.

"Come with me," Lucia shouts. "I can help."

She is furious, humiliated, she hunts in her memory, she tracks in her mind, and she stands on this broken street in the hope of finding Sarah again, or another.

And this is her last unresting place, the last place she will ever know.

A NOTE ON SOURCES

I first heard the story of Andreina Schwegler-Torré from Thomas Buomberger, whose account of the Swiss art trade in the last world war, *Kunstraub, Raubkunst* (Zurich, 1998), has a full account of that lady's crimes. Without Thomas's generous help, this book could not have been written. It is, however, the story of another woman: Lucia Müller-Rossi, who exists only in fiction.

It developed through many conversations with witnesses to these periods, and historians who have studied them; I owe many of these meetings to the help of Mario Pelli and Anna Ehrensperger. It was fed by dozens of memoirs, diaries, biographies, and studies, including: *Skeleton of Justice,* by Edith Roper and Clara Leiser (New York, 1941); *Between Dignity and Despair: Jewish Life in Nazi Germany,* by Marion A. Kaplan (New York, 1998); *Berlin Diaries: 1940–1945,* by Marie Vassiltchikov (New York, 1987); *The Klemperer Diaries 1933–1945,* by Victor Klemperer (London, 2000); *Guns and Barbed Wire: A Child Survives the Holocaust,* by Thomas Geve (Chicago, 1987); *Diary of a Nightmare: Berlin 1942–1945,* by Ursula von Kardorff (New York, 1966); *While Berlin Burns: The Diary of Hans-Georg von Studnitz 1943–1945* (Englewood Cliffs, N.J., 1964); *Blood and Banquets: A Berlin Social Diary,* by Bella Fromm (New York, 1990); *Shadows Over My Berlin,* by Heidi Scriba Vance (Middletown, Conn., 1996); *Mixed Blessings: An Almost Ordinary Life in Hitler's Germany,* by Heinz R. Kuehn (Athens, Ga., 1988); *Albert Speer: His Battle With the Truth,* by Gitta Sereny (London, 1995); *The Architect of Genocide: Himmler and the Final Solution,* by Richard Breitman (Hanover, N.H., 1992); *The Kersten Memoirs 1940–1945,* by

Felix Kersten (London, 1956); *The Fall of Berlin,* by Anthony Read and David Fisher (New York, 1995); *Berlin im Zweiten Weltkreig,* by Hans Dieter Schäfer (Munich, 1985); *Resistance of the Heart: Intermarriage and the Rosenstrasse Protest in Nazi Germany,* by Nathan Stoltzfus (New York, 1996); *The UFA Story,* by Klaus Kreimeier (New York, 1996); *Opel at War,* by Eckhart Bartels (West Chester, Penn., 1991), and other volumes in this series on Ford, Mercedes, and Volkswagen; *Il Faut Encore Avaler La Suisse,* by Klaus Urner (Geneva, 1996); *The Lifeboat Is Full,* by Alfred A. Häsler (New York, 1969); *Sketchbook 1946–1949,* by Max Frisch (New York, 1977); *Correspondance* of Max Frisch and Friedrich Dürrenmatt, presented by Peter Rüedi (Geneva, 1999); *Ces Messieurs de Berne 1939–1945,* by Claude Mossé (Paris, 1997); papers by Malcolm Pender, Regina Wecker, Gianni Haver, and Joy Charnley in *Switzerland and War,* edited by Joy Charnley and Malcolm Pender (Bern, 1999); papers by Luc Van Dongen, Josef Mooser, André Lasserre, and Rudolf Jaun in *Switzerland and the Second World War,* edited by George Kreis (London, 2000); papers by Wilfried Fiedler, Georg Kreis, and Matthias Frehner in *Das Geschäft mit der Raubkunst: Fakten, Thesen, Hintergründe,* edited by Matthias Frehner (Zurich, 1998); *Revendication de biens spoliés,* by Jean-Pierre Grenier (Bern, 1946), and other Swiss government reports on stolen art (Bern/Prague, 1948); *Le banquier noir,* by François Genoud (Paris, 1996); *L'Ombre Rouge: Suisse-URSS 1943–1944, Le Débat Politique en Suisse,* by Sophie Pavillon (Lausanne, 1999); *The Book of Zurich,* by Edwin Arnet and Hans Kasser (Zurich, 1954); *Il Banchiere Eretico: La Singolare Vita di Raffaele Mattioli,* by Giancarlo Galli (Milan, 1998); *Le Donne nel regime Fascista,* by Victoria de Grazia (Venice, 1993; originally published in English); *Italian Industrialists from Liberalism to Fascism,* by Franklin Hugh Adler (Cambridge, 1995); extracts from essays by Vincente Blasco Ibáñez, Karel Čapek, and André Suarès in *Milano e L'Europa,* edited by Attilio Brilli (Milan, 1997). The dates and places of publication are correct for the editions that I consulted.

I owe particular thanks to the staff of the *Nederlands Instituut voor Oorlogsdocumentatie* in Amsterdam; to Minister Lukas Beglinger of the Political Division of the Swiss Federal Department of Foreign Affairs *(Eidgenössiches Departement für Auswärtige Angelegenheiten)* in Bern; and to Dr. Peter Pfrunder, director of the *Schweizerische Stiftung für die Photographie* in Zurich.

Of course, none of these is responsible for what I've made of my story. But since it is founded in terrible events whose scale and even reality some people continue to deny, I have made sure that no public event in this book—that is, no trial, no crime, and no betrayal— is without a close, factual counterpart.